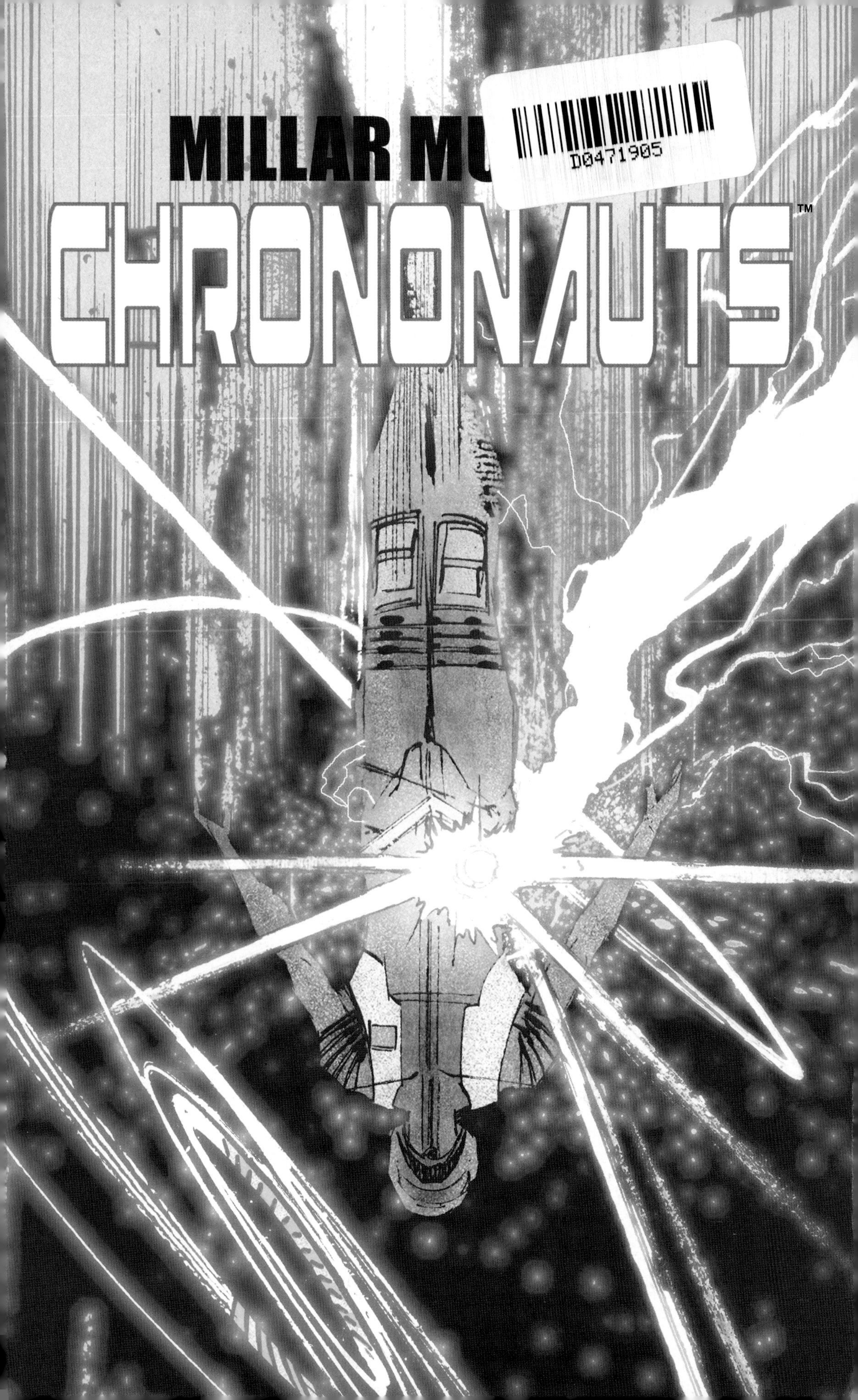
MILLAR
CHRONONAUTS™

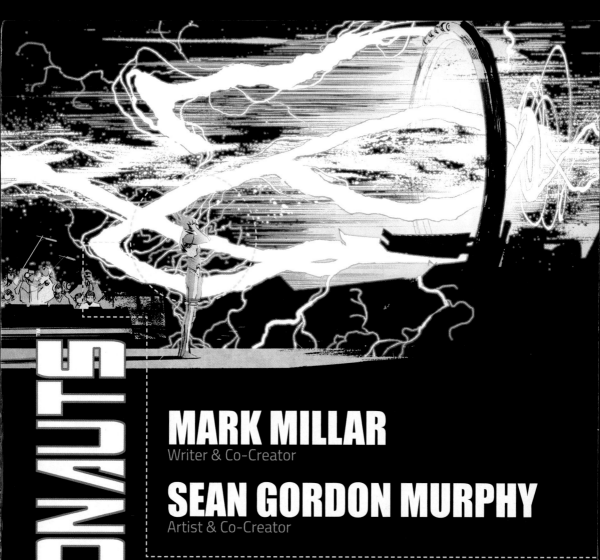

CHRONONAUTS

MARK MILLAR
Writer & Co-Creator

SEAN GORDON MURPHY
Artist & Co-Creator

MATT HOLLINGSWORTH
Color Artist

CHRIS ELIOPOULOS
Letterer

MELINA MIKULIĆ - Collection Designer
PETER DOHERTY & **DREW GILL** - Production
NICOLE BOOSE - Editor
JIM O'HARA - Special Thanks

IMAGE COMICS, INC.
Robert Kirkman – Chief Operating Officer
Erik Larsen – Chief Financial Officer
Todd McFarlane – President
Marc Silvestri – Chief Executive Officer
Jim Valentino – Vice-President

Eric Stephenson – Publisher
Corey Murphy – Director of Sales
Jeremy Sullivan – Director of Digital Sales
Kat Salazar – Director of PR & Marketing
Emily Miller – Director of Operations
Branwyn Bigglestone – Senior Accounts Manager
Sarah Mello – Accounts Manager
Drew Gill – Art Director
Jonathan Chan – Production Manager
Meredith Wallace – Print Manager
Randy Okamura – Marketing Production Designer
David Brothers – Branding Manager
Ally Power – Content Manager
Addison Duke – Production Artist
Vincent Kukua – Production Artist
Sasha Head – Production Artist
Tricia Ramos – Production Artist
Emilio Bautista – Sales Assistant
Chloe Ramos-Peterson – Administrative Assistant
IMAGECOMICS.COM

CHAPTER ONE

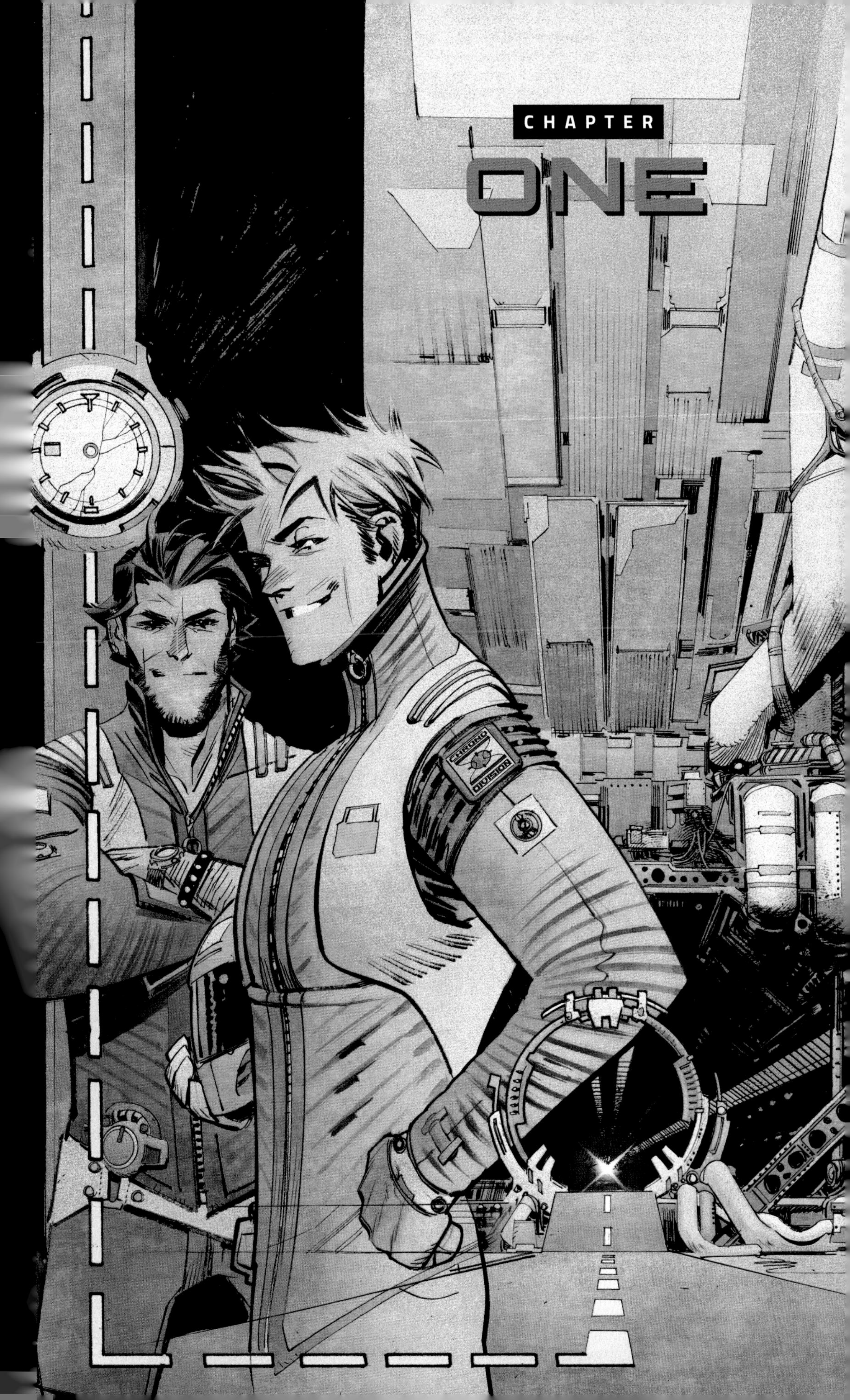
CHRONO DIVISION

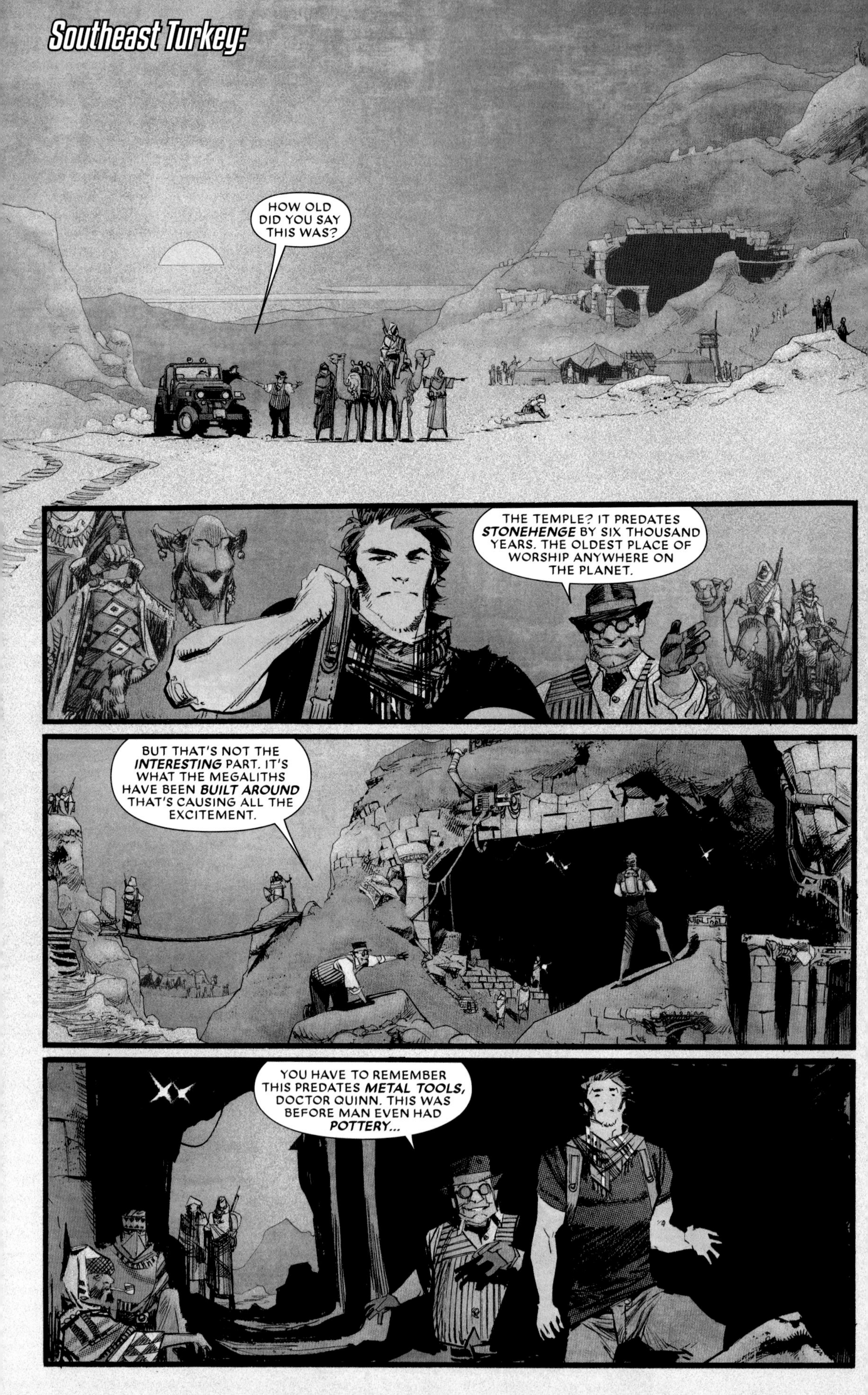
Southeast Turkey:
HOW OLD DID YOU SAY THIS WAS?
THE TEMPLE? IT PREDATES STONEHENGE BY SIX THOUSAND YEARS. THE OLDEST PLACE OF WORSHIP ANYWHERE ON THE PLANET.
BUT THAT'S NOT THE INTERESTING PART. IT'S WHAT THE MEGALITHS HAVE BEEN BUILT AROUND THAT'S CAUSING ALL THE EXCITEMENT.
YOU HAVE TO REMEMBER THIS PREDATES METAL TOOLS, DOCTOR QUINN. THIS WAS BEFORE MAN EVEN HAD POTTERY...

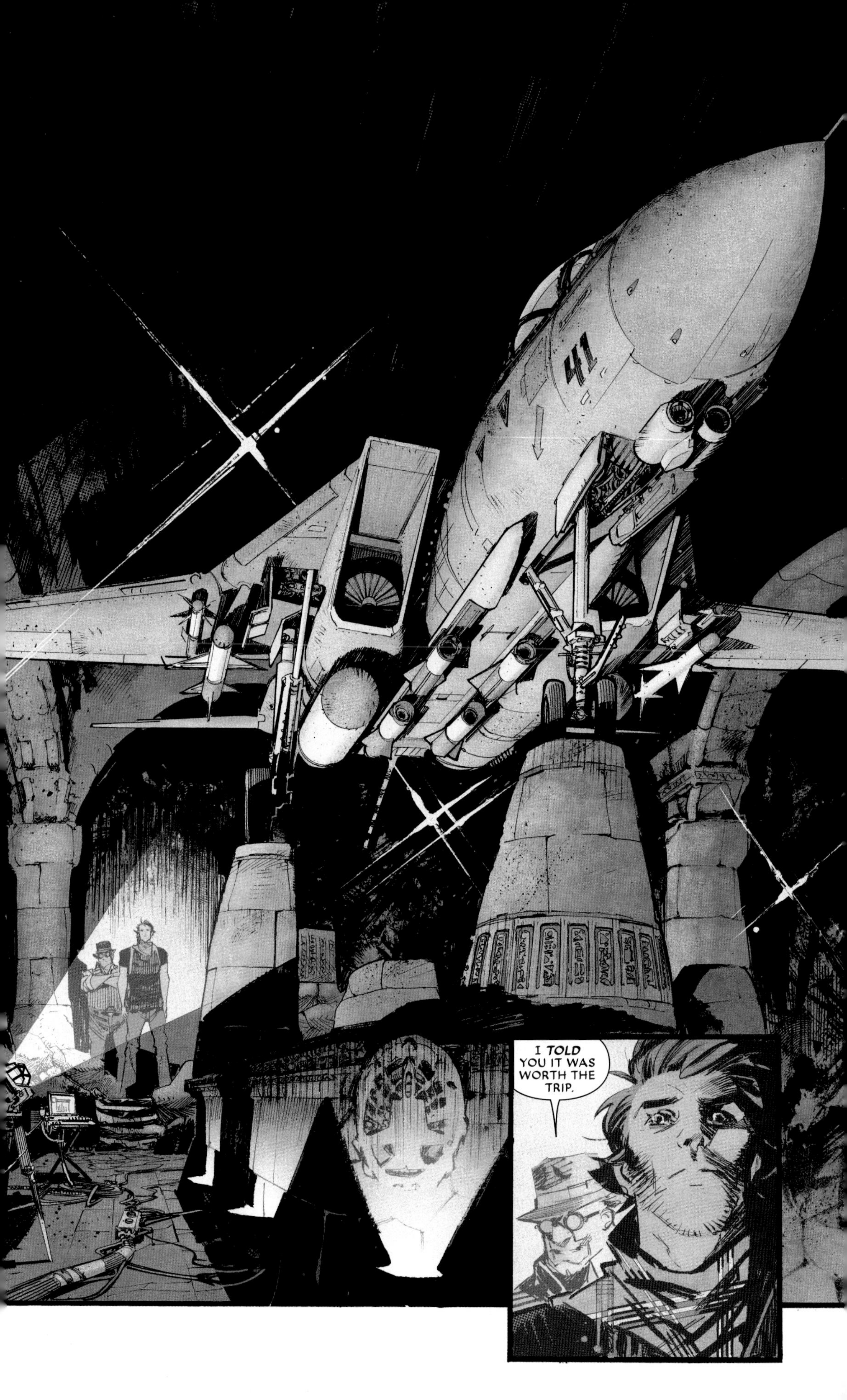
I *TOLD* YOU IT WAS WORTH THE TRIP.

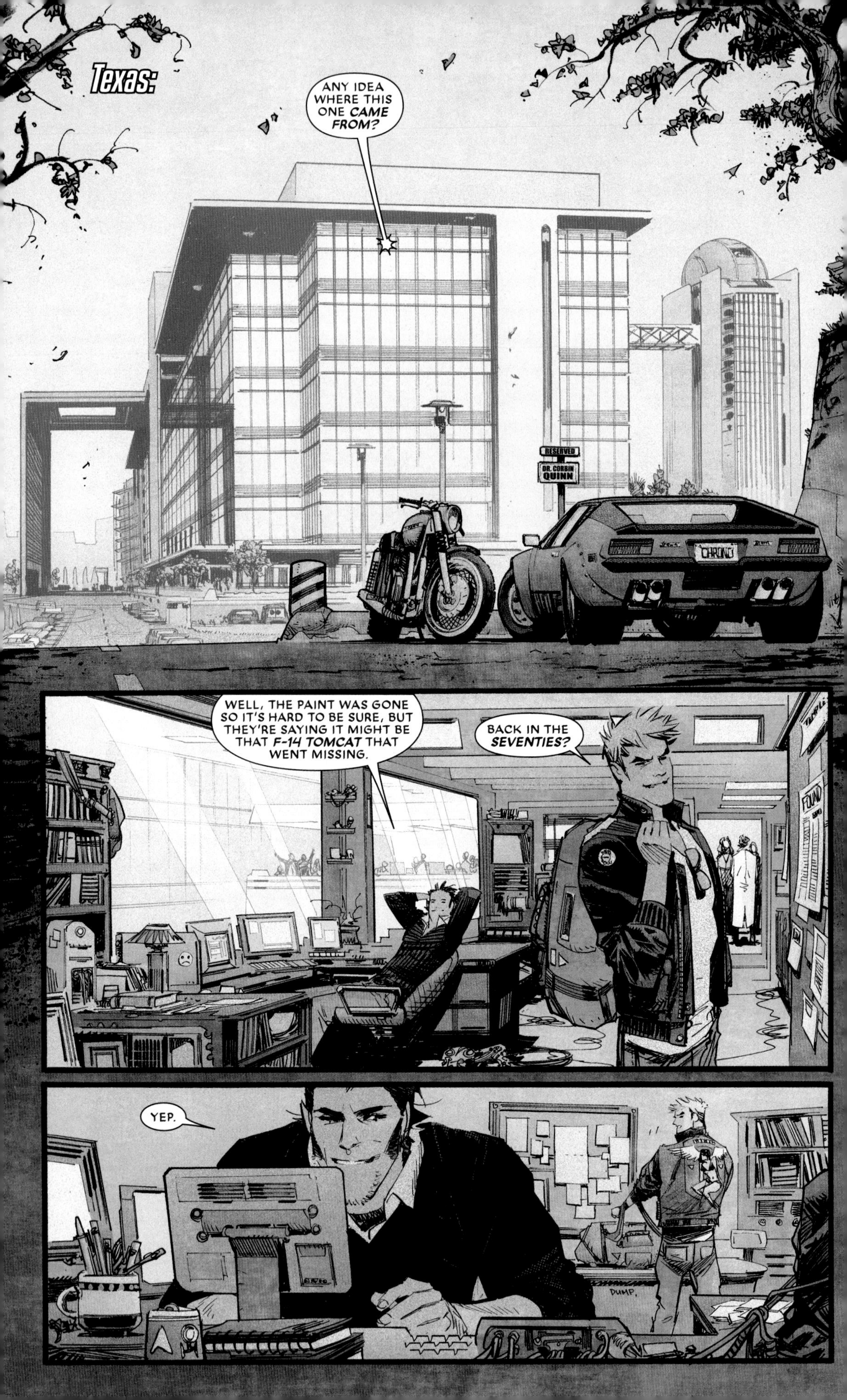
Texas:
ANY IDEA WHERE THIS ONE CAME FROM?
RESERVED
DR. CORBIN QUINN
CHRONO
WELL, THE PAINT WAS GONE SO IT'S HARD TO BE SURE, BUT THEY'RE SAYING IT MIGHT BE THAT F-14 TOMCAT THAT WENT MISSING.
BACK IN THE SEVENTIES?
FOUND
YEP.
DUMP.

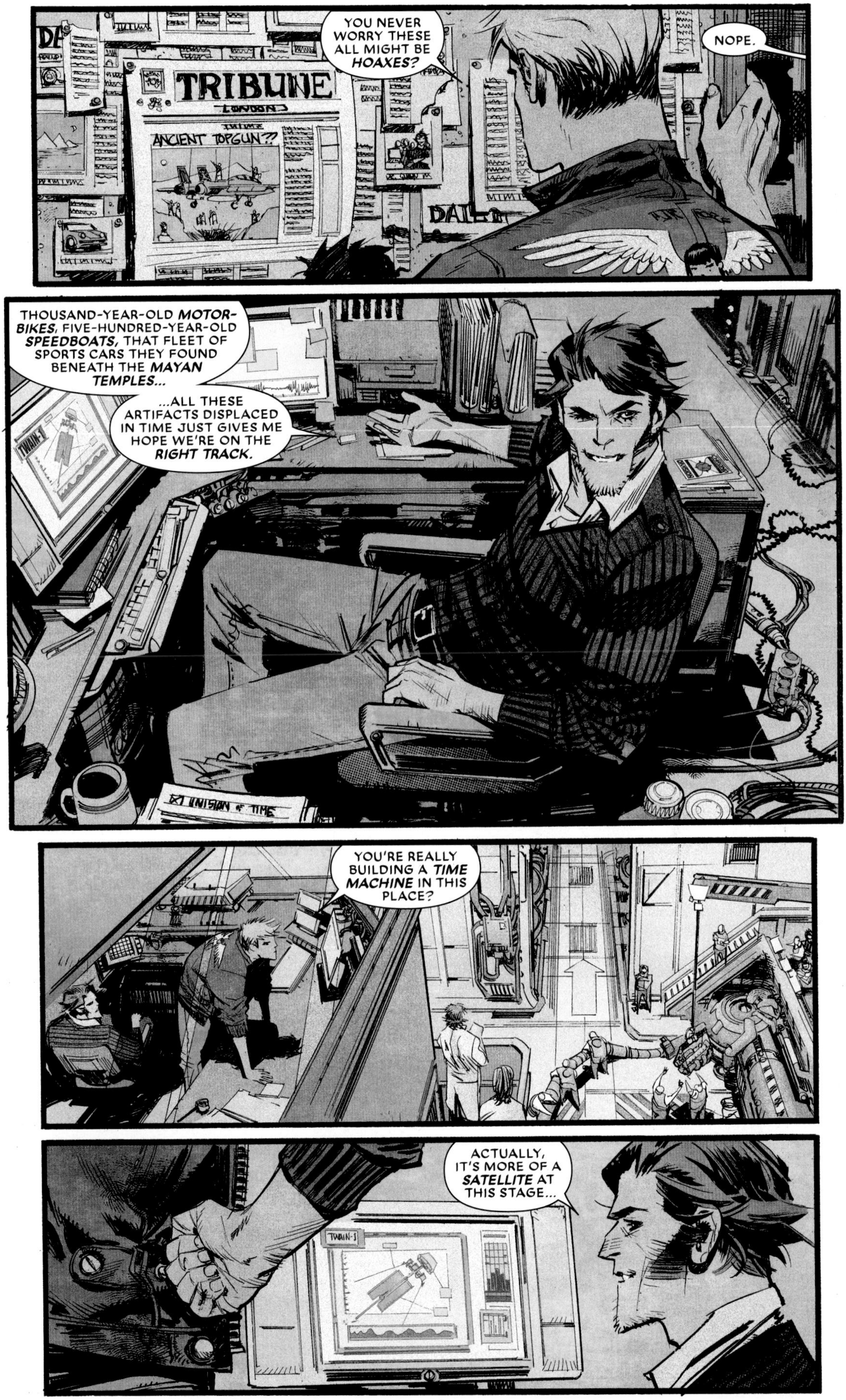
TRIBUNE
ANCIENT TOPGUN??
YOU NEVER WORRY THESE ALL MIGHT BE *HOAXES?*
NOPE.
THOUSAND-YEAR-OLD *MOTOR-BIKES,* FIVE-HUNDRED-YEAR-OLD *SPEEDBOATS,* THAT FLEET OF SPORTS CARS THEY FOUND BENEATH THE *MAYAN TEMPLES...*
...ALL THESE ARTIFACTS DISPLACED IN TIME JUST GIVES ME HOPE WE'RE ON THE *RIGHT TRACK.*
TWAIN-1
UNISON OF TIME
YOU'RE REALLY BUILDING A *TIME MACHINE* IN THIS PLACE?
ACTUALLY, IT'S MORE OF A *SATELLITE* AT THIS STAGE...
TWAIN-1

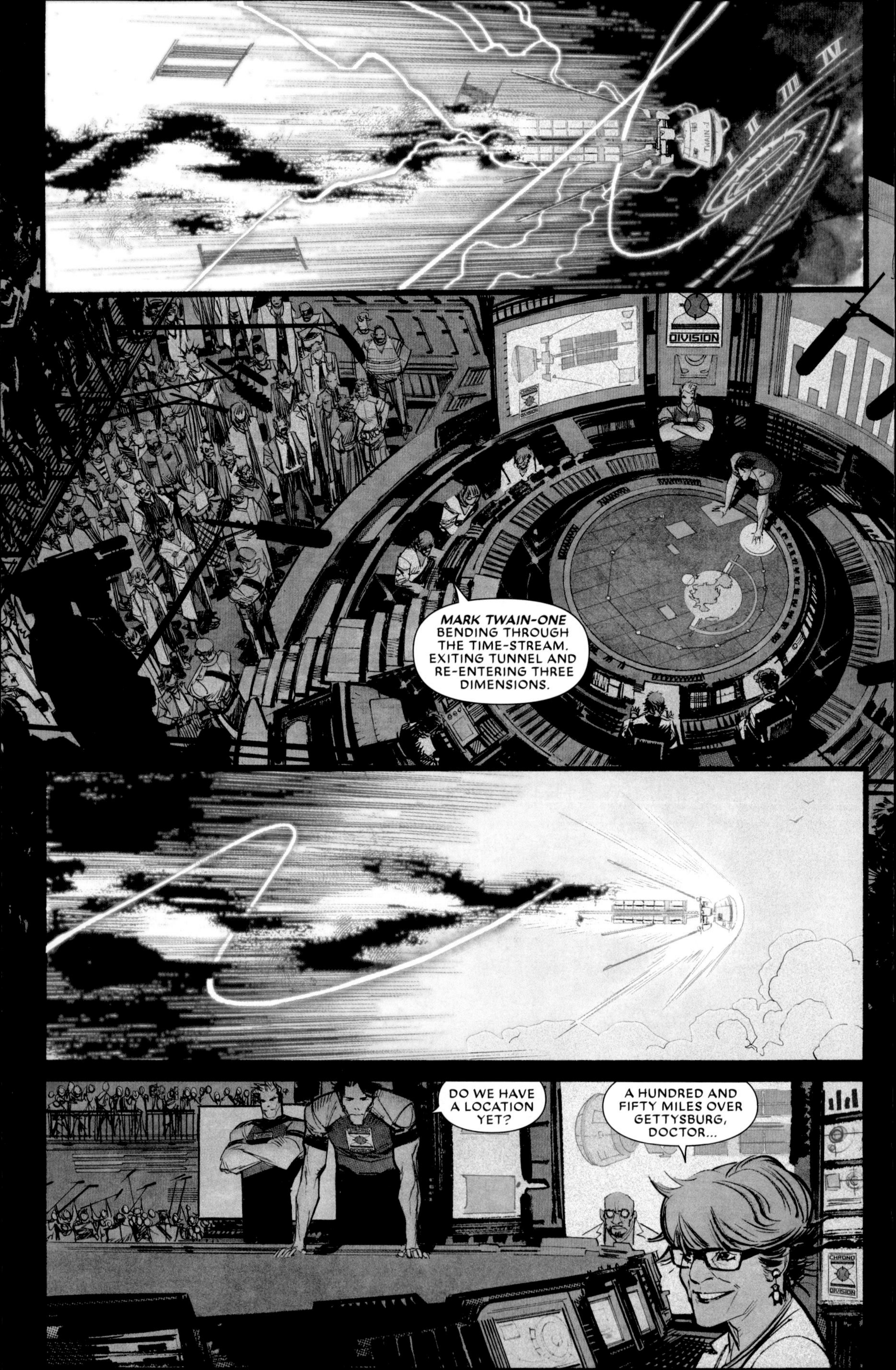
TWAIN-1
DIVISION
MARK TWAIN-ONE BENDING THROUGH THE TIME-STREAM. EXITING TUNNEL AND RE-ENTERING THREE DIMENSIONS.
DO WE HAVE A LOCATION YET?
A HUNDRED AND FIFTY MILES OVER GETTYSBURG, DOCTOR...
CHRONO DIVISION

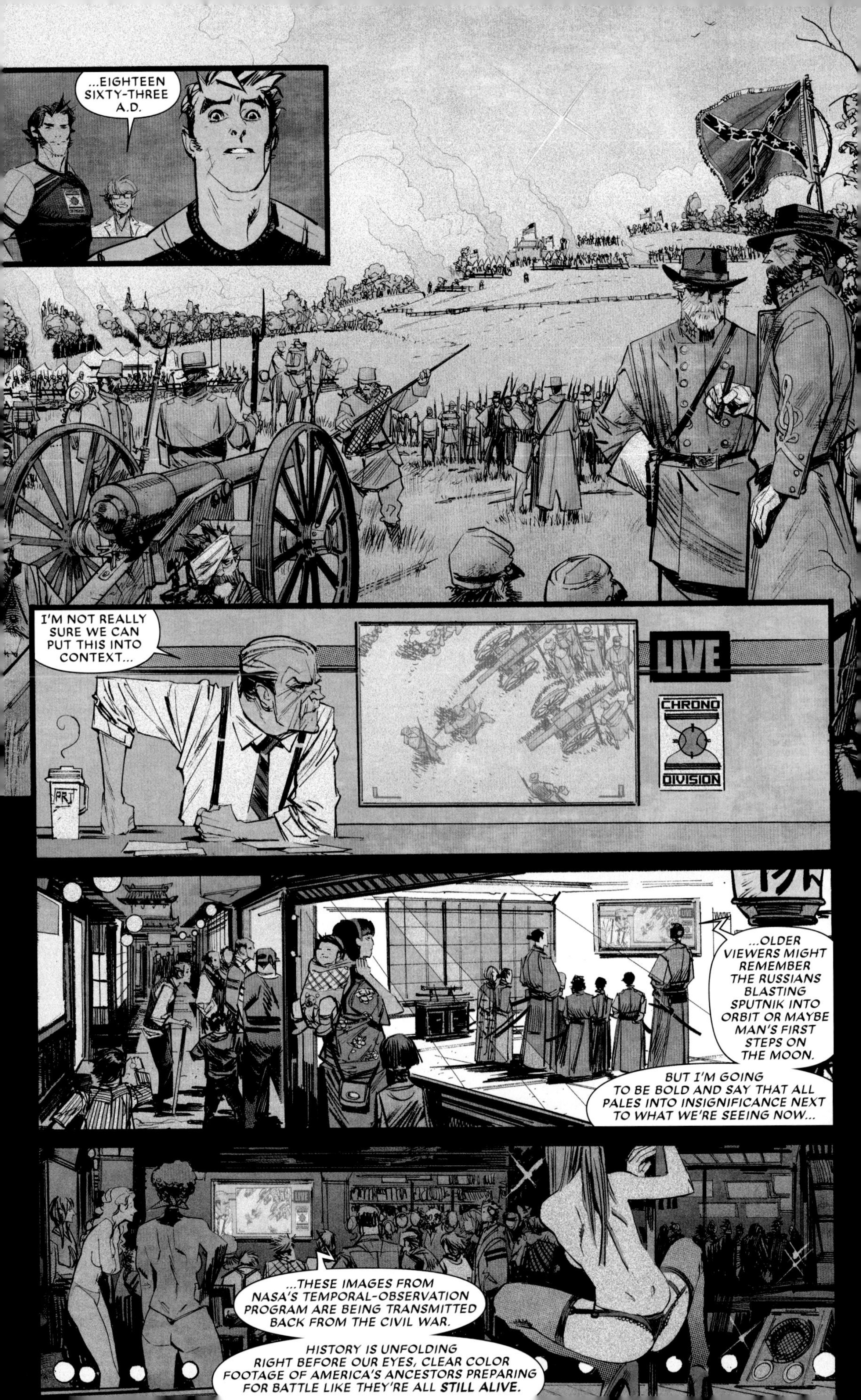
...EIGHTEEN SIXTY-THREE A.D.
I'M NOT REALLY SURE WE CAN PUT THIS INTO CONTEXT...
LIVE
CHRONO DIVISION
...OLDER VIEWERS MIGHT REMEMBER THE RUSSIANS BLASTING SPUTNIK INTO ORBIT OR MAYBE MAN'S FIRST STEPS ON THE MOON.
BUT I'M GOING TO BE BOLD AND SAY THAT ALL PALES INTO INSIGNIFICANCE NEXT TO WHAT WE'RE SEEING NOW...
...THESE IMAGES FROM NASA'S TEMPORAL-OBSERVATION PROGRAM ARE BEING TRANSMITTED BACK FROM THE CIVIL WAR.
HISTORY IS UNFOLDING RIGHT BEFORE OUR EYES, CLEAR COLOR FOOTAGE OF AMERICA'S ANCESTORS PREPARING FOR BATTLE LIKE THEY'RE ALL STILL ALIVE.

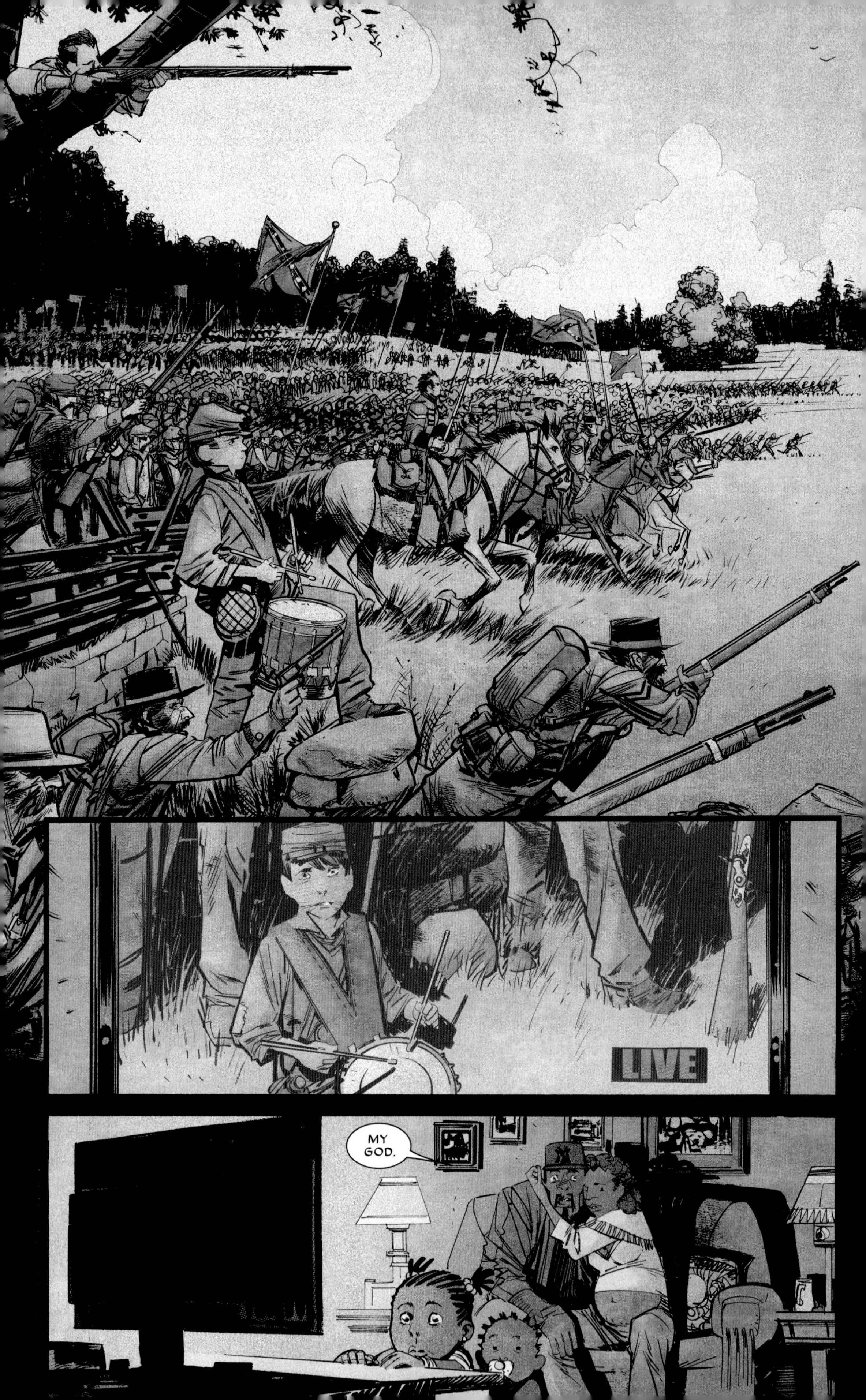
LIVE
MY GOD.

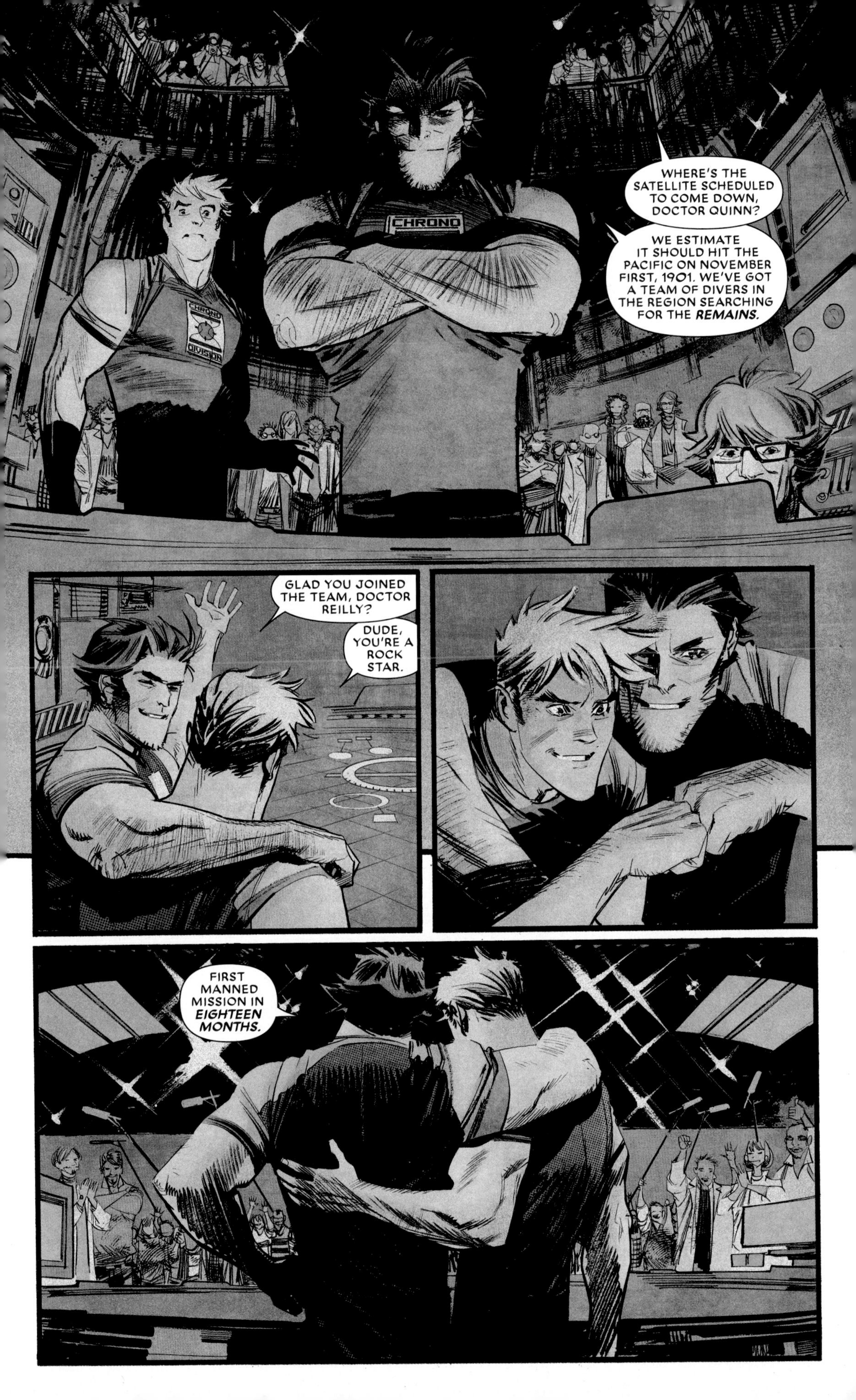
WHERE'S THE SATELLITE SCHEDULED TO COME DOWN, DOCTOR QUINN?
WE ESTIMATE IT SHOULD HIT THE PACIFIC ON NOVEMBER FIRST, 1901. WE'VE GOT A TEAM OF DIVERS IN THE REGION SEARCHING FOR THE *REMAINS.*
GLAD YOU JOINED THE TEAM, DOCTOR REILLY?
DUDE, YOU'RE A ROCK STAR.
FIRST MANNED MISSION IN *EIGHTEEN MONTHS.*

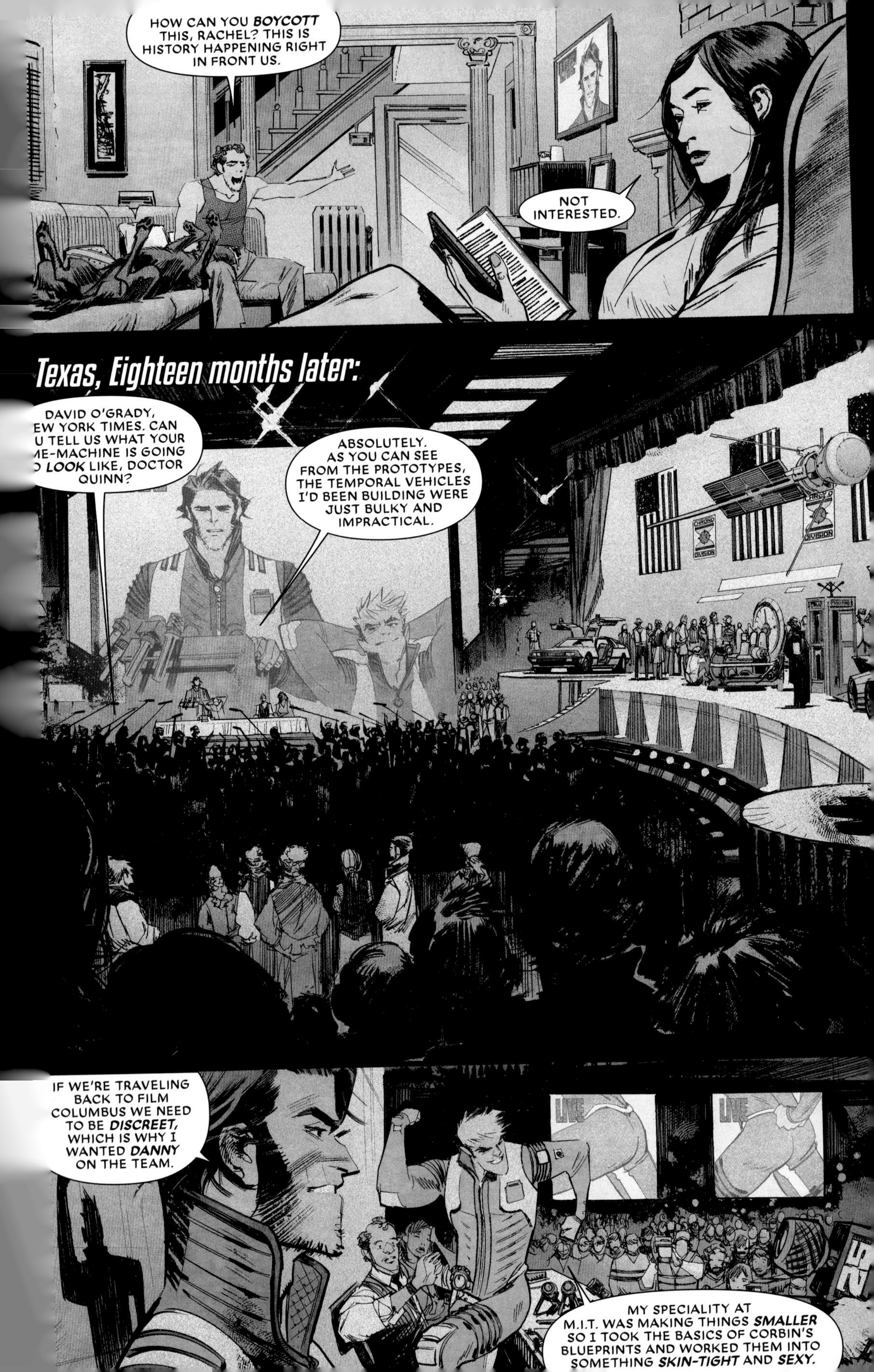
HOW CAN YOU BOYCOTT THIS, RACHEL? THIS IS HISTORY HAPPENING RIGHT IN FRONT US.
NOT INTERESTED.
Texas, Eighteen months later:
DAVID O'GRADY, EW YORK TIMES. CAN U TELL US WHAT YOUR ME-MACHINE IS GOING D LOOK LIKE, DOCTOR QUINN?
ABSOLUTELY. AS YOU CAN SEE FROM THE PROTOTYPES, THE TEMPORAL VEHICLES I'D BEEN BUILDING WERE JUST BULKY AND IMPRACTICAL.
CHRONO DIVISION
IF WE'RE TRAVELING BACK TO FILM COLUMBUS WE NEED TO BE DISCREET, WHICH IS WHY I WANTED DANNY ON THE TEAM.
LIVE
LIVE
MY SPECIALITY AT M.I.T. WAS MAKING THINGS SMALLER SO I TOOK THE BASICS OF CORBIN'S BLUEPRINTS AND WORKED THEM INTO SOMETHING SKIN-TIGHT AND SEXY.

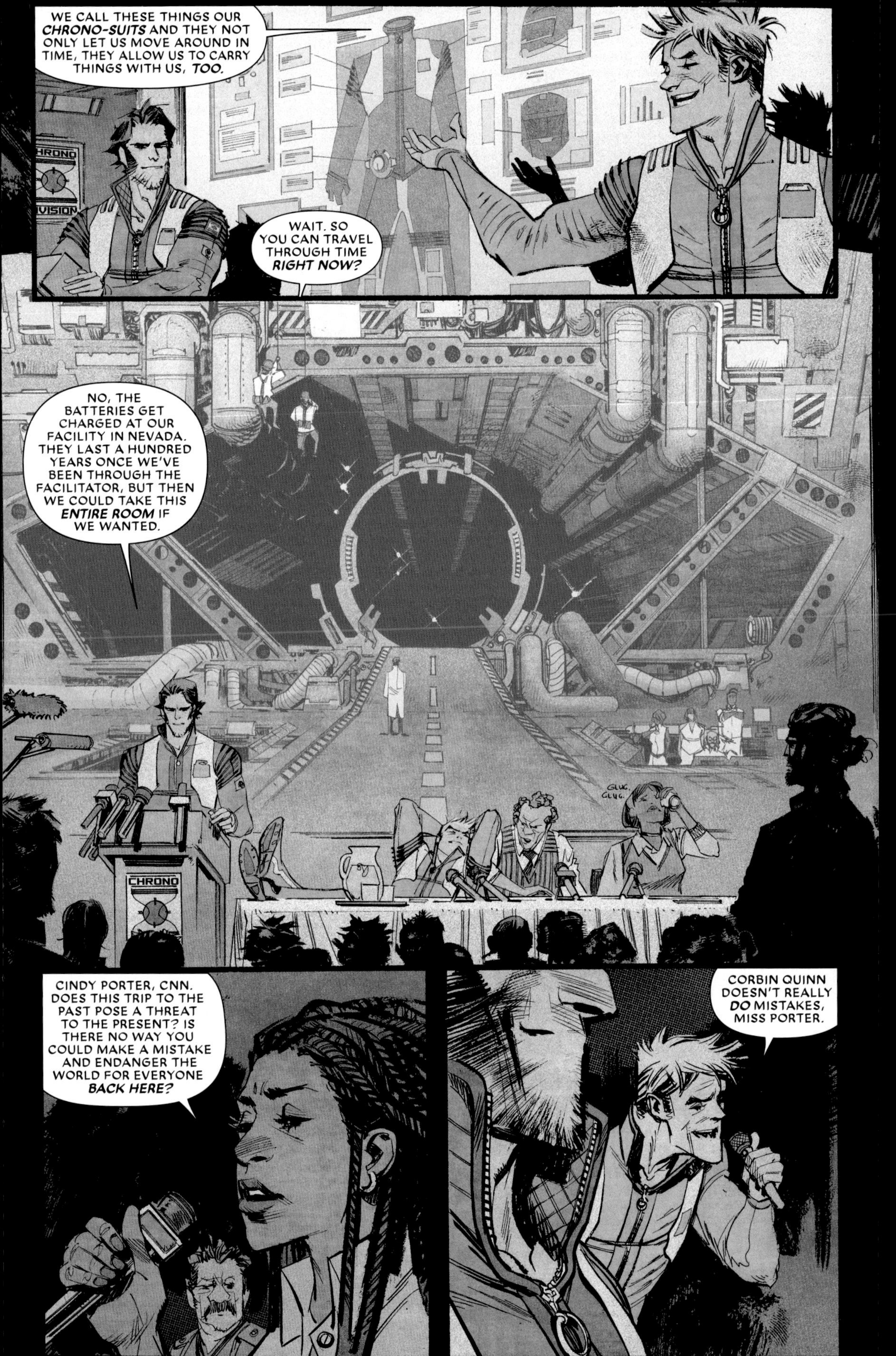
WE CALL THESE THINGS OUR *CHRONO-SUITS* AND THEY NOT ONLY LET US MOVE AROUND IN TIME, THEY ALLOW US TO CARRY THINGS WITH US, *TOO.*
CHRONO
DIVISION
WAIT. SO YOU CAN TRAVEL THROUGH TIME *RIGHT NOW?*
NO, THE BATTERIES GET CHARGED AT OUR FACILITY IN NEVADA. THEY LAST A HUNDRED YEARS ONCE WE'VE BEEN THROUGH THE FACILITATOR, BUT THEN WE COULD TAKE THIS *ENTIRE ROOM* IF WE WANTED.
GLUG. GLUG.
CHRONO
CINDY PORTER, CNN. DOES THIS TRIP TO THE PAST POSE A THREAT TO THE PRESENT? IS THERE NO WAY YOU COULD MAKE A MISTAKE AND ENDANGER THE WORLD FOR EVERYONE *BACK HERE?*
CORBIN QUINN DOESN'T REALLY *DO* MISTAKES, MISS PORTER.

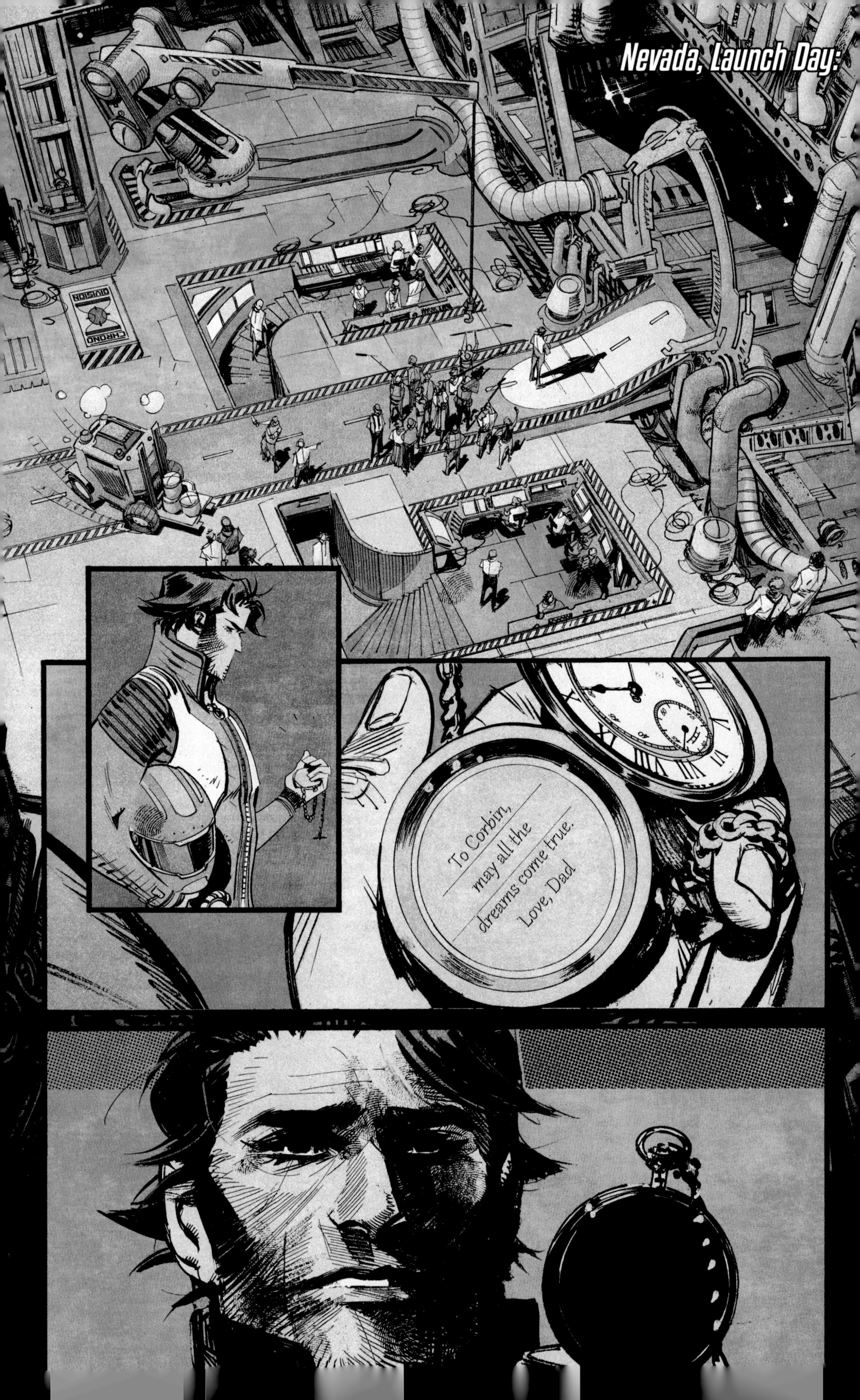
Nevada, Launch Day:
CHRONO DIVISION
To Corbin, may all the dreams come true. Love, Dad

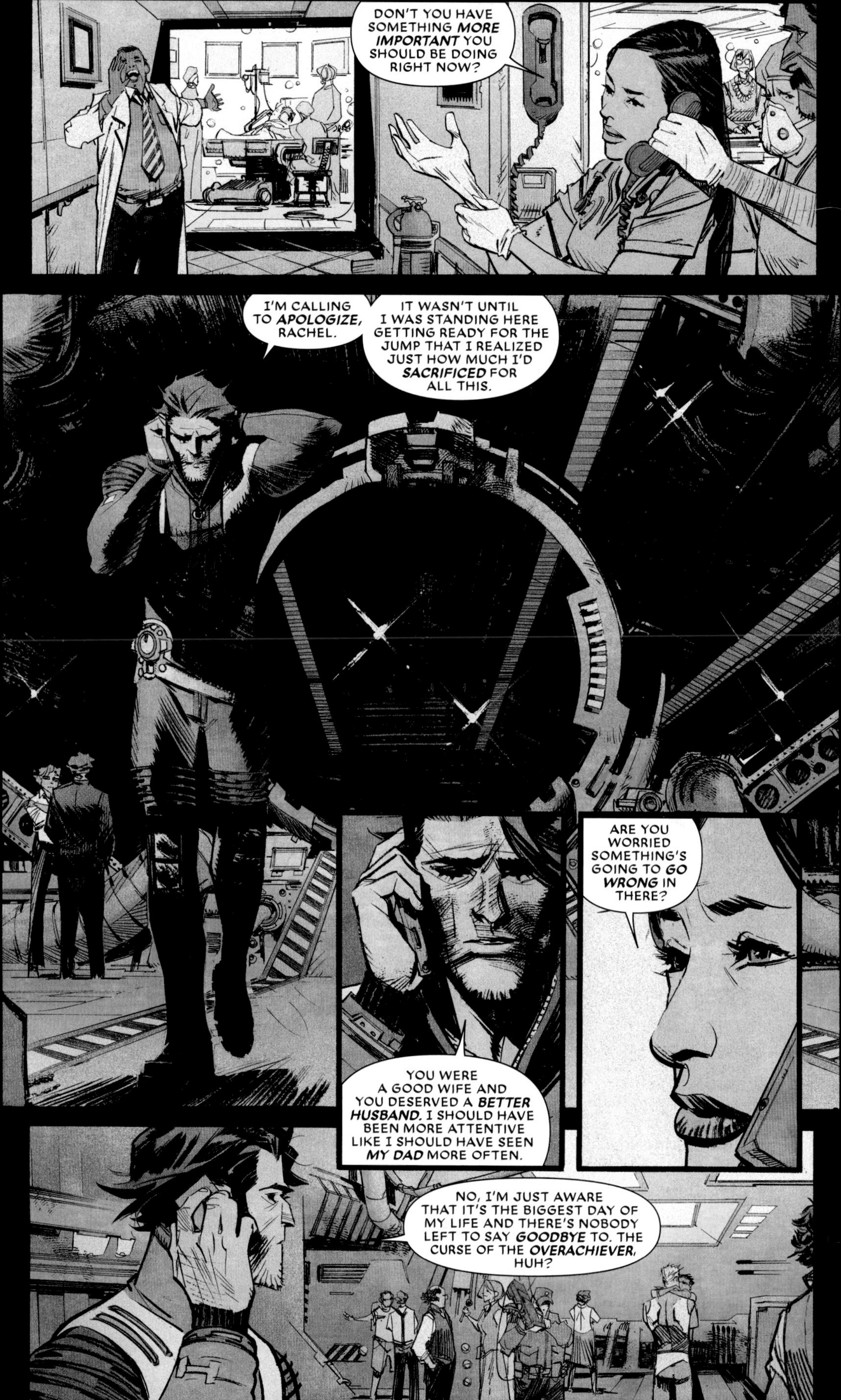

DON'T YOU HAVE SOMETHING MORE IMPORTANT YOU SHOULD BE DOING RIGHT NOW?
I'M CALLING TO APOLOGIZE, RACHEL.
IT WASN'T UNTIL I WAS STANDING HERE GETTING READY FOR THE JUMP THAT I REALIZED JUST HOW MUCH I'D SACRIFICED FOR ALL THIS.
ARE YOU WORRIED SOMETHING'S GOING TO GO WRONG IN THERE?
YOU WERE A GOOD WIFE AND YOU DESERVED A BETTER HUSBAND. I SHOULD HAVE BEEN MORE ATTENTIVE LIKE I SHOULD HAVE SEEN MY DAD MORE OFTEN.
NO, I'M JUST AWARE THAT IT'S THE BIGGEST DAY OF MY LIFE AND THERE'S NOBODY LEFT TO SAY GOODBYE TO. THE CURSE OF THE OVERACHIEVER, HUH?

HOW COULD YOU LEAVE ME FOR THAT *SLEAZY LAWYER?*

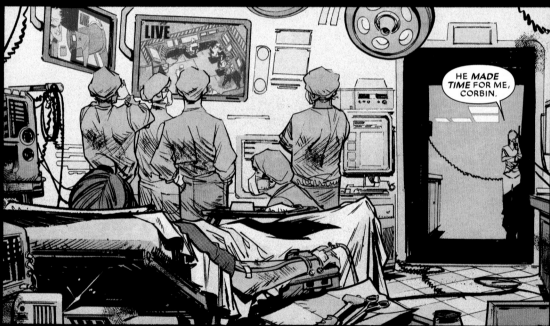

HE *MADE TIME* FOR ME, CORBIN.

UH, TIME-JUMP IN T-MINUS FIVE, DOCTOR REILLY.

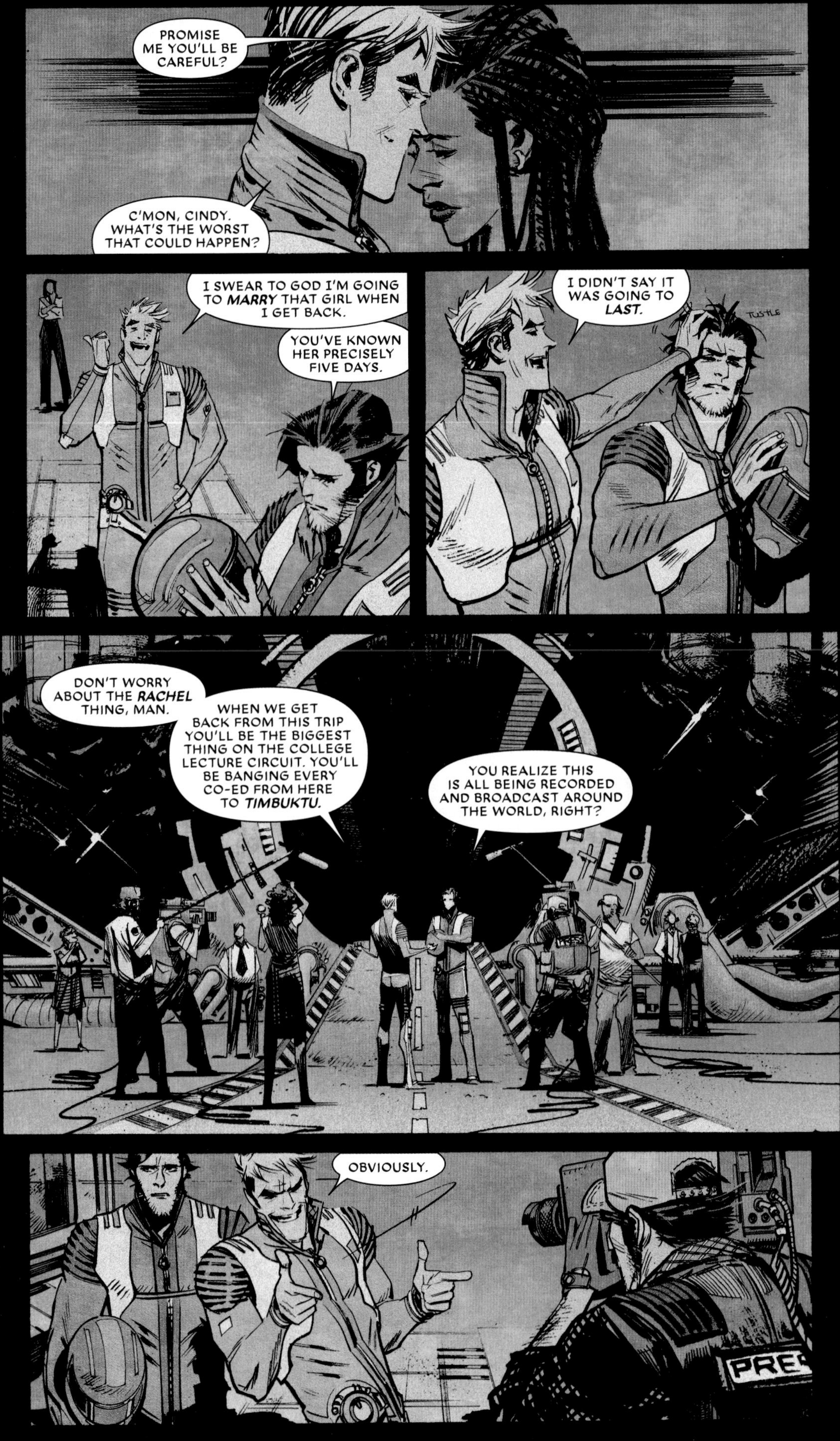
PROMISE ME YOU'LL BE CAREFUL?
C'MON, CINDY. WHAT'S THE WORST THAT COULD HAPPEN?
I SWEAR TO GOD I'M GOING TO MARRY THAT GIRL WHEN I GET BACK.
YOU'VE KNOWN HER PRECISELY FIVE DAYS.
I DIDN'T SAY IT WAS GOING TO LAST.
TUSSLE
DON'T WORRY ABOUT THE RACHEL THING, MAN.
WHEN WE GET BACK FROM THIS TRIP YOU'LL BE THE BIGGEST THING ON THE COLLEGE LECTURE CIRCUIT. YOU'LL BE BANGING EVERY CO-ED FROM HERE TO TIMBUKTU.
YOU REALIZE THIS IS ALL BEING RECORDED AND BROADCAST AROUND THE WORLD, RIGHT?
OBVIOUSLY.
PRES

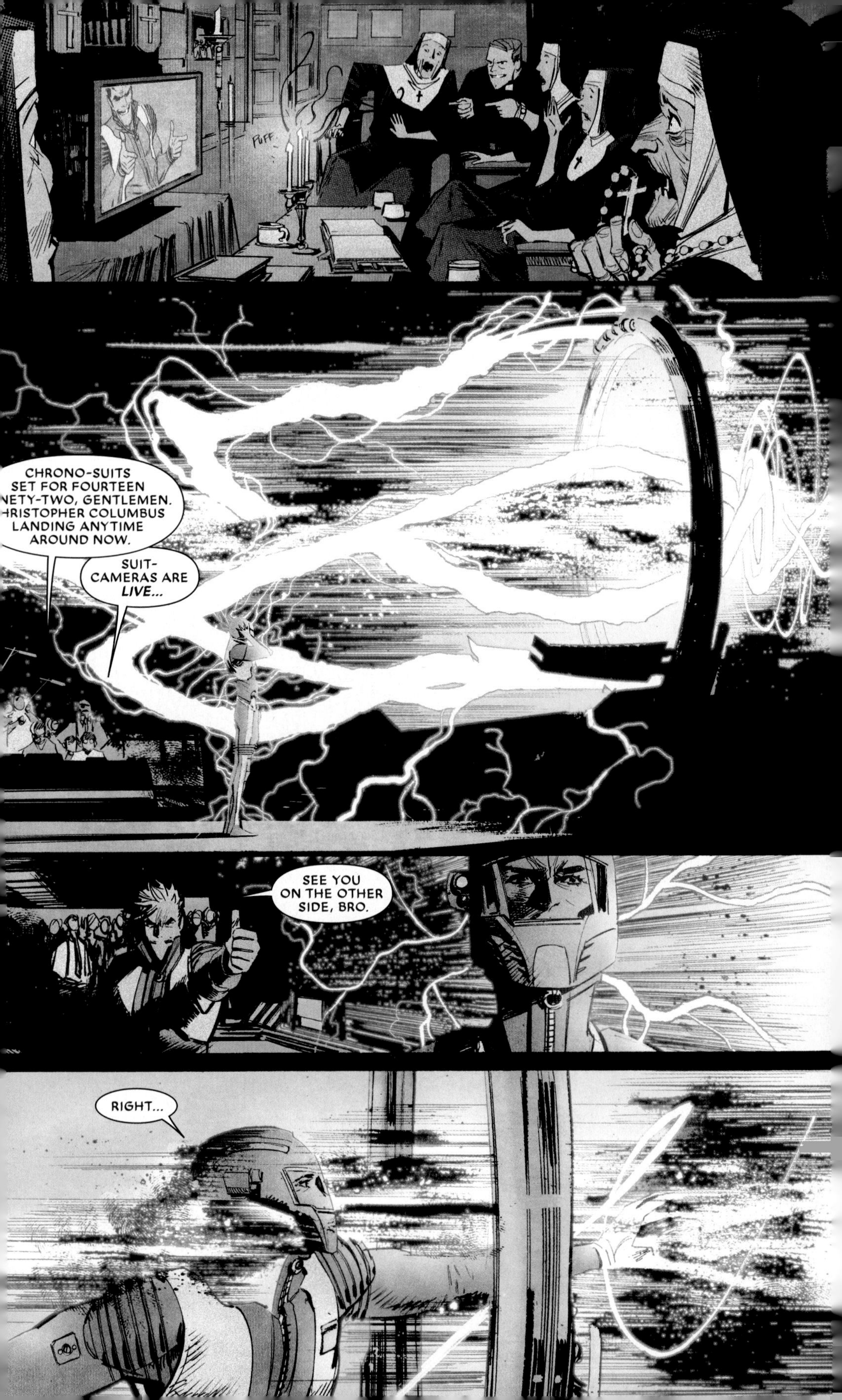
PUFF
CHRONO-SUITS SET FOR FOURTEEN NETY-TWO, GENTLEMEN. HRISTOPHER COLUMBUS LANDING ANYTIME AROUND NOW.
SUIT-CAMERAS ARE *LIVE...*
SEE YOU ON THE OTHER SIDE, BRO.
RIGHT...

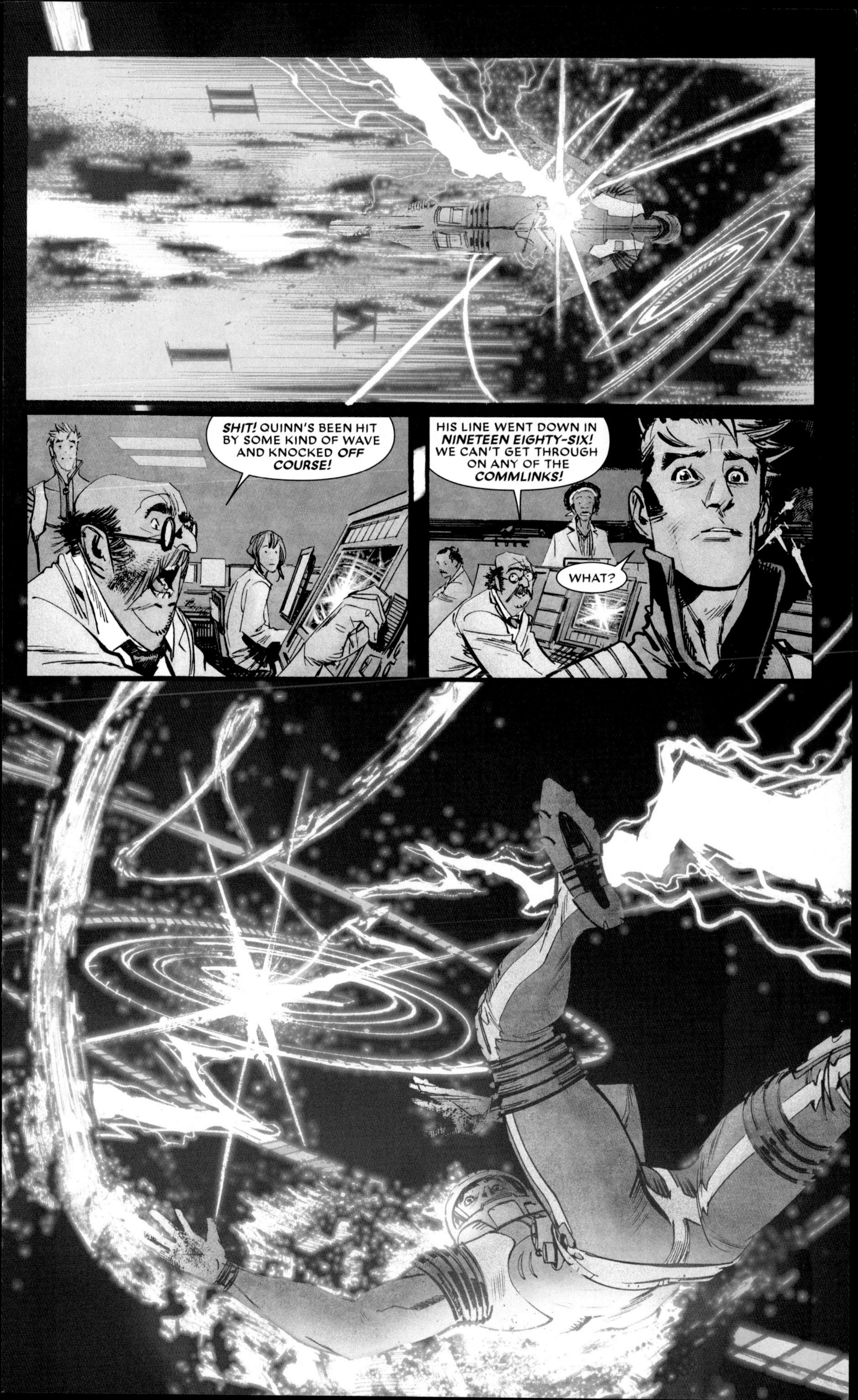
SHIT! QUINN'S BEEN HIT BY SOME KIND OF WAVE AND KNOCKED OFF COURSE!
HIS LINE WENT DOWN IN NINETEEN EIGHTY-SIX! WE CAN'T GET THROUGH ON ANY OF THE COMMLINKS!
WHAT?

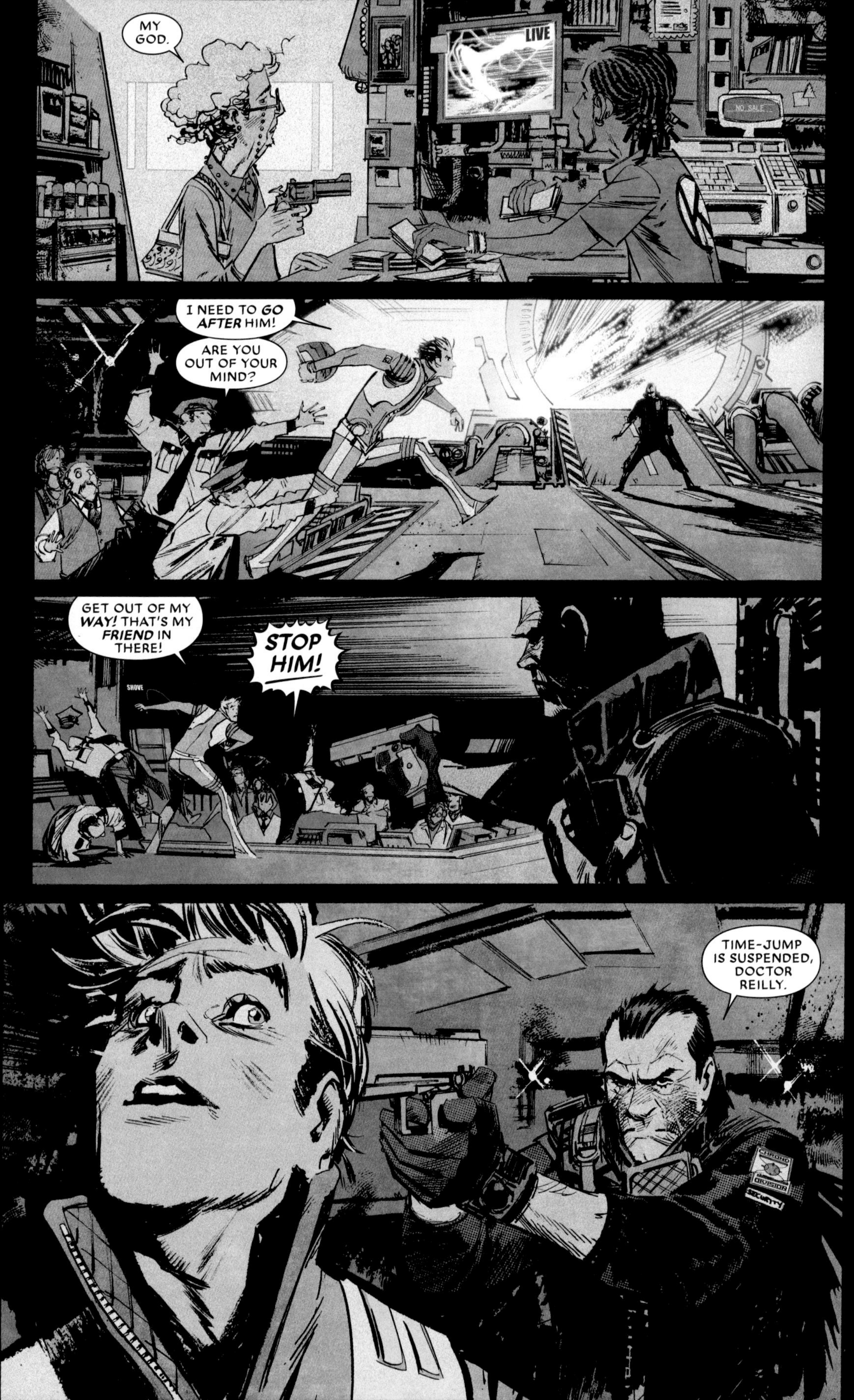
MY GOD.
LIVE
NO SALE
I NEED TO GO AFTER HIM!
ARE YOU OUT OF YOUR MIND?
GET OUT OF MY WAY! THAT'S MY FRIEND IN THERE!
SHOVE
STOP HIM!
TIME-JUMP IS SUSPENDED, DOCTOR REILLY.

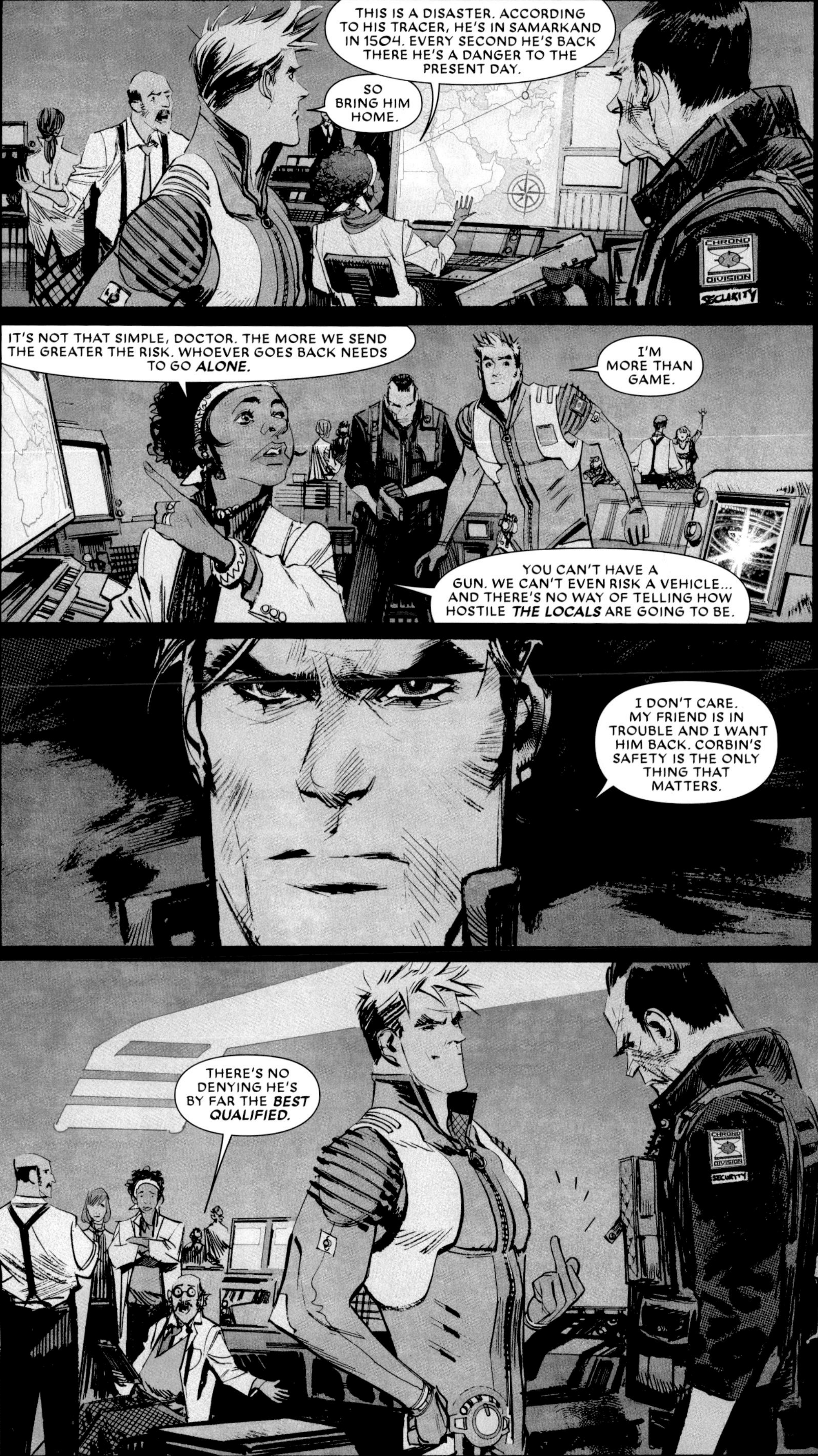
THIS IS A DISASTER. ACCORDING TO HIS TRACER, HE'S IN SAMARKAND IN 1504. EVERY SECOND HE'S BACK THERE HE'S A DANGER TO THE PRESENT DAY.
SO BRING HIM HOME.
CHRONO DIVISION SECURITY
IT'S NOT THAT SIMPLE, DOCTOR. THE MORE WE SEND THE GREATER THE RISK. WHOEVER GOES BACK NEEDS TO GO *ALONE.*
I'M MORE THAN GAME.
YOU CAN'T HAVE A GUN. WE CAN'T EVEN RISK A VEHICLE... AND THERE'S NO WAY OF TELLING HOW HOSTILE *THE LOCALS* ARE GOING TO BE.
I DON'T CARE. MY FRIEND IS IN TROUBLE AND I WANT HIM BACK. CORBIN'S SAFETY IS THE ONLY THING THAT MATTERS.
THERE'S NO DENYING HE'S BY FAR THE *BEST QUALIFIED.*
CHRONO DIVISION SECURITY

OKAY, FIRE IT UP.

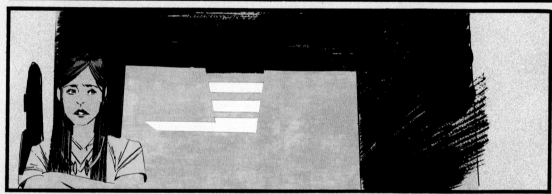

I'LL STAY IN TOUCH THROUGH THE FOUR-D LINK, BUT I DON'T ANTICIPATE ANY COMPLICATIONS. AS SOON AS I FIND HIM I'LL BRING HIM STRAIGHT BACK. WE WON'T BE HANGING AROUND.

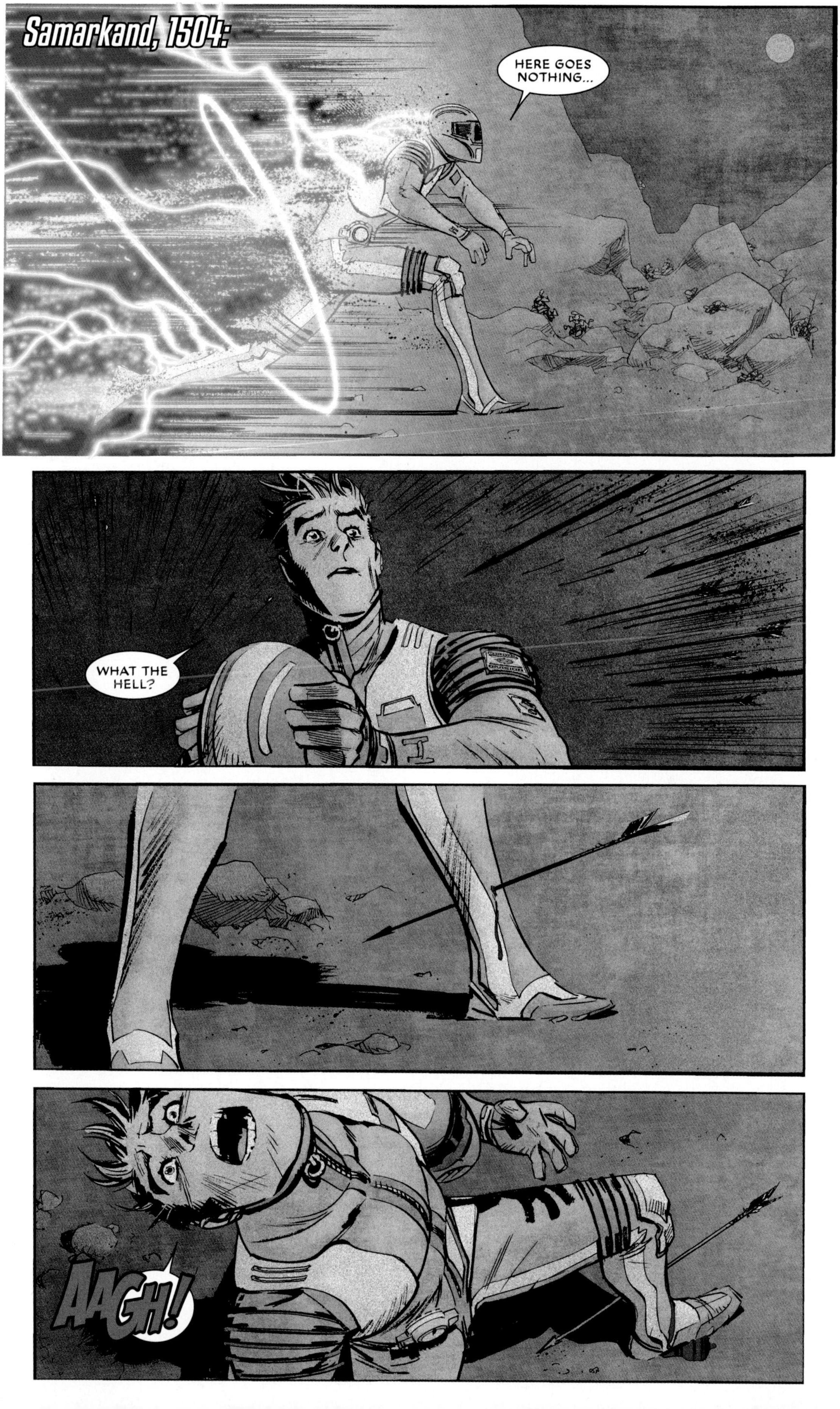
Samarkand, 1504:
HERE GOES NOTHING...
WHAT THE HELL?
AAGH!

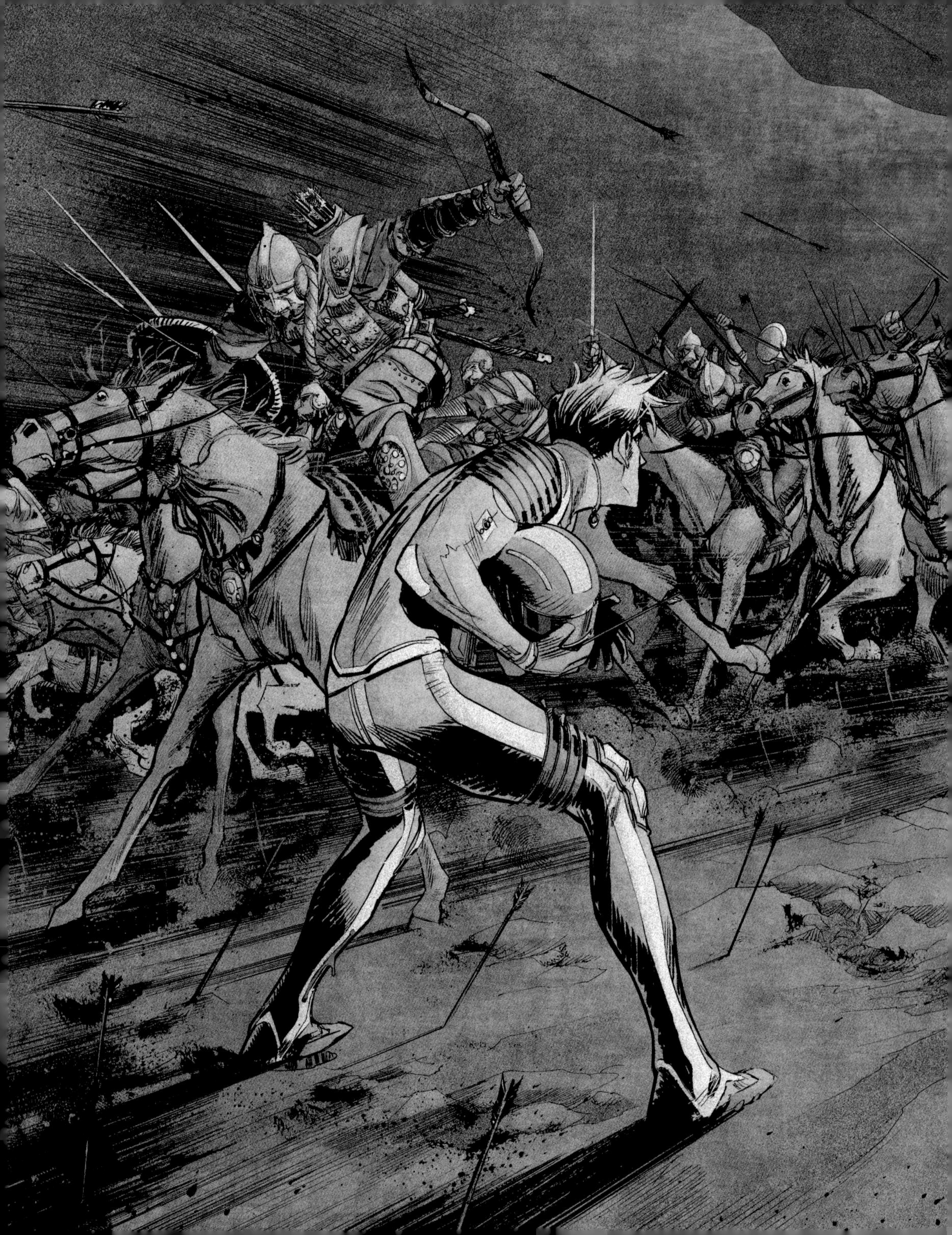

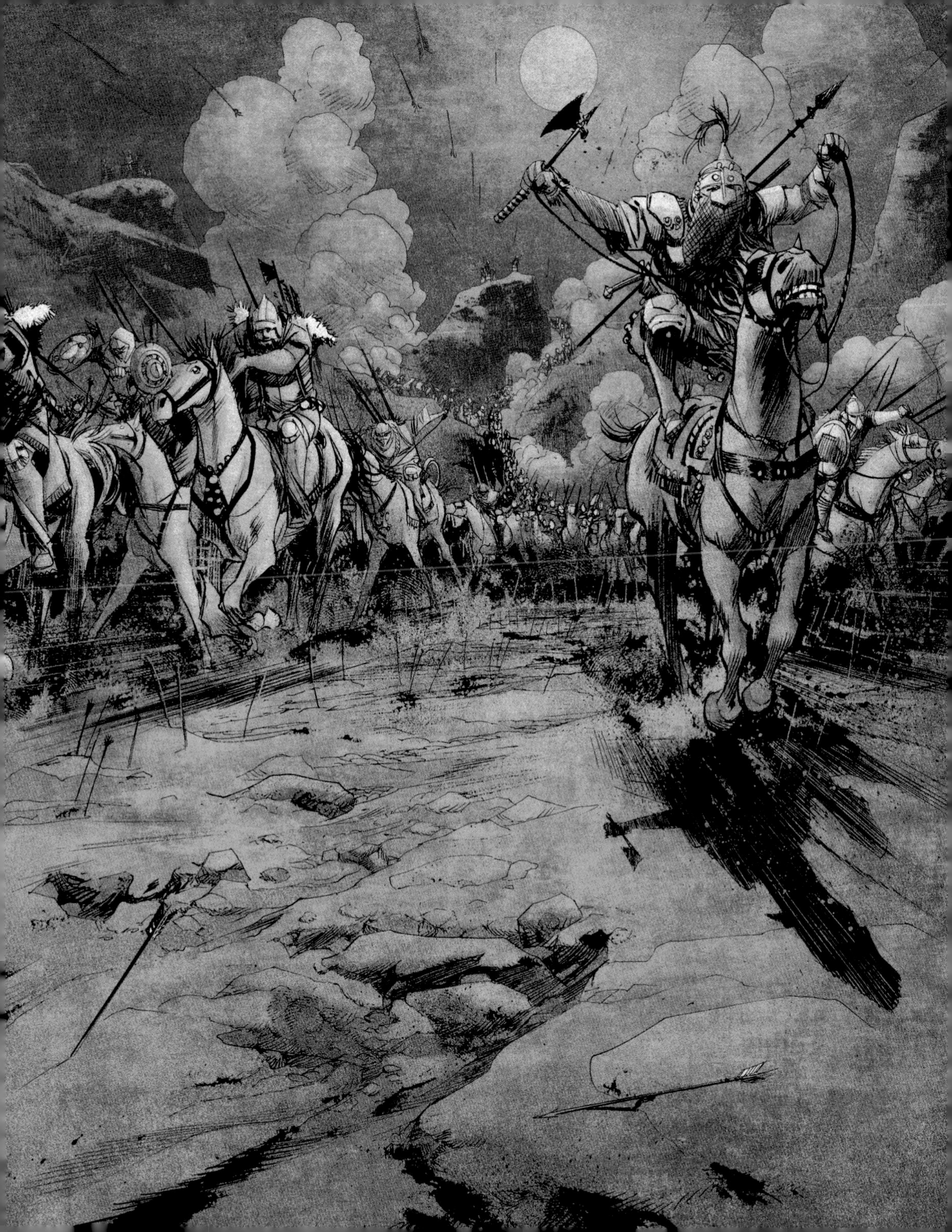

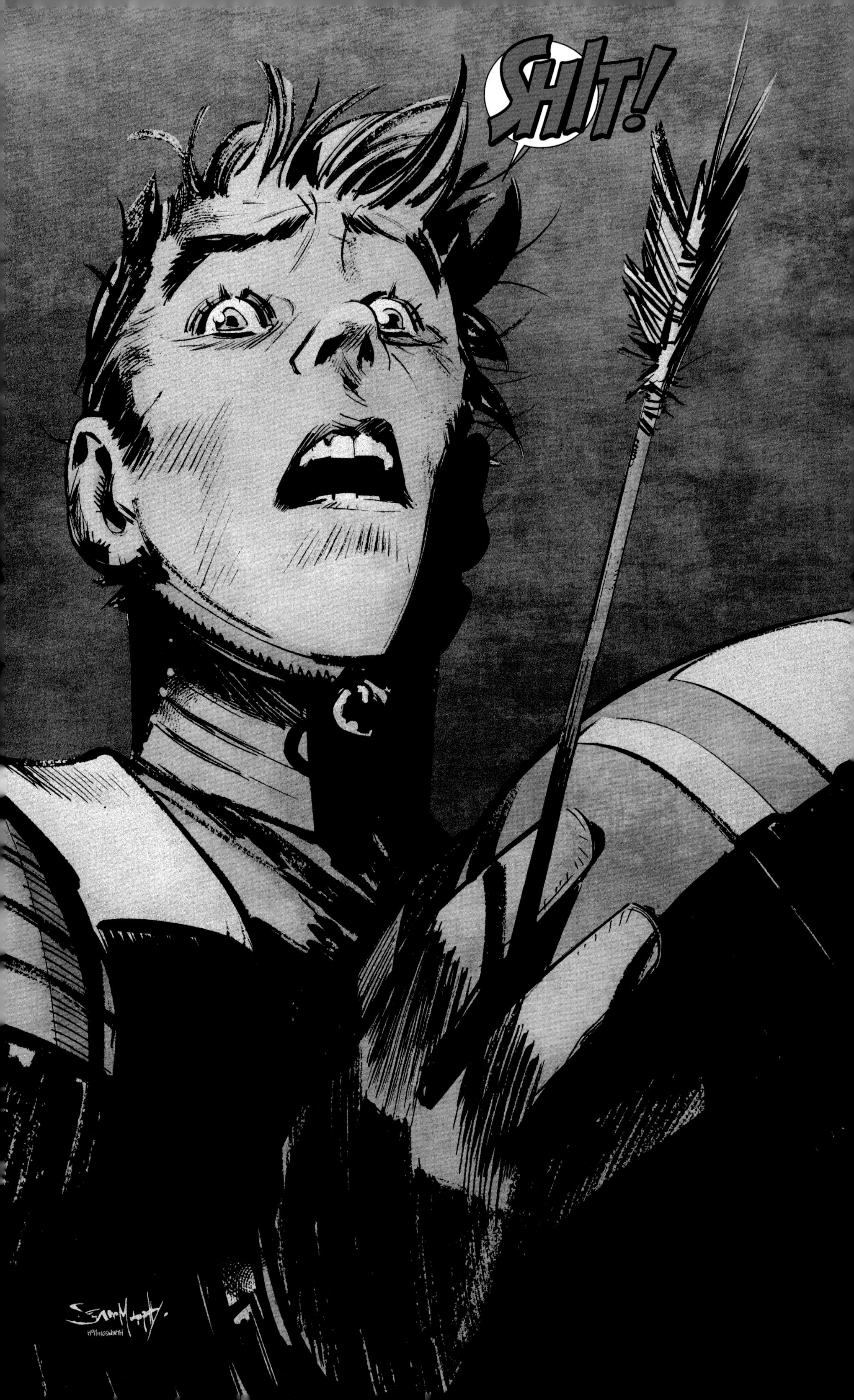
SHIT!

TWO

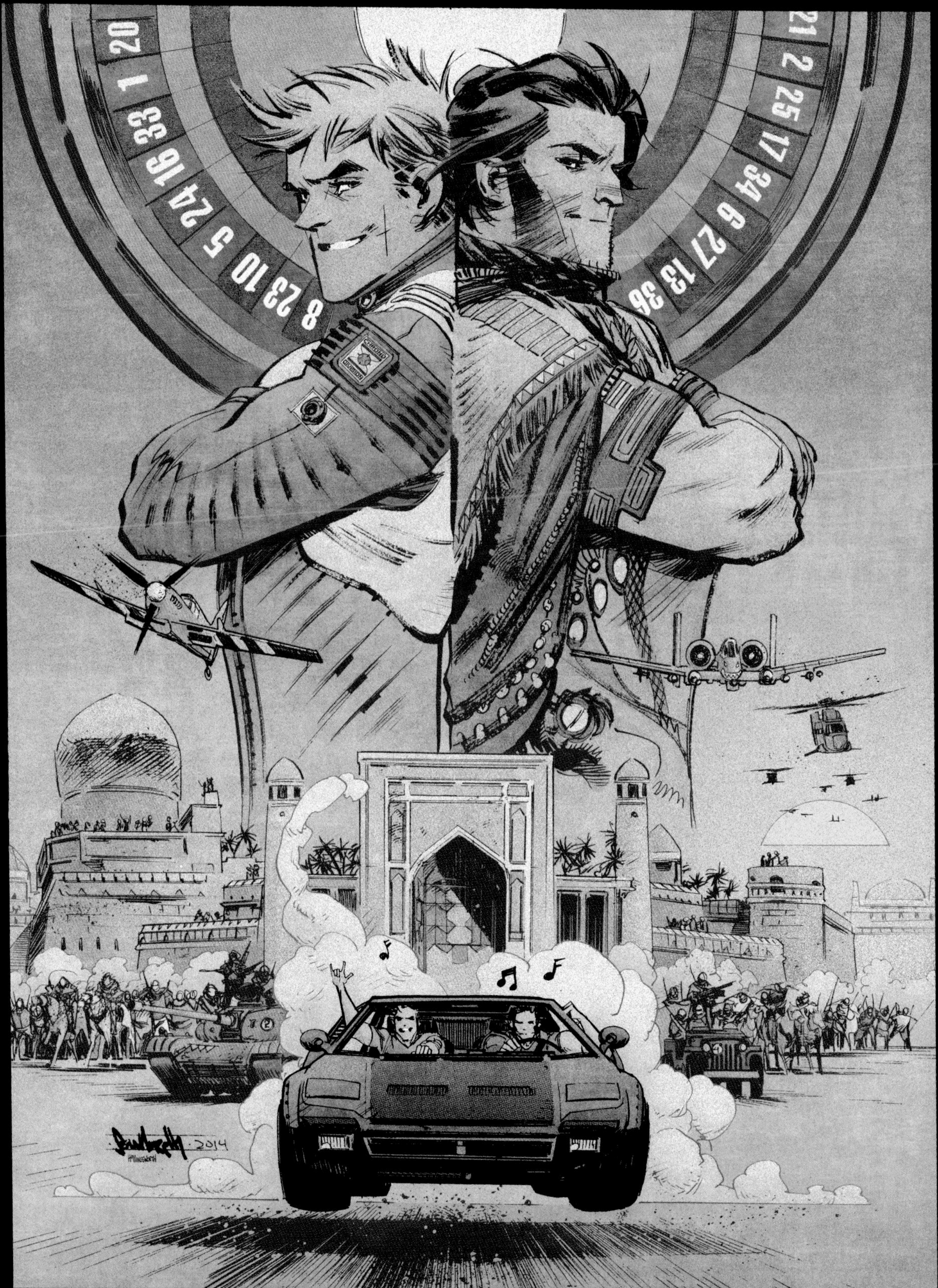

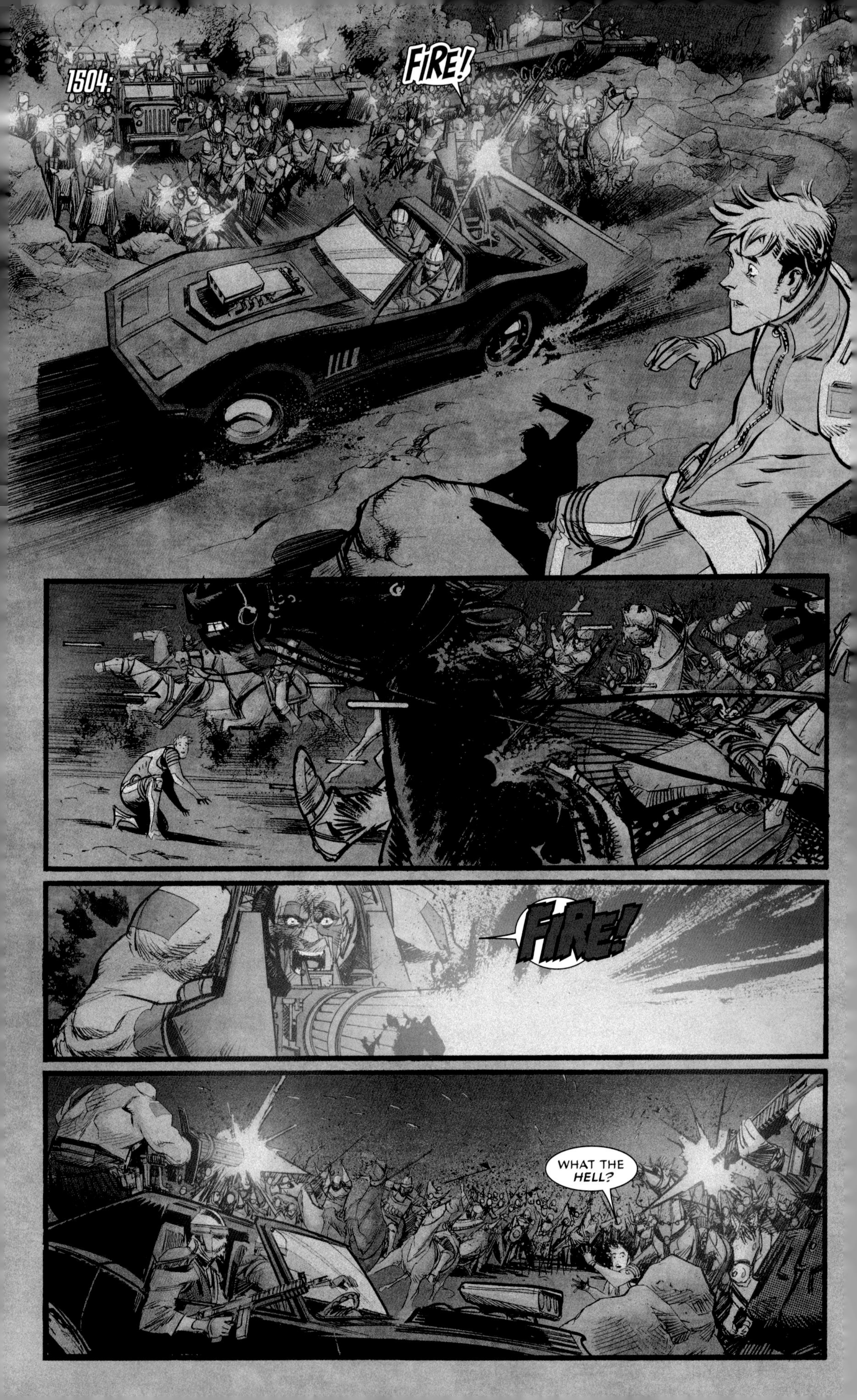
1504:
FIRE!
FIRE!
WHAT THE HELL?

STOP! I'M HERE ON A RESCUE MISSION!
THAT'S RIGHT, YOU COWARDS! FLEE TO YOUR WHORES AND TELL THEM WE'RE UNBEATABLE! OUR CITY'S WALLS WILL NOT BE BREACHED!

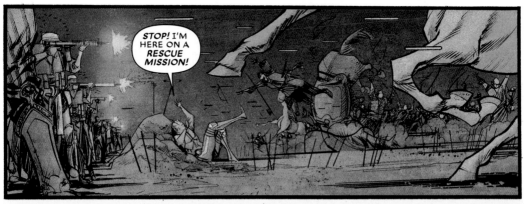

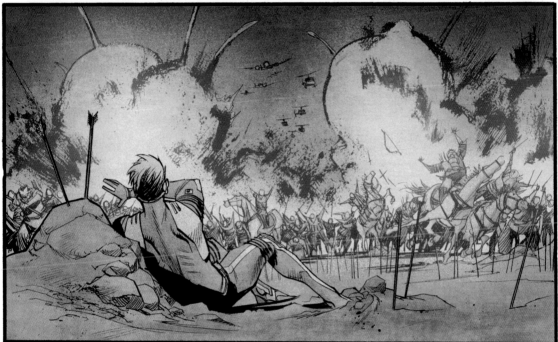

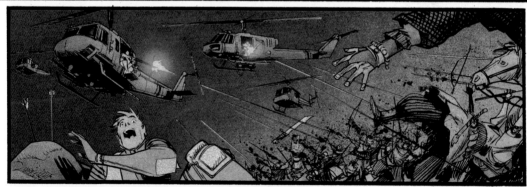

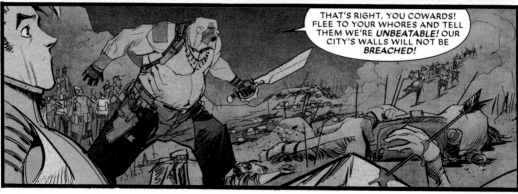

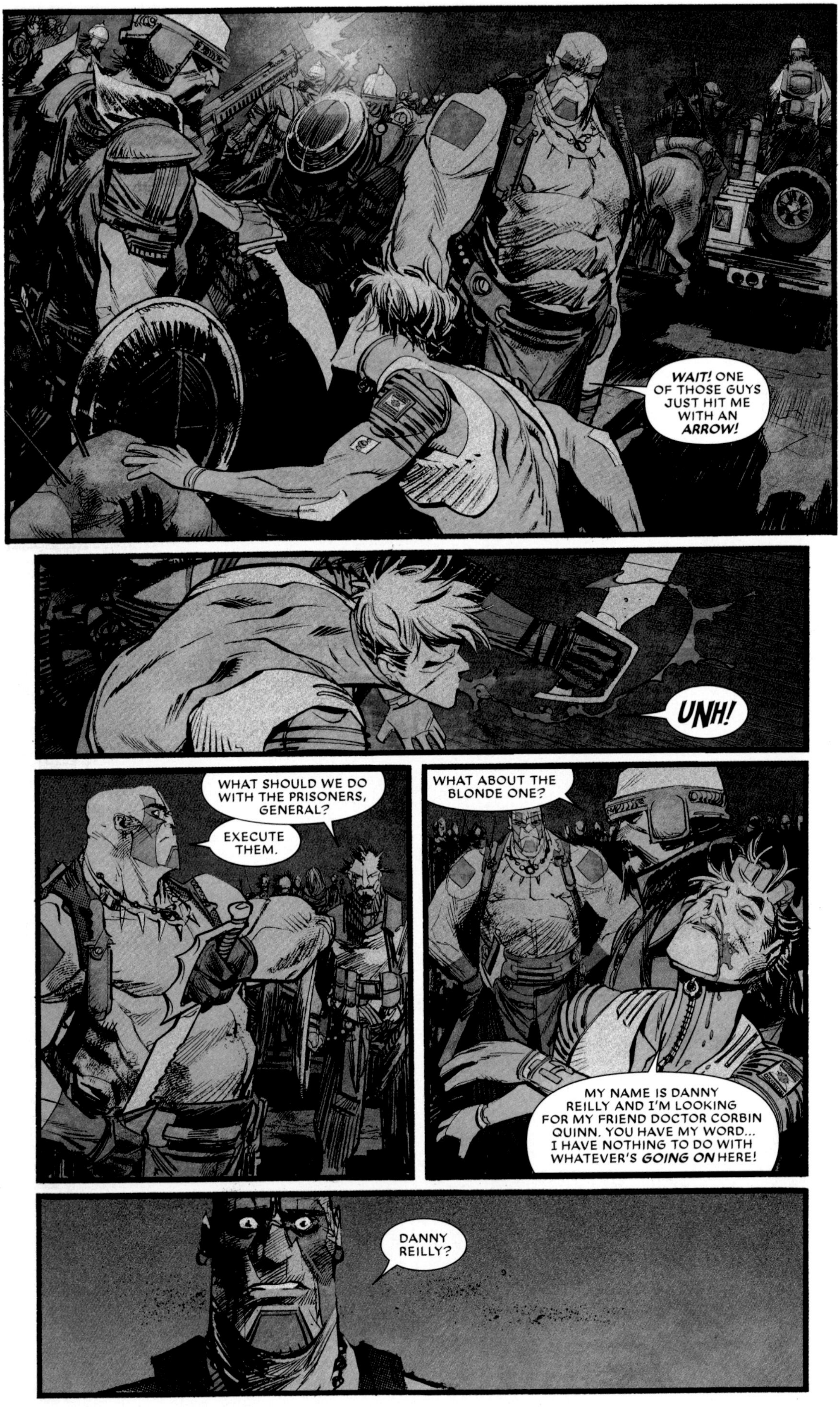
WAIT! ONE OF THOSE GUYS JUST HIT ME WITH AN ARROW!
UNH!
WHAT SHOULD WE DO WITH THE PRISONERS, GENERAL?
EXECUTE THEM.
WHAT ABOUT THE BLONDE ONE?
MY NAME IS DANNY REILLY AND I'M LOOKING FOR MY FRIEND DOCTOR CORBIN QUINN. YOU HAVE MY WORD... I HAVE NOTHING TO DO WITH WHATEVER'S GOING ON HERE!
DANNY REILLY?

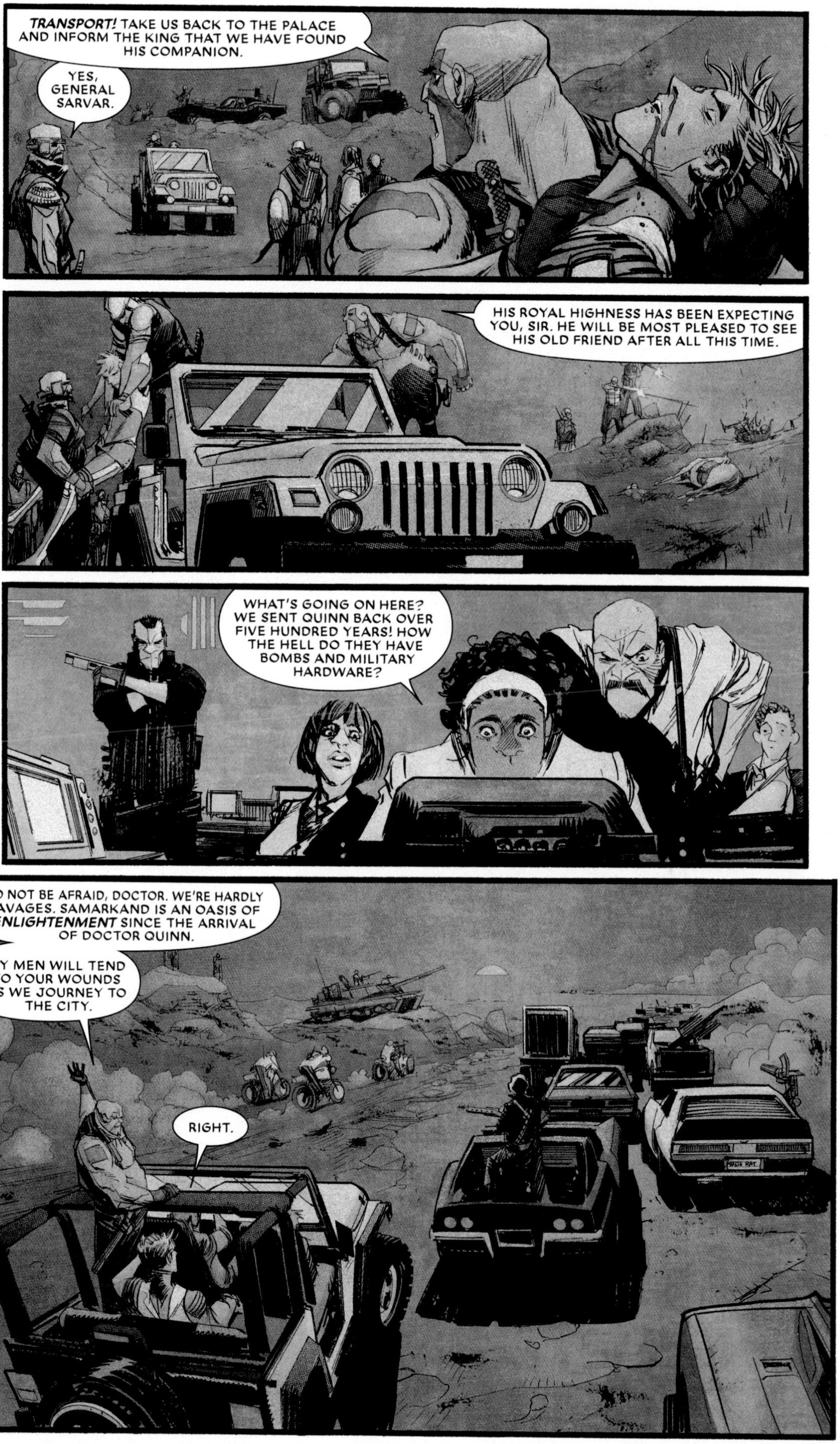
TRANSPORT! TAKE US BACK TO THE PALACE AND INFORM THE KING THAT WE HAVE FOUND HIS COMPANION.
YES, GENERAL SARVAR.
HIS ROYAL HIGHNESS HAS BEEN EXPECTING YOU, SIR. HE WILL BE MOST PLEASED TO SEE HIS OLD FRIEND AFTER ALL THIS TIME.
WHAT'S GOING ON HERE? WE SENT QUINN BACK OVER FIVE HUNDRED YEARS! HOW THE HELL DO THEY HAVE BOMBS AND MILITARY HARDWARE?
DO NOT BE AFRAID, DOCTOR. WE'RE HARDLY SAVAGES. SAMARKAND IS AN OASIS OF ENLIGHTENMENT SINCE THE ARRIVAL OF DOCTOR QUINN.
MY MEN WILL TEND TO YOUR WOUNDS AS WE JOURNEY TO THE CITY.
RIGHT.

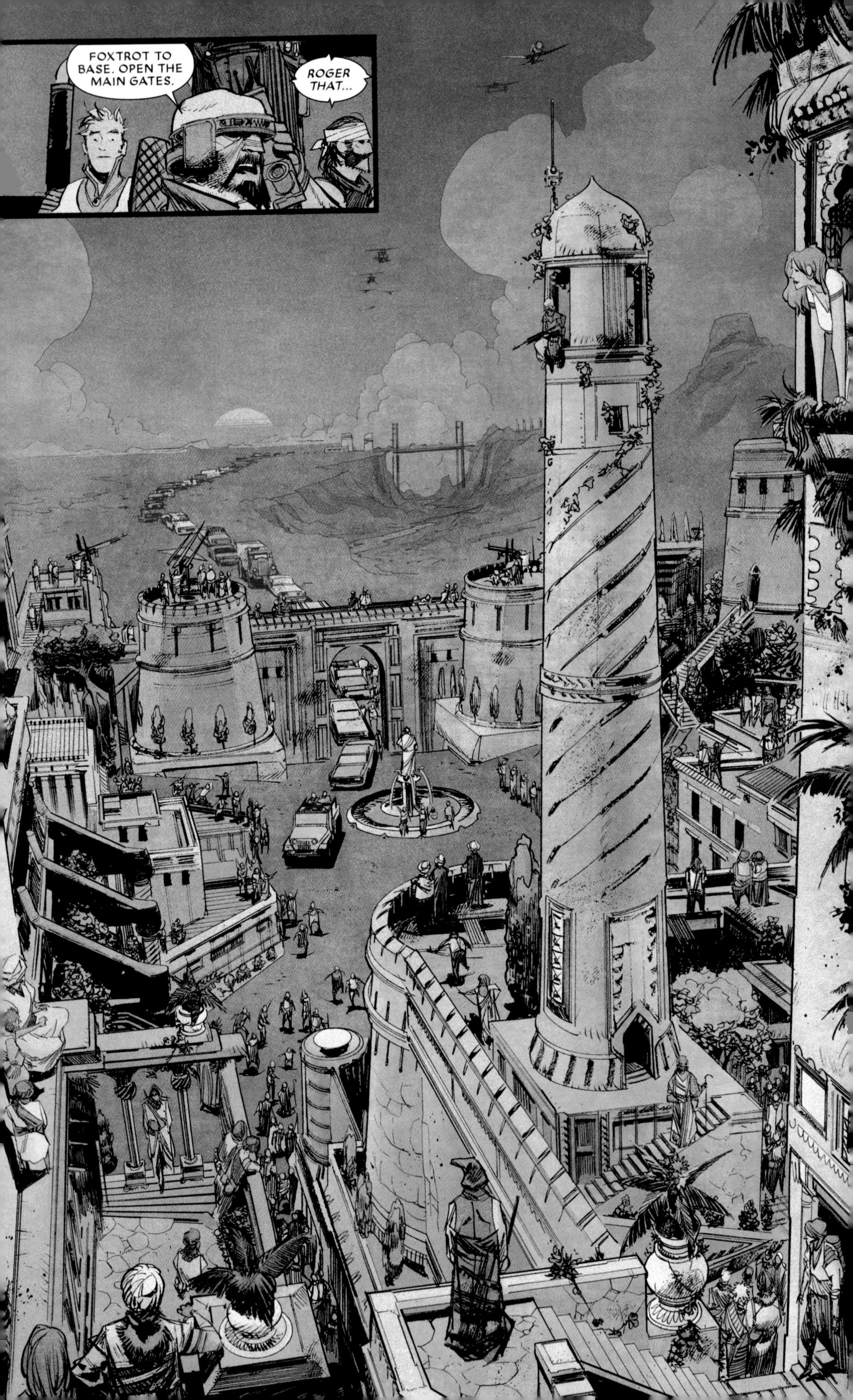
FOXTROT TO BASE. OPEN THE MAIN GATES.
ROGER THAT...

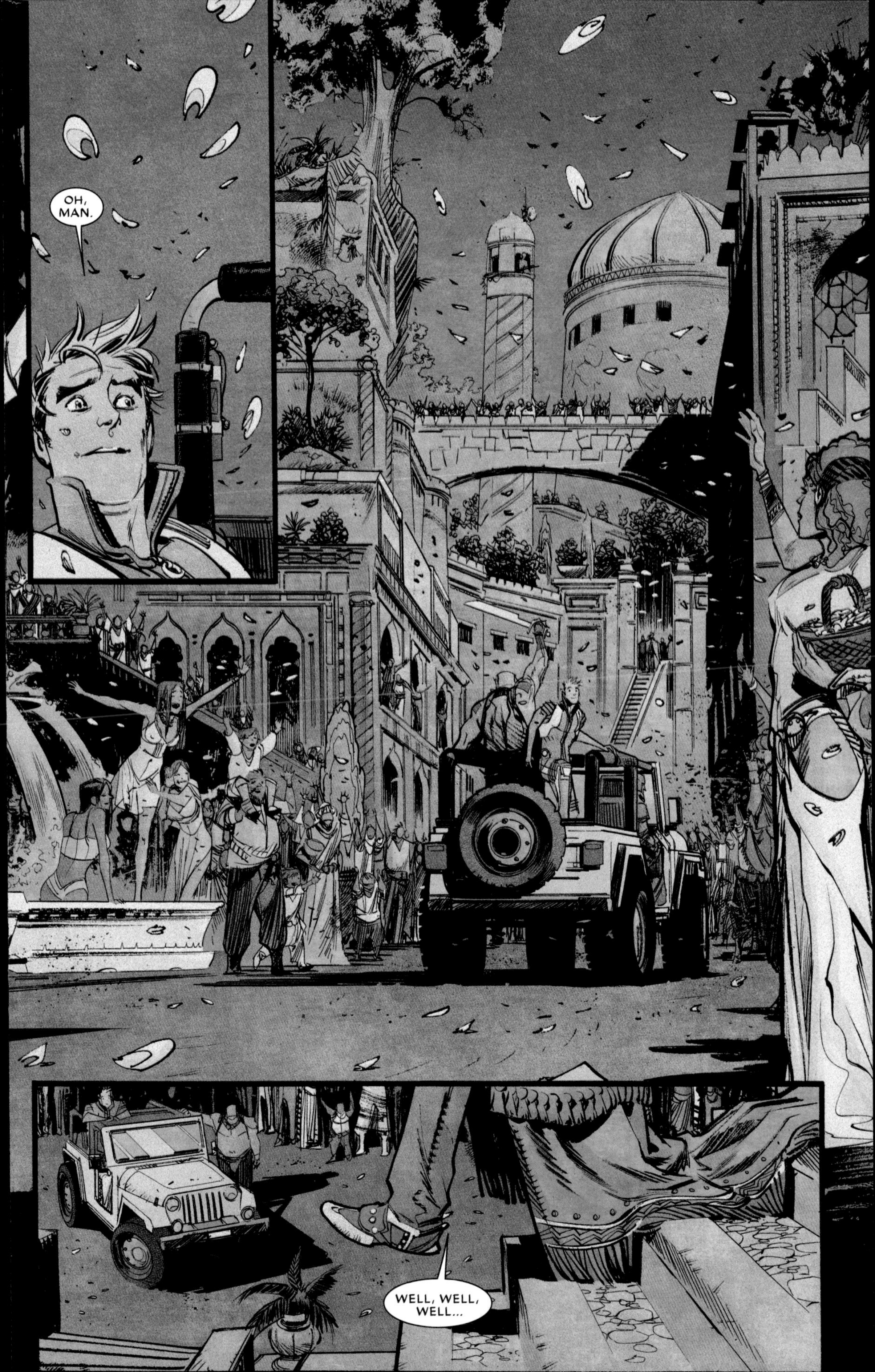
OH, MAN.
WELL, WELL, WELL...

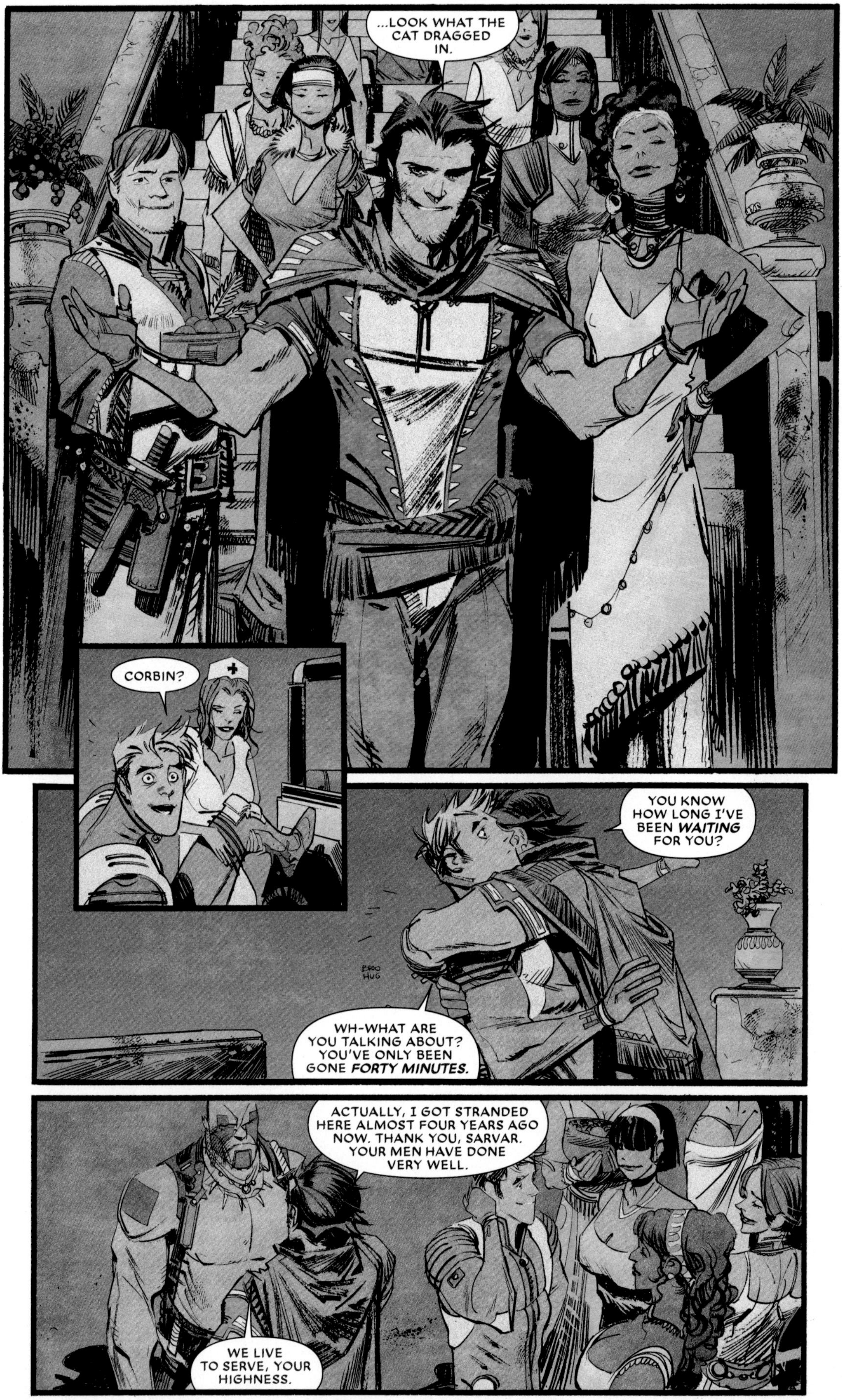
...LOOK WHAT THE CAT DRAGGED IN.
CORBIN?
YOU KNOW HOW LONG I'VE BEEN *WAITING* FOR YOU?
BRO HUG
WH-WHAT ARE YOU TALKING ABOUT? YOU'VE ONLY BEEN GONE *FORTY MINUTES.*
ACTUALLY, I GOT STRANDED HERE ALMOST FOUR YEARS AGO NOW. THANK YOU, SARVAR. YOUR MEN HAVE DONE VERY WELL.
WE LIVE TO SERVE, YOUR HIGHNESS.

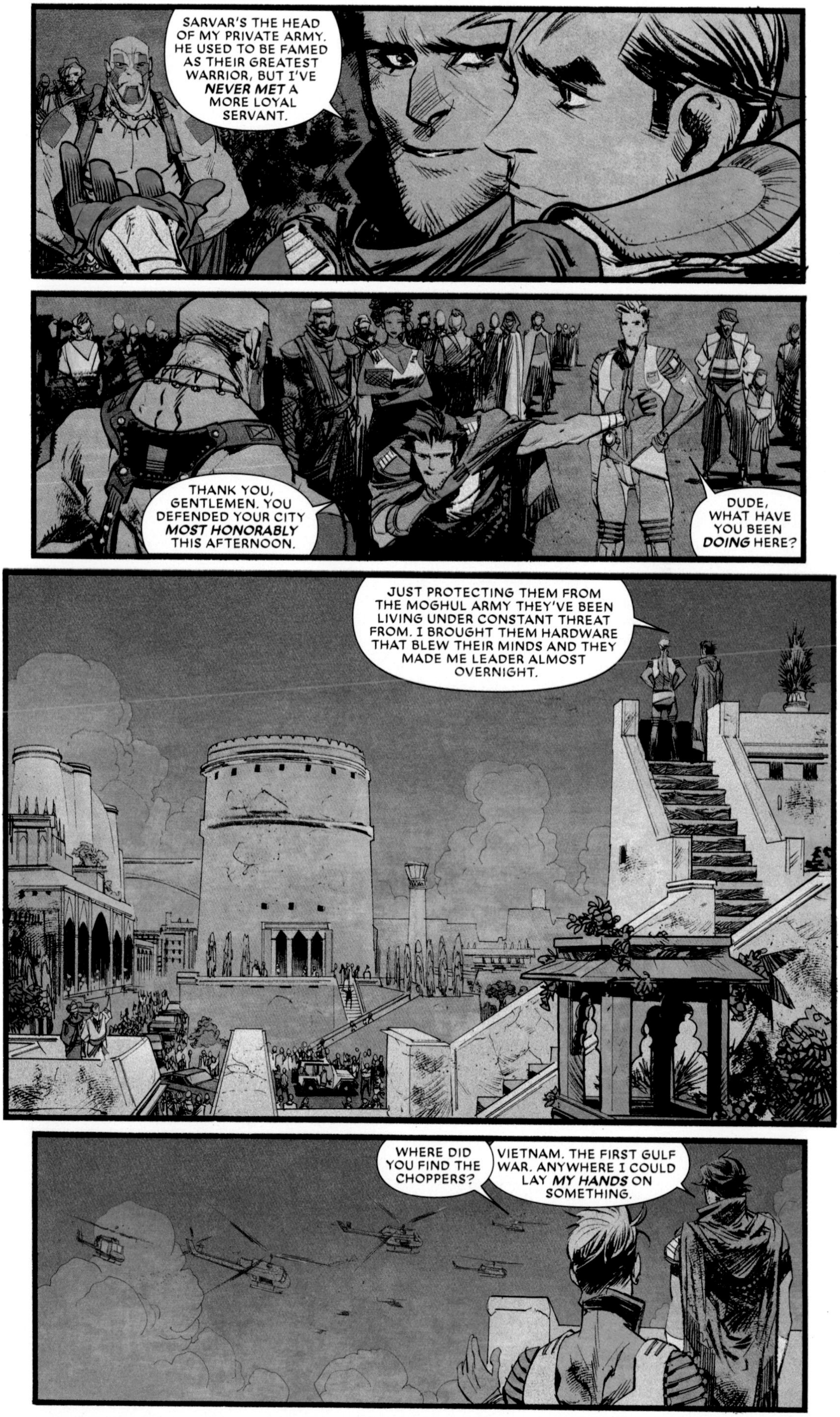
SARVAR'S THE HEAD OF MY PRIVATE ARMY. HE USED TO BE FAMED AS THEIR GREATEST WARRIOR, BUT I'VE ***NEVER MET*** A MORE LOYAL SERVANT.
THANK YOU, GENTLEMEN. YOU DEFENDED YOUR CITY ***MOST HONORABLY*** THIS AFTERNOON.
DUDE, WHAT HAVE YOU BEEN ***DOING*** HERE?
JUST PROTECTING THEM FROM THE MOGHUL ARMY THEY'VE BEEN LIVING UNDER CONSTANT THREAT FROM. I BROUGHT THEM HARDWARE THAT BLEW THEIR MINDS AND THEY MADE ME LEADER ALMOST OVERNIGHT.
WHERE DID YOU FIND THE CHOPPERS?
VIETNAM. THE FIRST GULF WAR. ANYWHERE I COULD LAY ***MY HANDS*** ON SOMETHING.

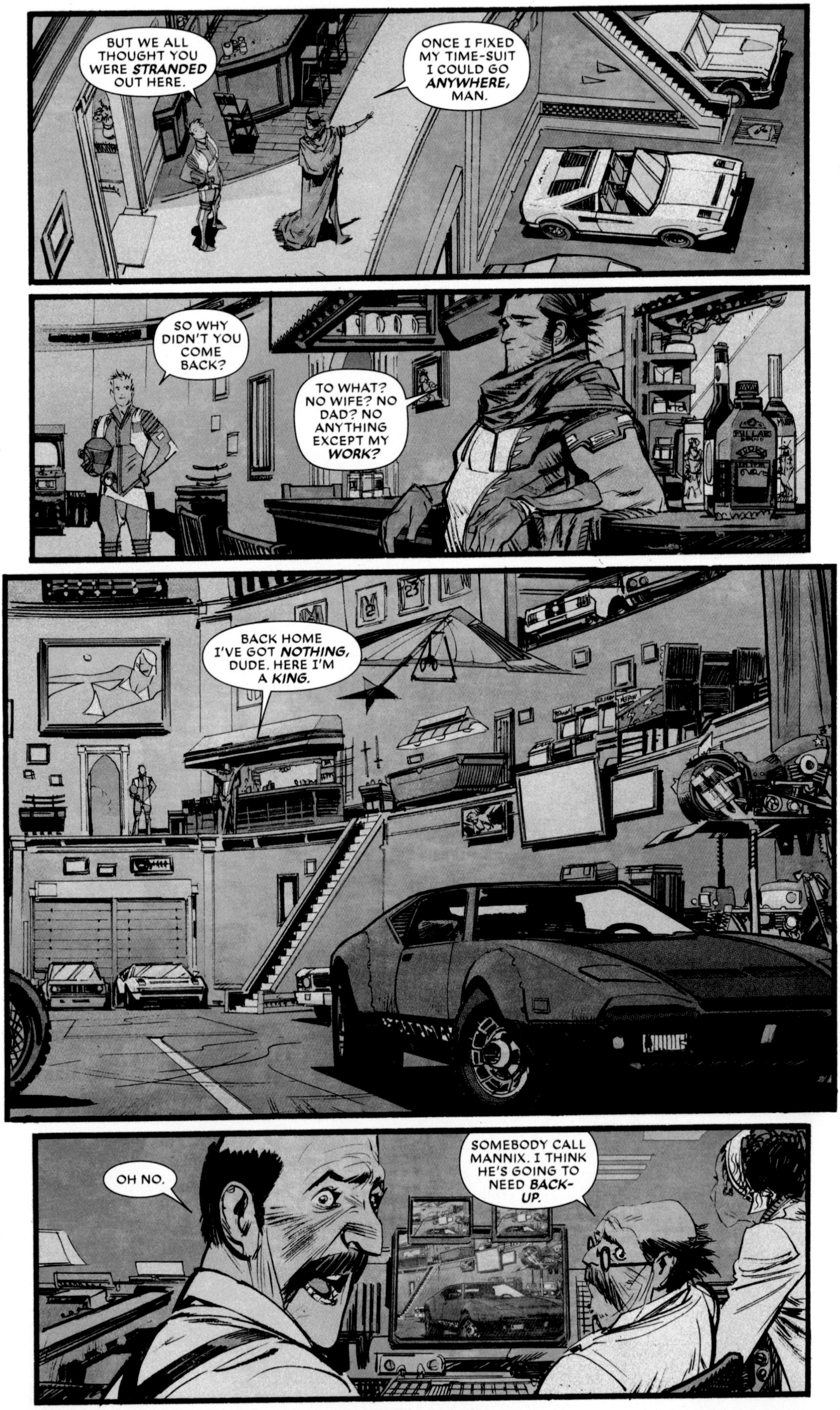
BUT WE ALL THOUGHT YOU WERE STRANDED OUT HERE.
ONCE I FIXED MY TIME-SUIT I COULD GO ANYWHERE, MAN.
SO WHY DIDN'T YOU COME BACK?
TO WHAT? NO WIFE? NO DAD? NO ANYTHING EXCEPT MY WORK?
BACK HOME I'VE GOT NOTHING, DUDE. HERE I'M A KING.
OH NO.
SOMEBODY CALL MANNIX. I THINK HE'S GOING TO NEED BACK-UP.

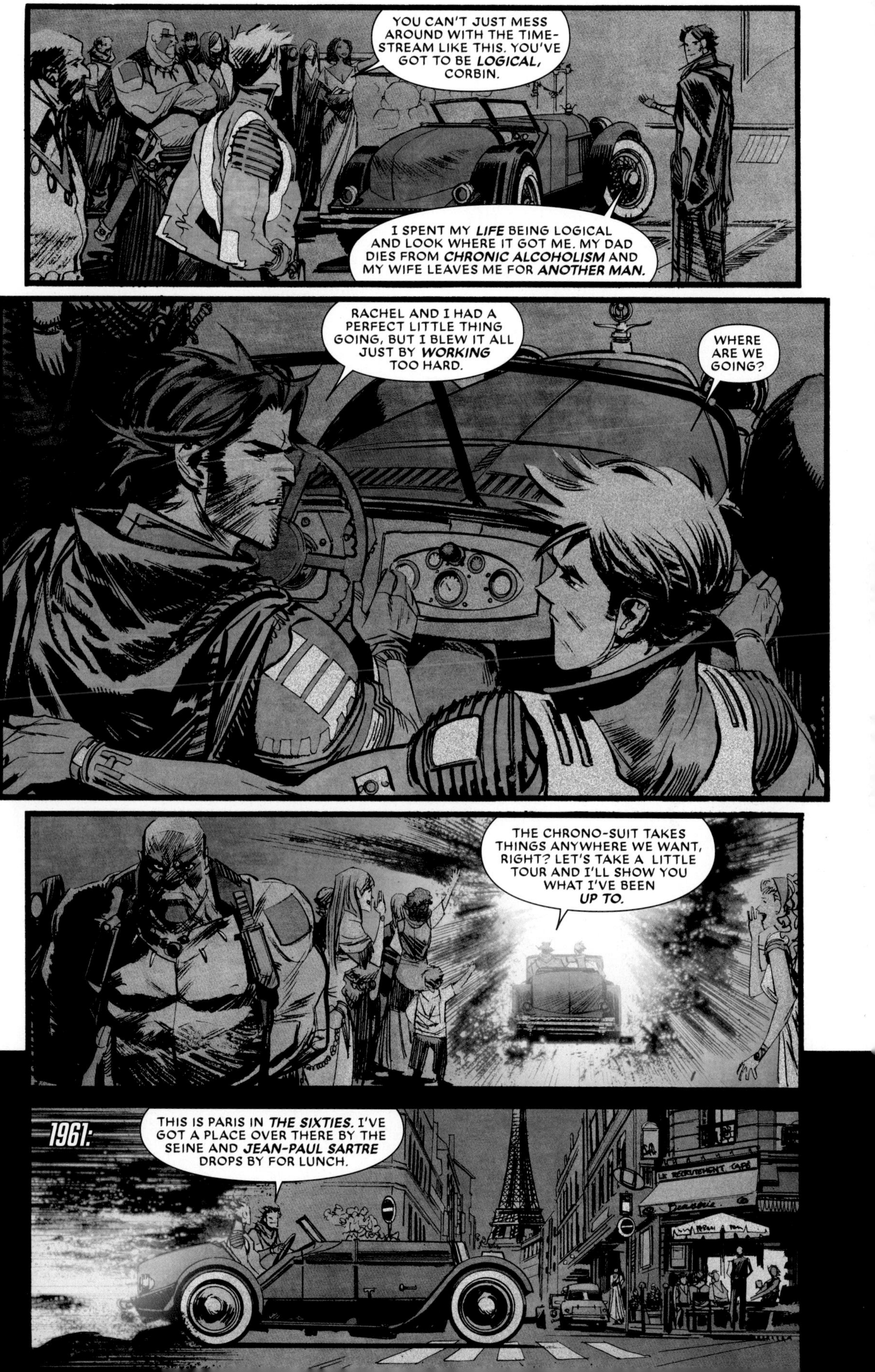
YOU CAN'T JUST MESS AROUND WITH THE TIME-STREAM LIKE THIS. YOU'VE GOT TO BE LOGICAL, CORBIN.
I SPENT MY LIFE BEING LOGICAL AND LOOK WHERE IT GOT ME. MY DAD DIES FROM CHRONIC ALCOHOLISM AND MY WIFE LEAVES ME FOR ANOTHER MAN.
RACHEL AND I HAD A PERFECT LITTLE THING GOING, BUT I BLEW IT ALL JUST BY WORKING TOO HARD.
WHERE ARE WE GOING?
THE CHRONO-SUIT TAKES THINGS ANYWHERE WE WANT, RIGHT? LET'S TAKE A LITTLE TOUR AND I'LL SHOW YOU WHAT I'VE BEEN UP TO.
1961:
THIS IS PARIS IN THE SIXTIES. I'VE GOT A PLACE OVER THERE BY THE SEINE AND JEAN-PAUL SARTRE DROPS BY FOR LUNCH.

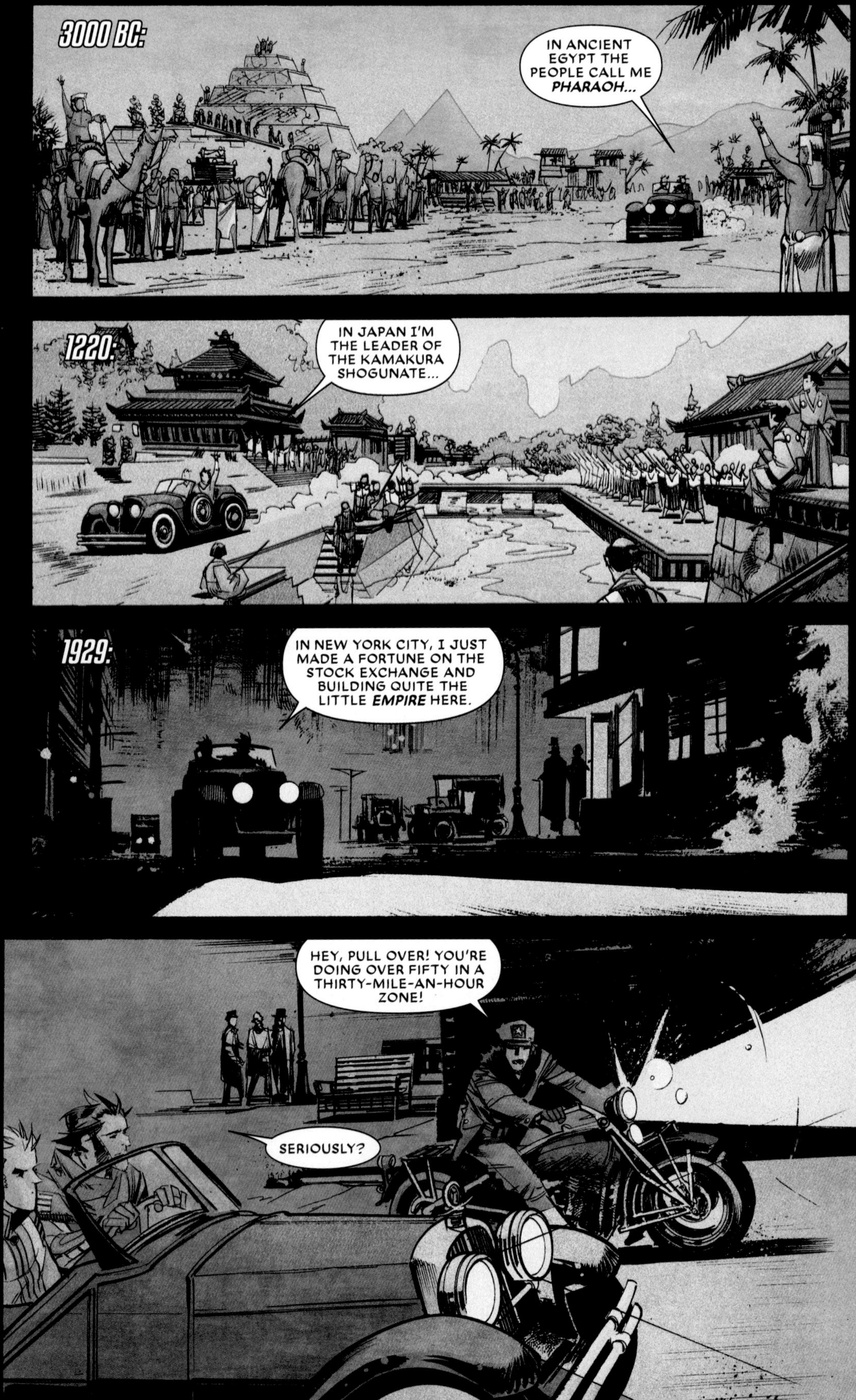
3000 BC:
IN ANCIENT EGYPT THE PEOPLE CALL ME *PHARAOH...*
1220:
IN JAPAN I'M THE LEADER OF THE KAMAKURA SHOGUNATE...
1929:
IN NEW YORK CITY, I JUST MADE A FORTUNE ON THE STOCK EXCHANGE AND BUILDING QUITE THE LITTLE *EMPIRE* HERE.
HEY, PULL OVER! YOU'RE DOING OVER FIFTY IN A THIRTY-MILE-AN-HOUR ZONE!
SERIOUSLY?

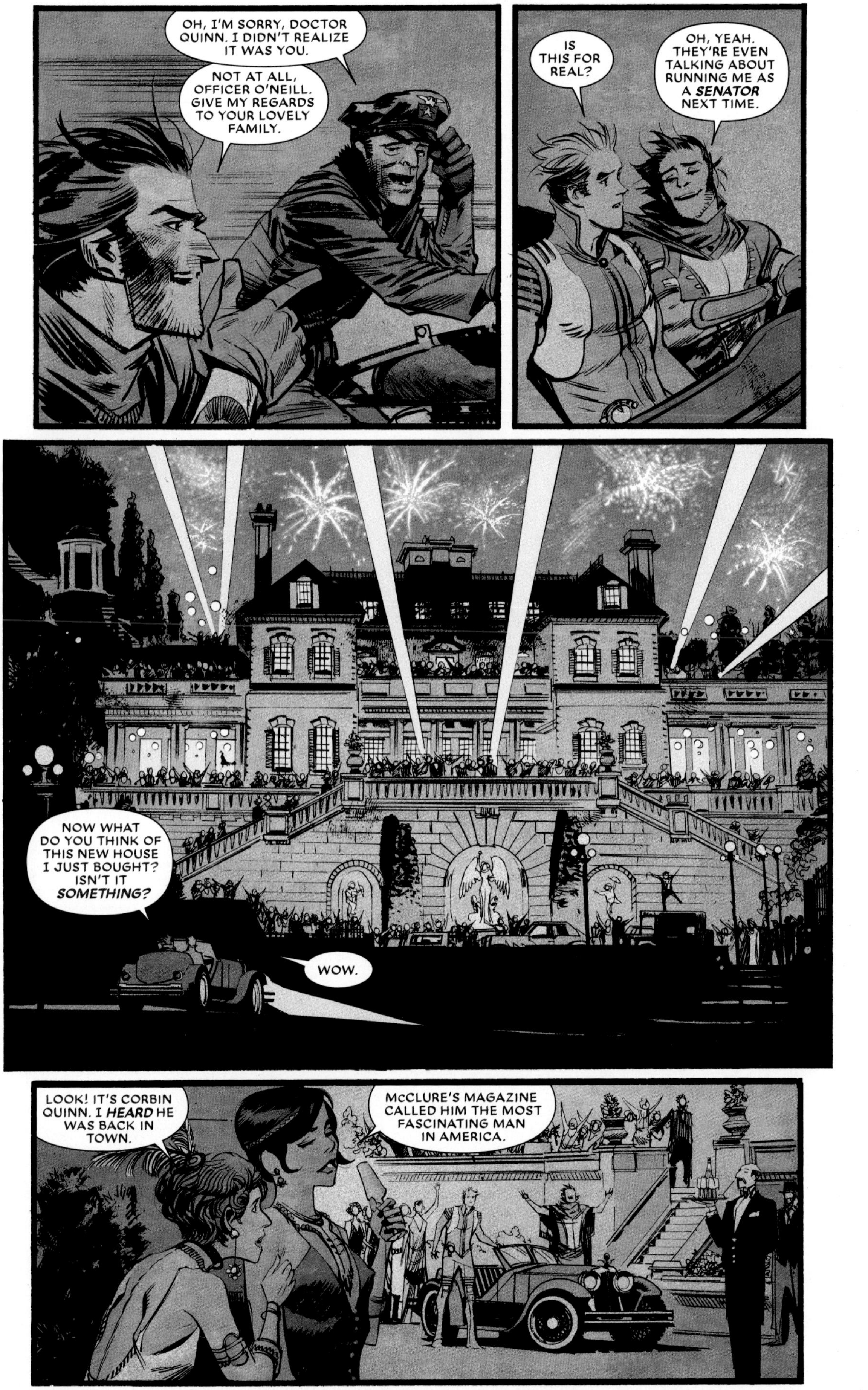
OH, I'M SORRY, DOCTOR QUINN. I DIDN'T REALIZE IT WAS YOU.
NOT AT ALL, OFFICER O'NEILL. GIVE MY REGARDS TO YOUR LOVELY FAMILY.
IS THIS FOR REAL?
OH, YEAH. THEY'RE EVEN TALKING ABOUT RUNNING ME AS A ***SENATOR*** NEXT TIME.
NOW WHAT DO YOU THINK OF THIS NEW HOUSE I JUST BOUGHT? ISN'T IT ***SOMETHING?***
WOW.
LOOK! IT'S CORBIN QUINN. I ***HEARD*** HE WAS BACK IN TOWN.
McCLURE'S MAGAZINE CALLED HIM THE MOST FASCINATING MAN IN AMERICA.

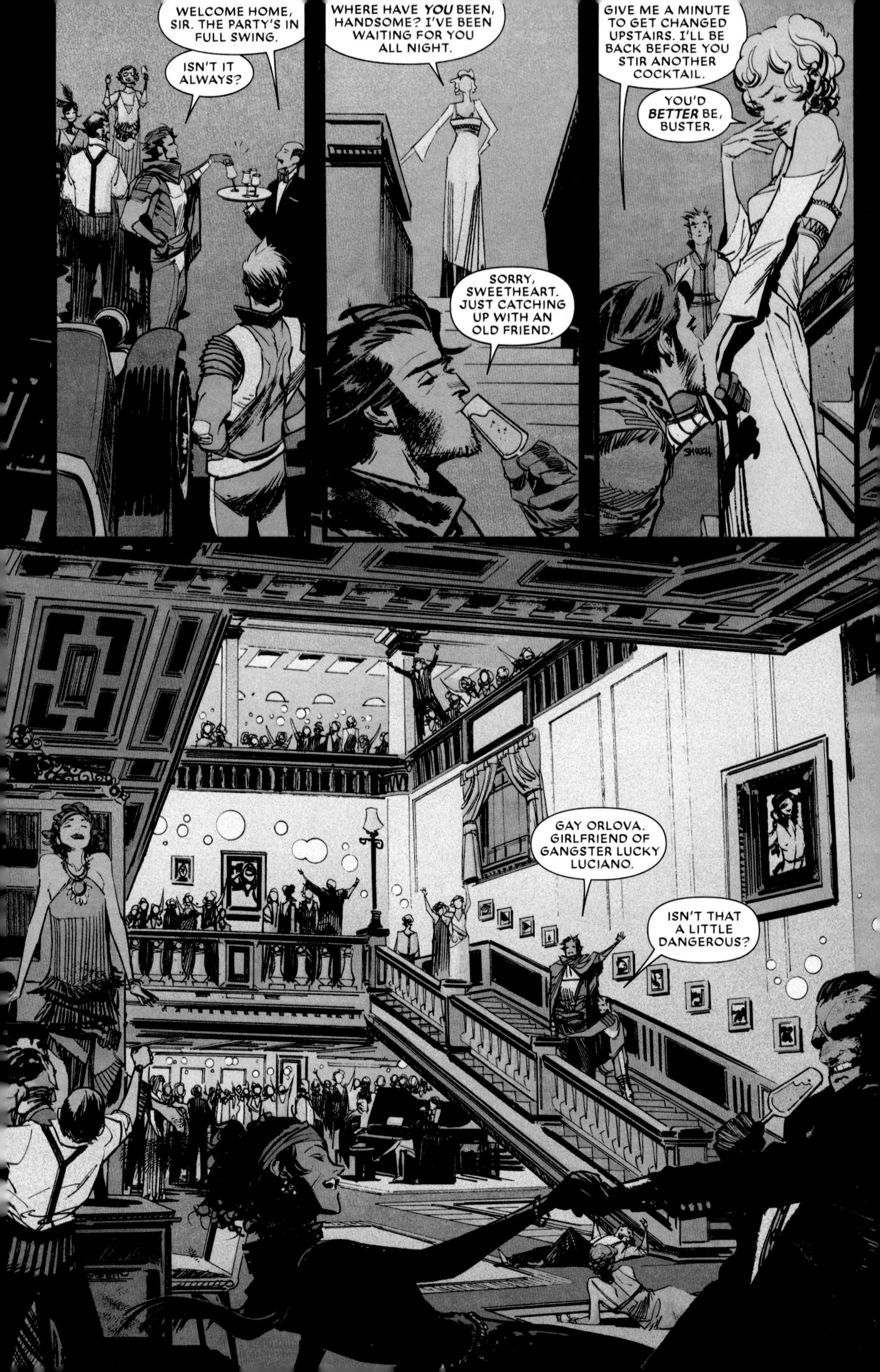
WELCOME HOME, SIR. THE PARTY'S IN FULL SWING.
ISN'T IT ALWAYS?
WHERE HAVE *YOU* BEEN, HANDSOME? I'VE BEEN WAITING FOR YOU ALL NIGHT.
SORRY, SWEETHEART. JUST CATCHING UP WITH AN OLD FRIEND.
GIVE ME A MINUTE TO GET CHANGED UPSTAIRS. I'LL BE BACK BEFORE YOU STIR ANOTHER COCKTAIL.
YOU'D *BETTER* BE, BUSTER.
GAY ORLOVA. GIRLFRIEND OF GANGSTER LUCKY LUCIANO.
ISN'T THAT A LITTLE DANGEROUS?

YEAH, BUT IT'S EXCITING.

THIS IS WHERE I KEEP THE CLOTHES FOR ALL MY DIFFERENT LIVES. I'VE GOT SO MANY GIRLS OUT THERE I NEED A CHART TO KEEP TRACK.

NAME	LIKES	DISLIKES	OTHER
NORMA JEAN BAKER	PRESIDENTS, BIRTHDAYS	BASEBALL, MISSIONARY	DON'T MENTION ROME
CLEOPATRA	SAND, FALCONRY	SNAKES	DON'T MENTION KID ROCK
SHERYL LEON	BEER, COWBOYS	CYCLING	EROTIC NOVELS
COLLEEN KATANA	PUPPIES, COFFEE, PUPPIES	HER ASSHOLE HUSBAND	DON'T TALK PLANES
AMELIA EARHART	TRAVEL, HAIRCUTS	HIEGHTS	
JOAN OF ARC	KNIVES, ARGUING	FIRE, BBQ's	LESBIAN??
GAY ORLOVA	DANGER	SEAFOOD	WATCH OUT FR-
TANA FORD	COMICS, PB J, POPCORN	MEN	LOVES MADDOW
BETTY PAGE	DANCING, TATTOOS	CIGARS	BE NICE !!
BETTY WHITE	SHUFFLEBOARD	REVERSE COWGIRL	BRING RIBBON CA-
BETSY ROSS	SEWING, ROCKING CHAIRS	BON JOVI	GEORGE WASHINGTO-

SCORE BOARD

IN NINETEEN FIFTY-ONE I'M DATING A STRUGGLING YOUNG ACTRESS CALLED NORMA JEAN BAKER. DO YOU REALIZE WHO THAT IS?

YOU'RE JOKING.

I'M LIVING THE LIFE WE'VE ALWAYS DREAMED OF, DANNY. SWITCH OFF THAT TRACKING DEVICE AND YOU COULD LIVE IT TOO.

WHAT?

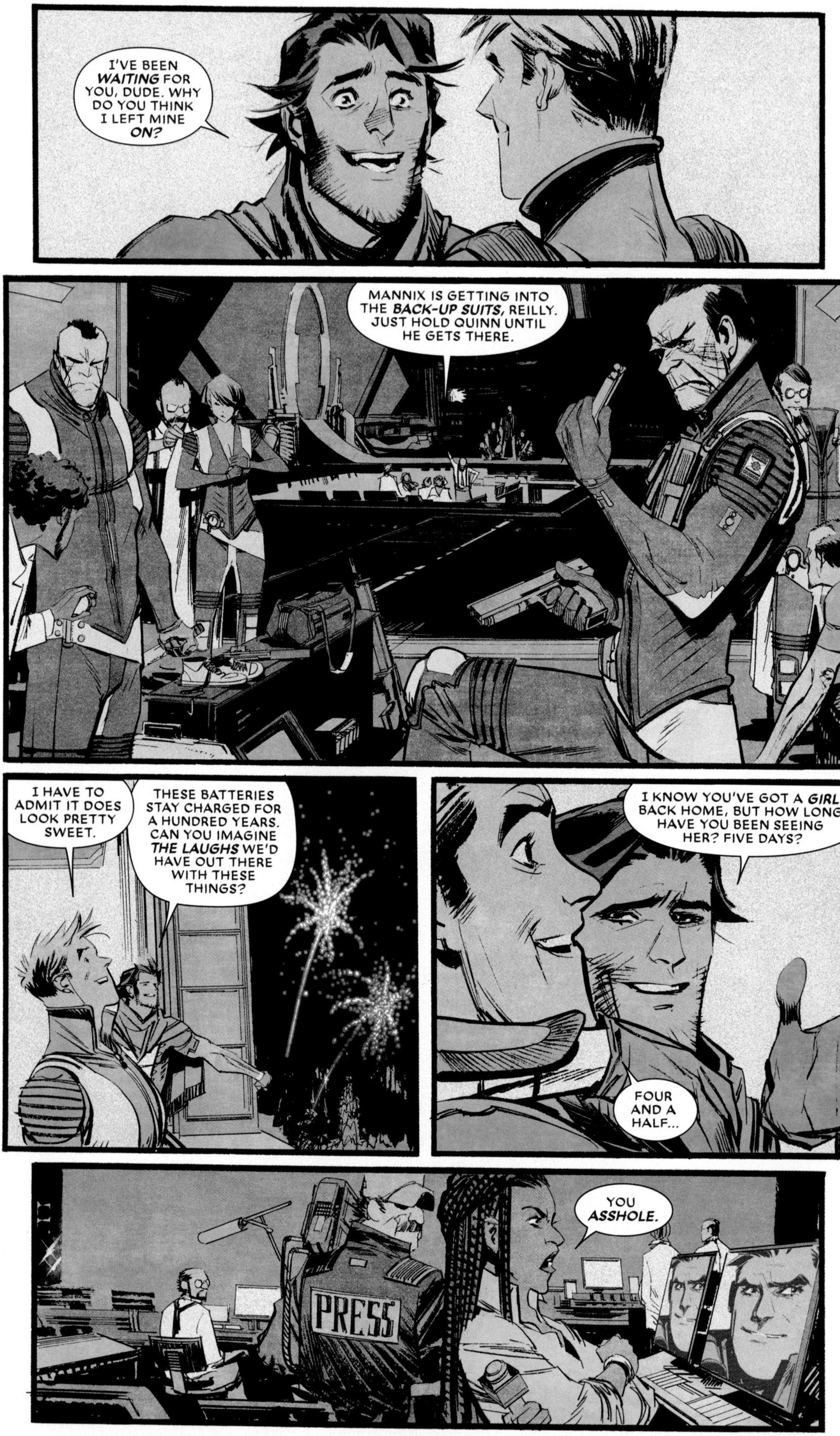
I'VE BEEN WAITING FOR YOU, DUDE. WHY DO YOU THINK I LEFT MINE ON?
MANNIX IS GETTING INTO THE BACK-UP SUITS, REILLY. JUST HOLD QUINN UNTIL HE GETS THERE.
I HAVE TO ADMIT IT DOES LOOK PRETTY SWEET.
THESE BATTERIES STAY CHARGED FOR A HUNDRED YEARS. CAN YOU IMAGINE THE LAUGHS WE'D HAVE OUT THERE WITH THESE THINGS?
I KNOW YOU'VE GOT A GIRL BACK HOME, BUT HOW LONG HAVE YOU BEEN SEEING HER? FIVE DAYS?
FOUR AND A HALF...
YOU ASSHOLE.
PRESS

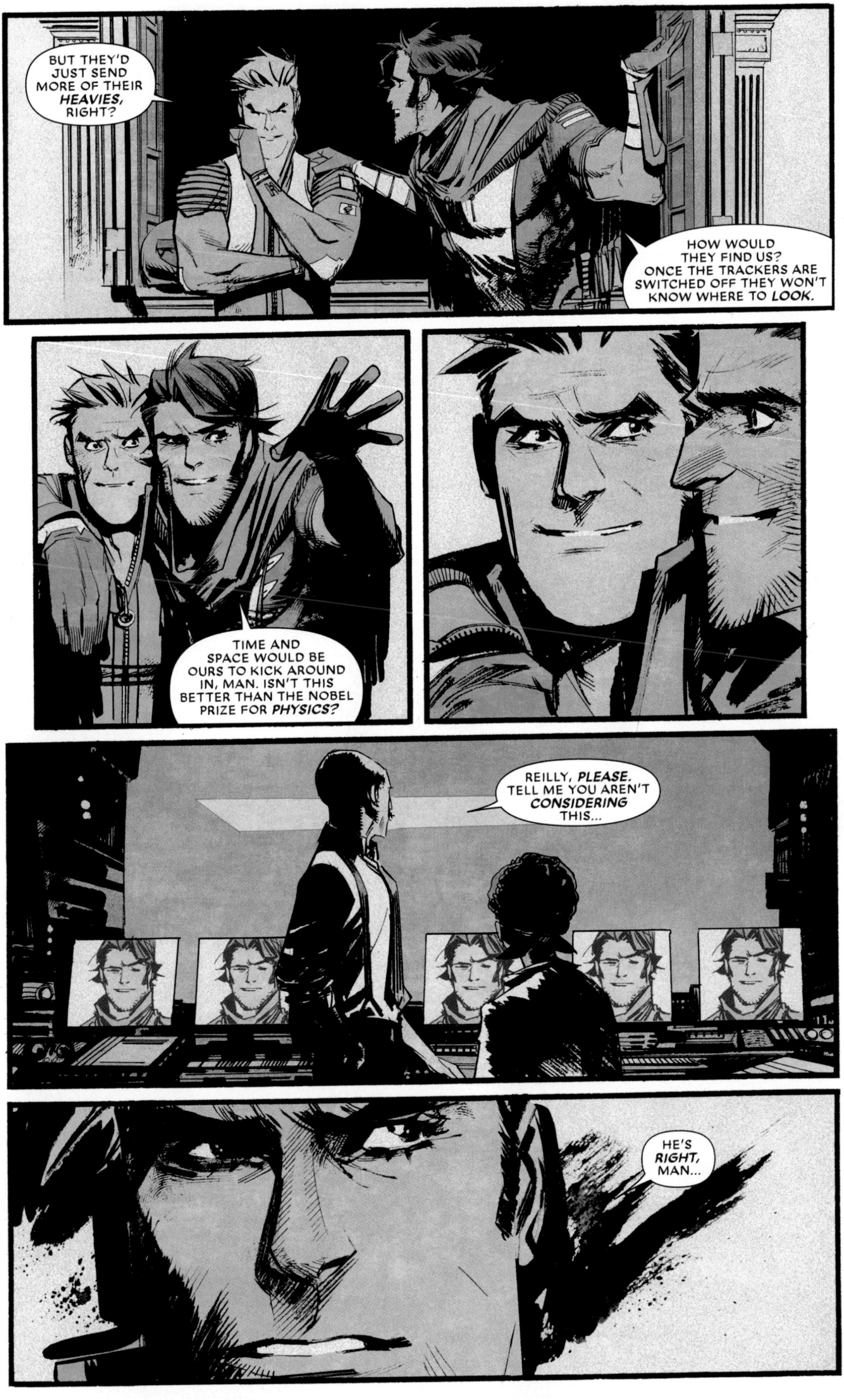

BUT THEY'D JUST SEND MORE OF THEIR *HEAVIES,* RIGHT?
HOW WOULD THEY FIND US? ONCE THE TRACKERS ARE SWITCHED OFF THEY WON'T KNOW WHERE TO *LOOK.*
TIME AND SPACE WOULD BE OURS TO KICK AROUND IN, MAN. ISN'T THIS BETTER THAN THE NOBEL PRIZE FOR *PHYSICS?*
REILLY, *PLEASE.* TELL ME YOU AREN'T *CONSIDERING* THIS...
HE'S *RIGHT,* MAN...

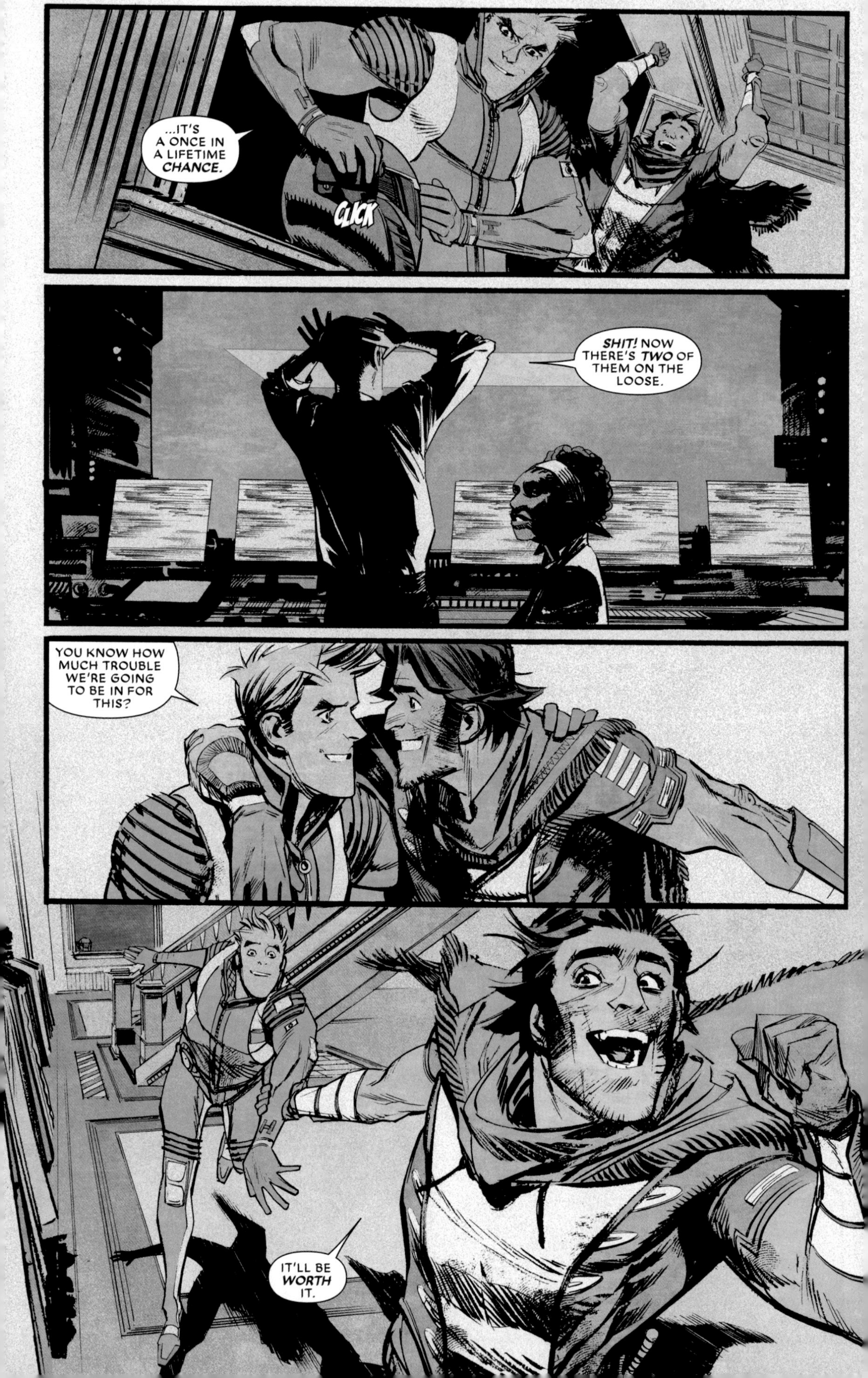
...IT'S A ONCE IN A LIFETIME CHANCE.
CLICK
SHIT! NOW THERE'S TWO OF THEM ON THE LOOSE.
YOU KNOW HOW MUCH TROUBLE WE'RE GOING TO BE IN FOR THIS?
IT'LL BE WORTH IT.

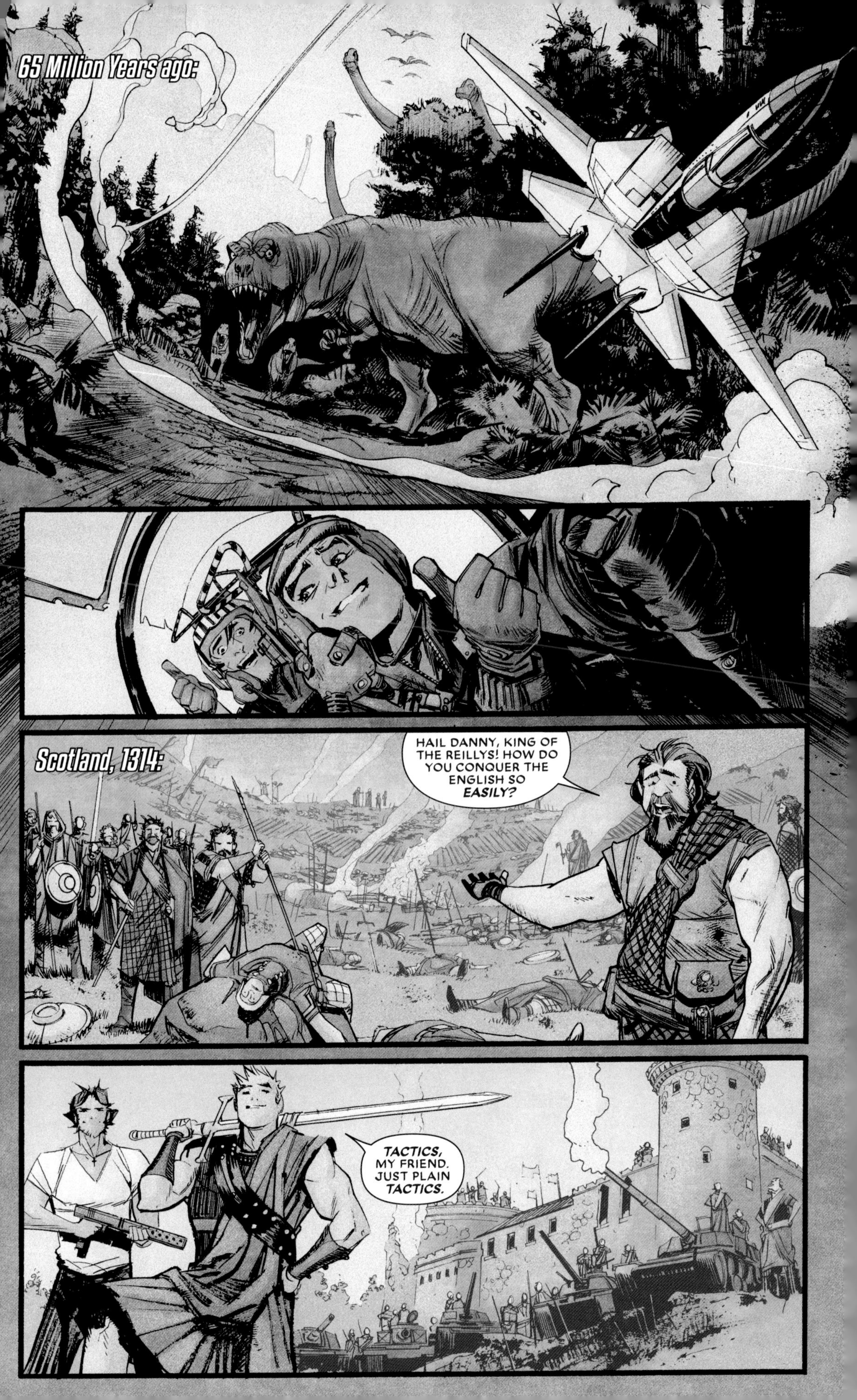
65 Million Years ago:
Scotland, 1314:
HAIL DANNY, KING OF THE REILLYS! HOW DO YOU CONQUER THE ENGLISH SO EASILY?
TACTICS, MY FRIEND. JUST PLAIN TACTICS.

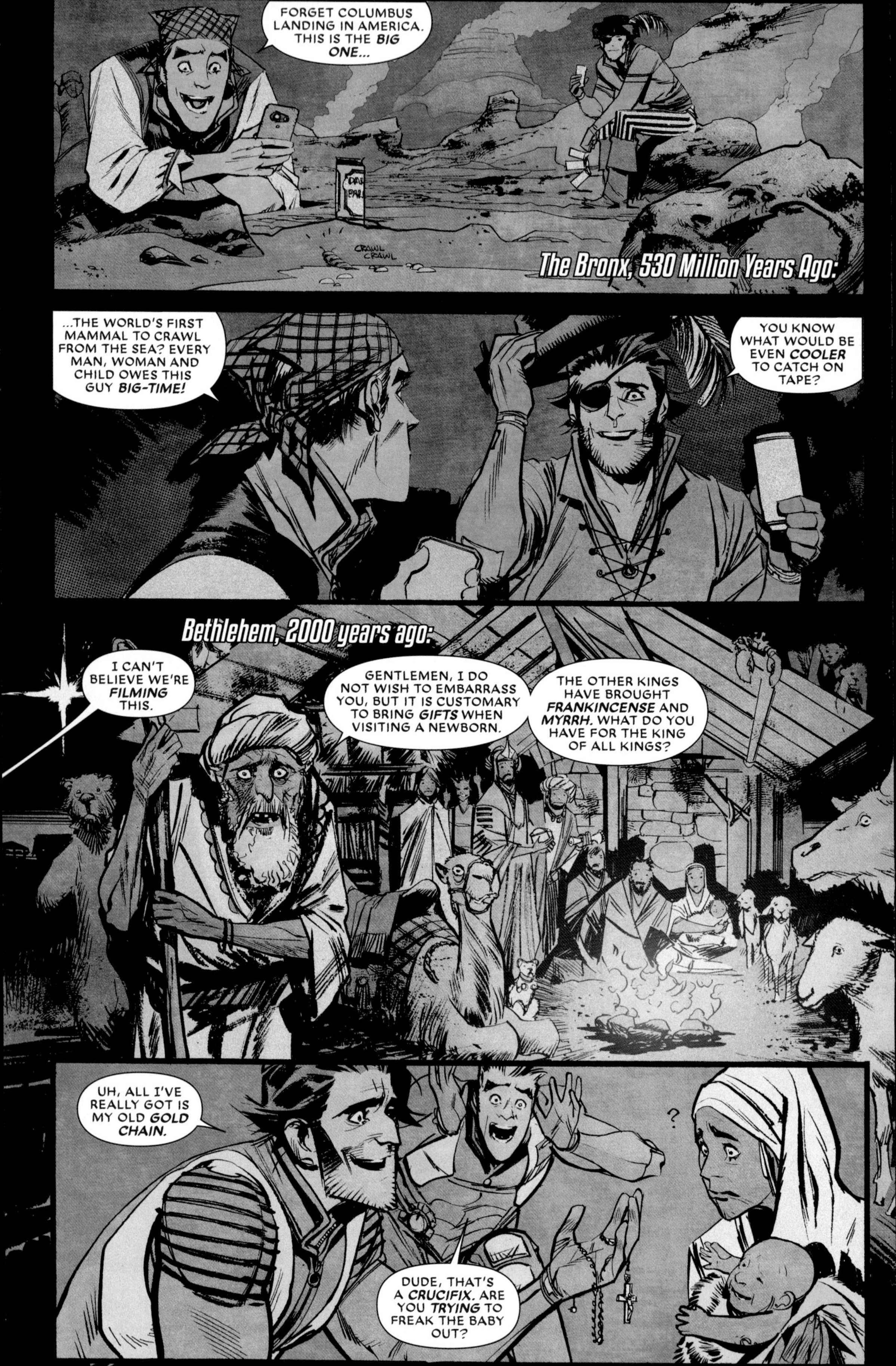
FORGET COLUMBUS LANDING IN AMERICA. THIS IS THE *BIG ONE...*
CRAWL CRAWL
The Bronx, 530 Million Years Ago:
...THE WORLD'S FIRST MAMMAL TO CRAWL FROM THE SEA? EVERY MAN, WOMAN AND CHILD OWES THIS GUY *BIG-TIME!*
YOU KNOW WHAT WOULD BE EVEN *COOLER* TO CATCH ON TAPE?
Bethlehem, 2000 years ago:
I CAN'T BELIEVE WE'RE *FILMING* THIS.
GENTLEMEN, I DO NOT WISH TO EMBARRASS YOU, BUT IT IS CUSTOMARY TO BRING *GIFTS* WHEN VISITING A NEWBORN.
THE OTHER KINGS HAVE BROUGHT *FRANKINCENSE* AND *MYRRH.* WHAT DO YOU HAVE FOR THE KING OF ALL KINGS?
UH, ALL I'VE REALLY GOT IS MY OLD *GOLD CHAIN.*
?
DUDE, THAT'S A *CRUCIFIX.* ARE YOU *TRYING* TO FREAK THE BABY OUT?

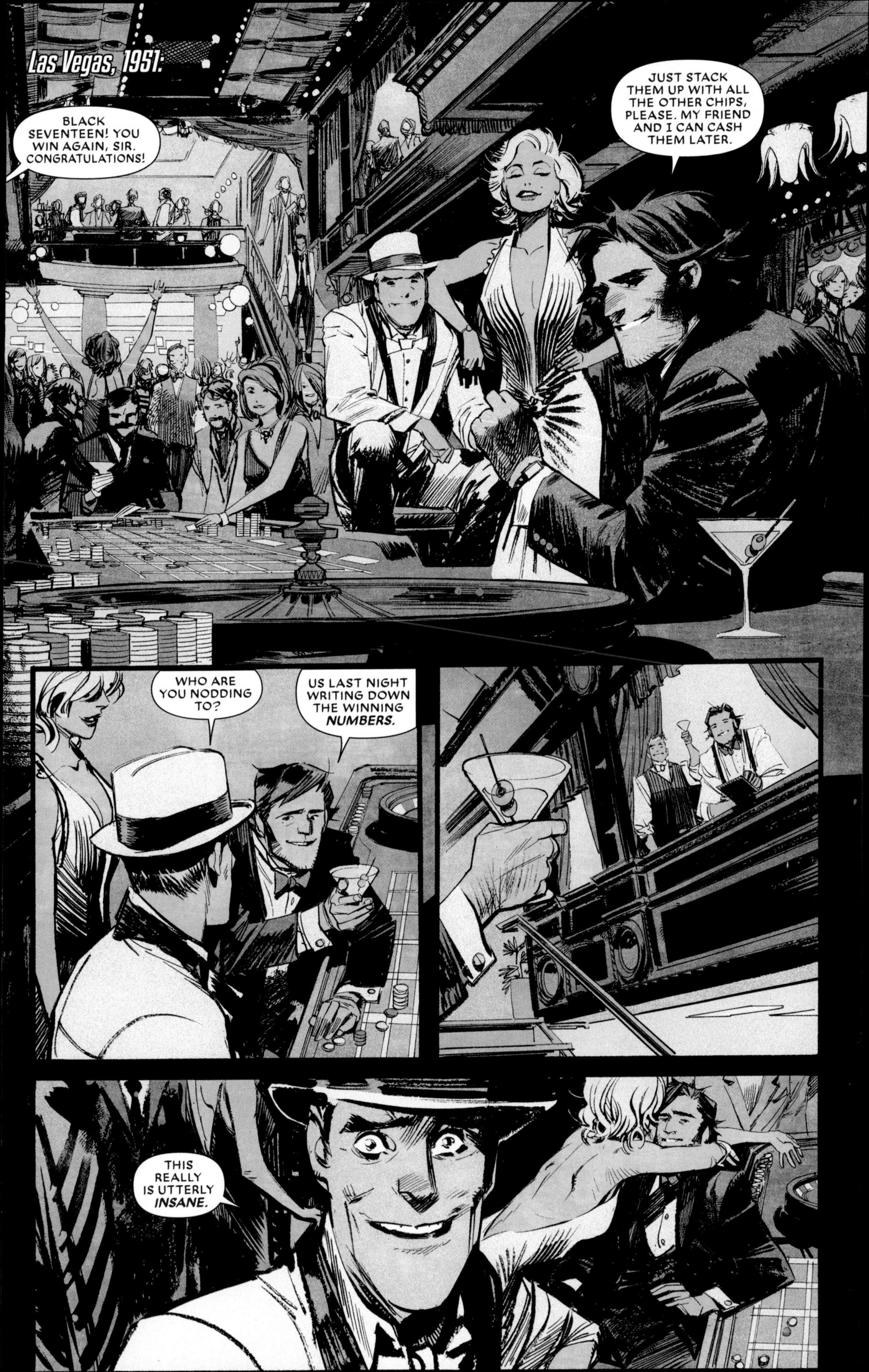
Las Vegas, 1951:
BLACK SEVENTEEN! YOU WIN AGAIN, SIR. CONGRATULATIONS!
JUST STACK THEM UP WITH ALL THE OTHER CHIPS, PLEASE. MY FRIEND AND I CAN CASH THEM LATER.
WHO ARE YOU NODDING TO?
US LAST NIGHT WRITING DOWN THE WINNING NUMBERS.
THIS REALLY IS UTTERLY INSANE.

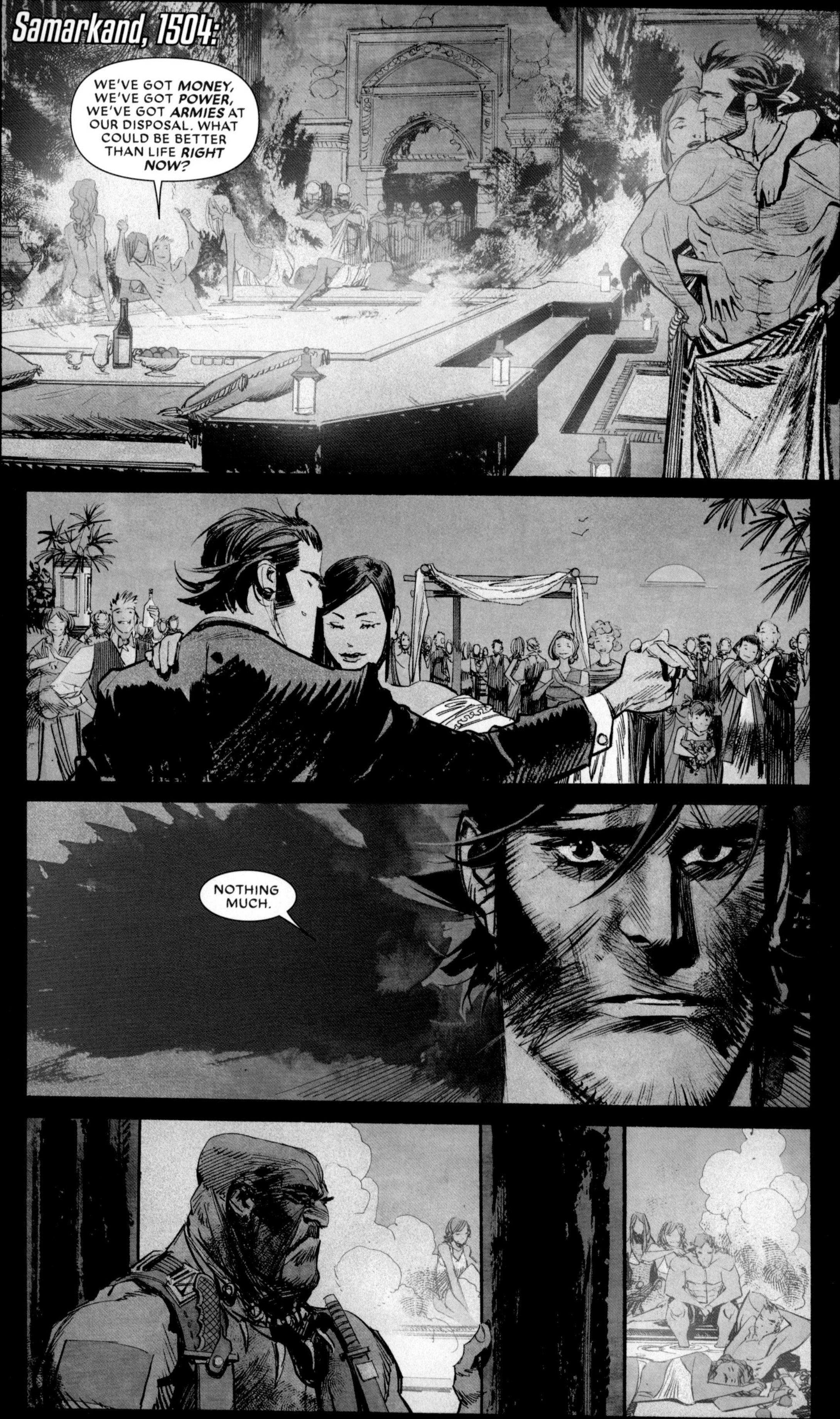
Samarkand, 1504:
WE'VE GOT MONEY, WE'VE GOT POWER, WE'VE GOT ARMIES AT OUR DISPOSAL. WHAT COULD BE BETTER THAN LIFE RIGHT NOW?
NOTHING MUCH.

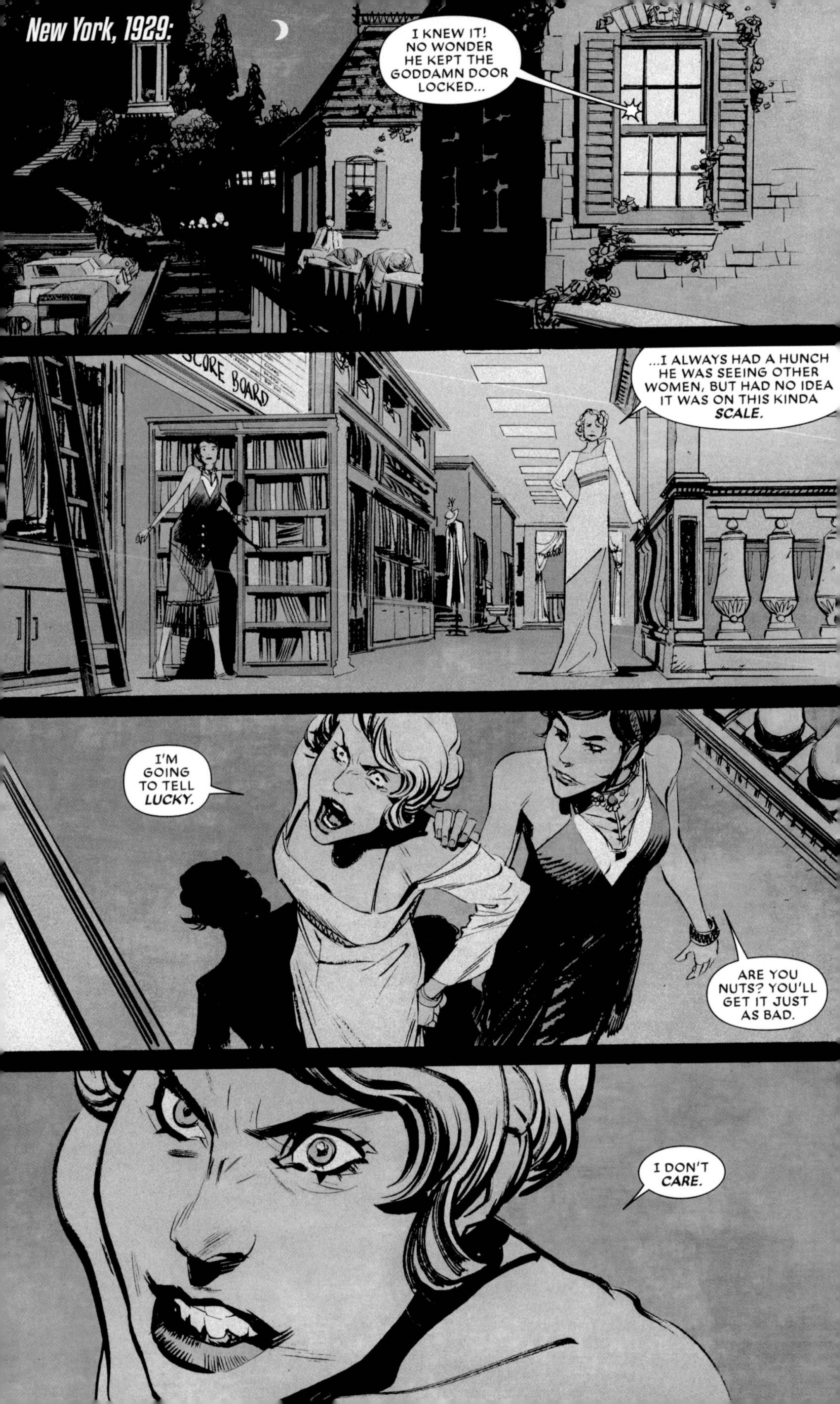
New York, 1929:
I KNEW IT! NO WONDER HE KEPT THE GODDAMN DOOR LOCKED...
SCORE BOARD
...I ALWAYS HAD A HUNCH HE WAS SEEING OTHER WOMEN, BUT HAD NO IDEA IT WAS ON THIS KINDA SCALE.
I'M GOING TO TELL LUCKY.
ARE YOU NUTS? YOU'LL GET IT JUST AS BAD.
I DON'T CARE.

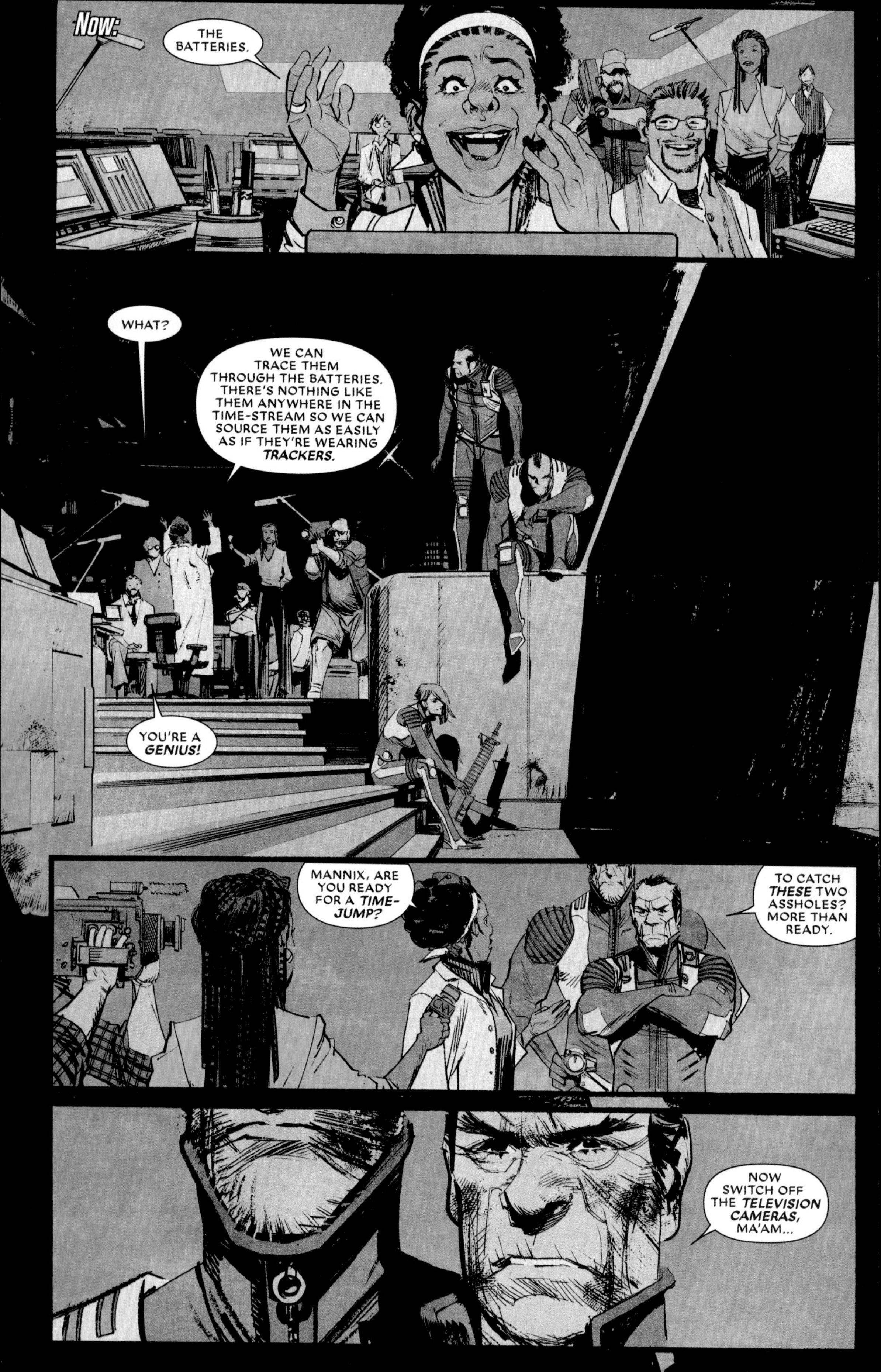
Now:
THE BATTERIES.
WHAT?
WE CAN TRACE THEM THROUGH THE BATTERIES. THERE'S NOTHING LIKE THEM ANYWHERE IN THE TIME-STREAM SO WE CAN SOURCE THEM AS EASILY AS IF THEY'RE WEARING TRACKERS.
YOU'RE A GENIUS!
MANNIX, ARE YOU READY FOR A TIME-JUMP?
TO CATCH THESE TWO ASSHOLES? MORE THAN READY.
NOW SWITCH OFF THE TELEVISION CAMERAS, MA'AM...

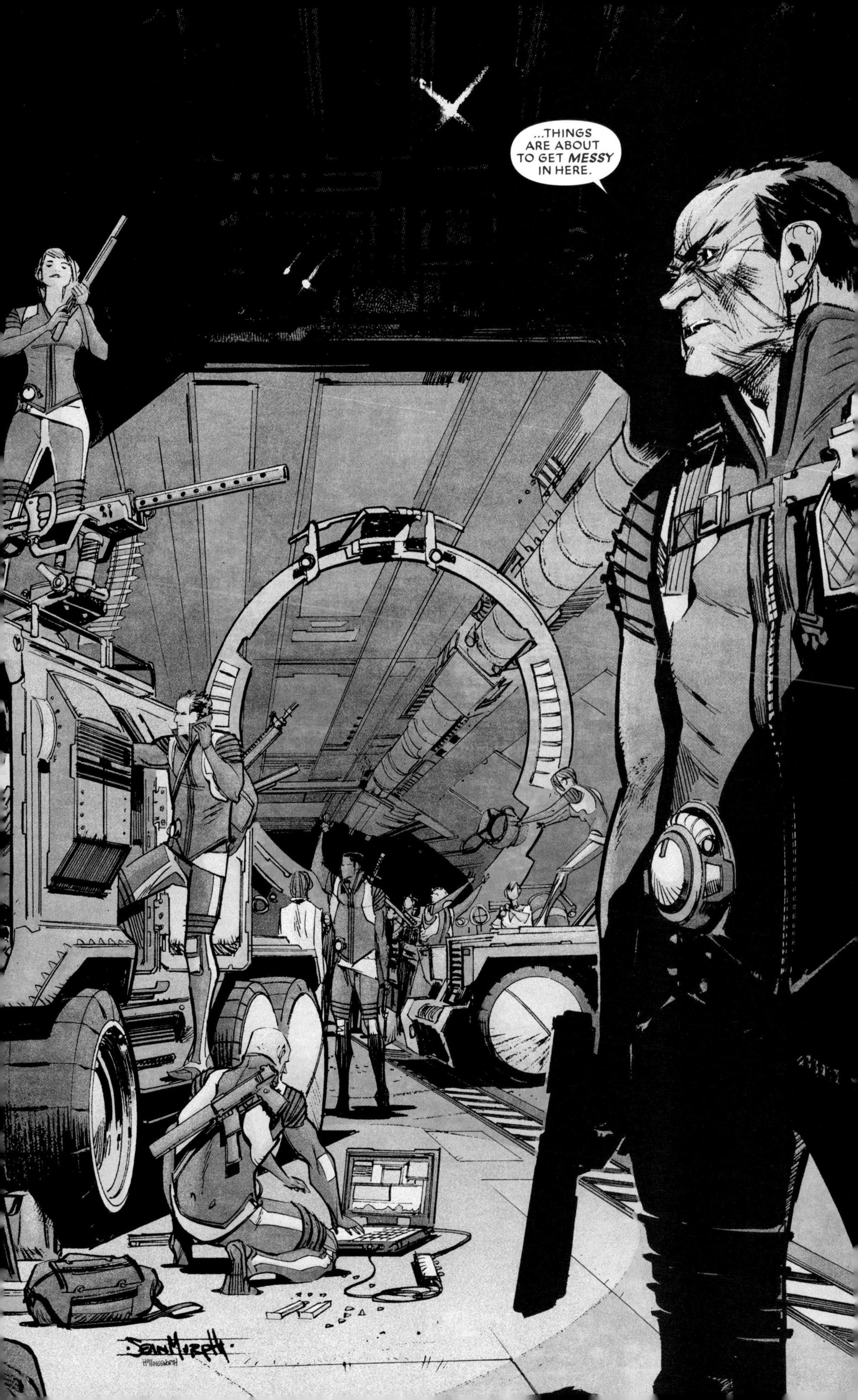
...THINGS ARE ABOUT TO GET MESSY IN HERE.
SEAN MURPHY
HOLLINGSWORTH

CHAPTER THREE

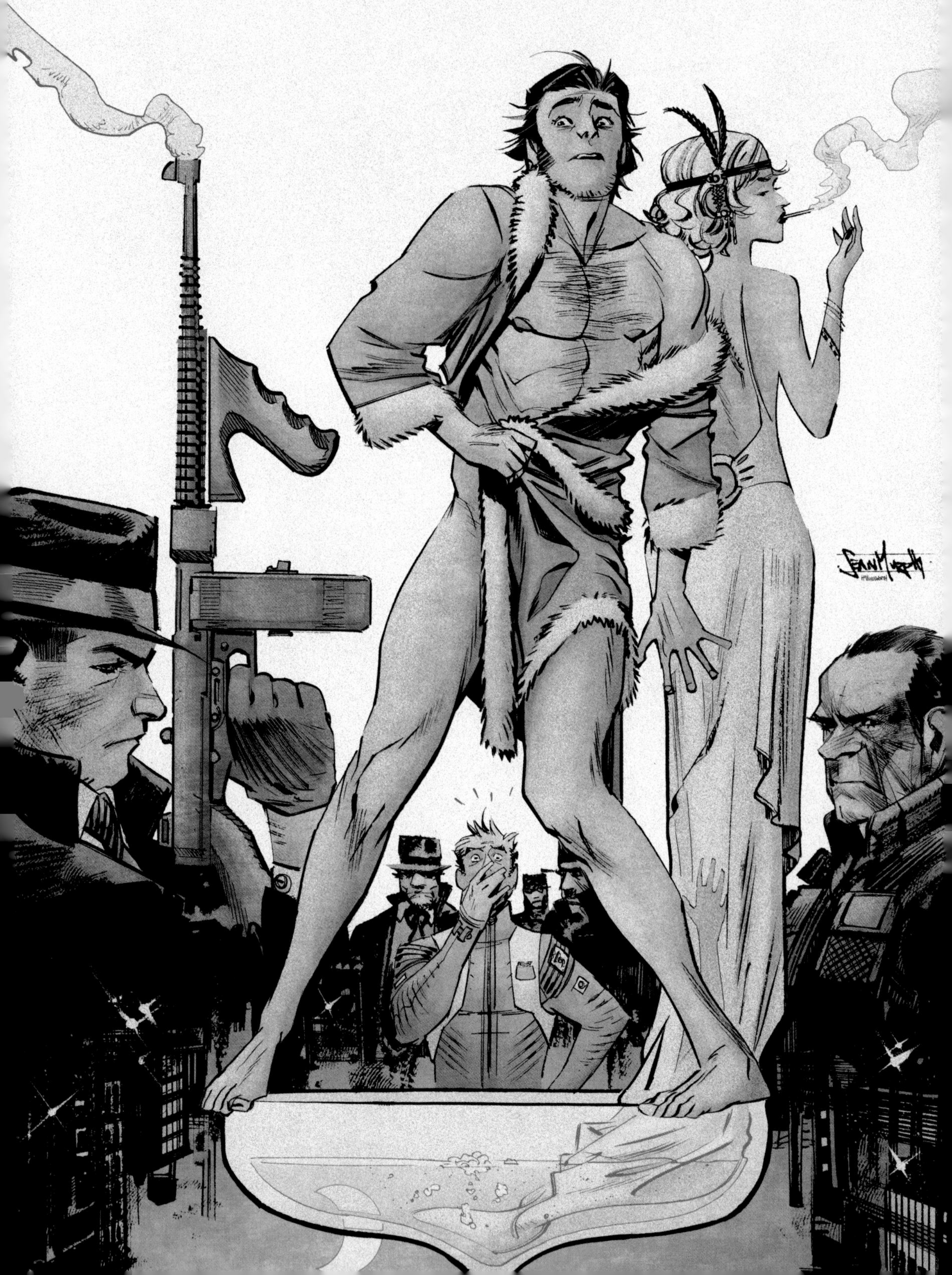

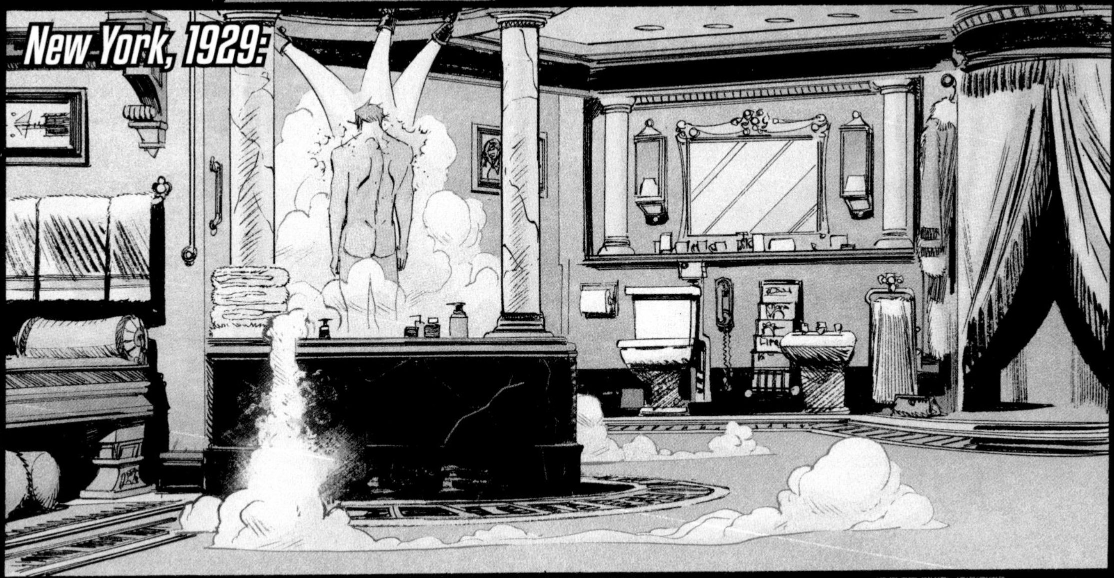
New York, 1929:

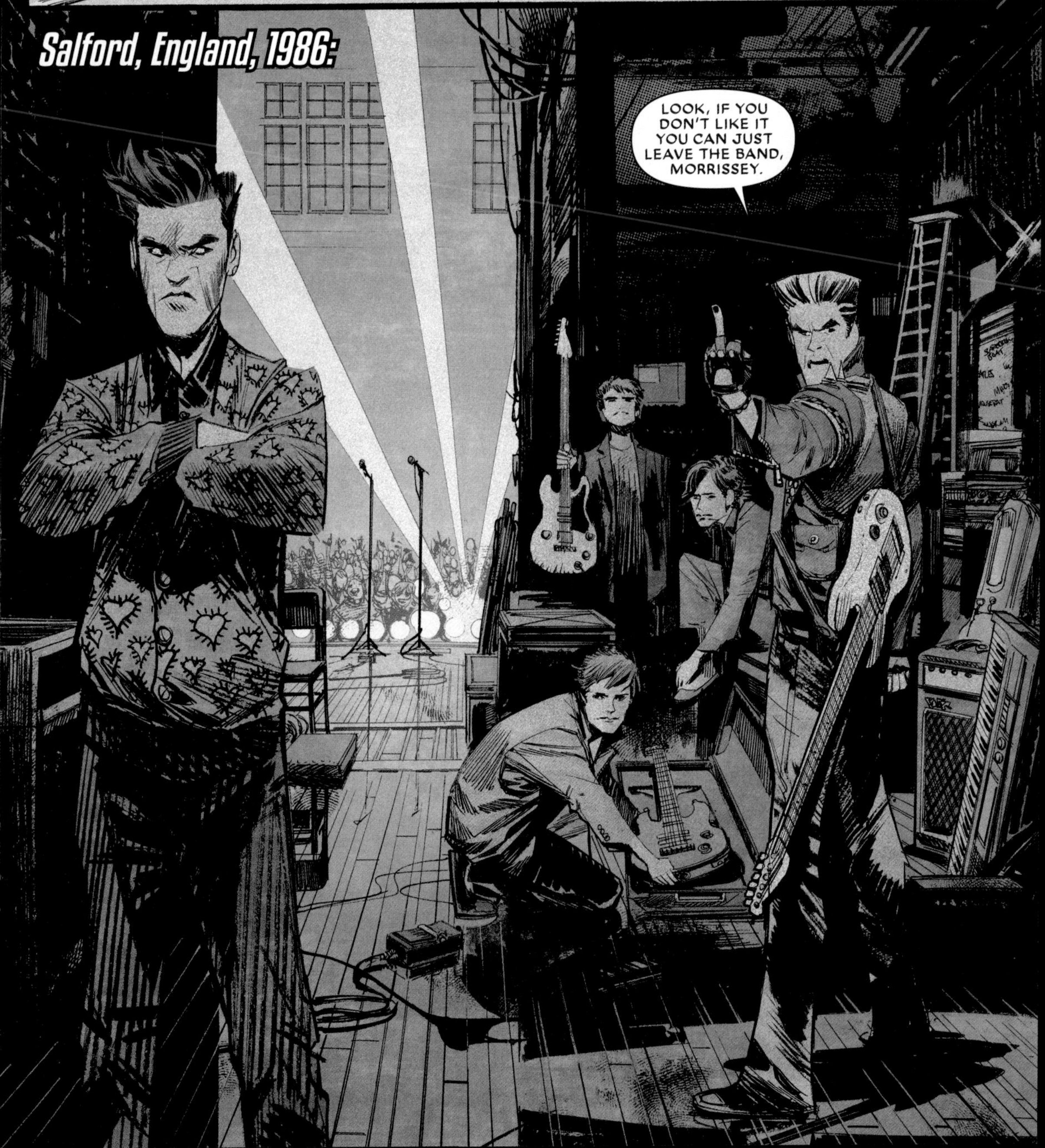
Salford, England, 1986:
LOOK, IF YOU DON'T LIKE IT YOU CAN JUST LEAVE THE BAND, MORRISSEY.

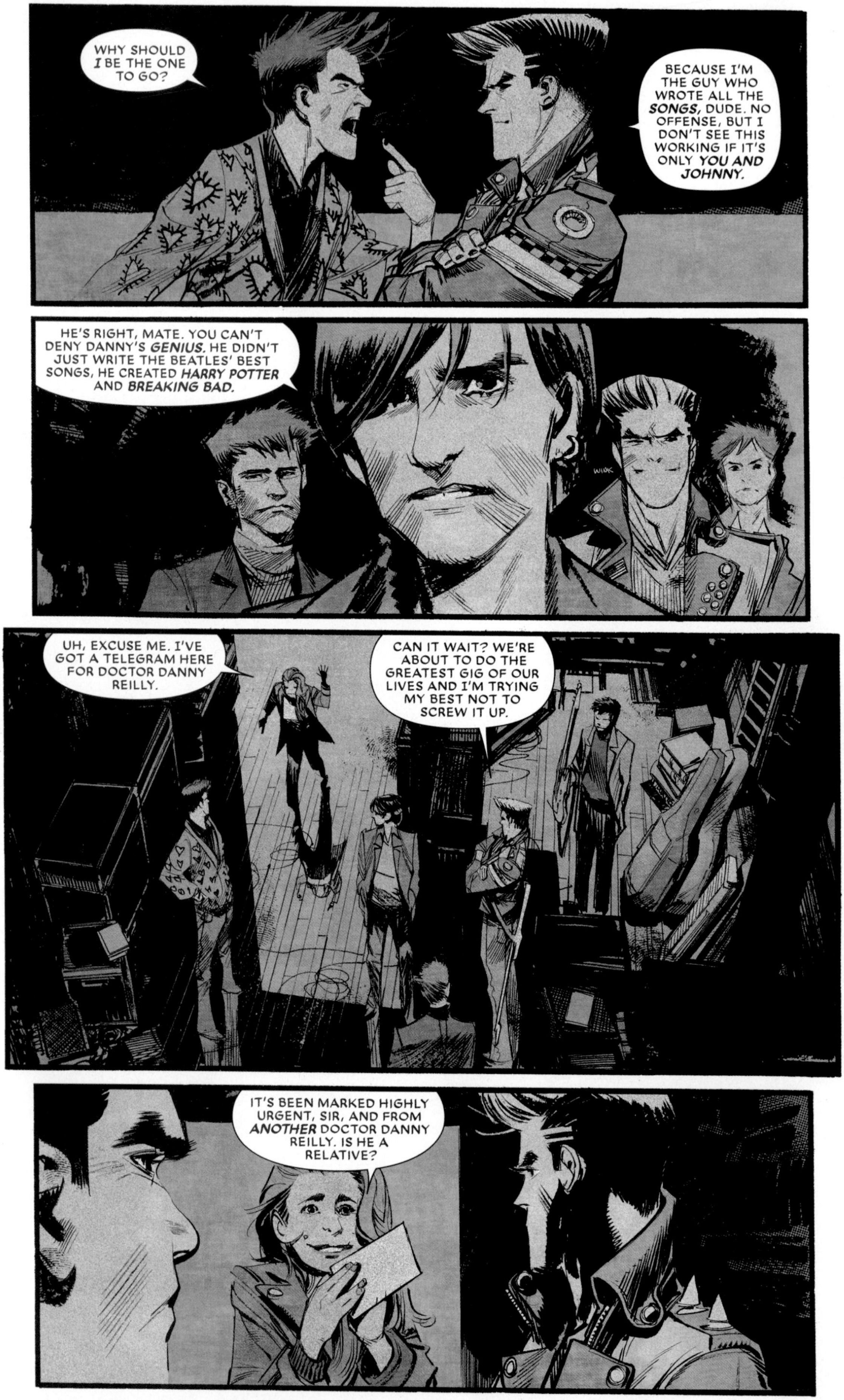
WHY SHOULD *I* BE THE ONE TO GO?
BECAUSE I'M THE GUY WHO WROTE ALL THE ***SONGS,*** DUDE. NO OFFENSE, BUT I DON'T SEE THIS WORKING IF IT'S ONLY ***YOU AND JOHNNY.***
HE'S RIGHT, MATE. YOU CAN'T DENY DANNY'S ***GENIUS.*** HE DIDN'T JUST WRITE THE BEATLES' BEST SONGS, HE CREATED ***HARRY POTTER*** AND ***BREAKING BAD.***
WINK
UH, EXCUSE ME. I'VE GOT A TELEGRAM HERE FOR DOCTOR DANNY REILLY.
CAN IT WAIT? WE'RE ABOUT TO DO THE GREATEST GIG OF OUR LIVES AND I'M TRYING MY BEST NOT TO SCREW IT UP.
IT'S BEEN MARKED HIGHLY URGENT, SIR, AND FROM ***ANOTHER*** DOCTOR DANNY REILLY. IS HE A RELATIVE?

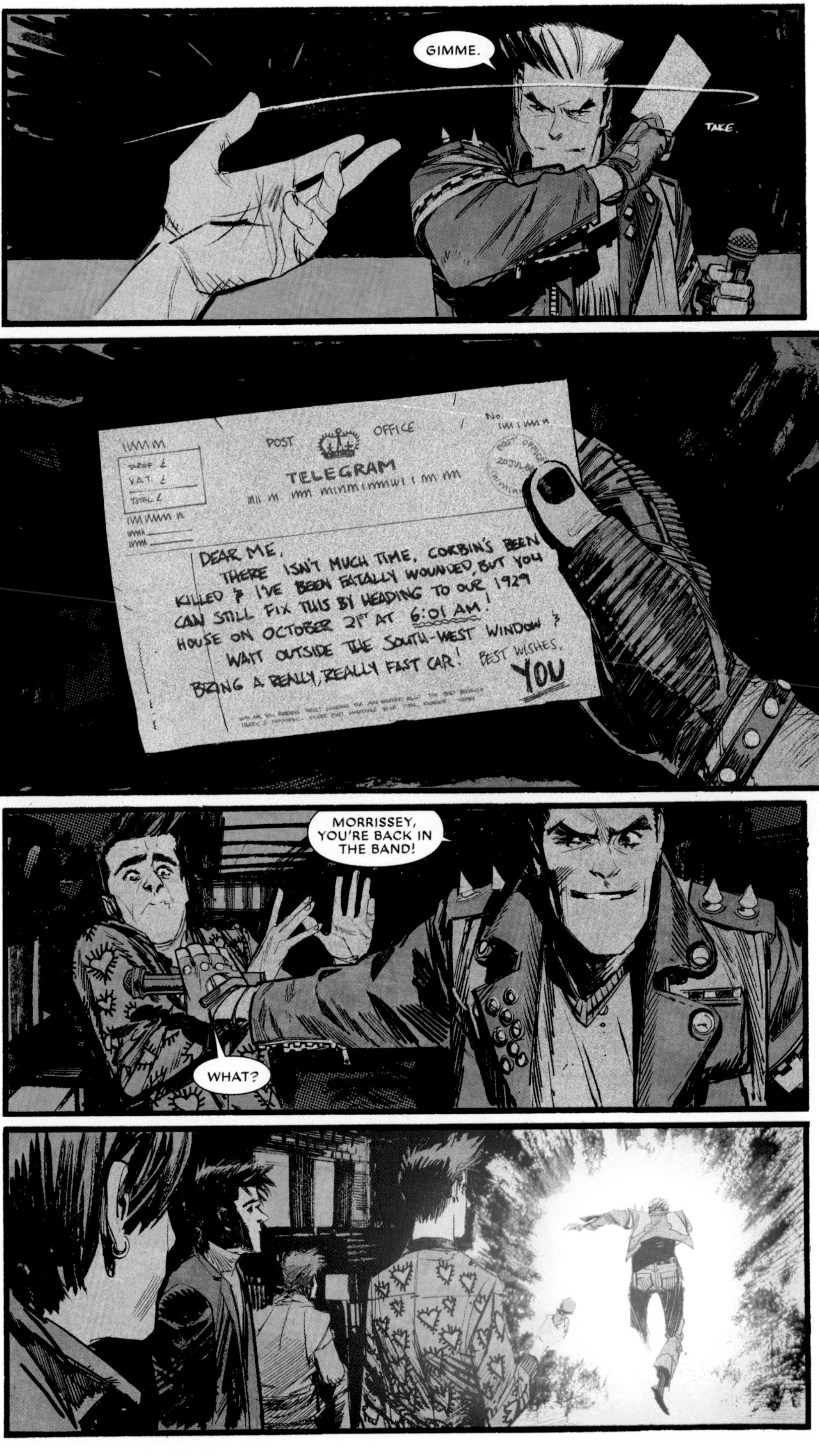
GIMME.
TAKE.
POST OFFICE
TELEGRAM
TARIFF £
V.A.T. £
TOTAL £
DEAR ME,
THERE ISN'T MUCH TIME. CORBIN'S BEEN KILLED & I'VE BEEN FATALLY WOUNDED, BUT YOU CAN STILL FIX THIS BY HEADING TO OUR 1929 HOUSE ON OCTOBER 21ST AT 6:01 AM!
WAIT OUTSIDE THE SOUTH-WEST WINDOW & BRING A REALLY, REALLY FAST CAR!
BEST WISHES,
YOU
MORRISSEY, YOU'RE BACK IN THE BAND!
WHAT?

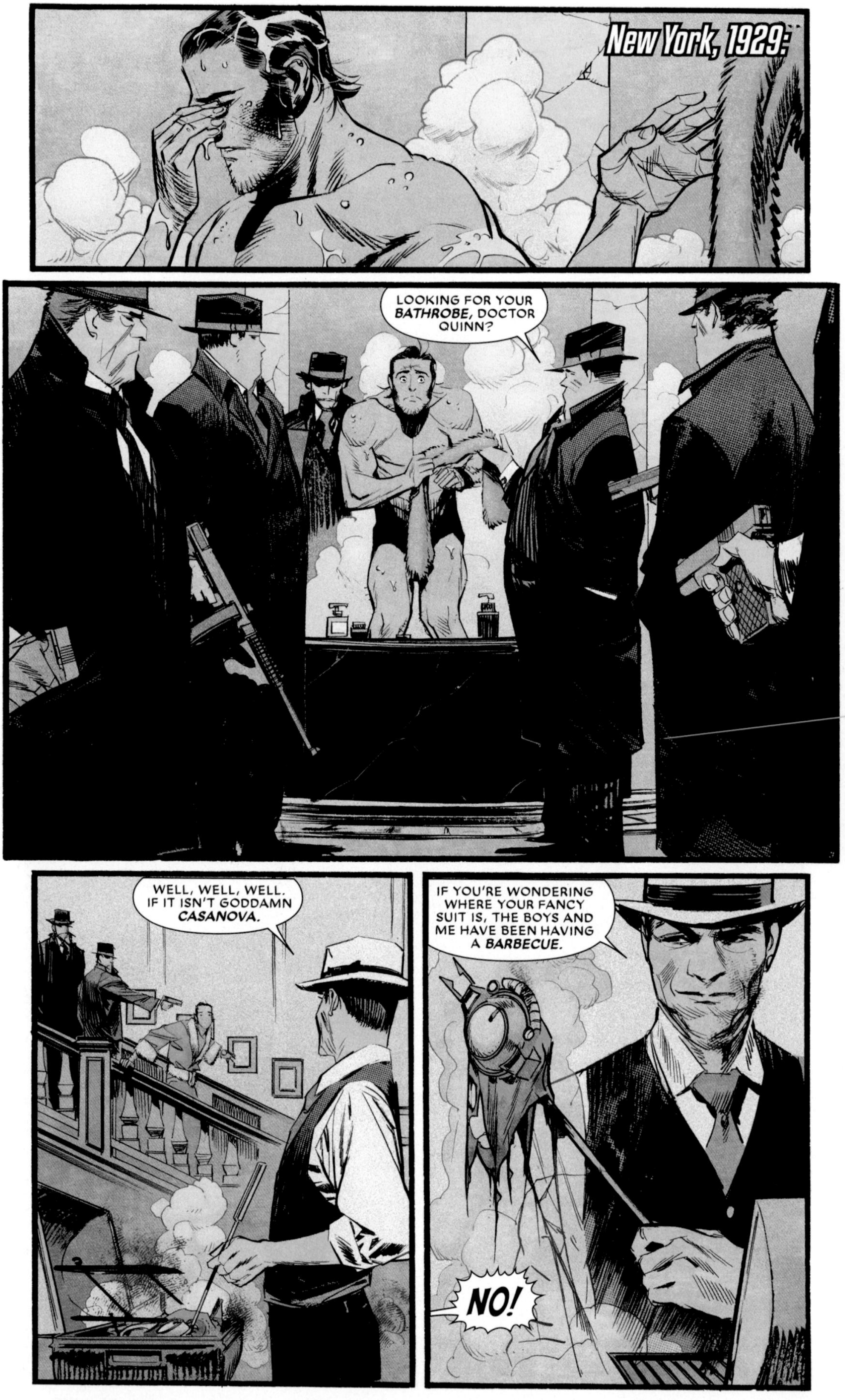
New York, 1929:
LOOKING FOR YOUR BATHROBE, DOCTOR QUINN?
WELL, WELL, WELL. IF IT ISN'T GODDAMN CASANOVA.
IF YOU'RE WONDERING WHERE YOUR FANCY SUIT IS, THE BOYS AND ME HAVE BEEN HAVING A BARBECUE.
NO!

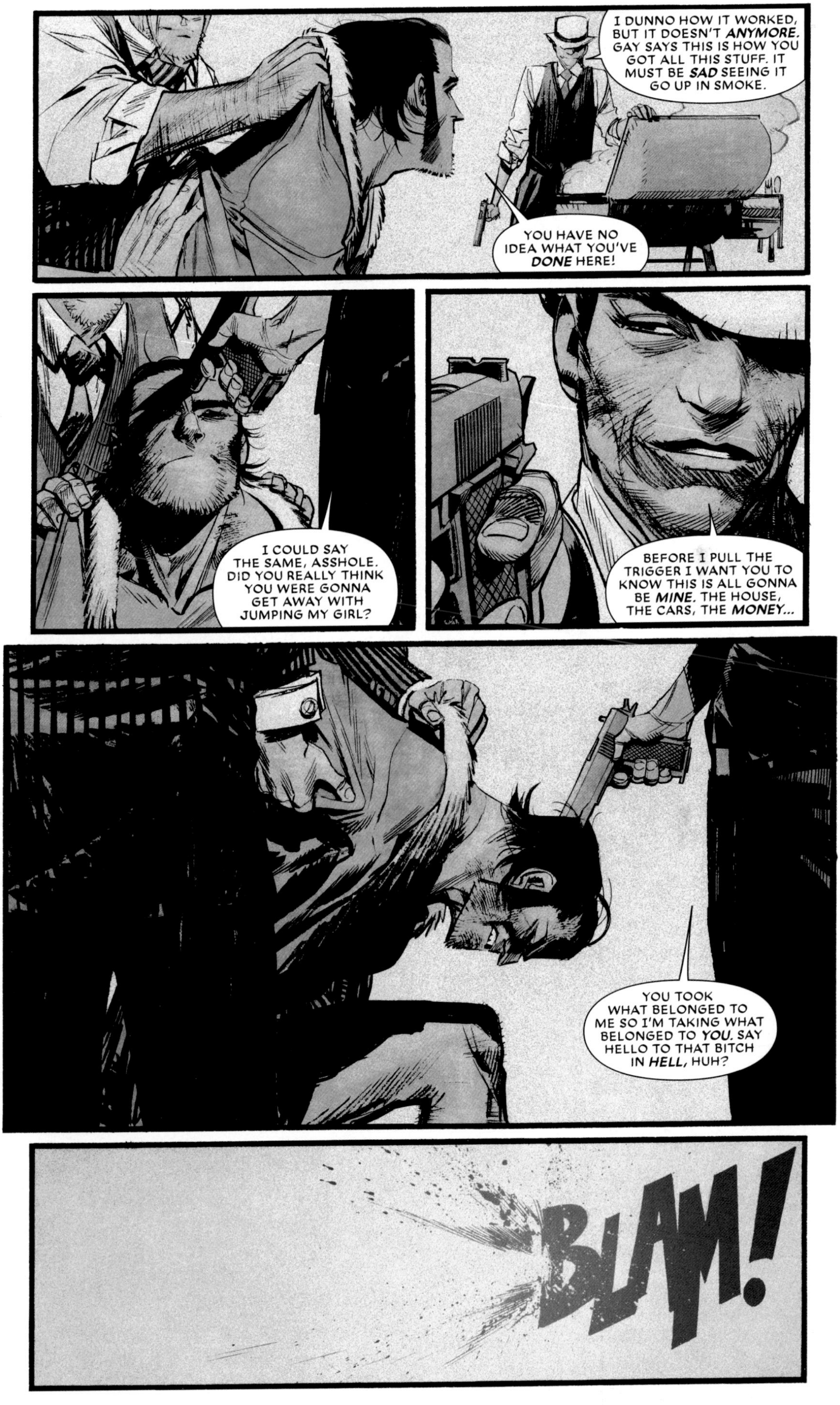
I DUNNO HOW IT WORKED, BUT IT DOESN'T ANYMORE. GAY SAYS THIS IS HOW YOU GOT ALL THIS STUFF. IT MUST BE SAD SEEING IT GO UP IN SMOKE.
YOU HAVE NO IDEA WHAT YOU'VE DONE HERE!
I COULD SAY THE SAME, ASSHOLE. DID YOU REALLY THINK YOU WERE GONNA GET AWAY WITH JUMPING MY GIRL?
BEFORE I PULL THE TRIGGER I WANT YOU TO KNOW THIS IS ALL GONNA BE MINE. THE HOUSE, THE CARS, THE MONEY...
YOU TOOK WHAT BELONGED TO ME SO I'M TAKING WHAT BELONGED TO YOU. SAY HELLO TO THAT BITCH IN HELL, HUH?
BLAM!

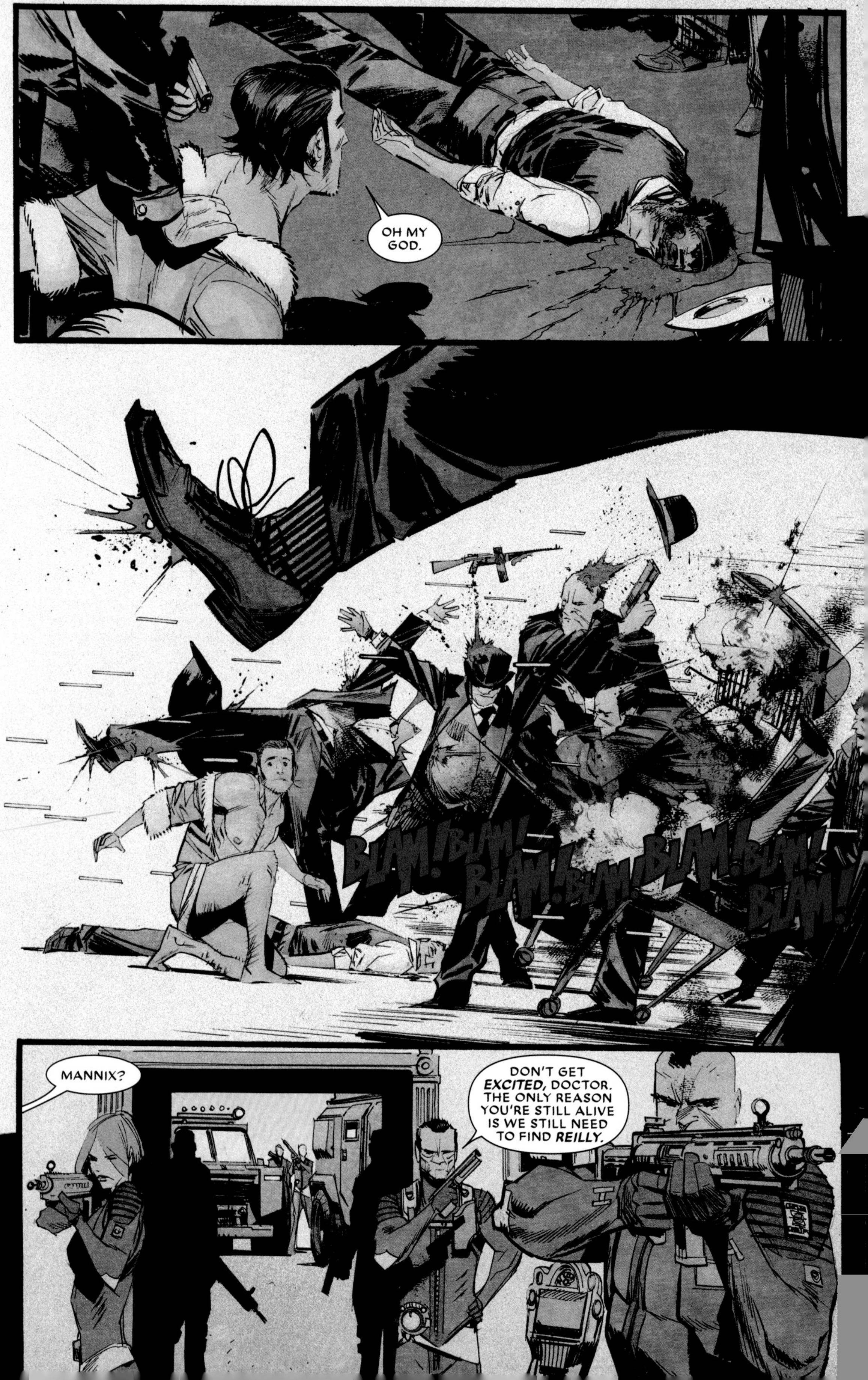
OH MY GOD.
BLAM! BLAM! BLAM! BLAM! BLAM! BLAM! BLAM! BLAM!
MANNIX?
DON'T GET *EXCITED,* DOCTOR. THE ONLY REASON YOU'RE STILL ALIVE IS WE STILL NEED TO FIND *REILLY.*

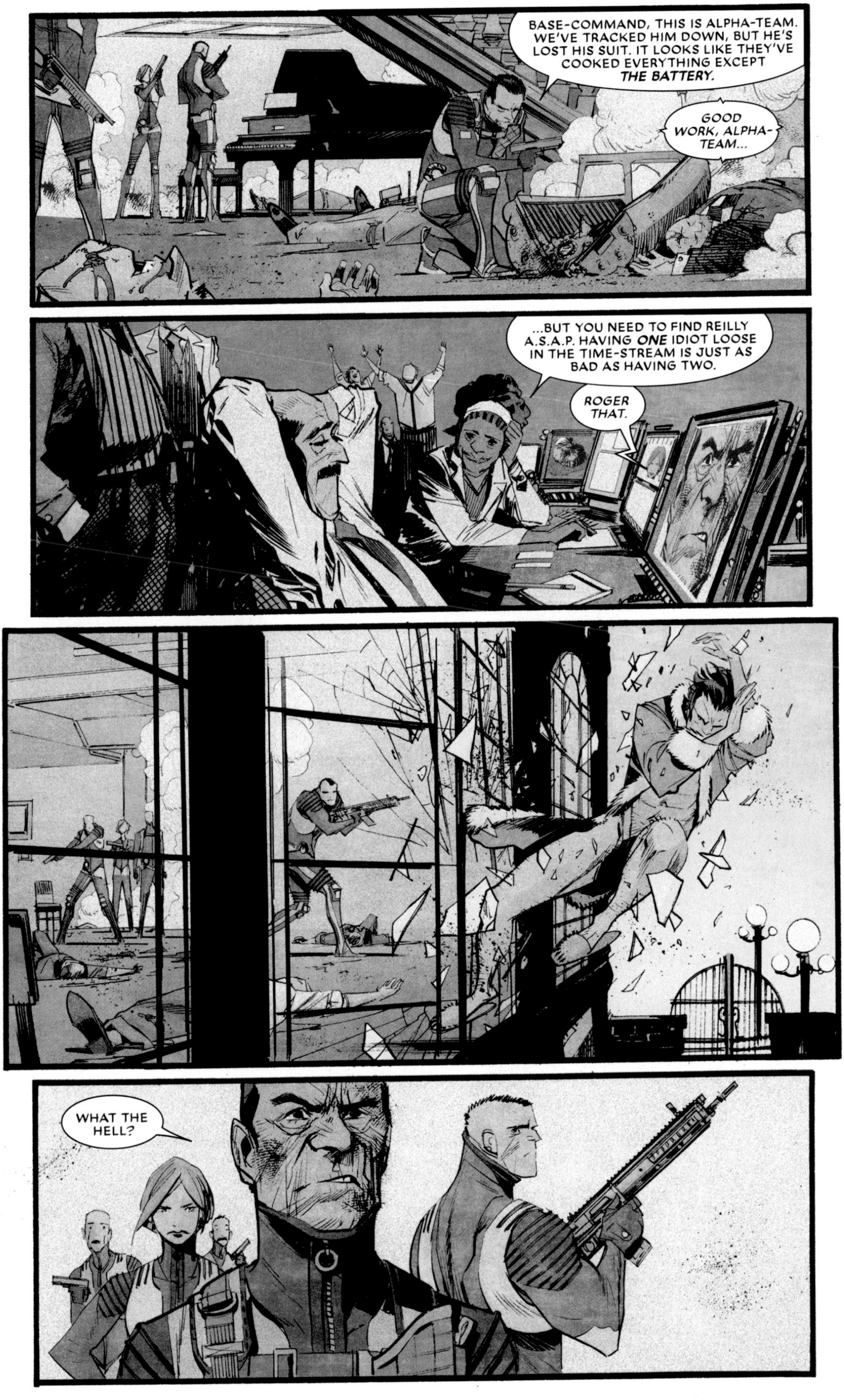
BASE-COMMAND, THIS IS ALPHA-TEAM. WE'VE TRACKED HIM DOWN, BUT HE'S LOST HIS SUIT. IT LOOKS LIKE THEY'VE COOKED EVERYTHING EXCEPT *THE BATTERY.*
GOOD WORK, ALPHA-TEAM...
...BUT YOU NEED TO FIND REILLY A.S.A.P. HAVING *ONE* IDIOT LOOSE IN THE TIME-STREAM IS JUST AS BAD AS HAVING TWO.
ROGER THAT.
WHAT THE HELL?

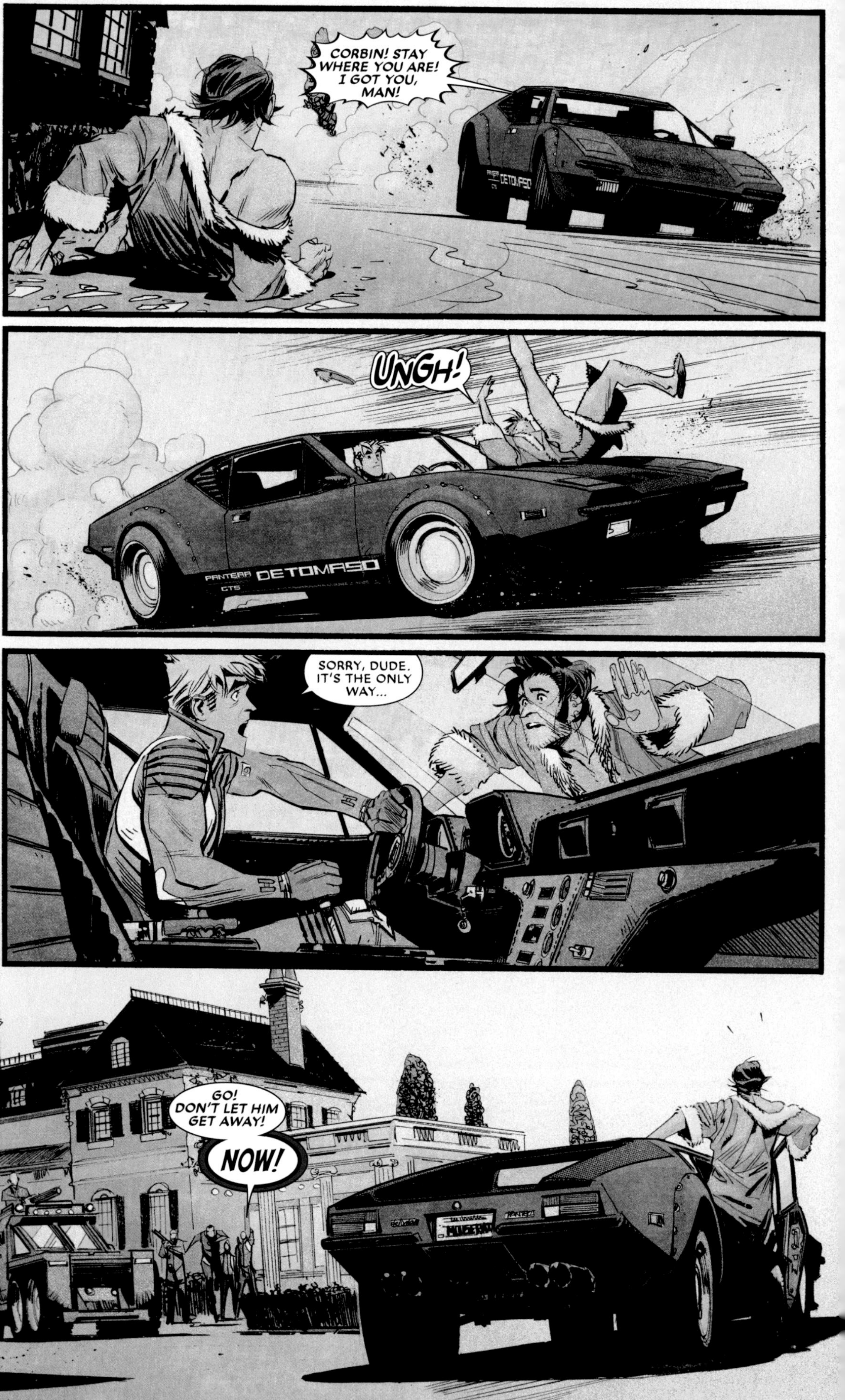
CORBIN! STAY WHERE YOU ARE! I GOT YOU, MAN!
UNGH!
PANTERA
DETOMASO
GTS
SORRY, DUDE. IT'S THE ONLY WAY...
GO! DON'T LET HIM GET AWAY!
NOW!

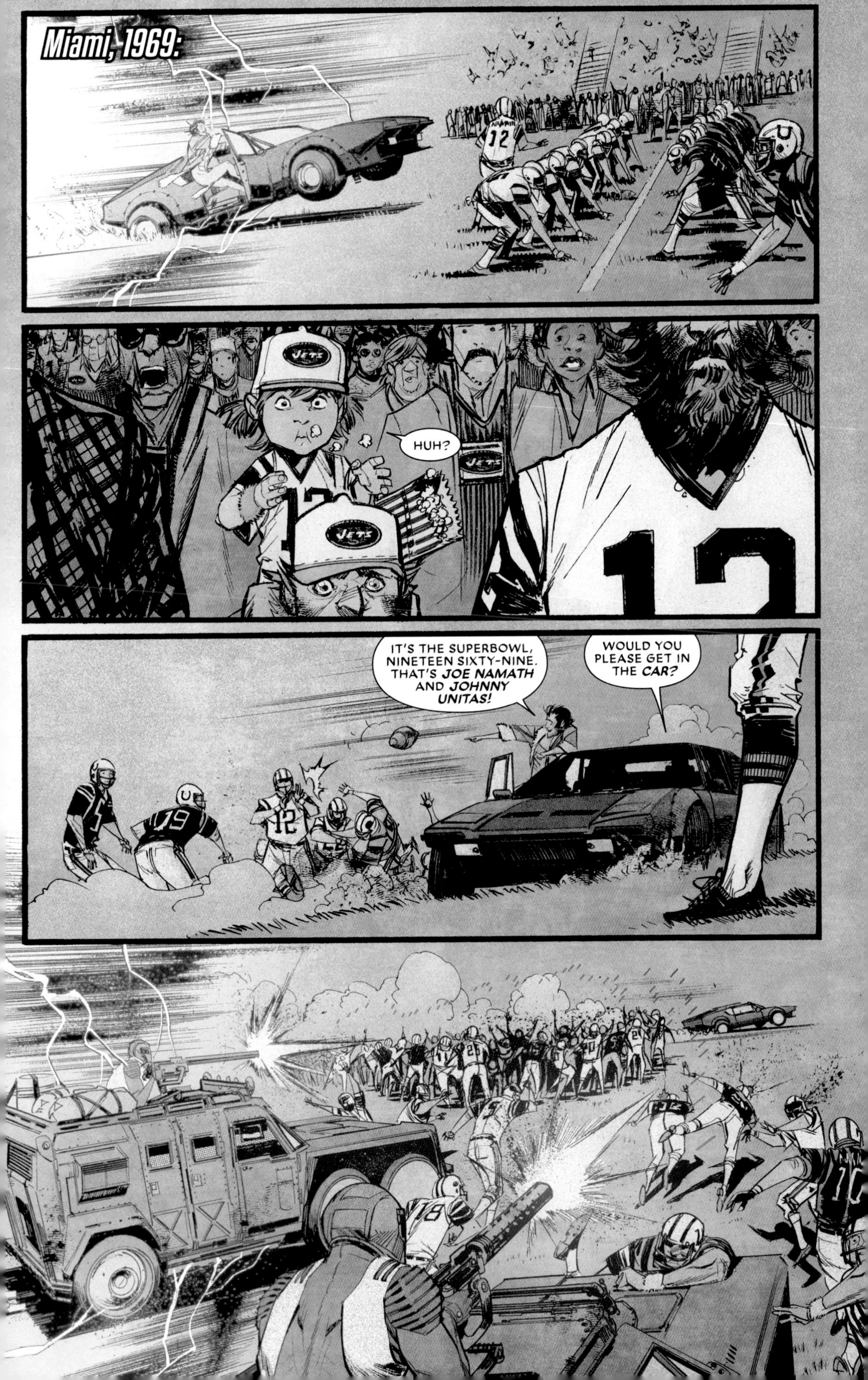
Miami, 1969:
HUH?
IT'S THE SUPERBOWL, NINETEEN SIXTY-NINE. THAT'S JOE NAMATH AND JOHNNY UNITAS!
WOULD YOU PLEASE GET IN THE CAR?

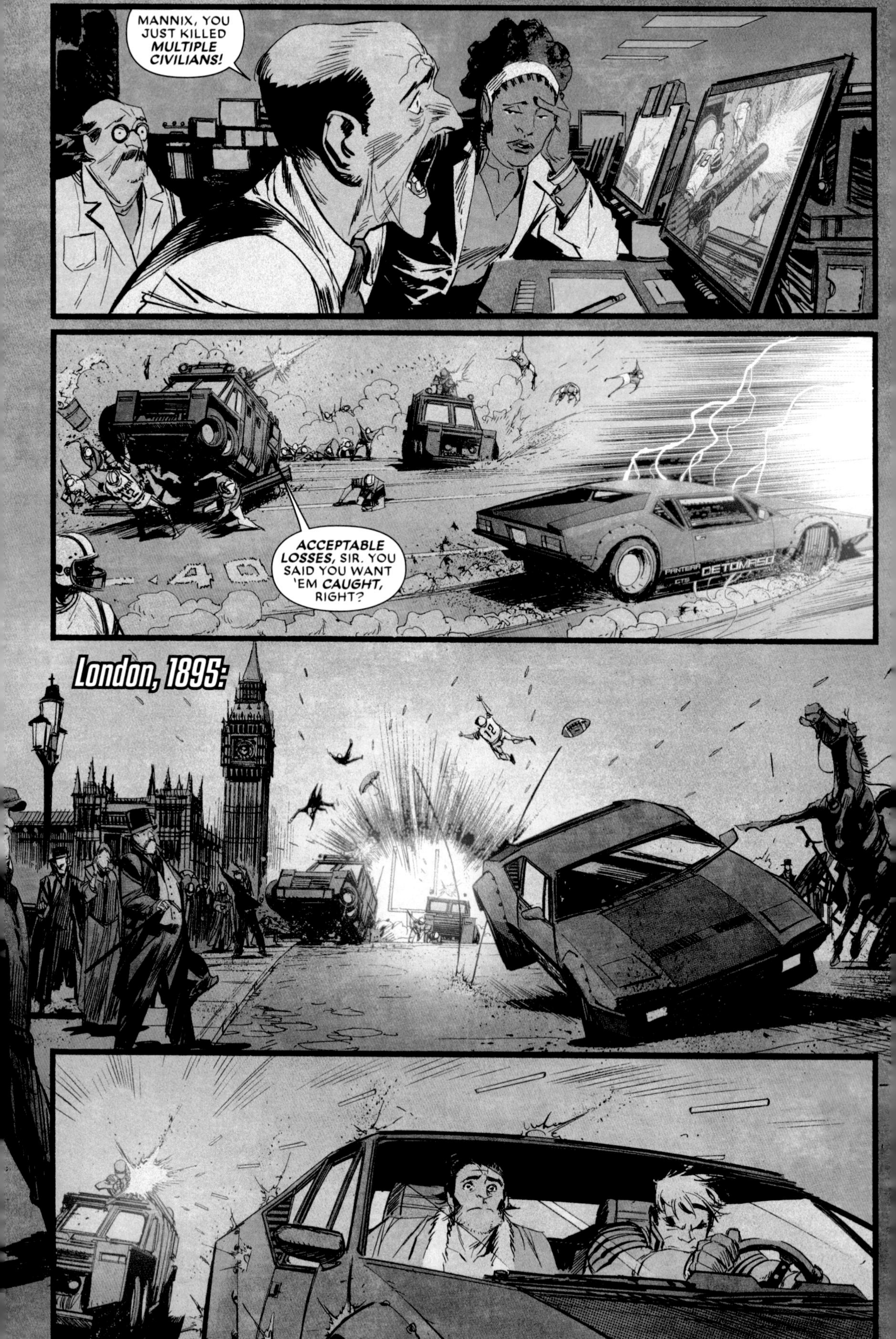
MANNIX, YOU JUST KILLED MULTIPLE CIVILIANS!
ACCEPTABLE LOSSES, SIR. YOU SAID YOU WANT 'EM CAUGHT, RIGHT?
PANTERA DETOMASO GTS
London, 1895:

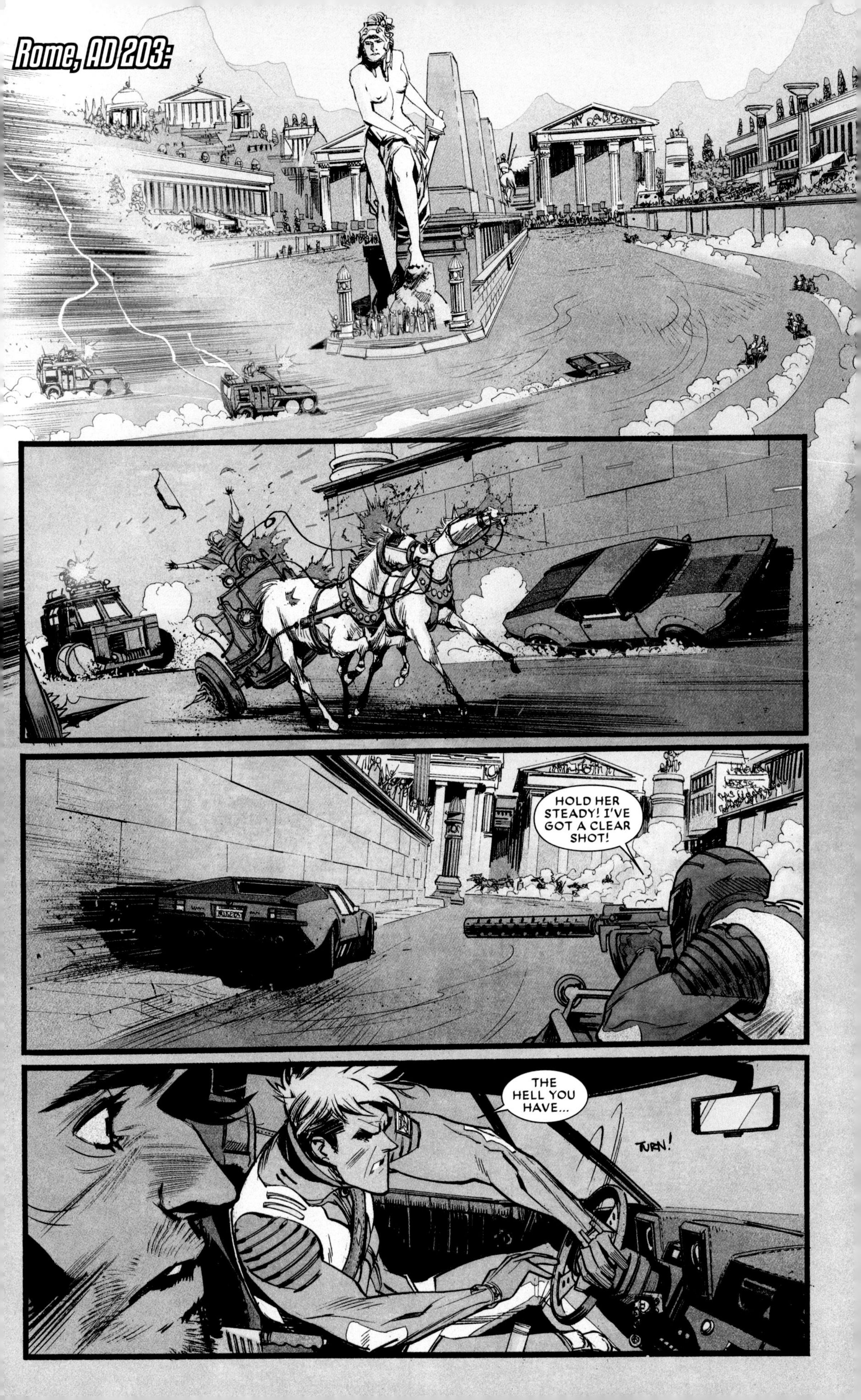
Rome, AD 203:
HOLD HER STEADY! I'VE GOT A CLEAR SHOT!
THE HELL YOU HAVE...
TURN!

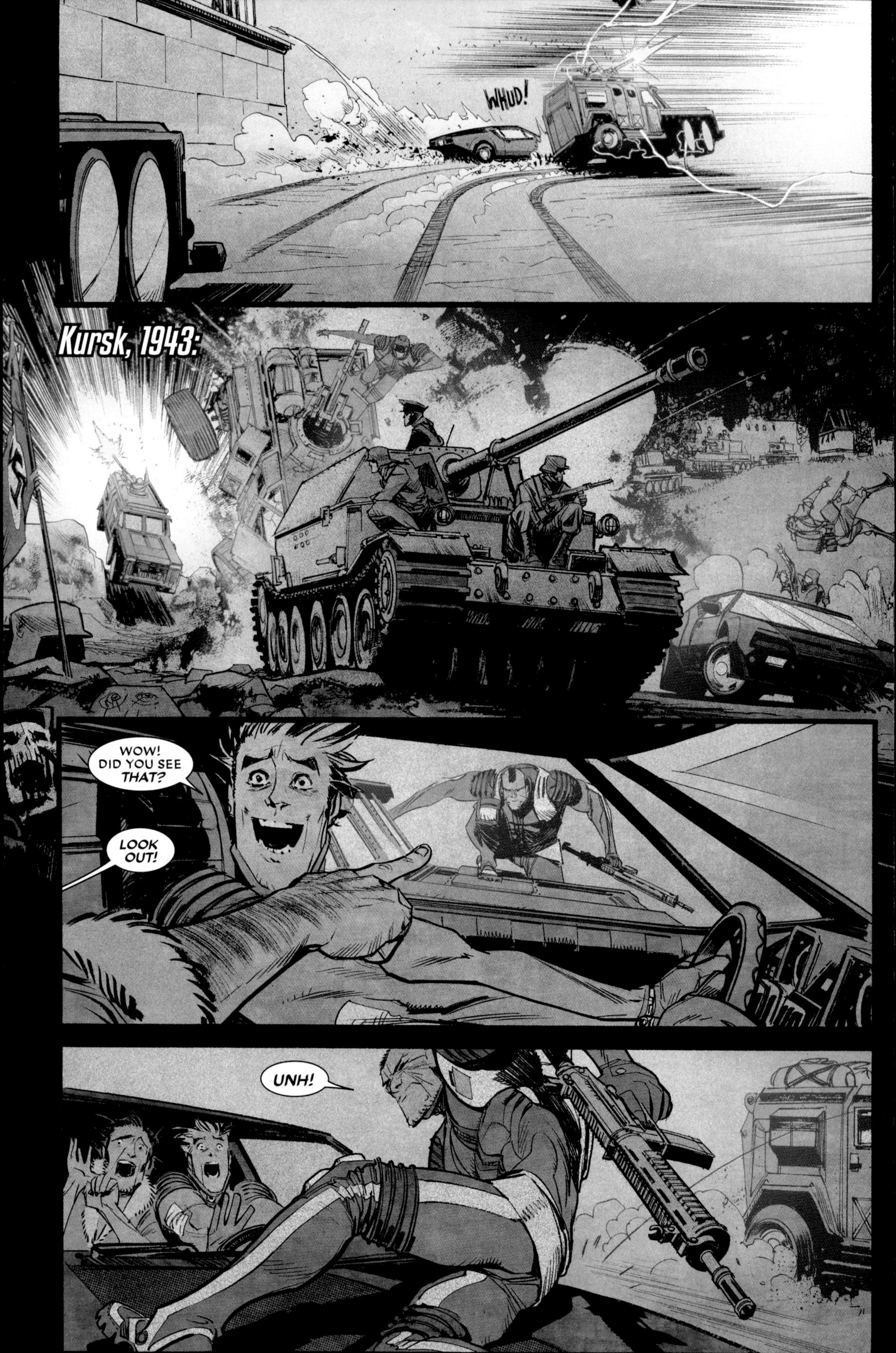
WHUD!
Kursk, 1943:
WOW! DID YOU SEE THAT?
LOOK OUT!
UNH!

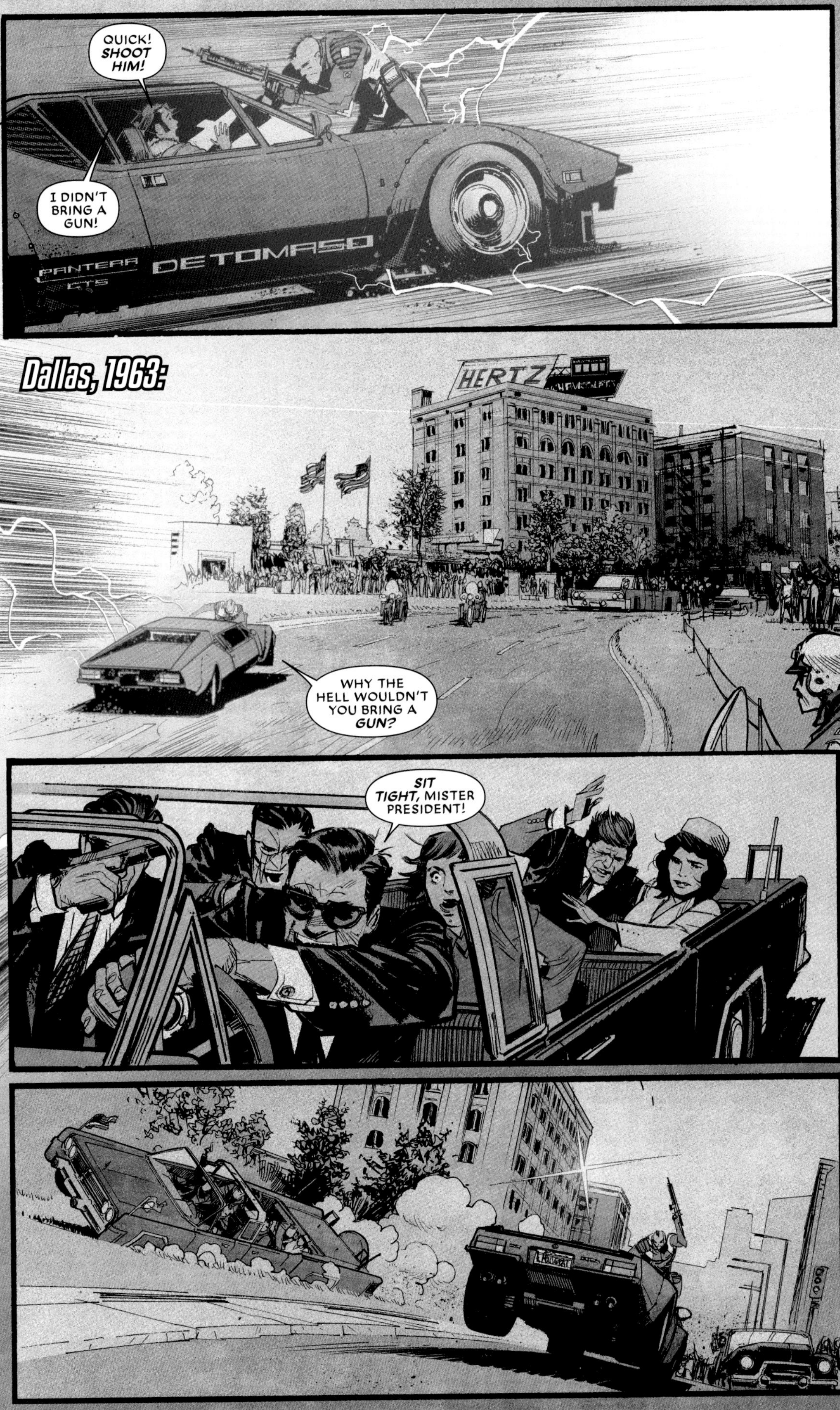
QUICK! SHOOT HIM!
I DIDN'T BRING A GUN!
PANTERA GTS
DETOMASO
Dallas, 1963:
HERTZ
WHY THE HELL WOULDN'T YOU BRING A GUN?
SIT TIGHT, MISTER PRESIDENT!

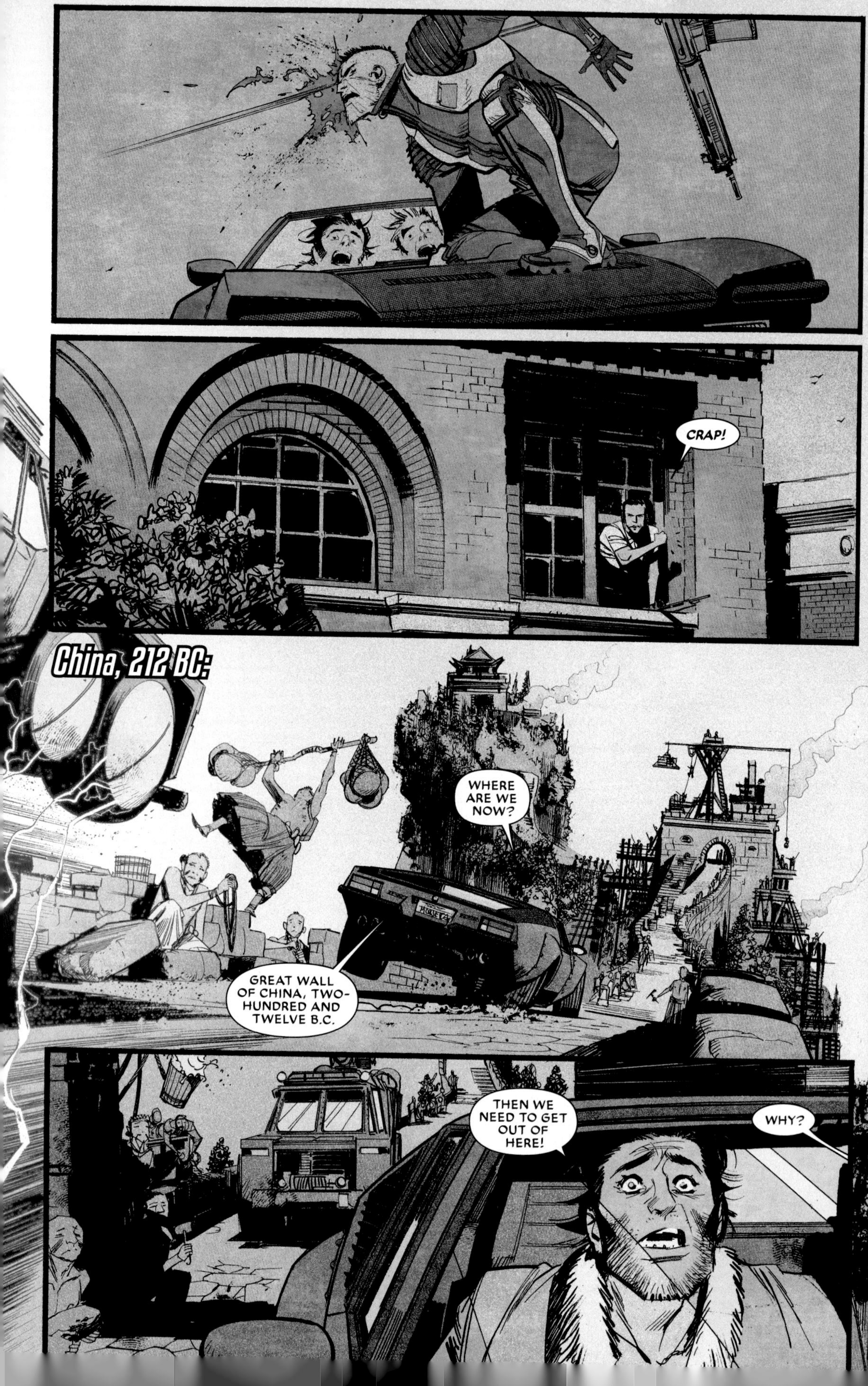
CRAP!
China, 212 BC:
WHERE ARE WE NOW?
GREAT WALL OF CHINA, TWO-HUNDRED AND TWELVE B.C.
THEN WE NEED TO GET OUT OF HERE!
WHY?

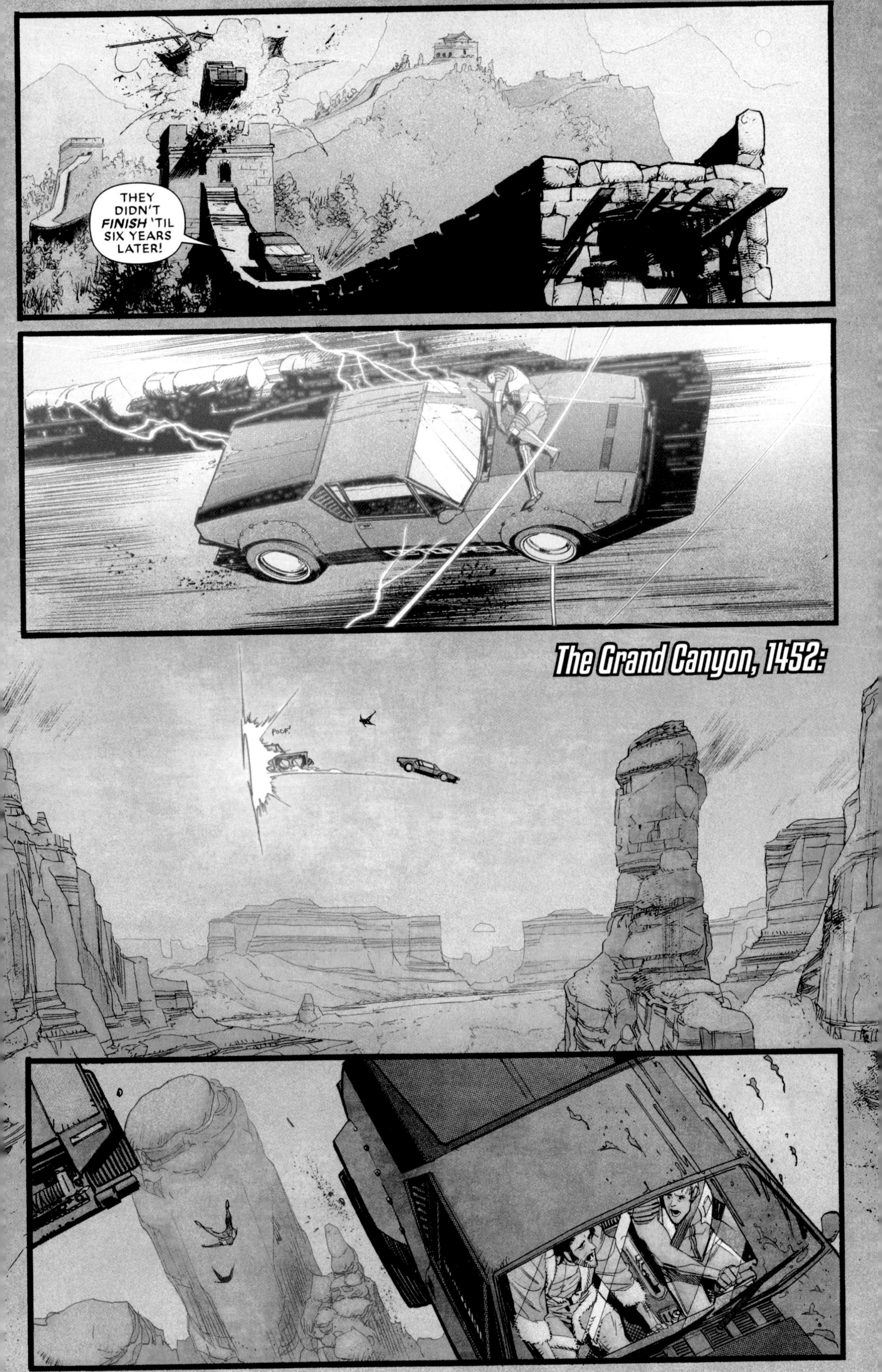
THEY DIDN'T FINISH 'TIL SIX YEARS LATER!
The Grand Canyon, 1452:
POOF!

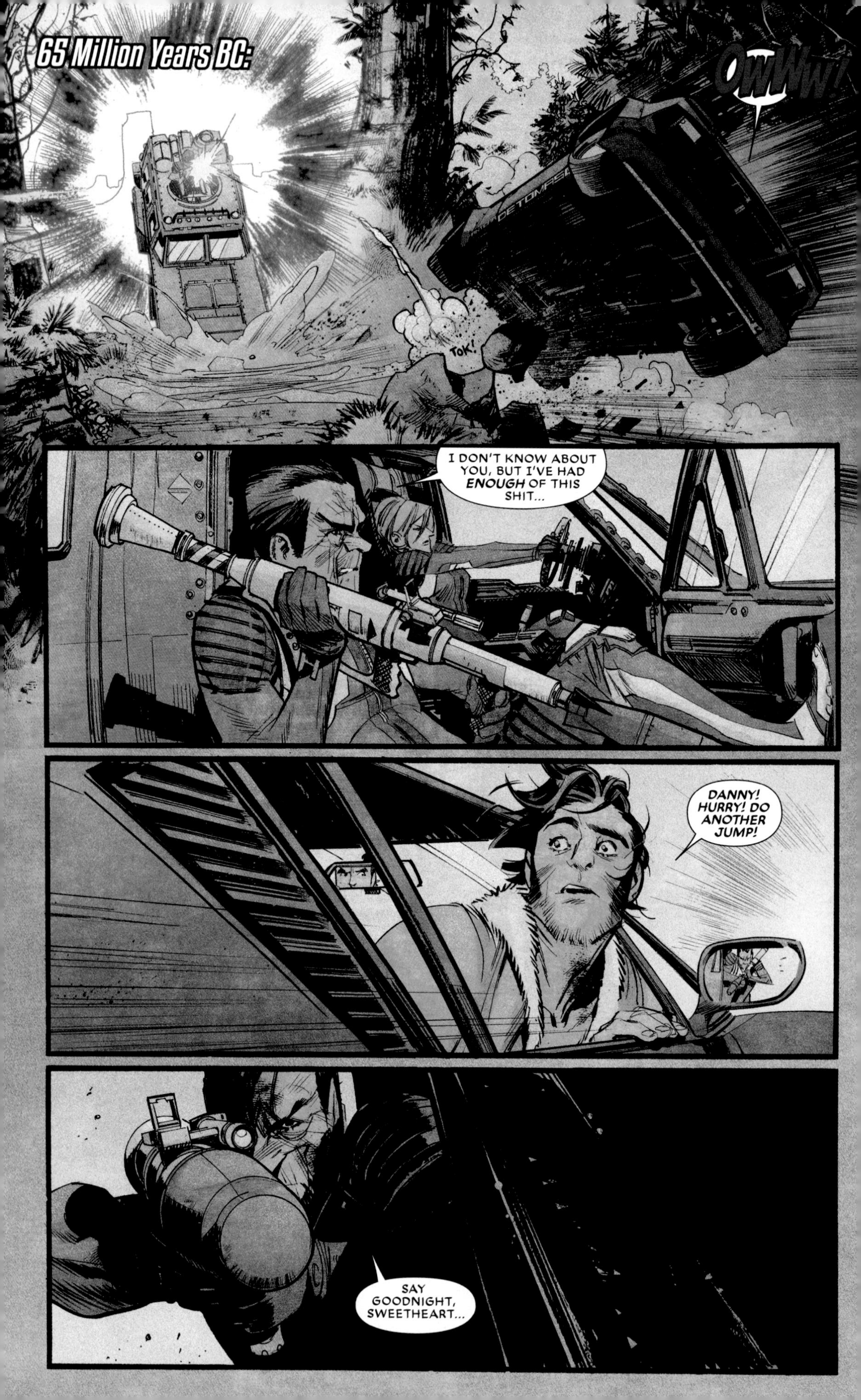
65 Million Years BC:
OWWW!
DETOMASO
TOK!
I DON'T KNOW ABOUT YOU, BUT I'VE HAD ENOUGH OF THIS SHIT...
DANNY! HURRY! DO ANOTHER JUMP!
SAY GOODNIGHT, SWEETHEART...

Samarkand, 1504:

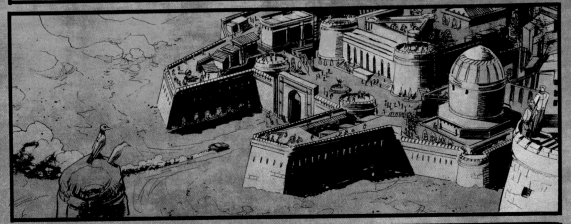

WOW.

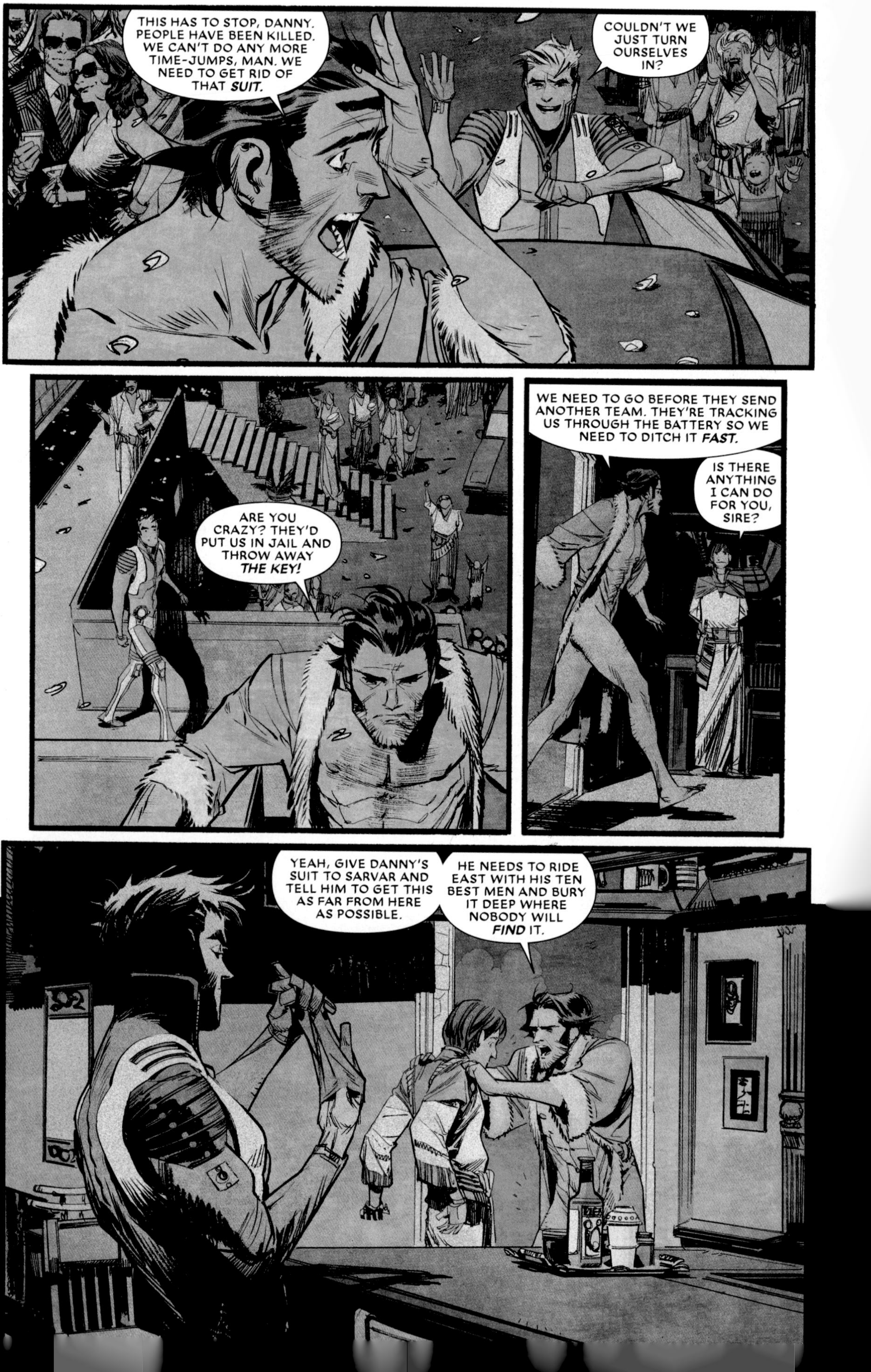
THIS HAS TO STOP, DANNY. PEOPLE HAVE BEEN KILLED. WE CAN'T DO ANY MORE TIME-JUMPS, MAN. WE NEED TO GET RID OF THAT SUIT.
COULDN'T WE JUST TURN OURSELVES IN?
ARE YOU CRAZY? THEY'D PUT US IN JAIL AND THROW AWAY THE KEY!
WE NEED TO GO BEFORE THEY SEND ANOTHER TEAM. THEY'RE TRACKING US THROUGH THE BATTERY SO WE NEED TO DITCH IT FAST.
IS THERE ANYTHING I CAN DO FOR YOU, SIRE?
YEAH, GIVE DANNY'S SUIT TO SARVAR AND TELL HIM TO GET THIS AS FAR FROM HERE AS POSSIBLE.
HE NEEDS TO RIDE EAST WITH HIS TEN BEST MEN AND BURY IT DEEP WHERE NOBODY WILL FIND IT.

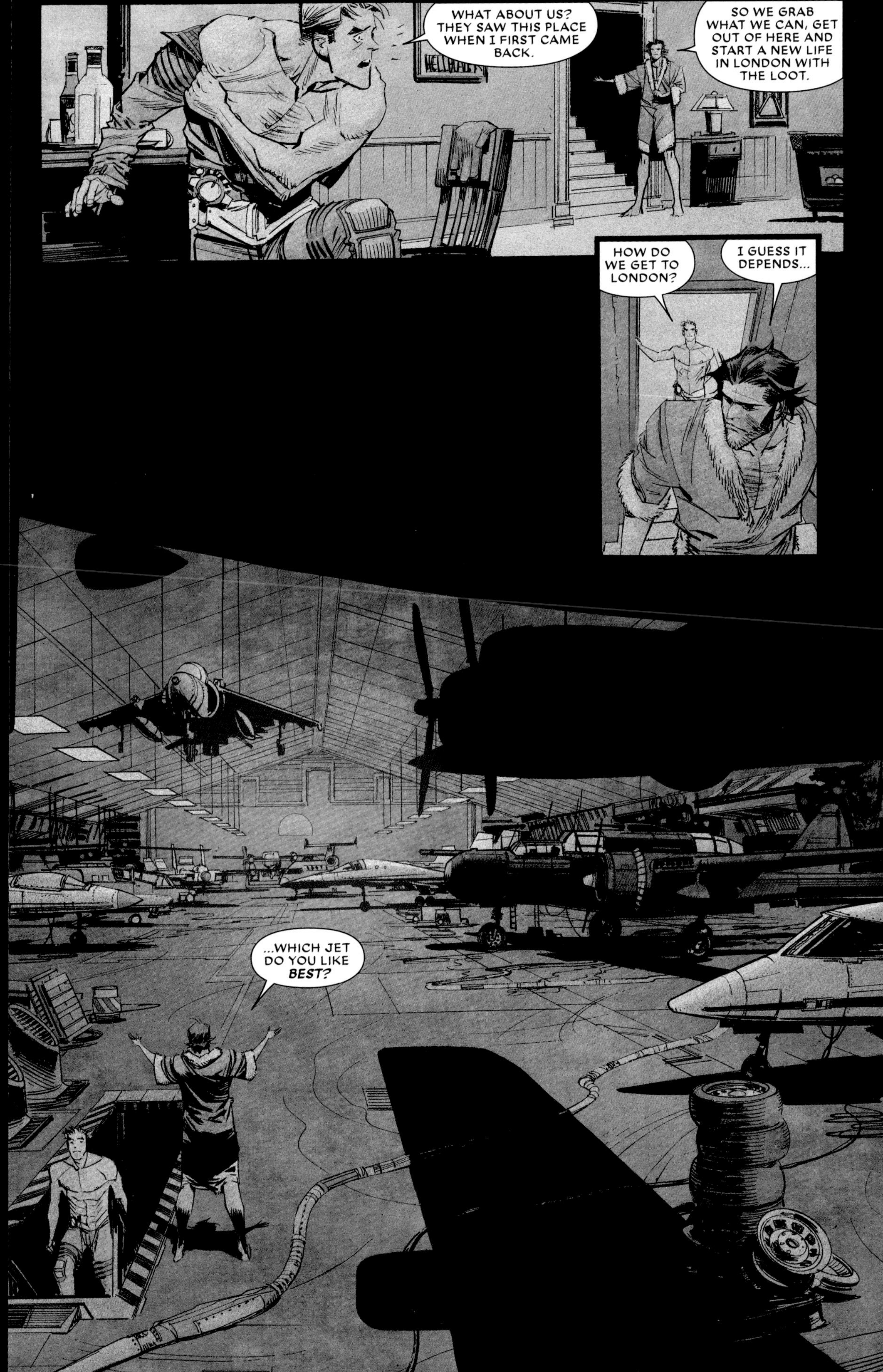
WHAT ABOUT US? THEY SAW THIS PLACE WHEN I FIRST CAME BACK.
SO WE GRAB WHAT WE CAN, GET OUT OF HERE AND START A NEW LIFE IN LONDON WITH THE LOOT.
HOW DO WE GET TO LONDON?
I GUESS IT DEPENDS...
...WHICH JET DO YOU LIKE *BEST?*

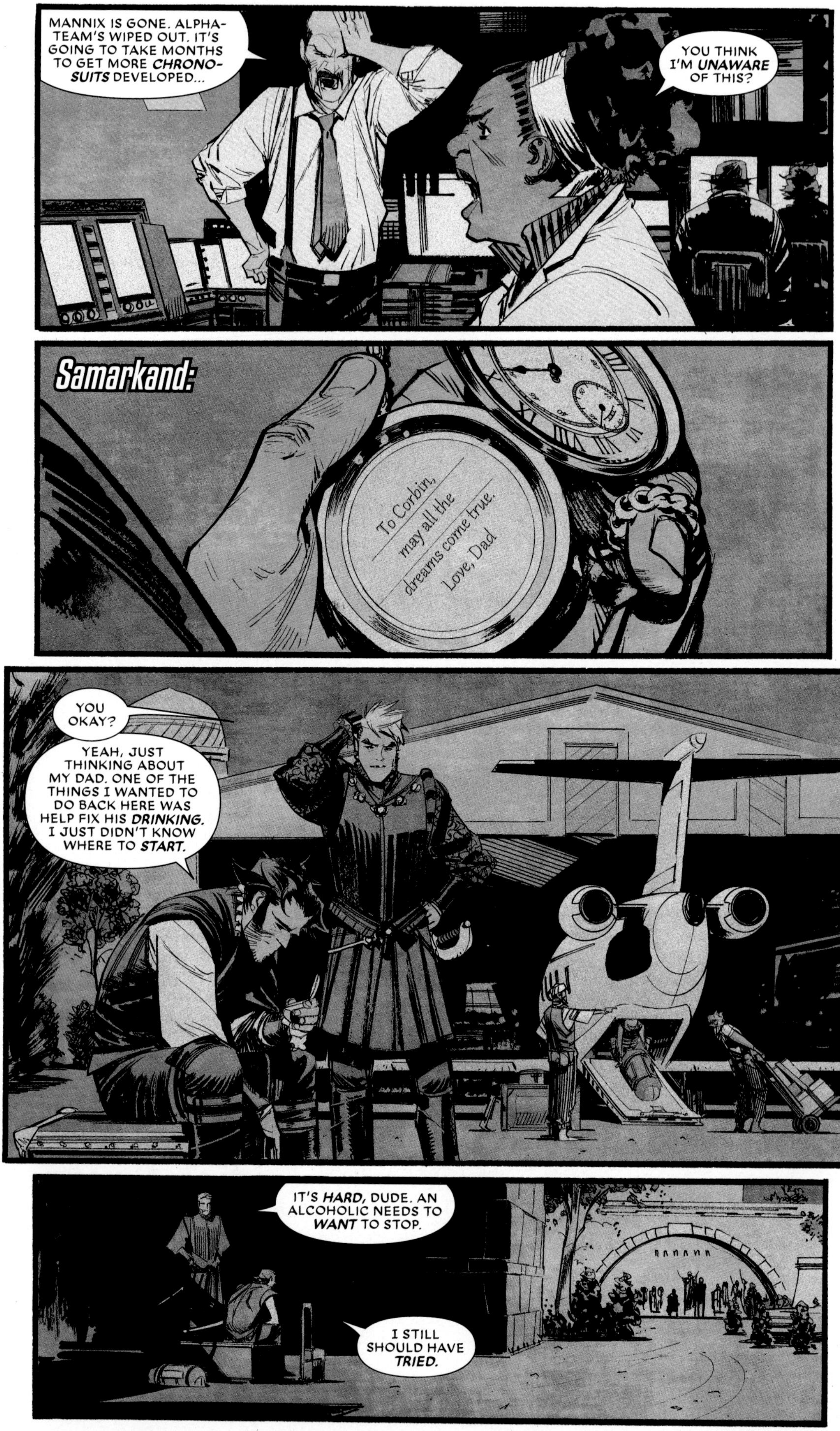
MANNIX IS GONE. ALPHA-TEAM'S WIPED OUT. IT'S GOING TO TAKE MONTHS TO GET MORE CHRONO-SUITS DEVELOPED...
YOU THINK I'M UNAWARE OF THIS?
Samarkand:
To Corbin, may all the dreams come true. Love, Dad
YOU OKAY?
YEAH, JUST THINKING ABOUT MY DAD. ONE OF THE THINGS I WANTED TO DO BACK HERE WAS HELP FIX HIS DRINKING. I JUST DIDN'T KNOW WHERE TO START.
IT'S HARD, DUDE. AN ALCOHOLIC NEEDS TO WANT TO STOP.
I STILL SHOULD HAVE TRIED.

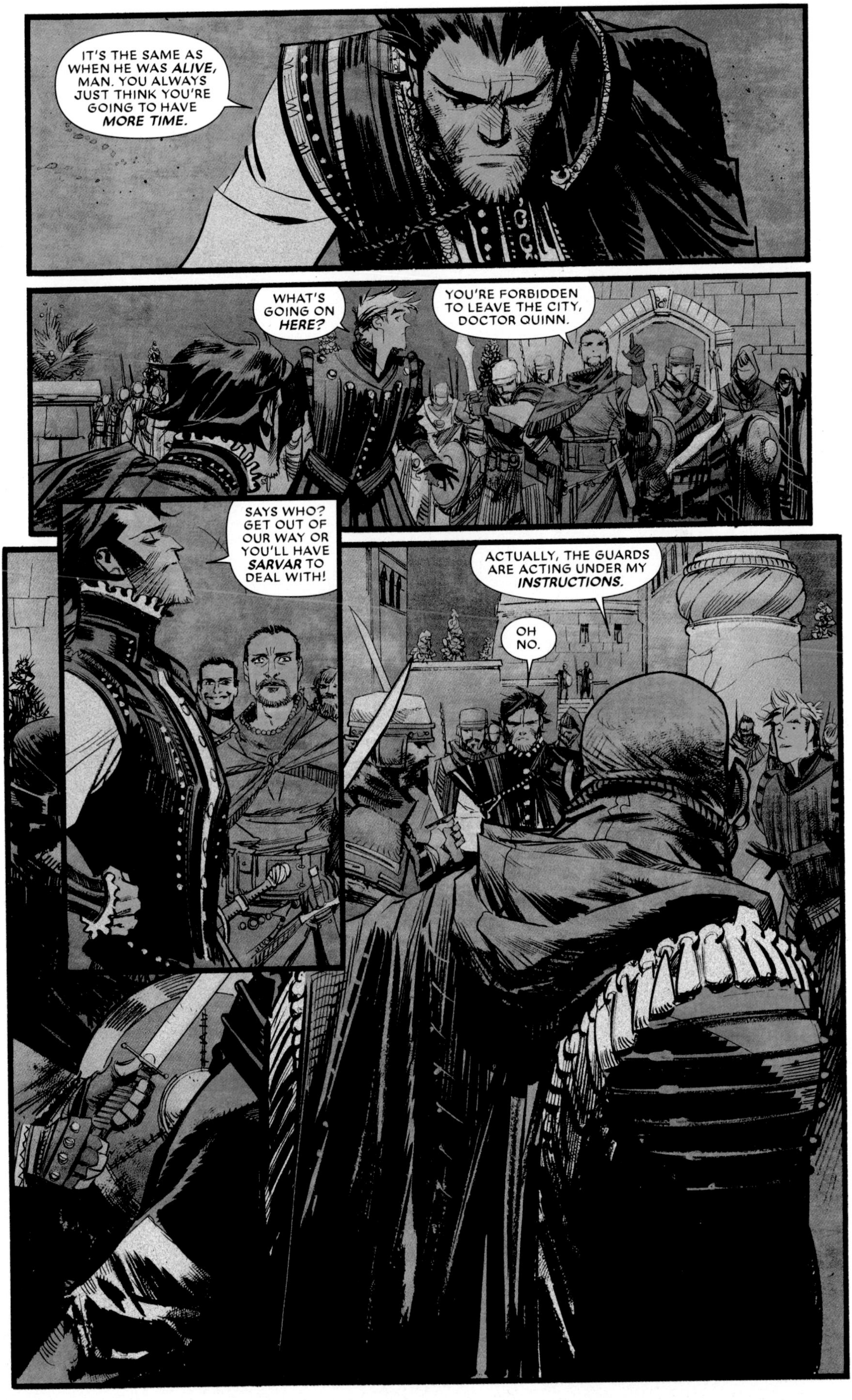
IT'S THE SAME AS WHEN HE WAS *ALIVE,* MAN. YOU ALWAYS JUST THINK YOU'RE GOING TO HAVE *MORE TIME.*
WHAT'S GOING ON *HERE?*
YOU'RE FORBIDDEN TO LEAVE THE CITY, DOCTOR QUINN.
SAYS WHO? GET OUT OF OUR WAY OR YOU'LL HAVE *SARVAR* TO DEAL WITH!
ACTUALLY, THE GUARDS ARE ACTING UNDER MY *INSTRUCTIONS.*
OH NO.

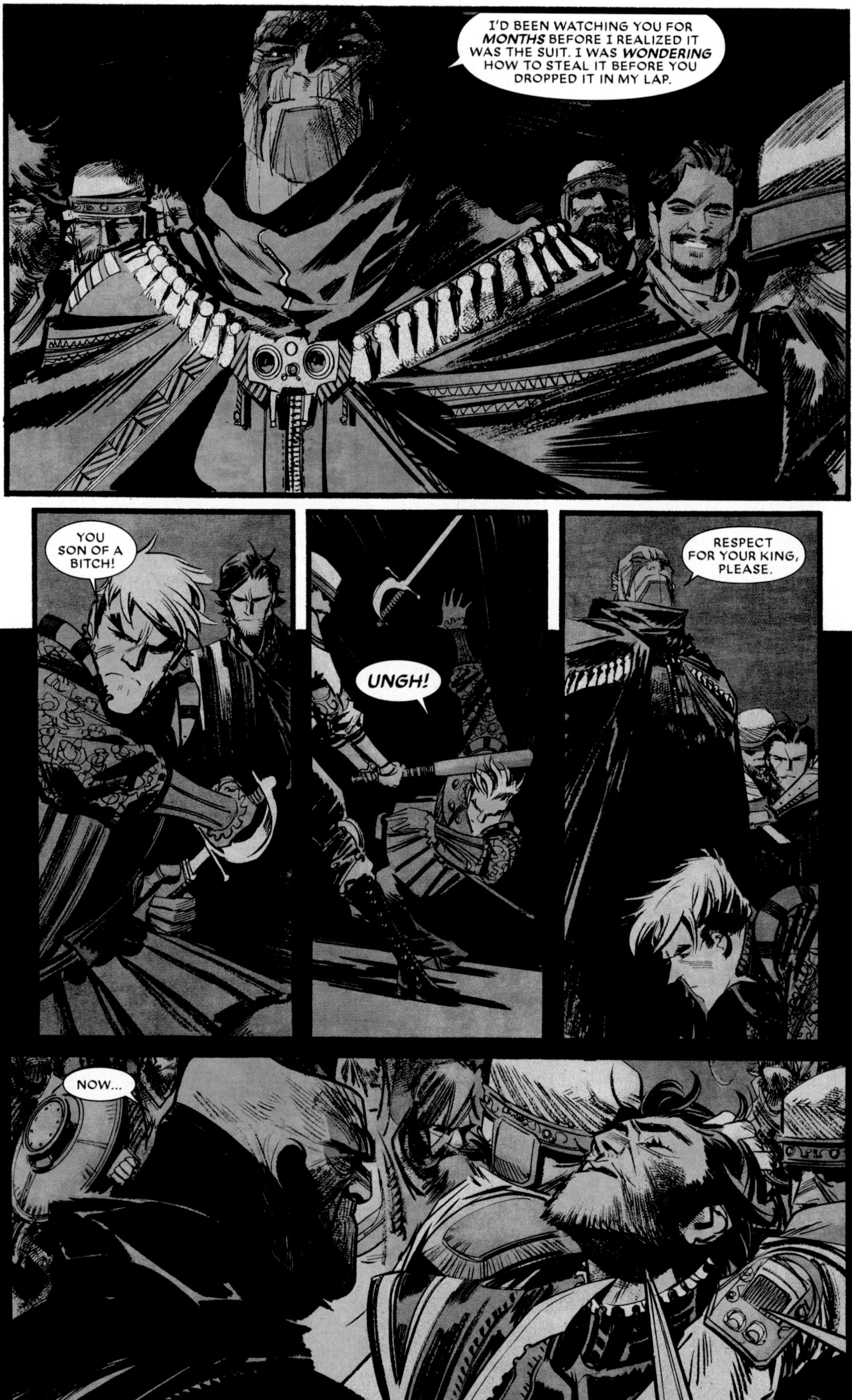
I'D BEEN WATCHING YOU FOR MONTHS BEFORE I REALIZED IT WAS THE SUIT. I WAS WONDERING HOW TO STEAL IT BEFORE YOU DROPPED IT IN MY LAP.
YOU SON OF A BITCH!
UNGH!
RESPECT FOR YOUR KING, PLEASE.
NOW...

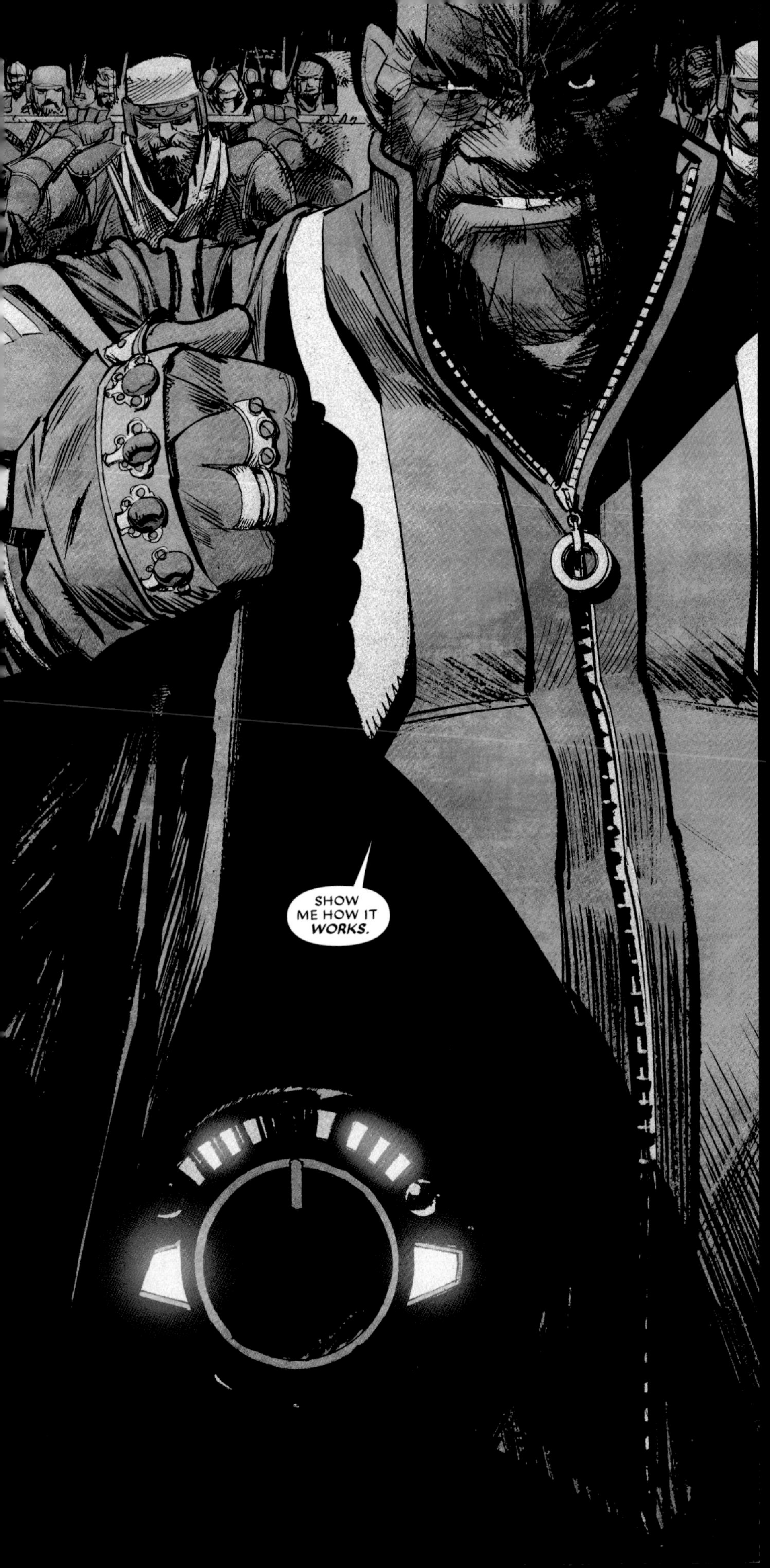
SHOW ME HOW IT *WORKS.*

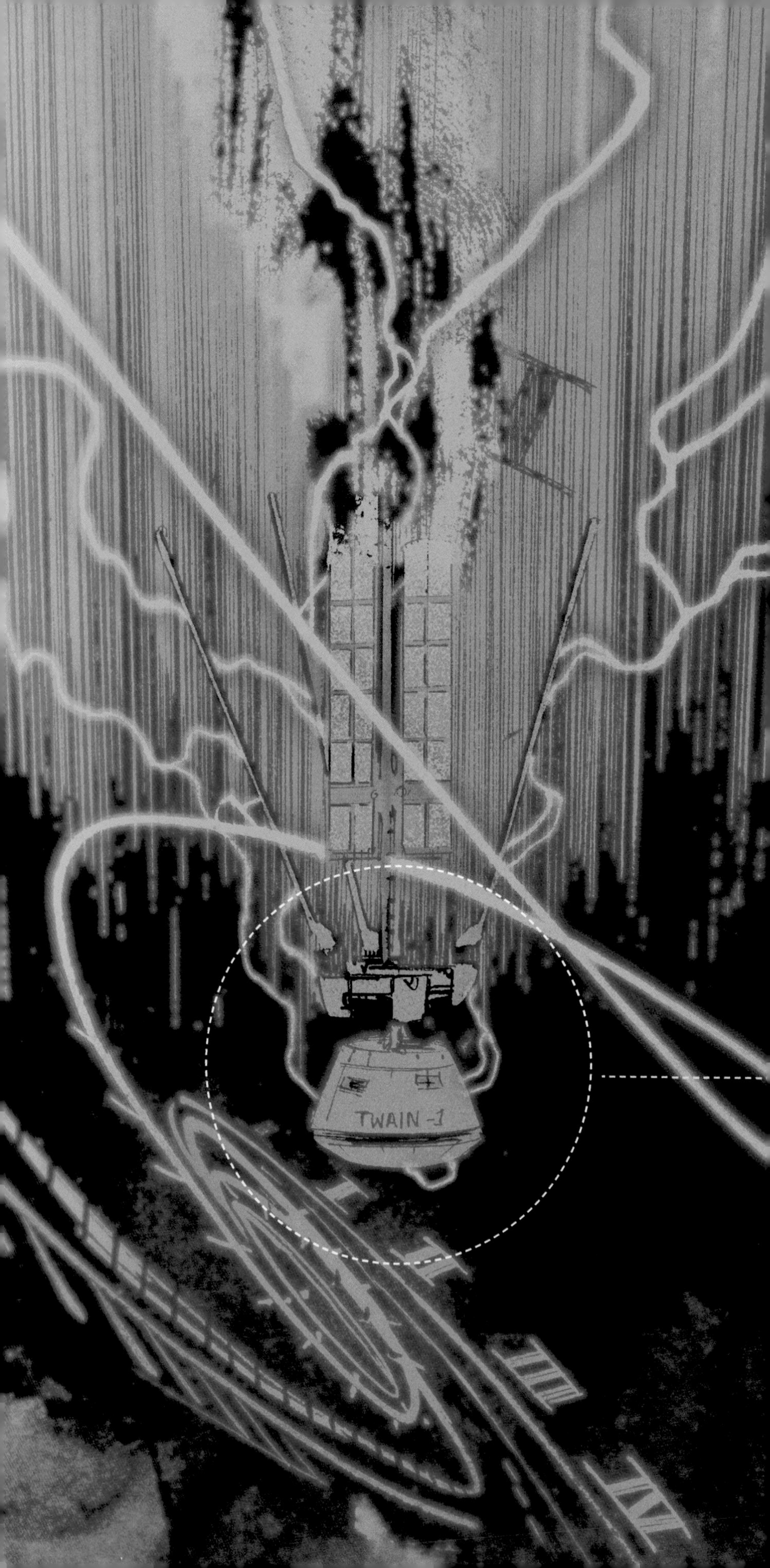
TWAIN-1

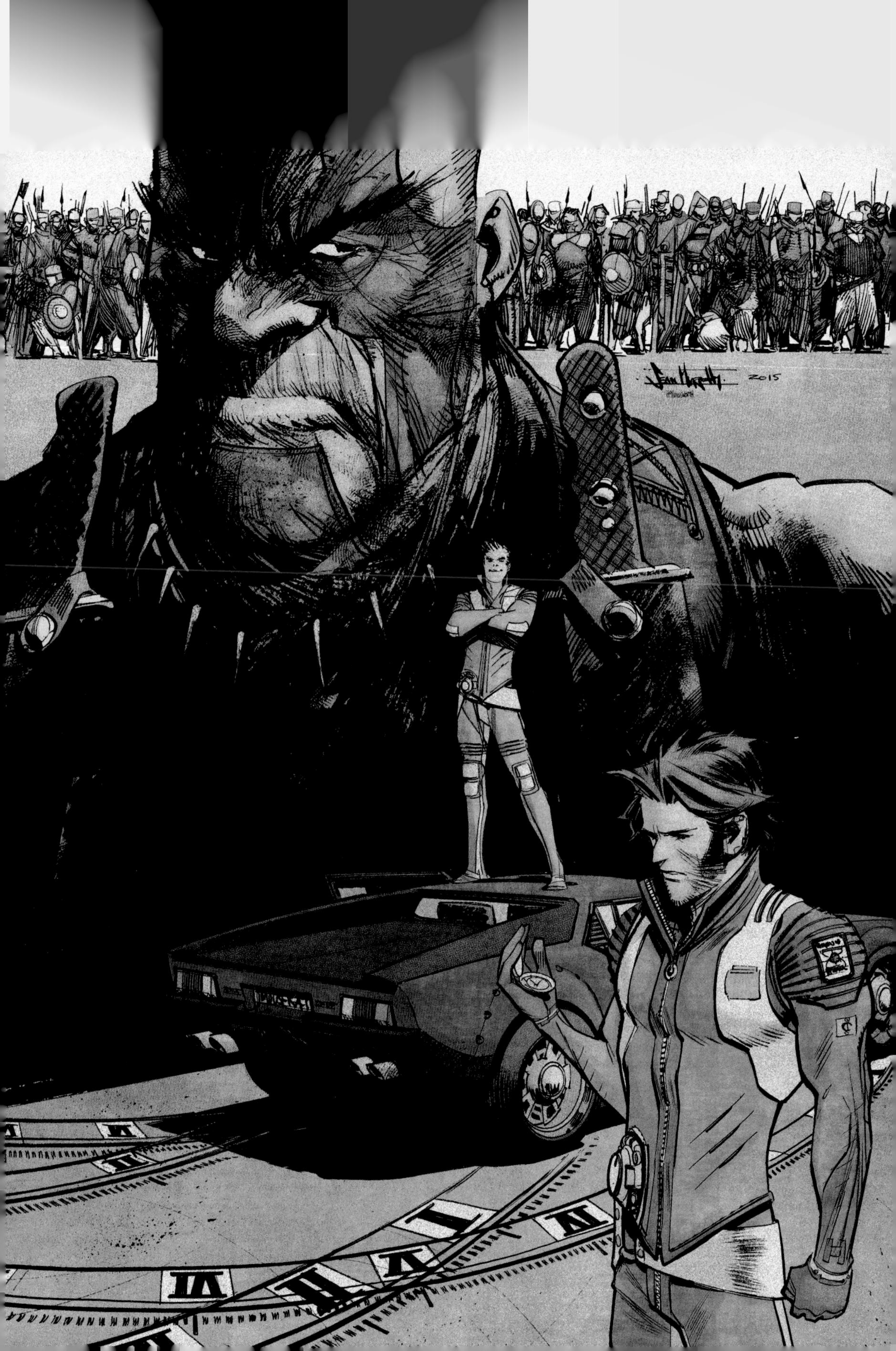

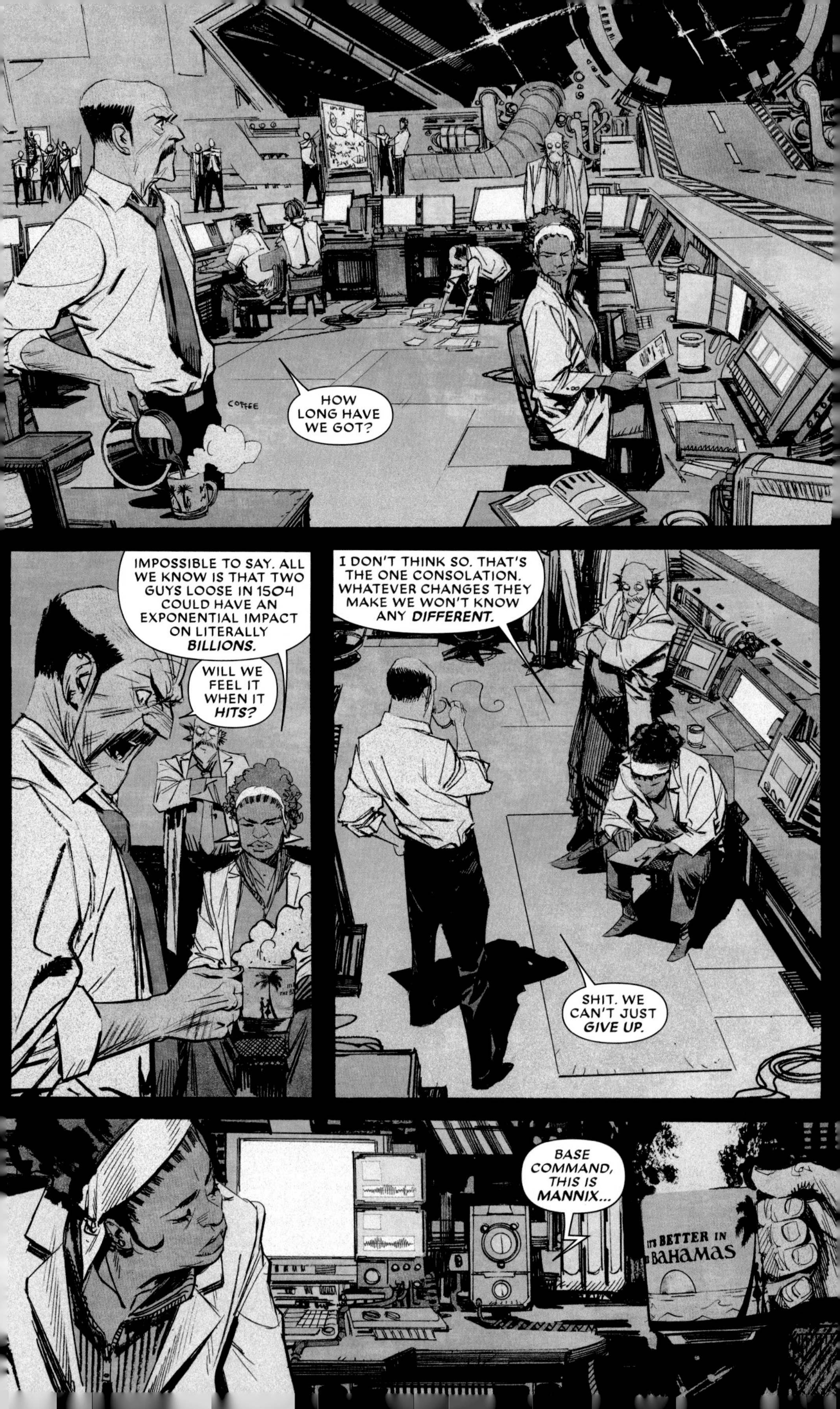
COFFEE
HOW LONG HAVE WE GOT?
IMPOSSIBLE TO SAY. ALL WE KNOW IS THAT TWO GUYS LOOSE IN 1504 COULD HAVE AN EXPONENTIAL IMPACT ON LITERALLY *BILLIONS.*
WILL WE FEEL IT WHEN IT *HITS?*
I DON'T THINK SO. THAT'S THE ONE CONSOLATION. WHATEVER CHANGES THEY MAKE WE WON'T KNOW ANY *DIFFERENT.*
SHIT. WE CAN'T JUST *GIVE UP.*
BASE COMMAND, THIS IS *MANNIX...*
IT'S BETTER IN
BAHAMAS

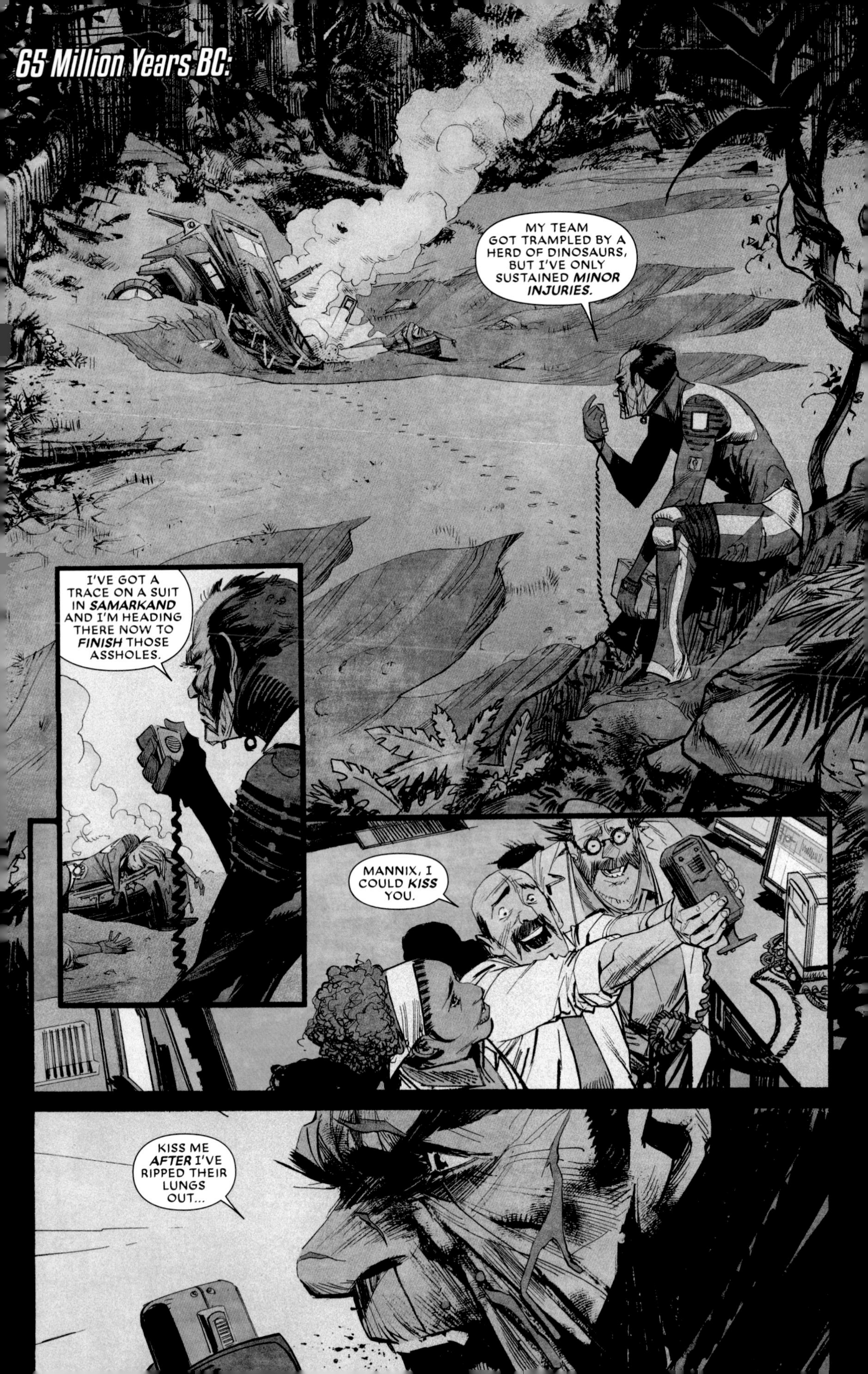
65 Million Years BC:
MY TEAM GOT TRAMPLED BY A HERD OF DINOSAURS, BUT I'VE ONLY SUSTAINED MINOR INJURIES.
I'VE GOT A TRACE ON A SUIT IN SAMARKAND AND I'M HEADING THERE NOW TO FINISH THOSE ASSHOLES.
MANNIX, I COULD KISS YOU.
KISS ME AFTER I'VE RIPPED THEIR LUNGS OUT...

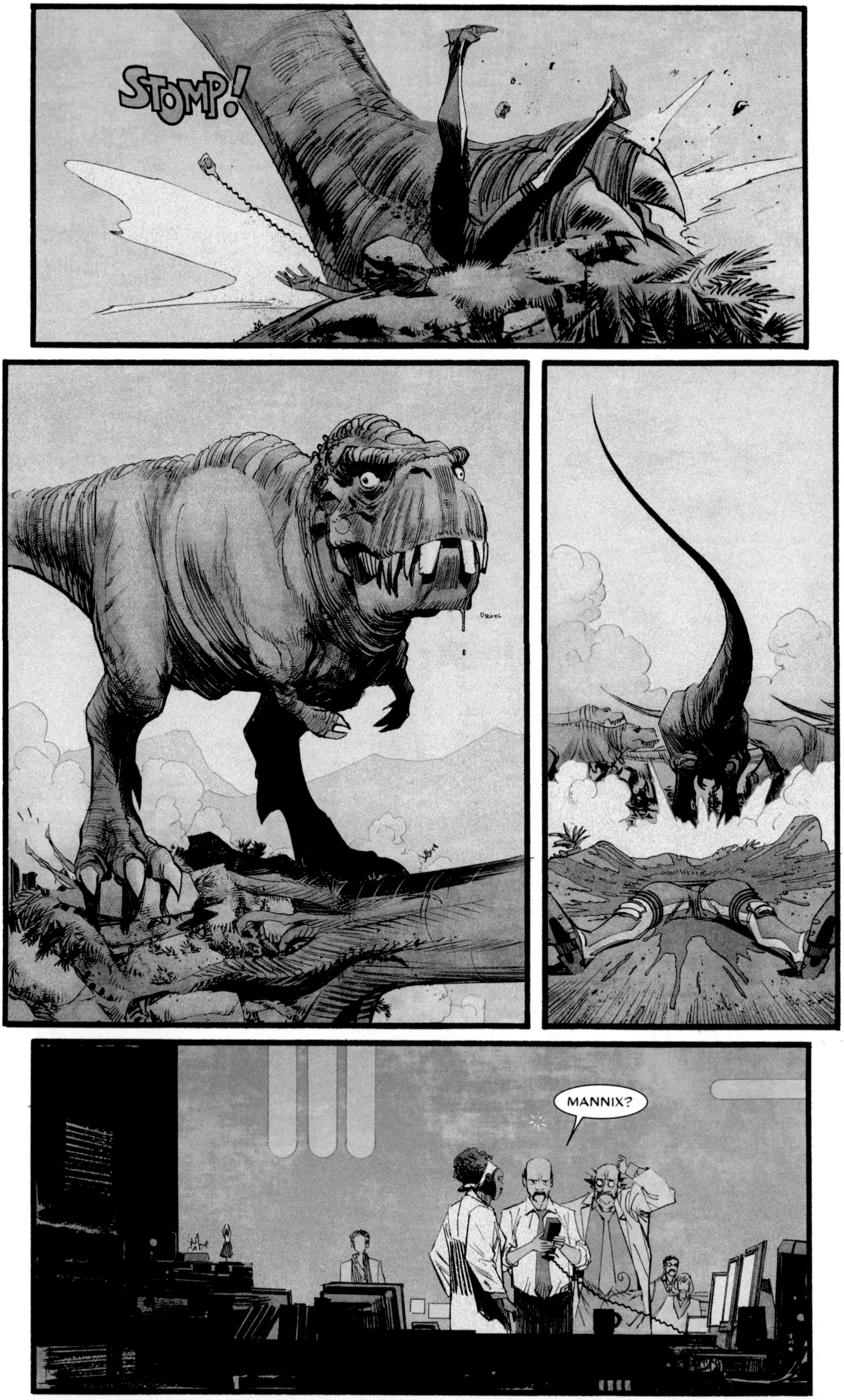
STOMP!
DROOL
MANNIX?

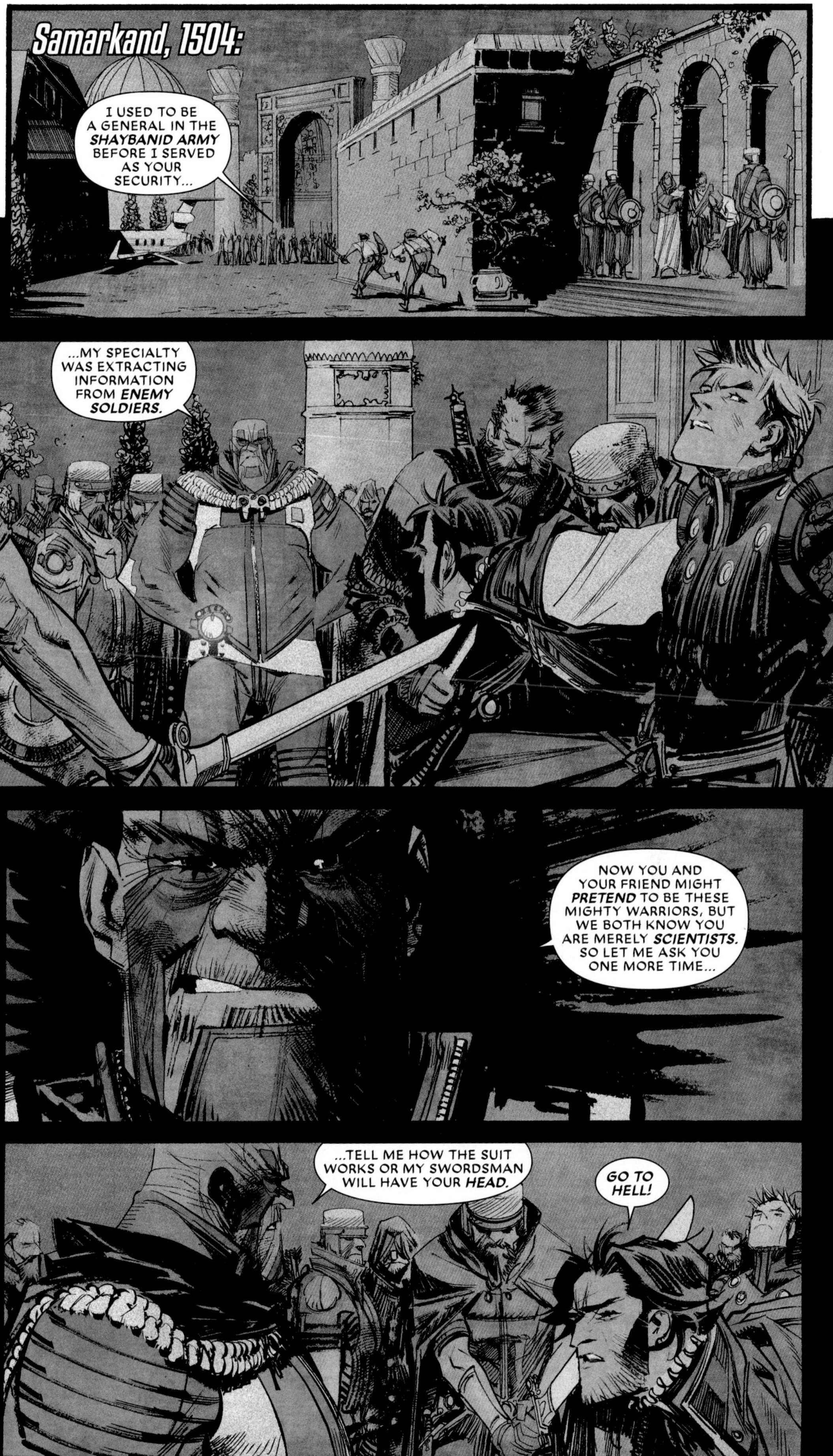
Samarkand, 1504:
I USED TO BE A GENERAL IN THE SHAYBANID ARMY BEFORE I SERVED AS YOUR SECURITY...
...MY SPECIALTY WAS EXTRACTING INFORMATION FROM ENEMY SOLDIERS.
NOW YOU AND YOUR FRIEND MIGHT PRETEND TO BE THESE MIGHTY WARRIORS, BUT WE BOTH KNOW YOU ARE MERELY SCIENTISTS. SO LET ME ASK YOU ONE MORE TIME...
...TELL ME HOW THE SUIT WORKS OR MY SWORDSMAN WILL HAVE YOUR HEAD.
GO TO HELL!

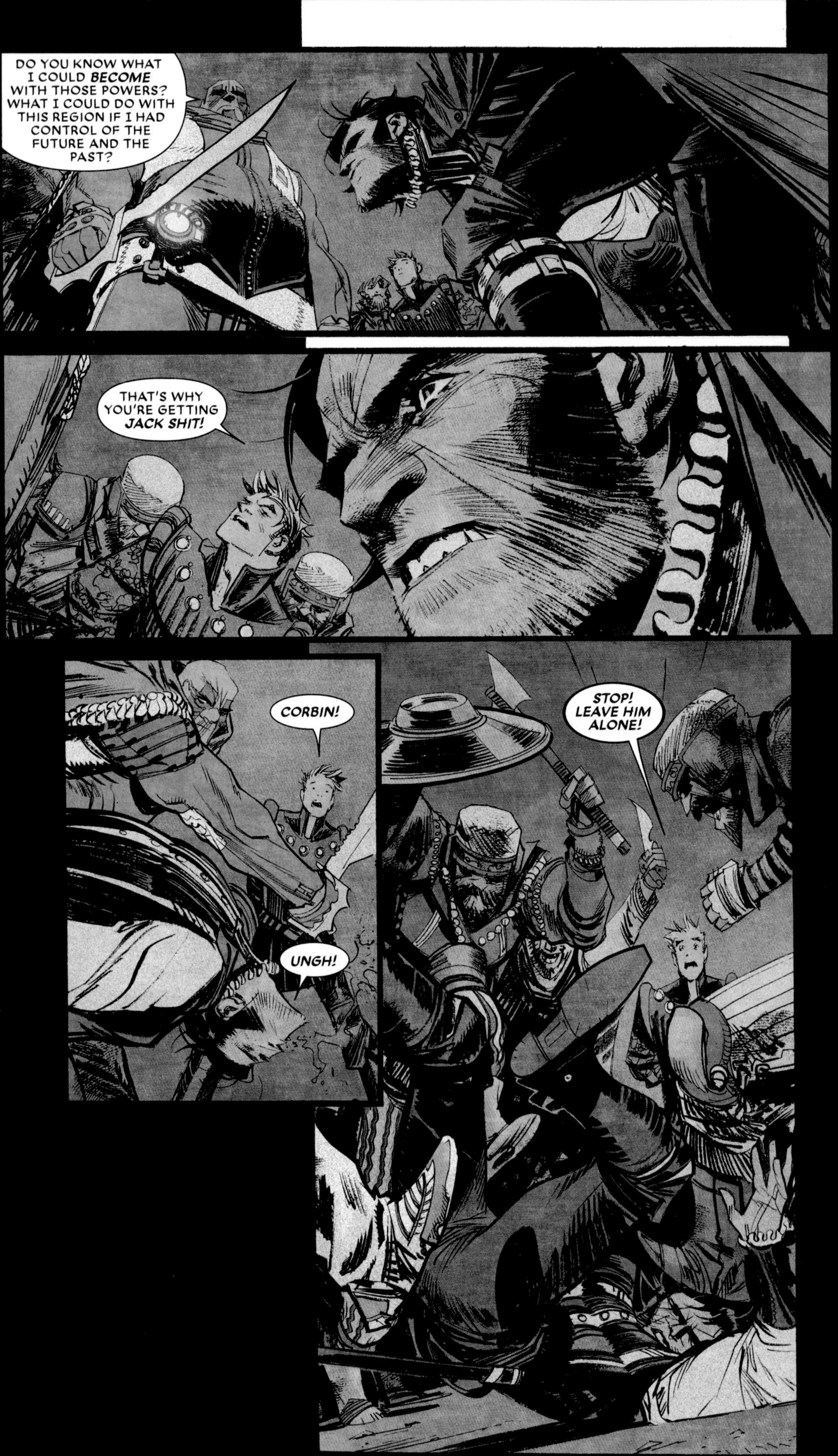
DO YOU KNOW WHAT I COULD BECOME WITH THOSE POWERS? WHAT I COULD DO WITH THIS REGION IF I HAD CONTROL OF THE FUTURE AND THE PAST?
THAT'S WHY YOU'RE GETTING JACK SHIT!
CORBIN!
UNGH!
STOP! LEAVE HIM ALONE!

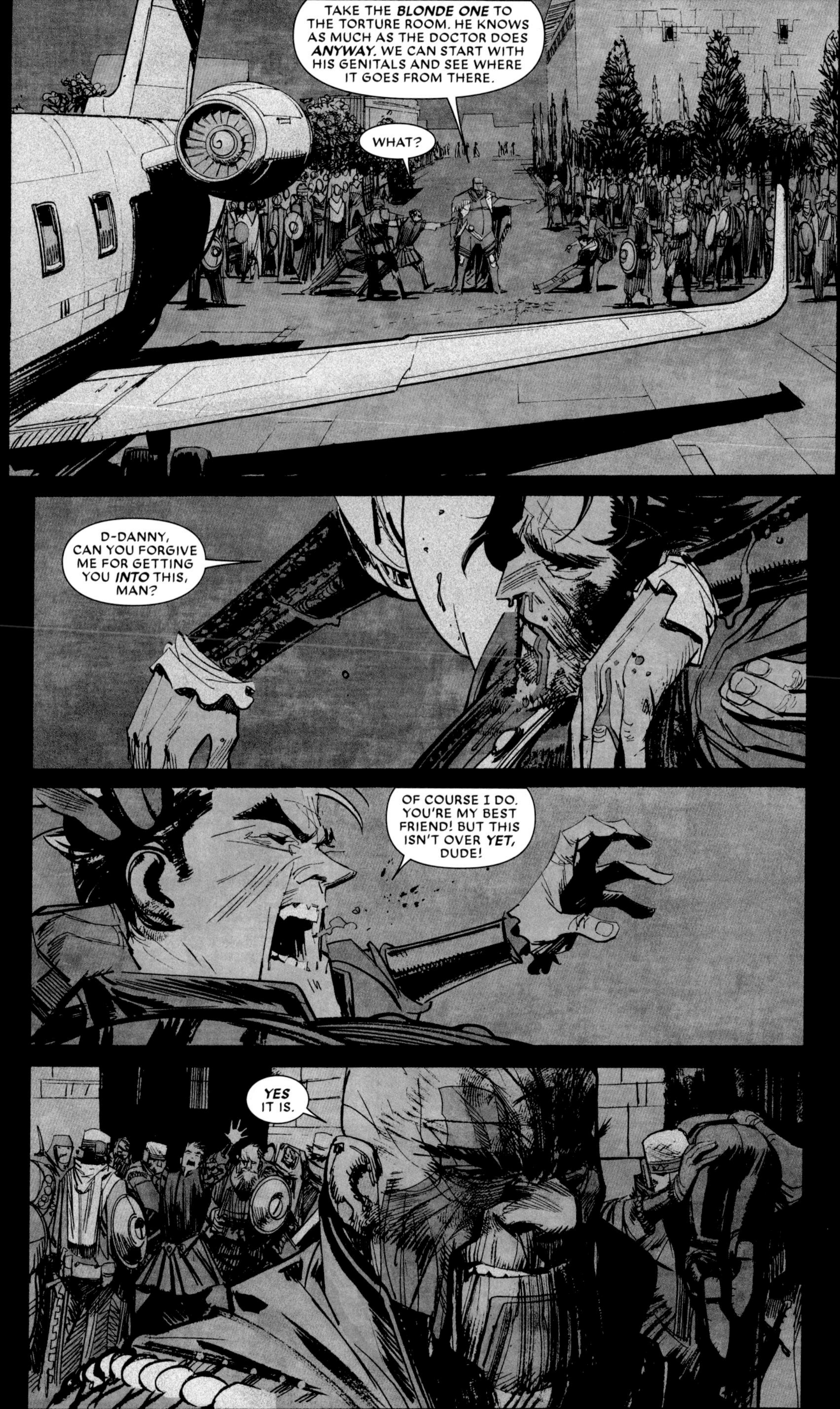
TAKE THE BLONDE ONE TO THE TORTURE ROOM. HE KNOWS AS MUCH AS THE DOCTOR DOES ANYWAY. WE CAN START WITH HIS GENITALS AND SEE WHERE IT GOES FROM THERE.
WHAT?
D-DANNY, CAN YOU FORGIVE ME FOR GETTING YOU INTO THIS, MAN?
OF COURSE I DO. YOU'RE MY BEST FRIEND! BUT THIS ISN'T OVER YET, DUDE!
YES IT IS.

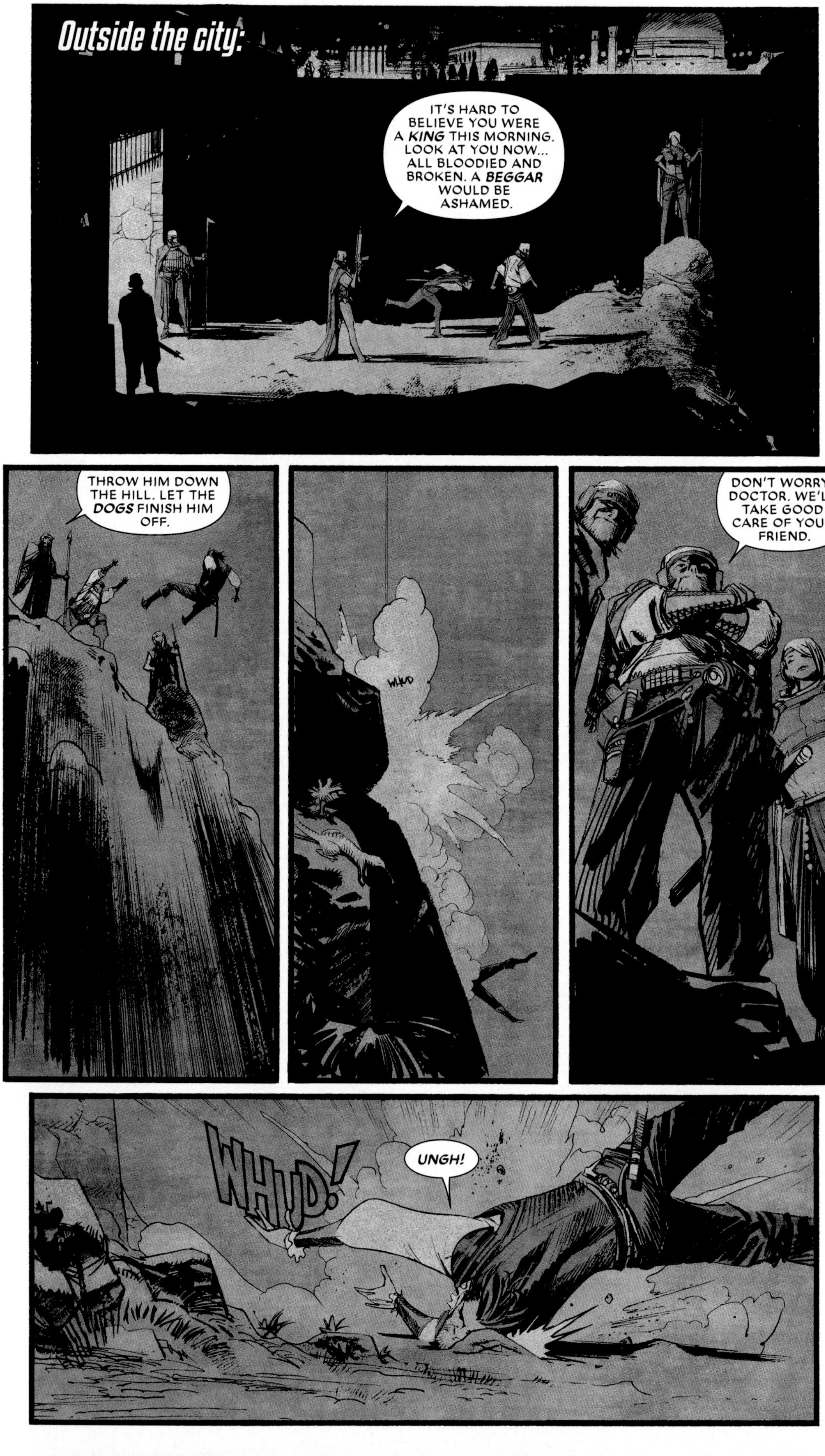
Outside the city:
IT'S HARD TO BELIEVE YOU WERE A KING THIS MORNING. LOOK AT YOU NOW... ALL BLOODIED AND BROKEN. A BEGGAR WOULD BE ASHAMED.
THROW HIM DOWN THE HILL. LET THE DOGS FINISH HIM OFF.
WHUD
DON'T WORRY, DOCTOR. WE'LL TAKE GOOD CARE OF YOUR FRIEND.
WHUD!
UNGH!

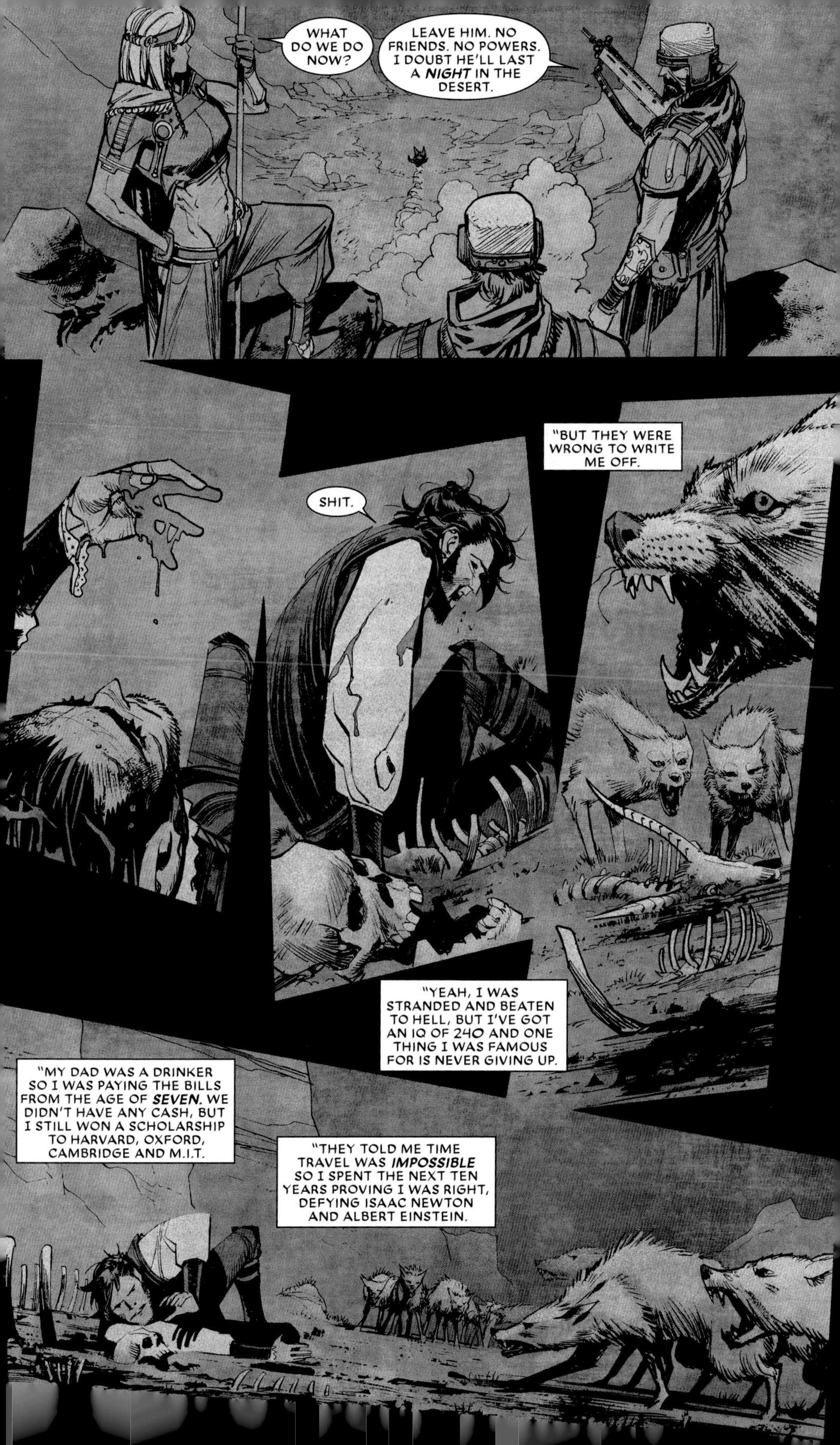
WHAT DO WE DO NOW?
LEAVE HIM. NO FRIENDS. NO POWERS. I DOUBT HE'LL LAST A *NIGHT* IN THE DESERT.
SHIT.
"BUT THEY WERE WRONG TO WRITE ME OFF.
"YEAH, I WAS STRANDED AND BEATEN TO HELL, BUT I'VE GOT AN IQ OF 240 AND ONE THING I WAS FAMOUS FOR IS NEVER GIVING UP.
"MY DAD WAS A DRINKER SO I WAS PAYING THE BILLS FROM THE AGE OF *SEVEN.* WE DIDN'T HAVE ANY CASH, BUT I STILL WON A SCHOLARSHIP TO HARVARD, OXFORD, CAMBRIDGE AND M.I.T.
"THEY TOLD ME TIME TRAVEL WAS *IMPOSSIBLE* SO I SPENT THE NEXT TEN YEARS PROVING I WAS RIGHT, DEFYING ISAAC NEWTON AND ALBERT EINSTEIN.

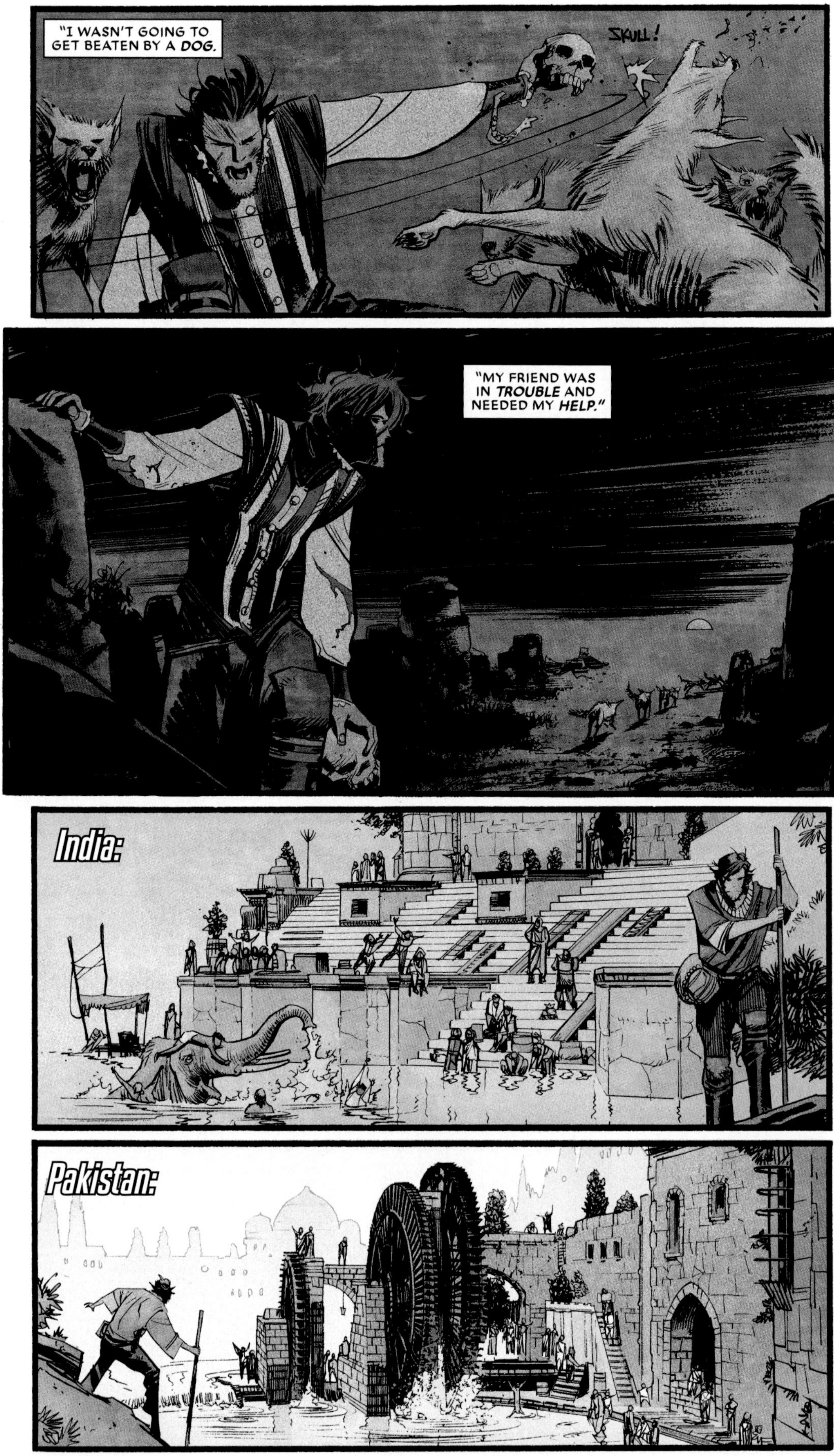
"I WASN'T GOING TO GET BEATEN BY A DOG.
SKULL!
"MY FRIEND WAS IN TROUBLE AND NEEDED MY HELP."
India:
Pakistan:

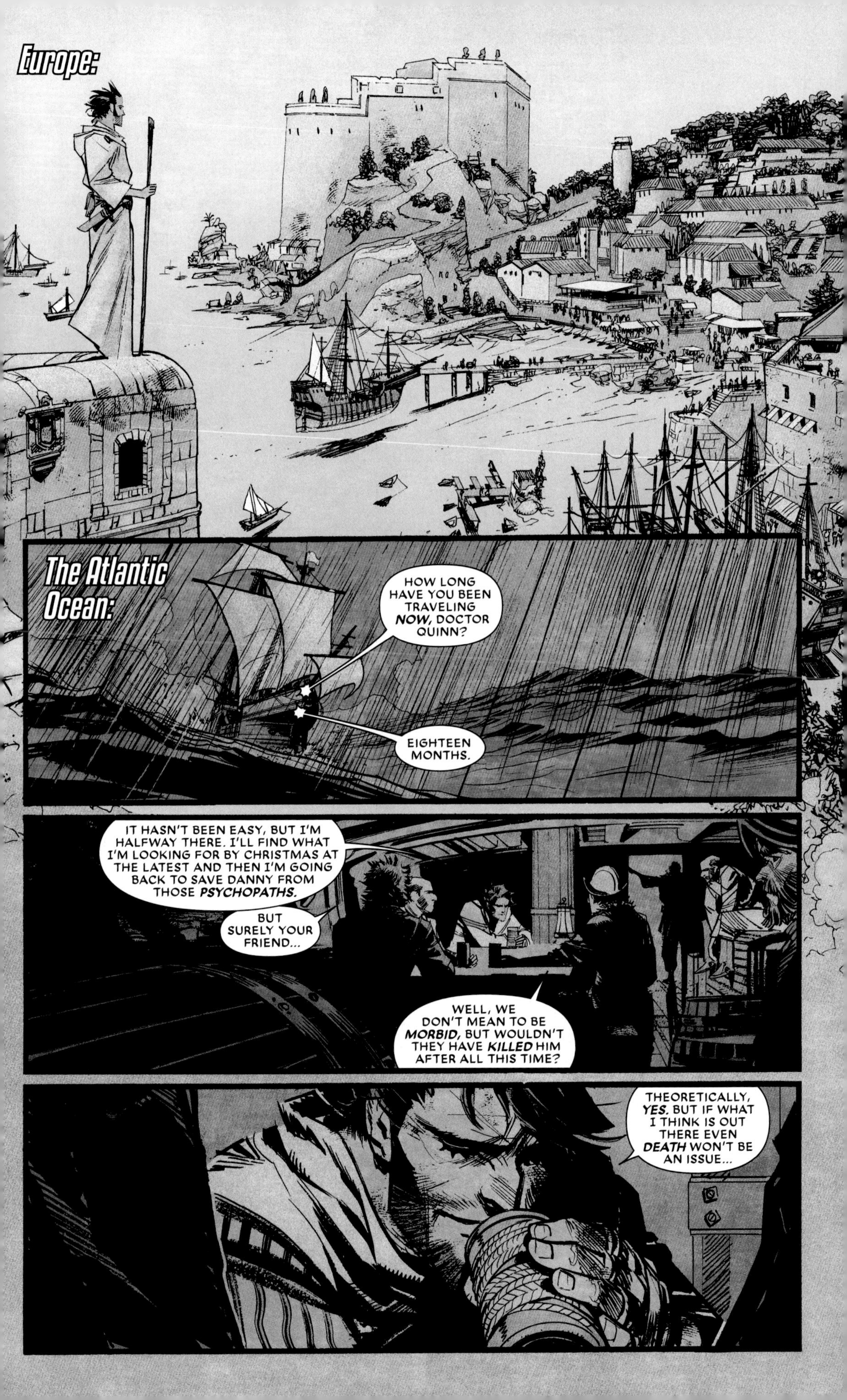
Europe:
The Atlantic Ocean:
HOW LONG HAVE YOU BEEN TRAVELING NOW, DOCTOR QUINN?
EIGHTEEN MONTHS.
IT HASN'T BEEN EASY, BUT I'M HALFWAY THERE. I'LL FIND WHAT I'M LOOKING FOR BY CHRISTMAS AT THE LATEST AND THEN I'M GOING BACK TO SAVE DANNY FROM THOSE PSYCHOPATHS.
BUT SURELY YOUR FRIEND...
WELL, WE DON'T MEAN TO BE MORBID, BUT WOULDN'T THEY HAVE KILLED HIM AFTER ALL THIS TIME?
THEORETICALLY, YES. BUT IF WHAT I THINK IS OUT THERE EVEN DEATH WON'T BE AN ISSUE...

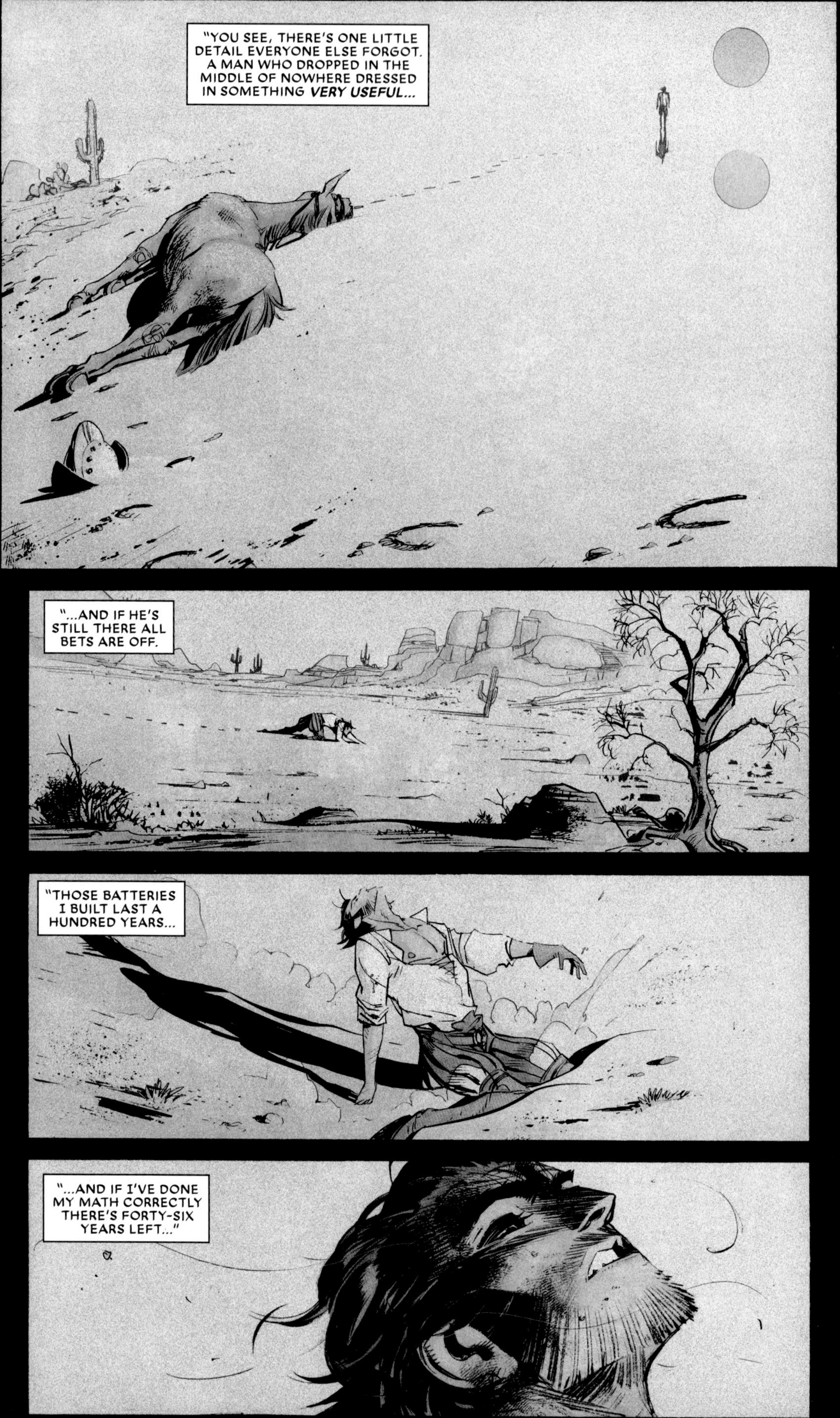
"YOU SEE, THERE'S ONE LITTLE DETAIL EVERYONE ELSE FORGOT. A MAN WHO DROPPED IN THE MIDDLE OF NOWHERE DRESSED IN SOMETHING *VERY USEFUL*...
"...AND IF HE'S STILL THERE ALL BETS ARE OFF.
"THOSE BATTERIES I BUILT LAST A HUNDRED YEARS...
"...AND IF I'VE DONE MY MATH CORRECTLY THERE'S FORTY-SIX YEARS LEFT..."

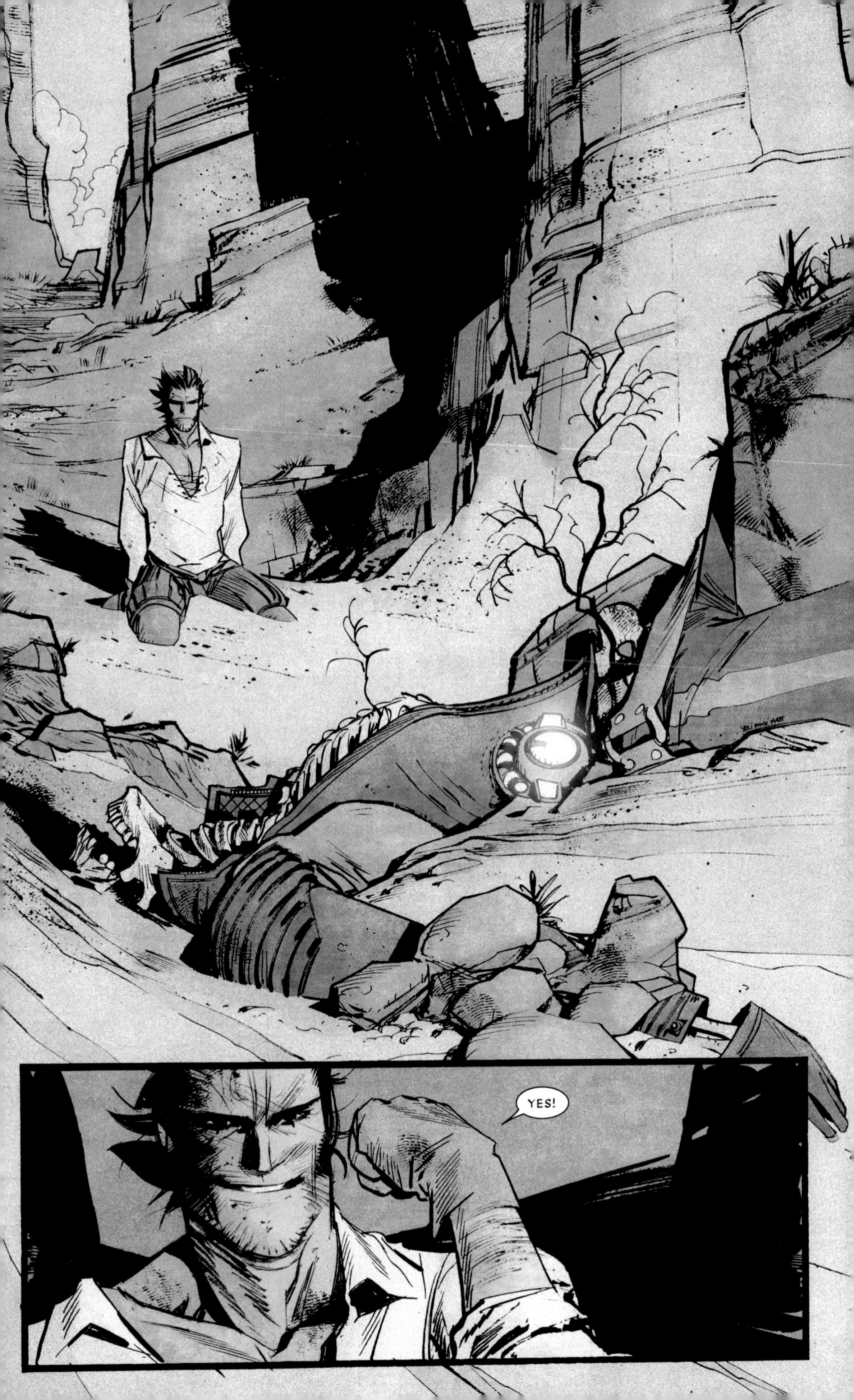
YOU ROCK MATT
YES!

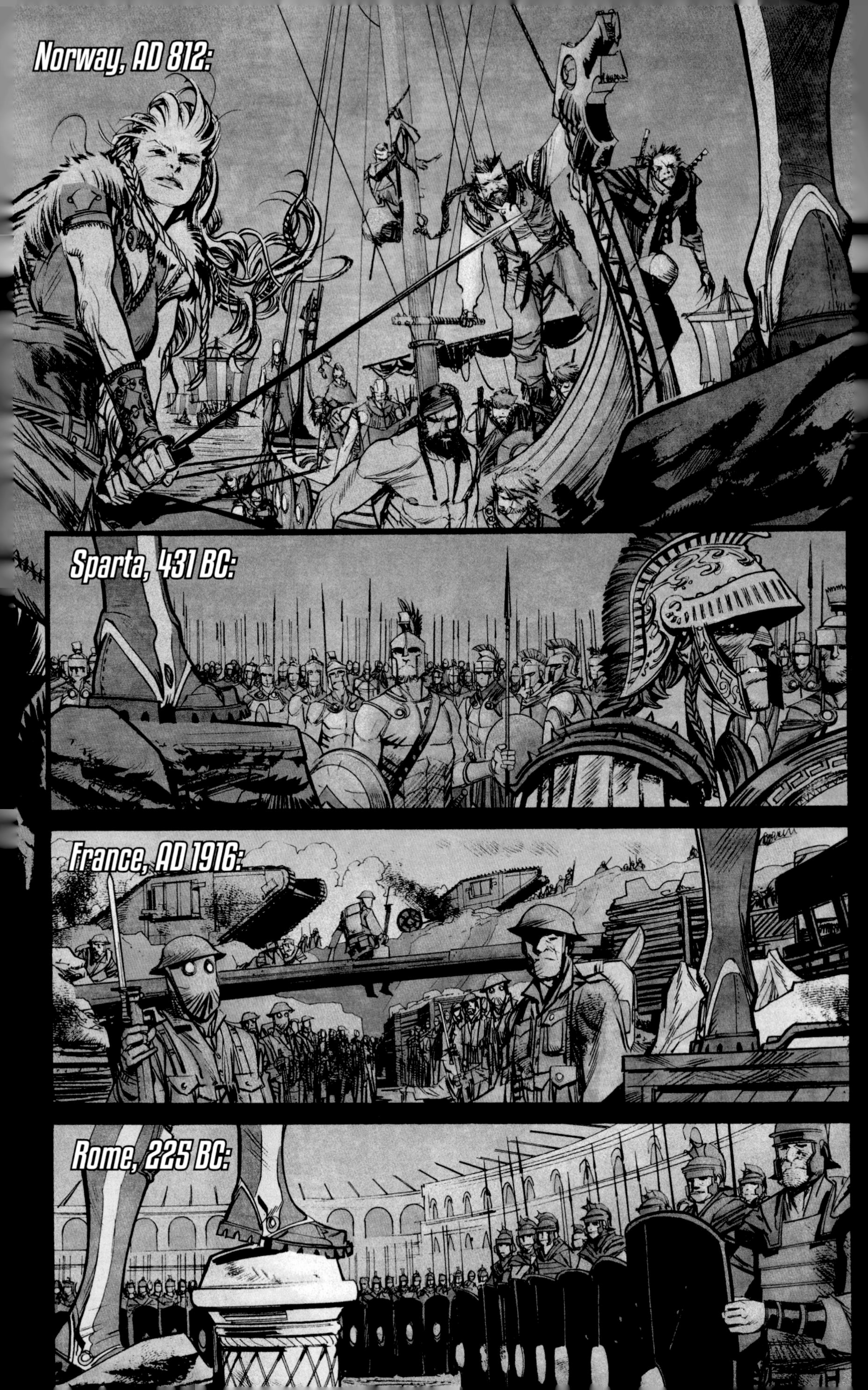
Norway, AD 812:
Sparta, 431 BC:
France, AD 1916:
Rome, 225 BC:

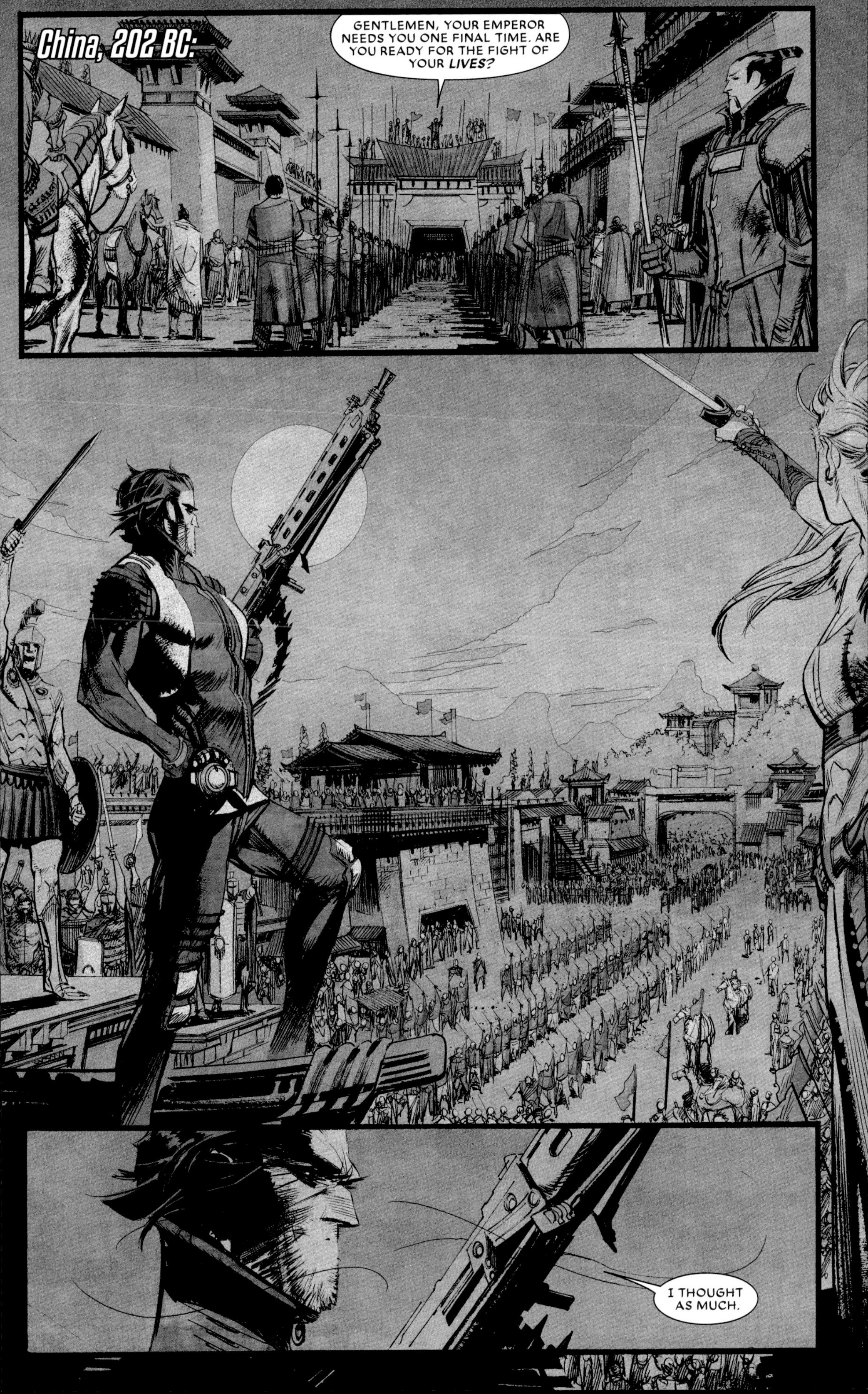
China, 202 BC:
GENTLEMEN, YOUR EMPEROR NEEDS YOU ONE FINAL TIME. ARE YOU READY FOR THE FIGHT OF YOUR *LIVES?*
I THOUGHT AS MUCH.

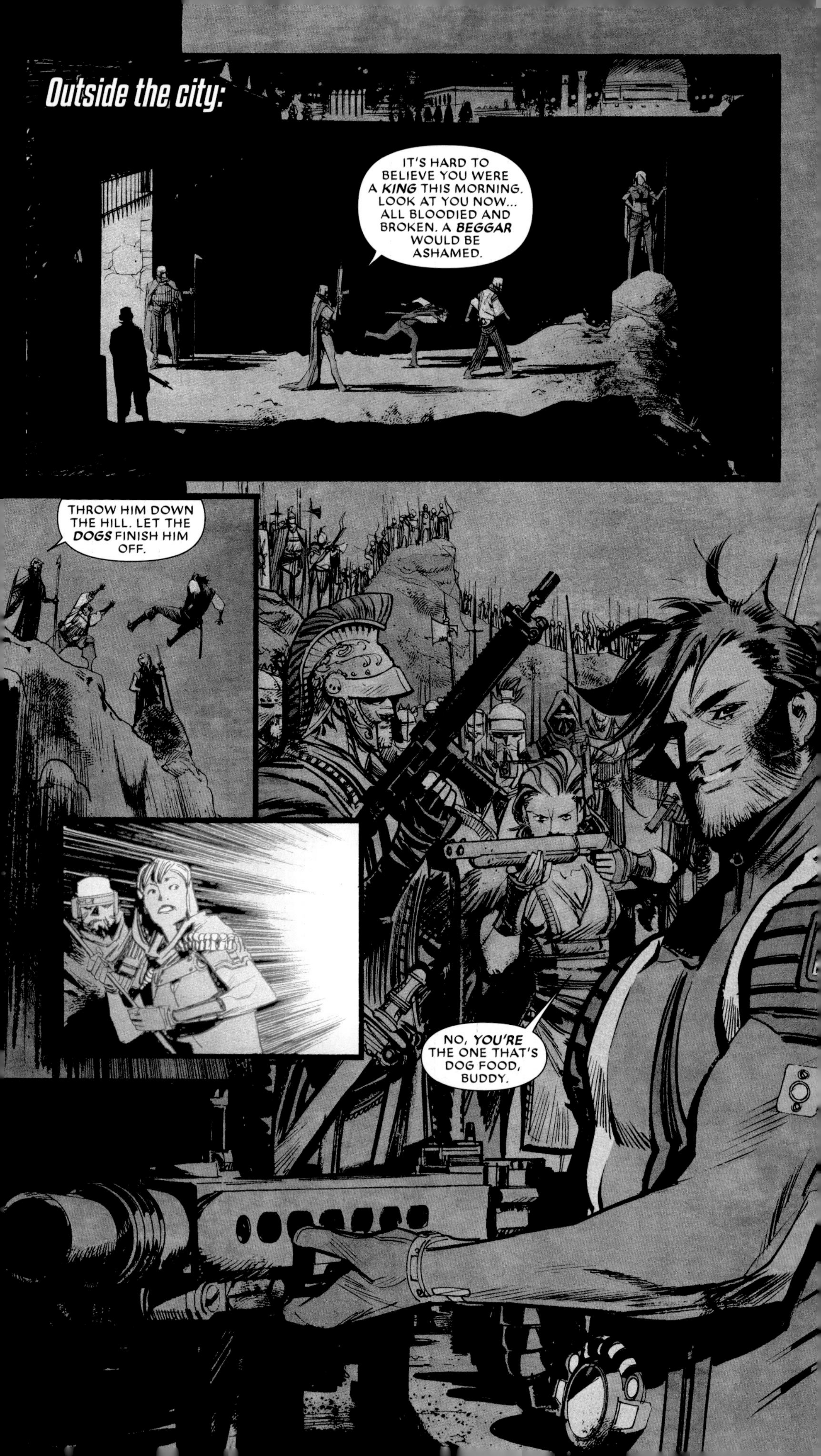
Outside the city:
IT'S HARD TO BELIEVE YOU WERE A KING THIS MORNING. LOOK AT YOU NOW... ALL BLOODIED AND BROKEN. A BEGGAR WOULD BE ASHAMED.
THROW HIM DOWN THE HILL. LET THE DOGS FINISH HIM OFF.
NO, YOU'RE THE ONE THAT'S DOG FOOD, BUDDY.

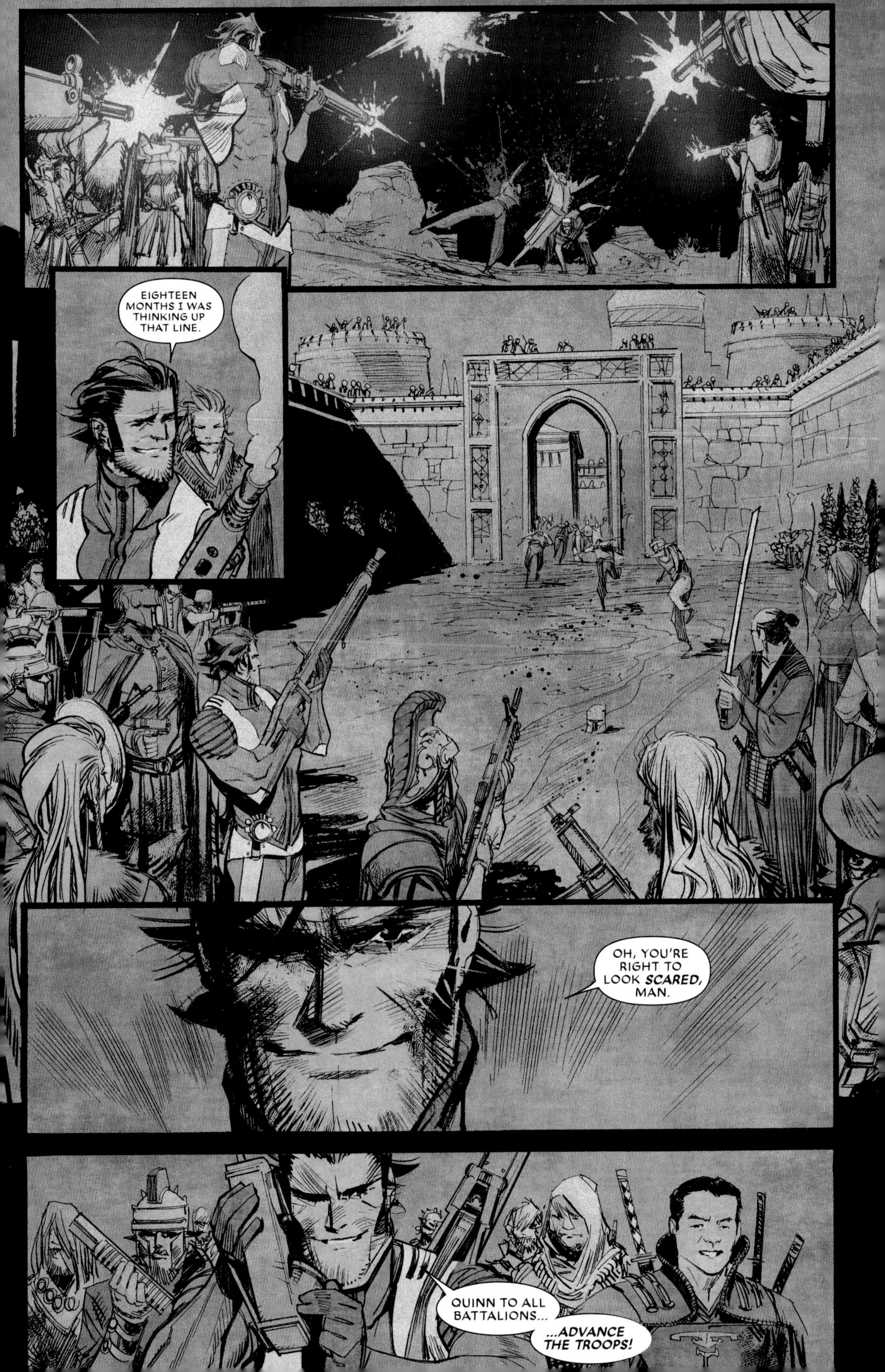
EIGHTEEN MONTHS I WAS THINKING UP THAT LINE.
OH, YOU'RE RIGHT TO LOOK SCARED, MAN.
QUINN TO ALL BATTALIONS...
...ADVANCE THE TROOPS!

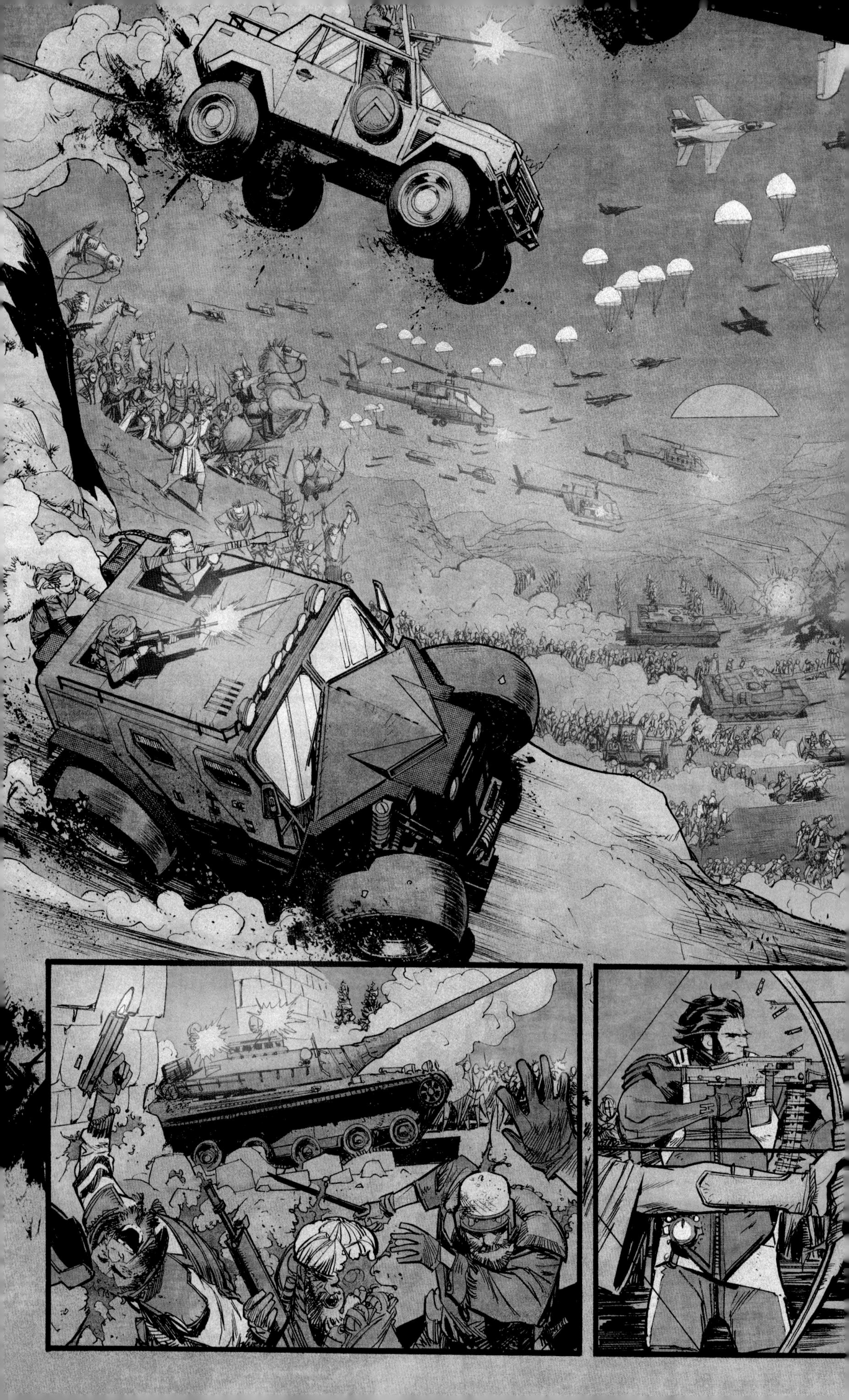

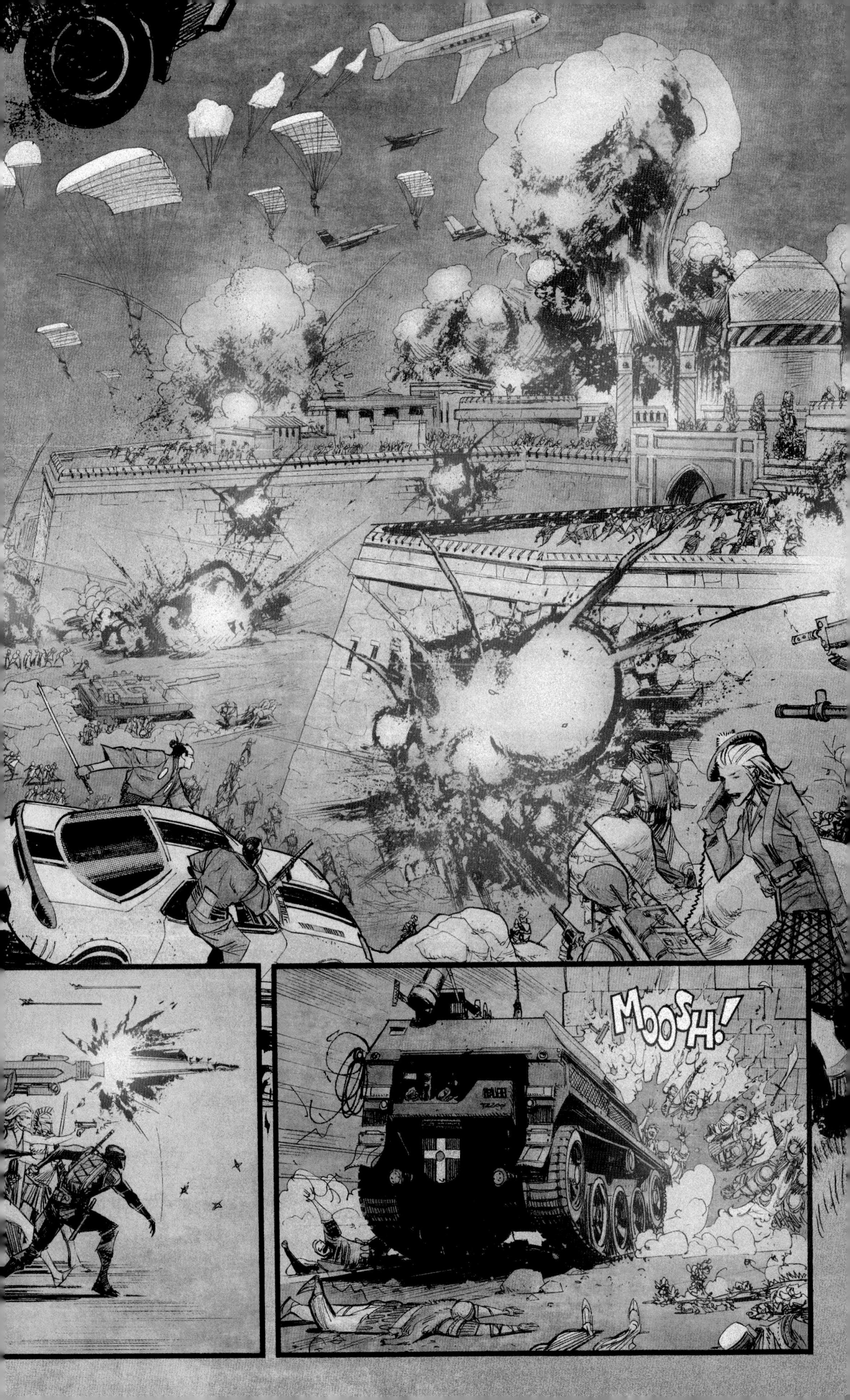
MOOSH!

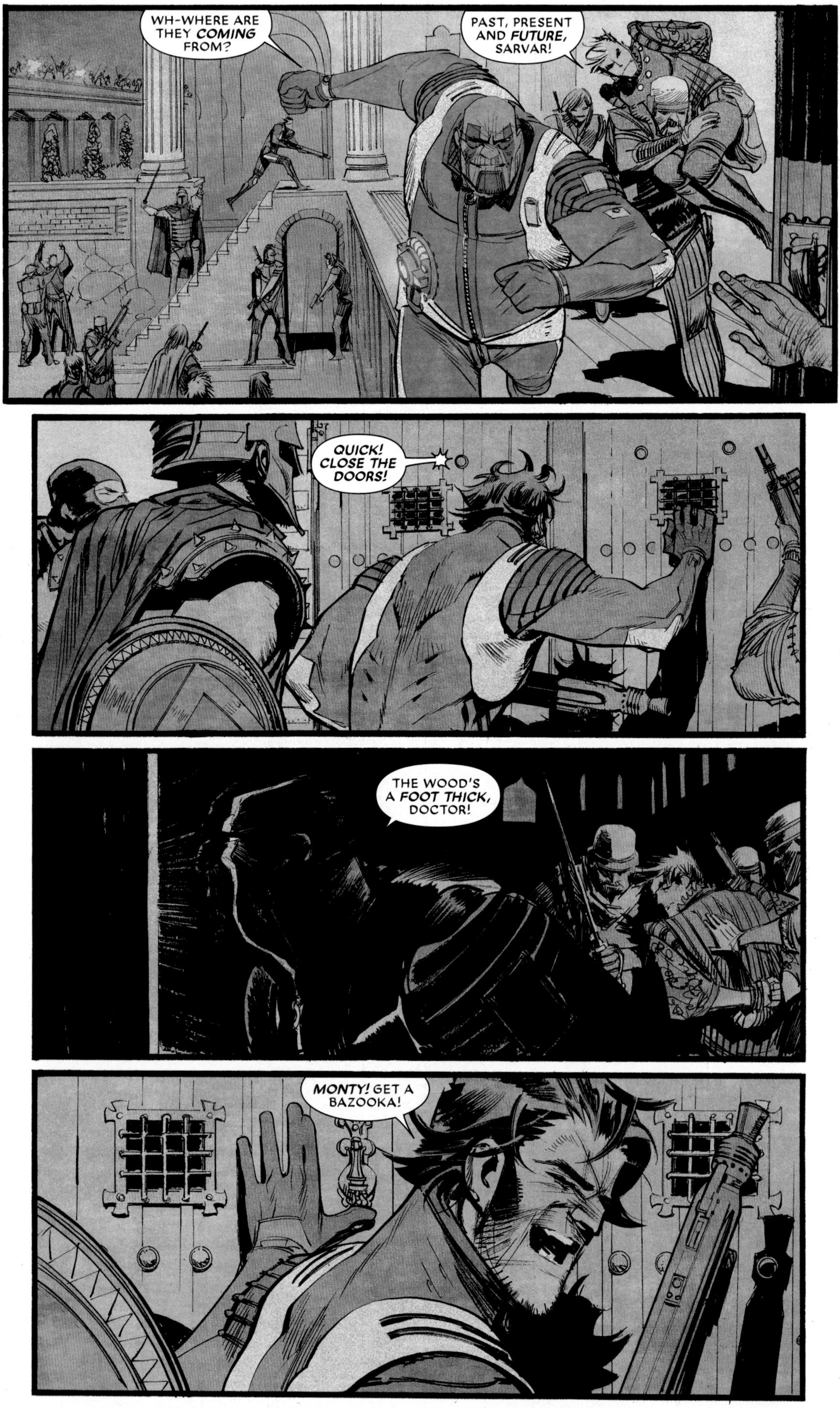
WH-WHERE ARE THEY COMING FROM?
PAST, PRESENT AND FUTURE, SARVAR!
QUICK! CLOSE THE DOORS!
THE WOOD'S A FOOT THICK, DOCTOR!
MONTY! GET A BAZOOKA!

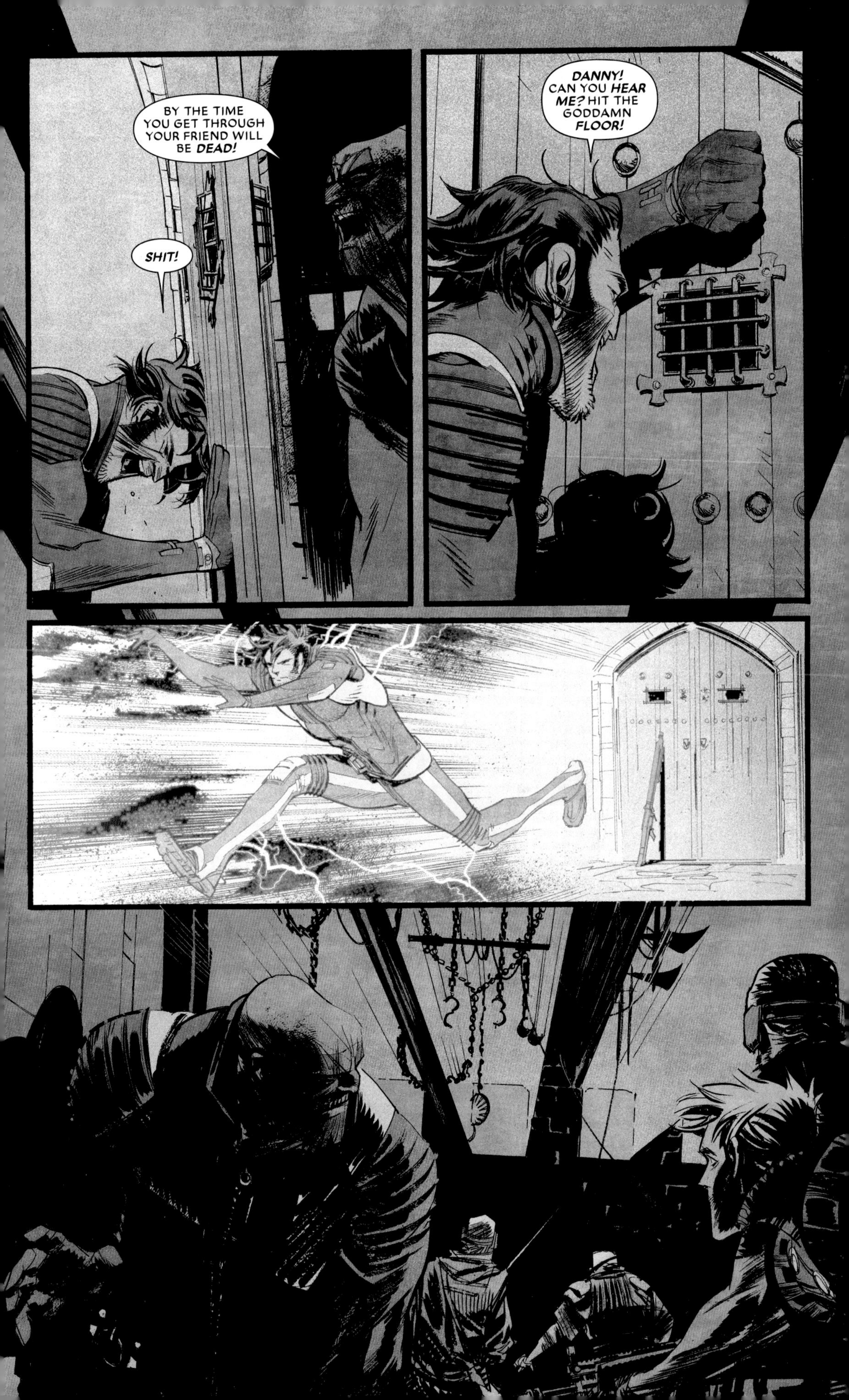
BY THE TIME YOU GET THROUGH YOUR FRIEND WILL BE DEAD!
SHIT!
DANNY! CAN YOU HEAR ME? HIT THE GODDAMN FLOOR!

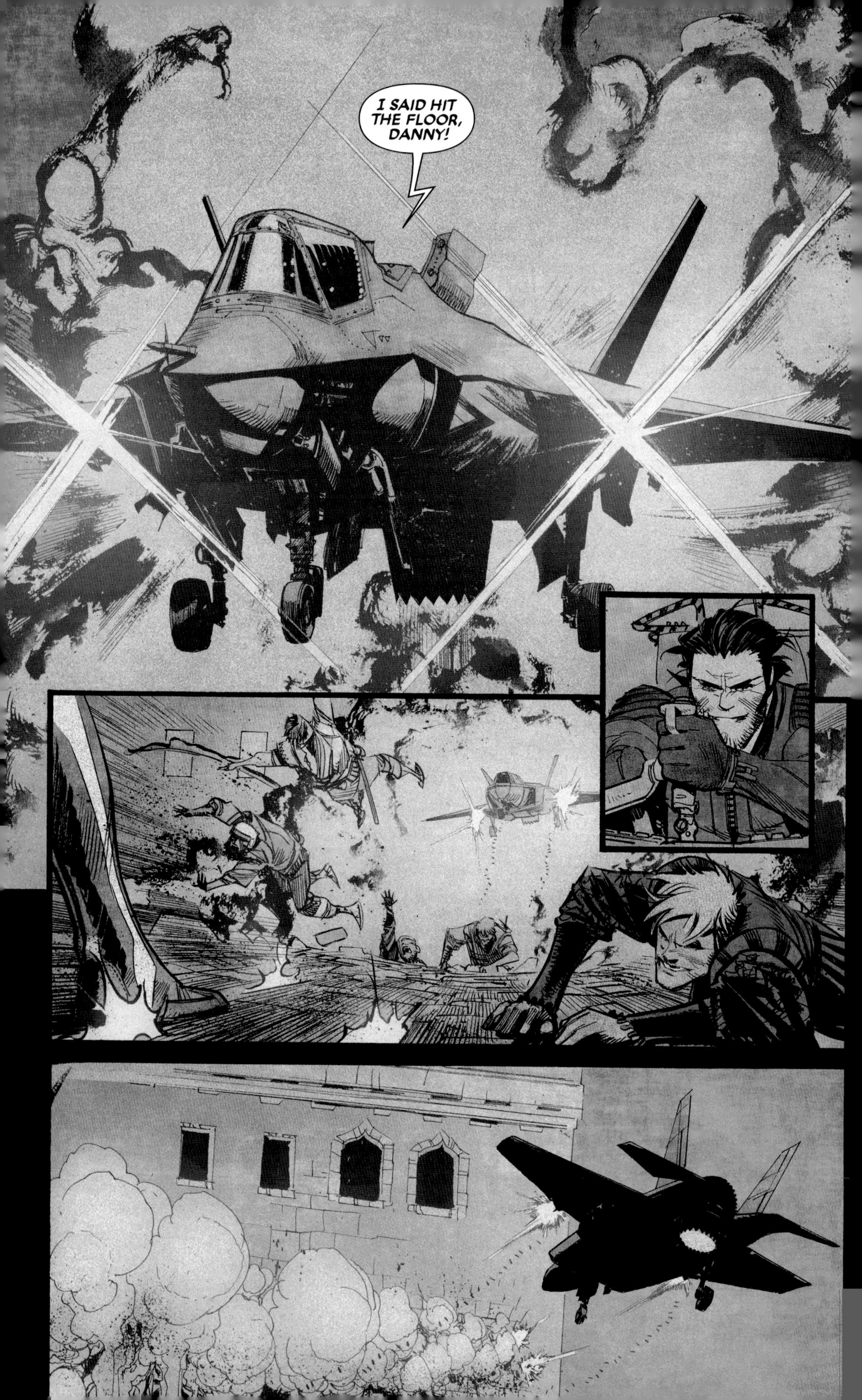
I SAID HIT THE FLOOR, DANNY!

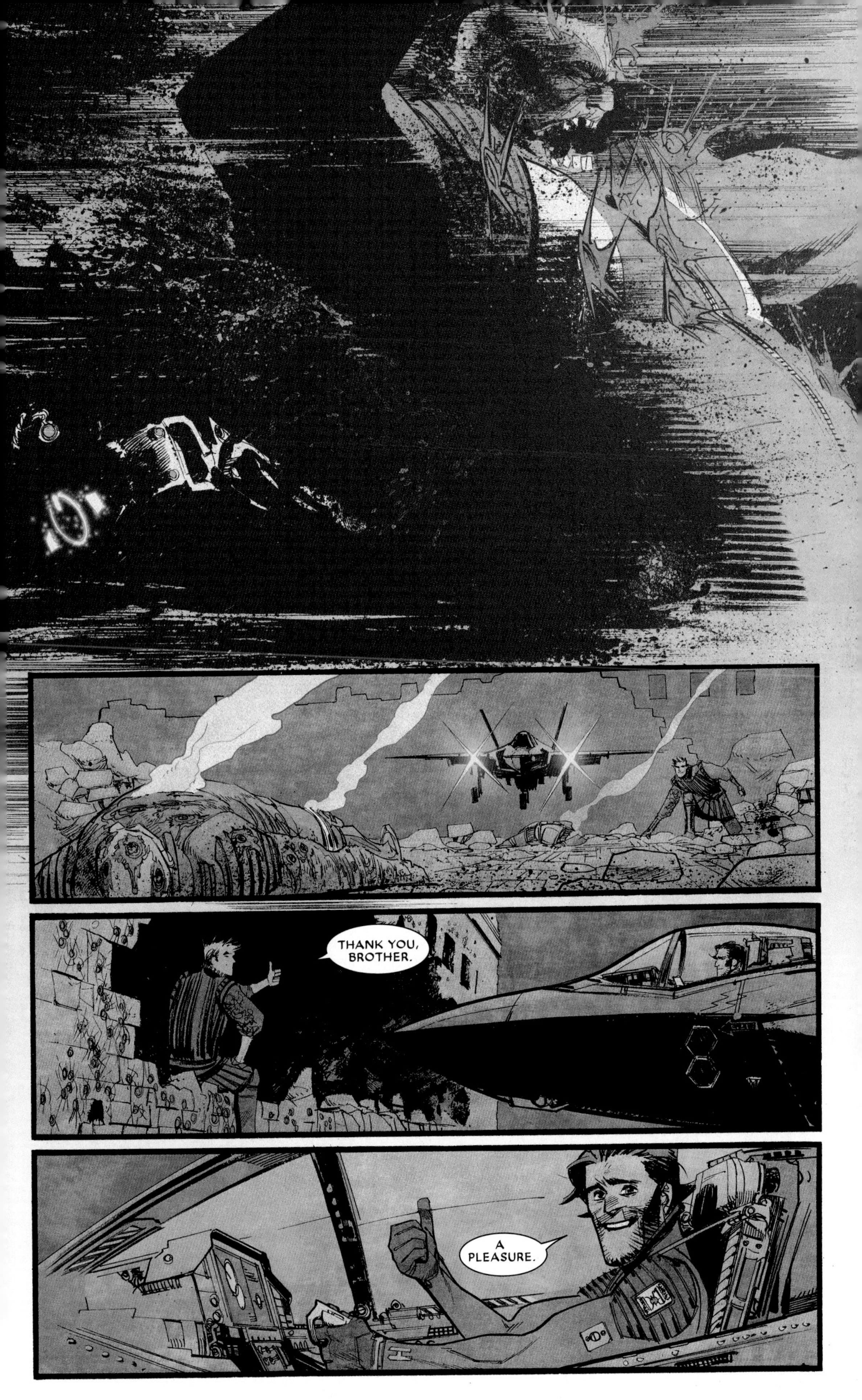
THANK YOU, BROTHER.
A PLEASURE.

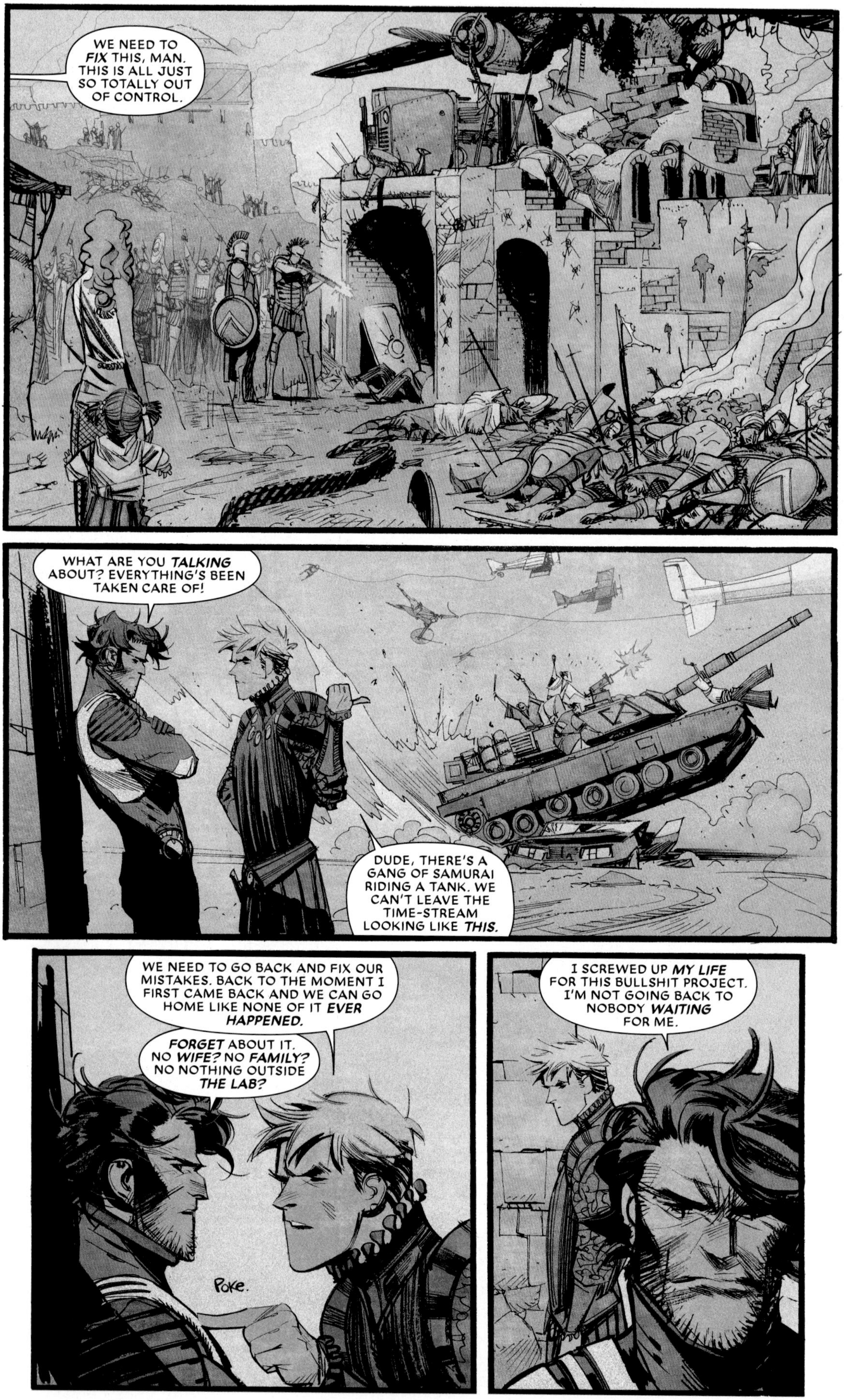
WE NEED TO FIX THIS, MAN. THIS IS ALL JUST SO TOTALLY OUT OF CONTROL.
WHAT ARE YOU TALKING ABOUT? EVERYTHING'S BEEN TAKEN CARE OF!
DUDE, THERE'S A GANG OF SAMURAI RIDING A TANK. WE CAN'T LEAVE THE TIME-STREAM LOOKING LIKE THIS.
WE NEED TO GO BACK AND FIX OUR MISTAKES. BACK TO THE MOMENT I FIRST CAME BACK AND WE CAN GO HOME LIKE NONE OF IT EVER HAPPENED.
FORGET ABOUT IT. NO WIFE? NO FAMILY? NO NOTHING OUTSIDE THE LAB?
POKE.
I SCREWED UP MY LIFE FOR THIS BULLSHIT PROJECT. I'M NOT GOING BACK TO NOBODY WAITING FOR ME.

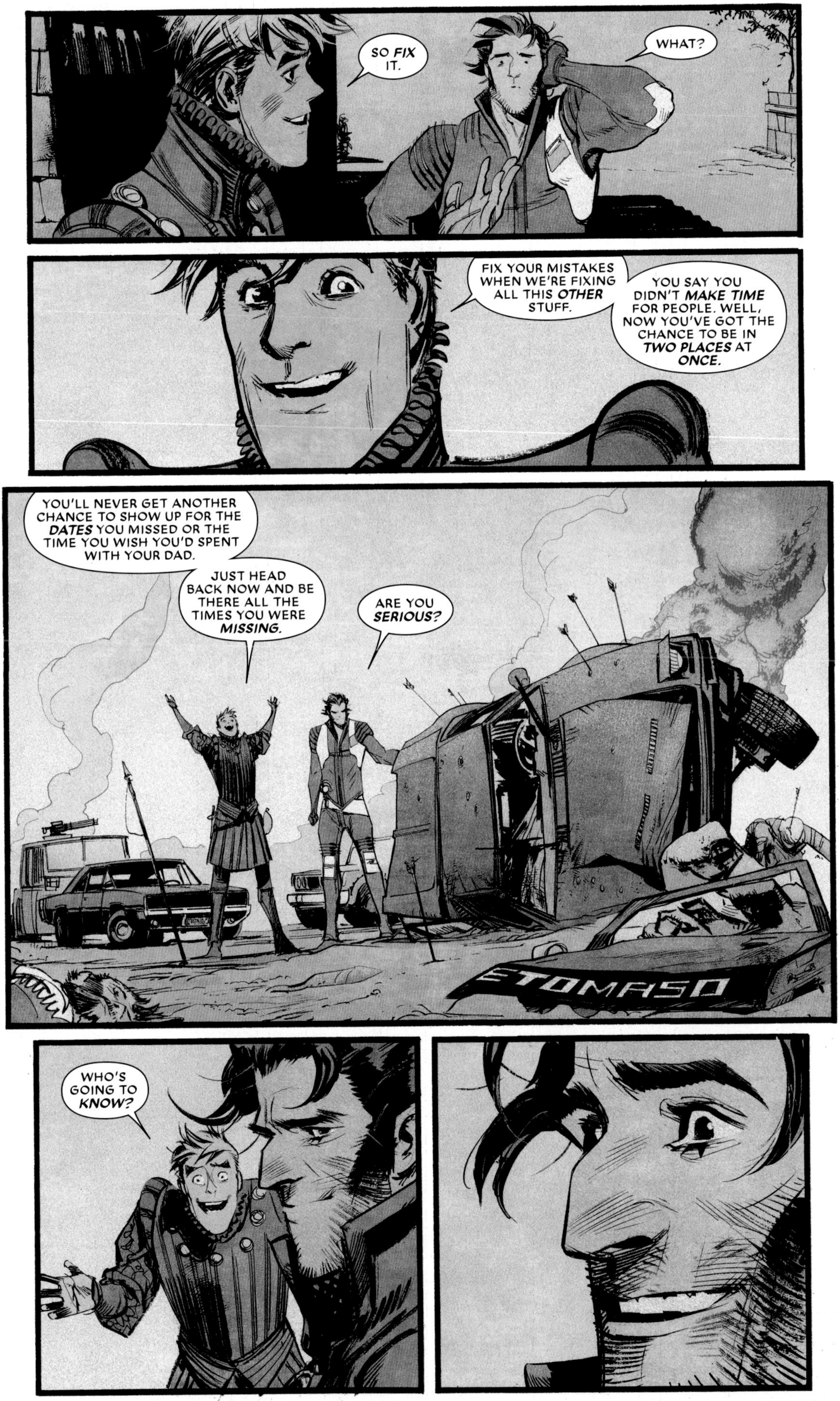
SO FIX IT.
WHAT?
FIX YOUR MISTAKES WHEN WE'RE FIXING ALL THIS OTHER STUFF.
YOU SAY YOU DIDN'T MAKE TIME FOR PEOPLE. WELL, NOW YOU'VE GOT THE CHANCE TO BE IN TWO PLACES AT ONCE.
YOU'LL NEVER GET ANOTHER CHANCE TO SHOW UP FOR THE DATES YOU MISSED OR THE TIME YOU WISH YOU'D SPENT WITH YOUR DAD.
JUST HEAD BACK NOW AND BE THERE ALL THE TIMES YOU WERE MISSING.
ARE YOU SERIOUS?
ETOMASO
WHO'S GOING TO KNOW?

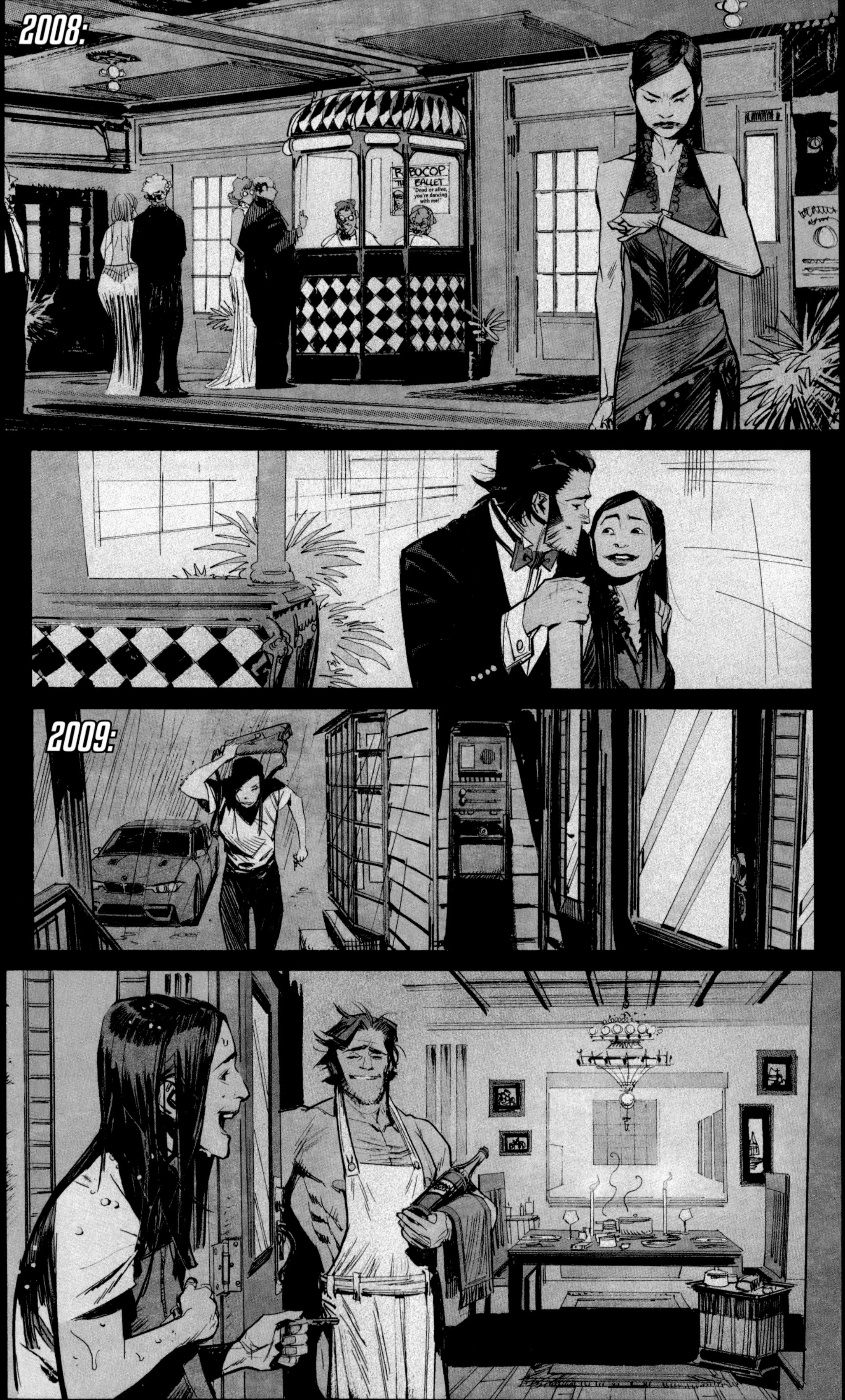
2008:
R BOCOP
TH BALLET
"Dead or alive, you're dancing with me!"
2009:

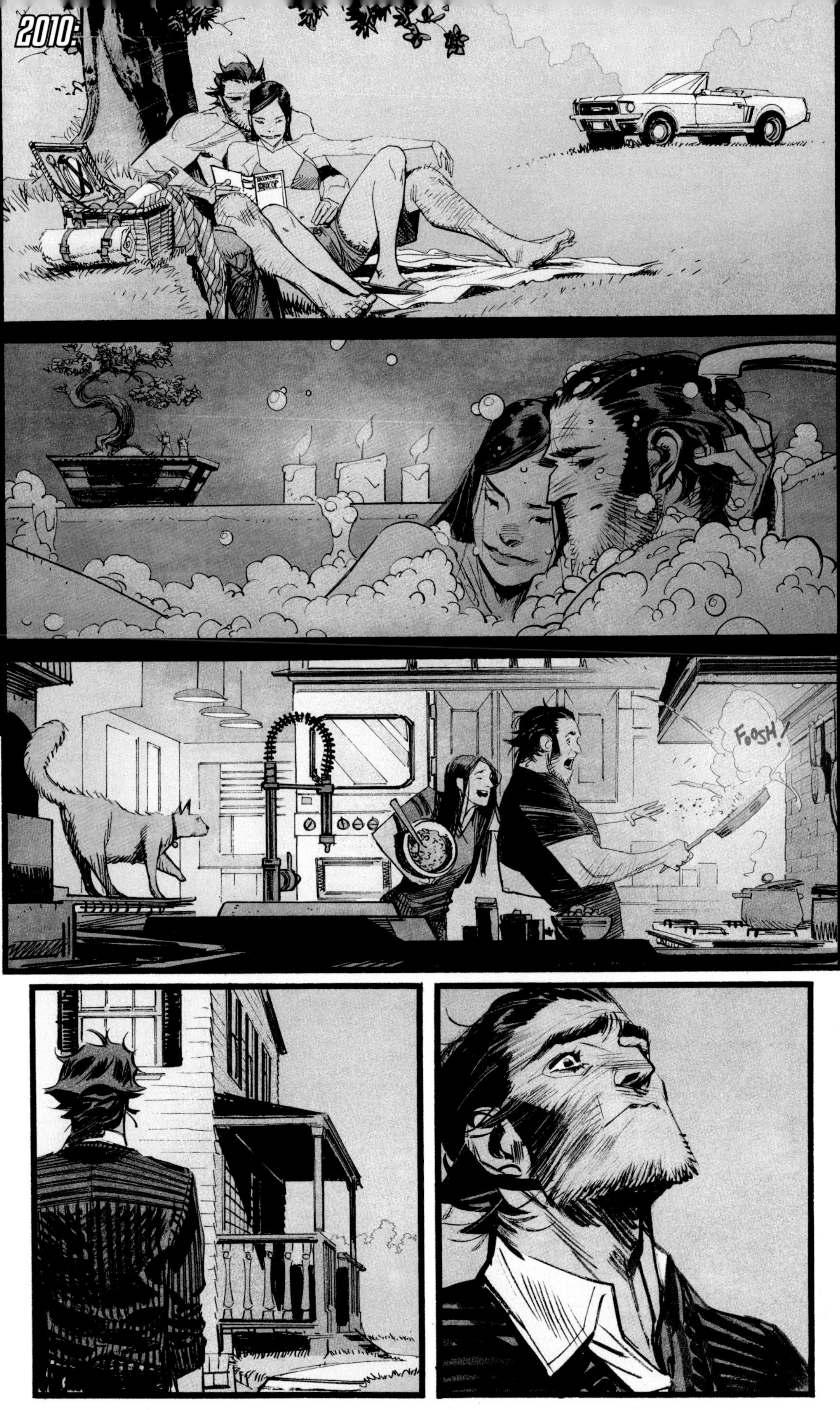
2010:
FOOSH!

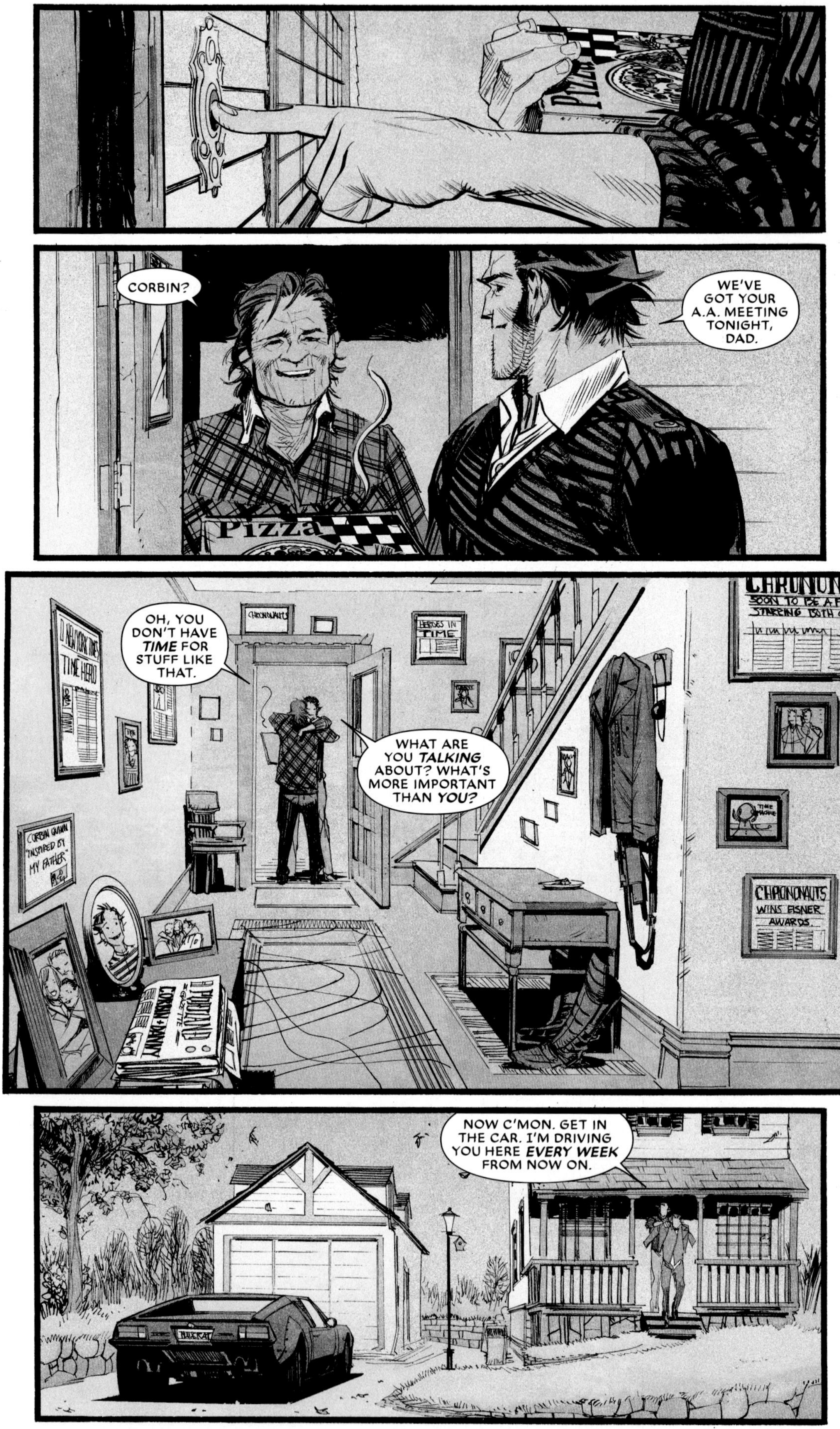
CORBIN?
WE'VE GOT YOUR A.A. MEETING TONIGHT, DAD.
OH, YOU DON'T HAVE *TIME* FOR STUFF LIKE THAT.
WHAT ARE YOU *TALKING* ABOUT? WHAT'S MORE IMPORTANT THAN *YOU?*
CHRONONAUTS WINS EISNER AWARDS
NOW C'MON. GET IN THE CAR. I'M DRIVING YOU HERE *EVERY WEEK* FROM NOW ON.

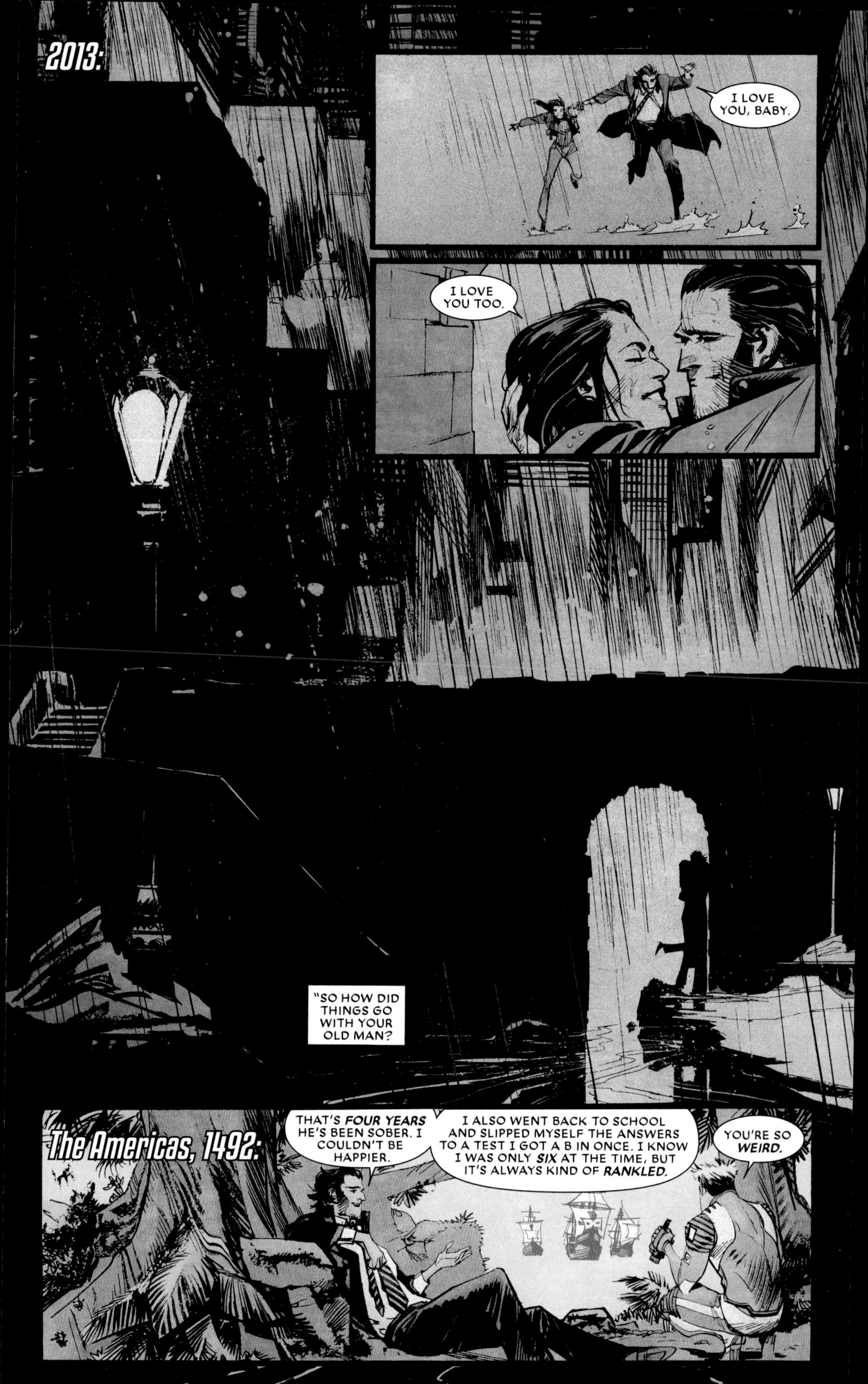
2013:
I LOVE YOU, BABY.
I LOVE YOU TOO.
"SO HOW DID THINGS GO WITH YOUR OLD MAN?
The Americas, 1492:
THAT'S FOUR YEARS HE'S BEEN SOBER. I COULDN'T BE HAPPIER.
I ALSO WENT BACK TO SCHOOL AND SLIPPED MYSELF THE ANSWERS TO A TEST I GOT A B IN ONCE. I KNOW I WAS ONLY SIX AT THE TIME, BUT IT'S ALWAYS KIND OF RANKLED.
YOU'RE SO WEIRD.

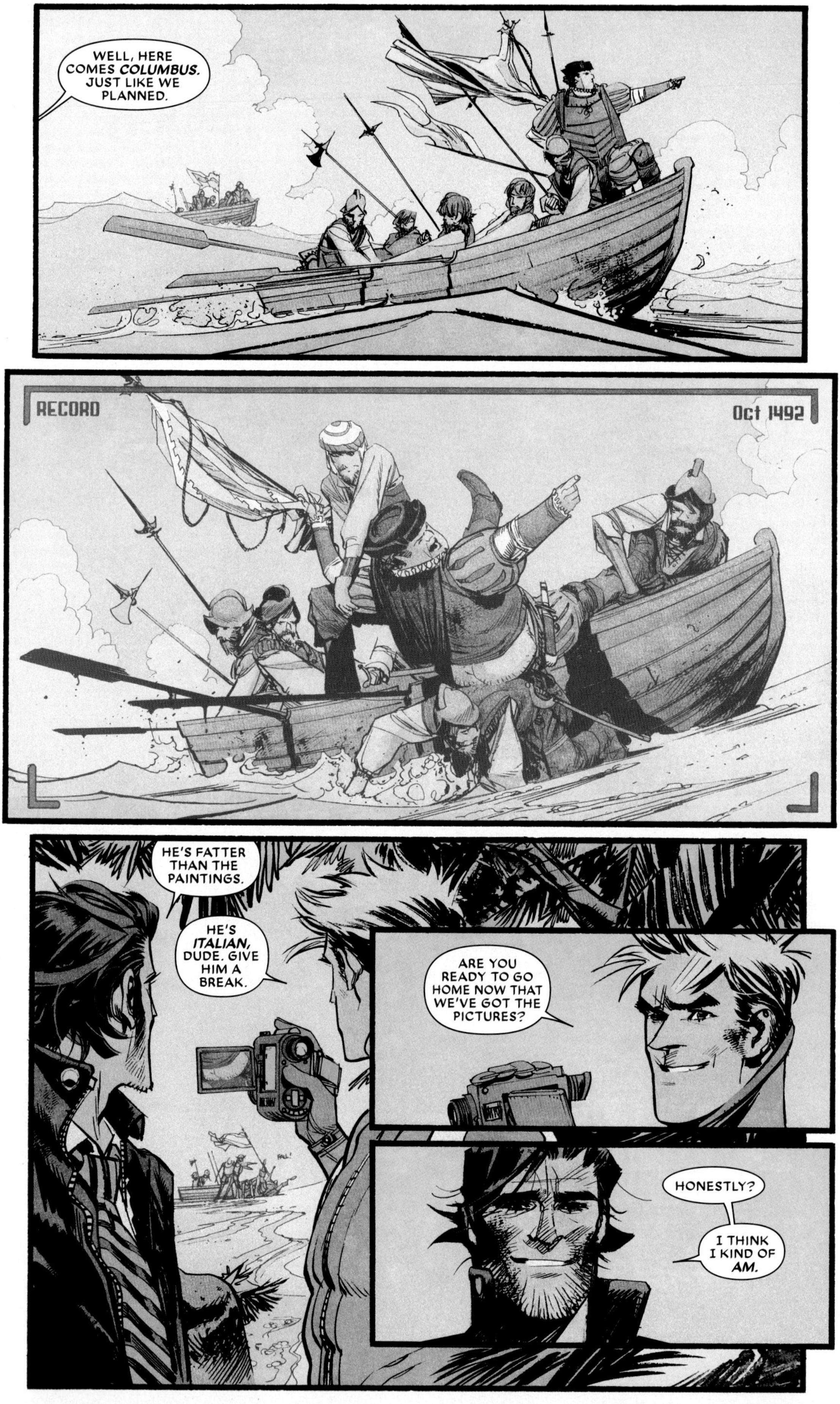
WELL, HERE COMES *COLUMBUS.* JUST LIKE WE PLANNED.
RECORD
Oct 1492
HE'S FATTER THAN THE PAINTINGS.
HE'S *ITALIAN,* DUDE. GIVE HIM A BREAK.
ARE YOU READY TO GO HOME NOW THAT WE'VE GOT THE PICTURES?
HONESTLY?
I THINK I KIND OF *AM.*

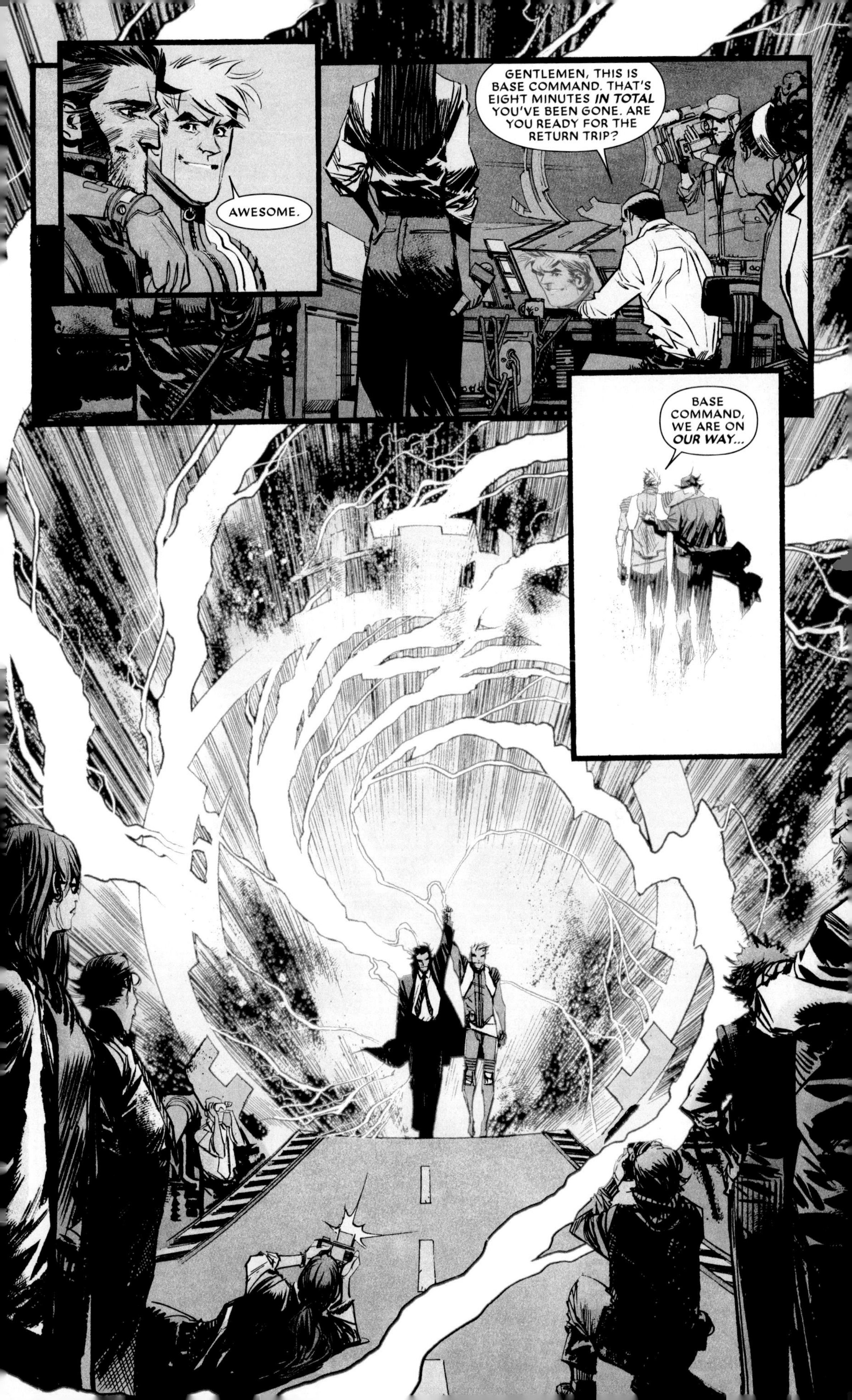
AWESOME.
GENTLEMEN, THIS IS BASE COMMAND. THAT'S EIGHT MINUTES *IN TOTAL* YOU'VE BEEN GONE. ARE YOU READY FOR THE RETURN TRIP?
BASE COMMAND, WE ARE ON *OUR WAY...*

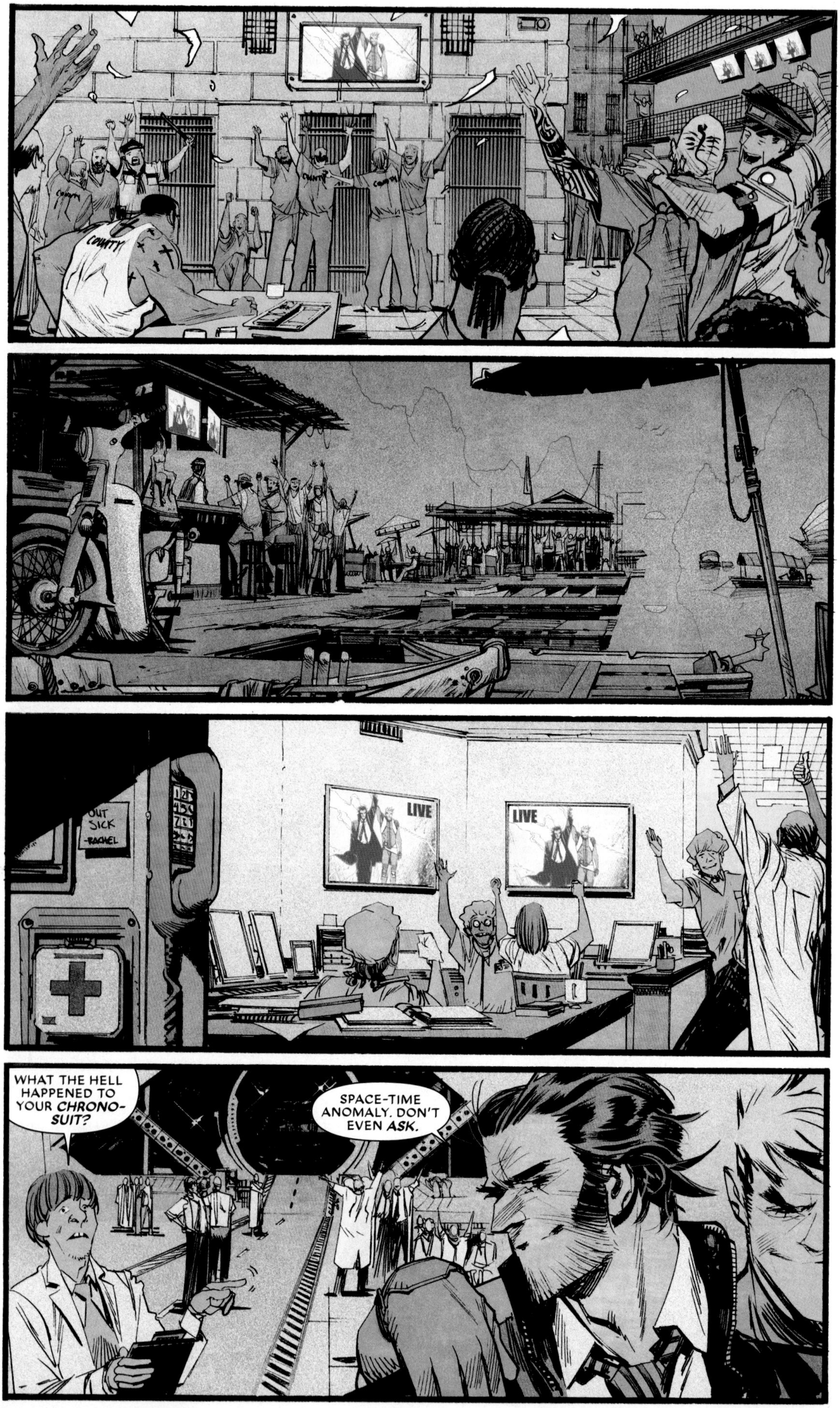
COUNTY
LIVE
LIVE
OUT SICK -RACHEL
WHAT THE HELL HAPPENED TO YOUR *CHRONO-SUIT?*
SPACE-TIME ANOMALY. DON'T EVEN *ASK.*

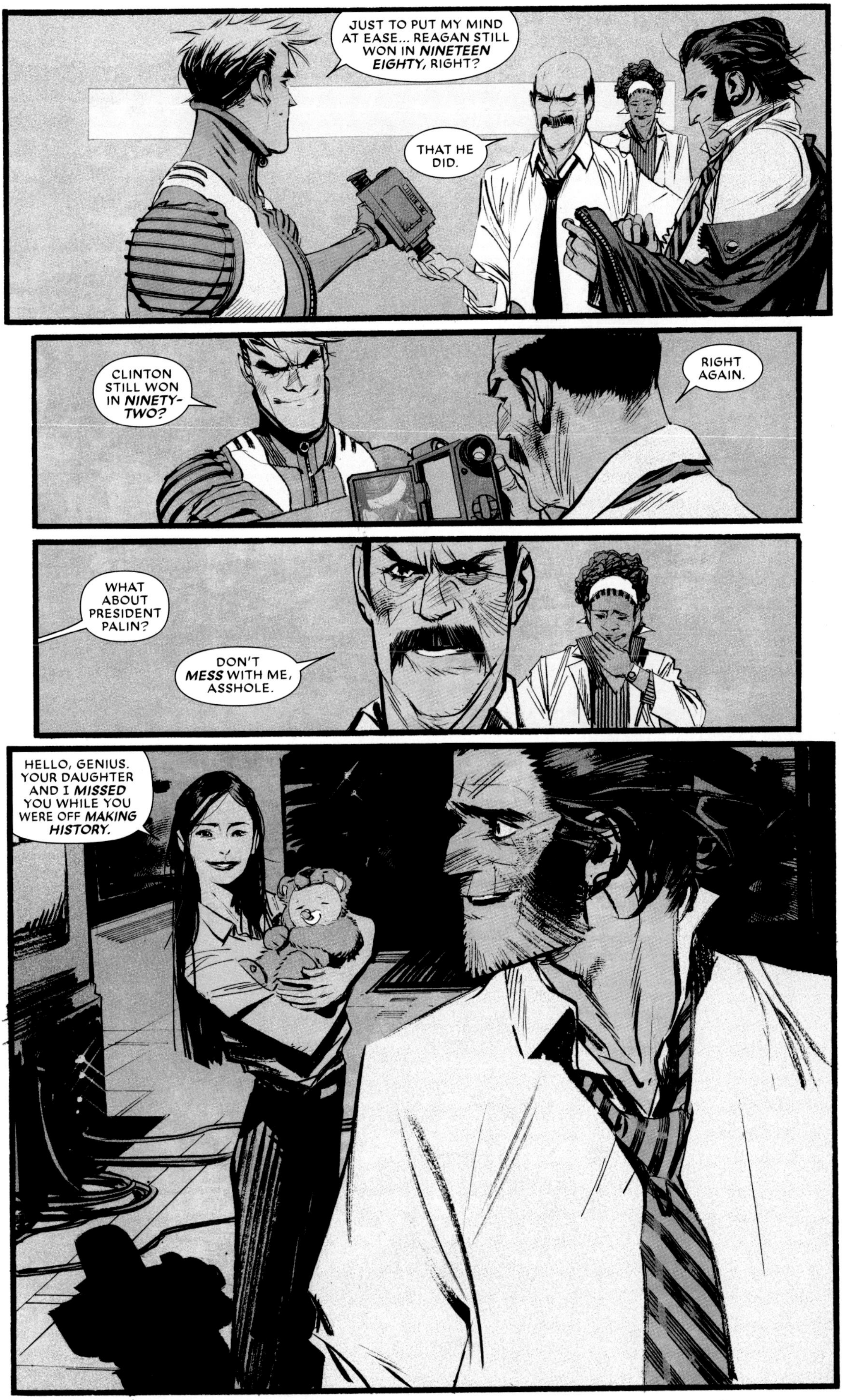
JUST TO PUT MY MIND AT EASE... REAGAN STILL WON IN NINETEEN EIGHTY, RIGHT?
THAT HE DID.
CLINTON STILL WON IN NINETY-TWO?
RIGHT AGAIN.
WHAT ABOUT PRESIDENT PALIN?
DON'T MESS WITH ME, ASSHOLE.
HELLO, GENIUS. YOUR DAUGHTER AND I MISSED YOU WHILE YOU WERE OFF MAKING HISTORY.

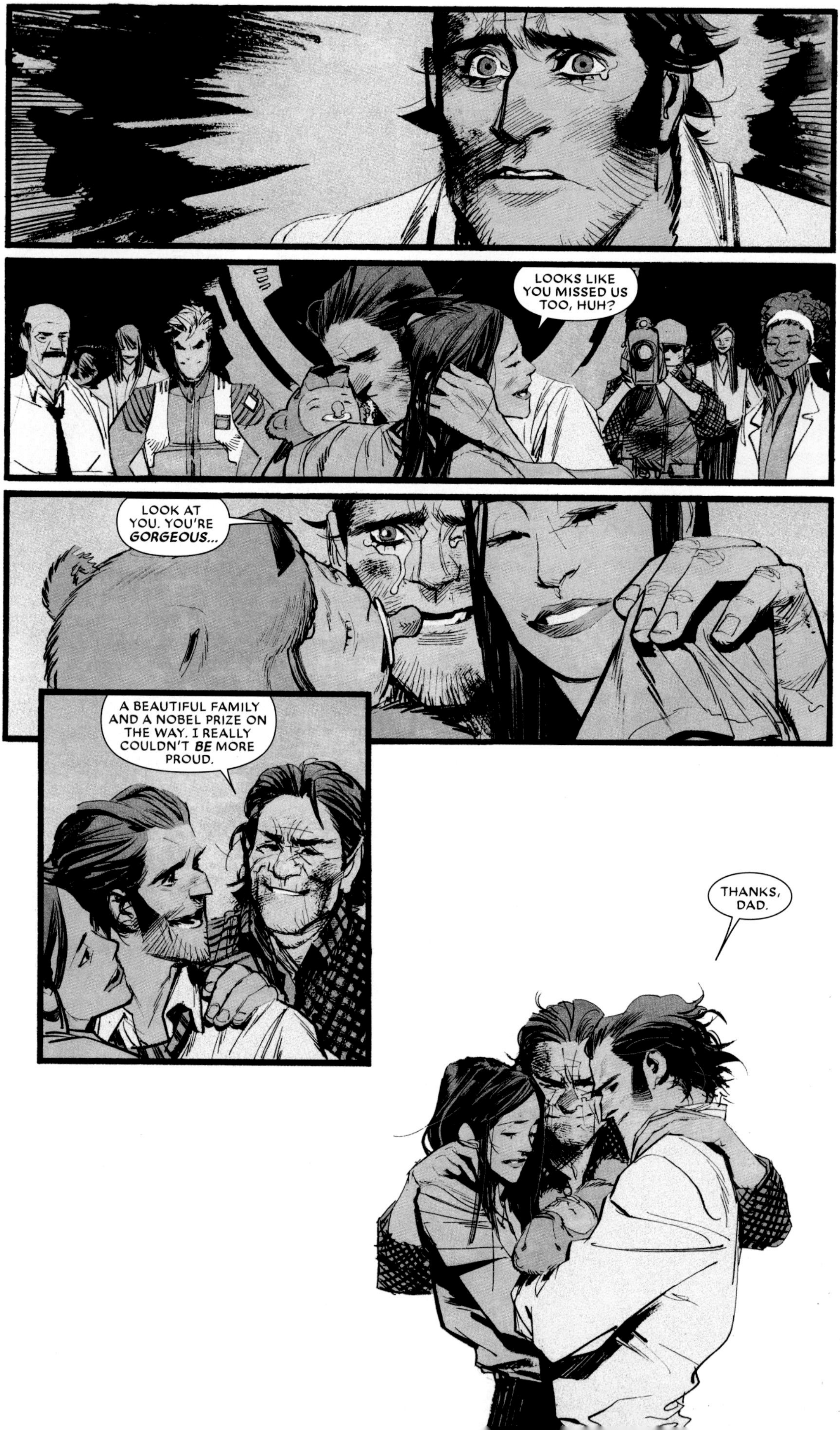
LOOKS LIKE YOU MISSED US TOO, HUH?
LOOK AT YOU. YOU'RE *GORGEOUS...*
A BEAUTIFUL FAMILY AND A NOBEL PRIZE ON THE WAY. I REALLY COULDN'T ***BE*** MORE PROUD.
THANKS, DAD.

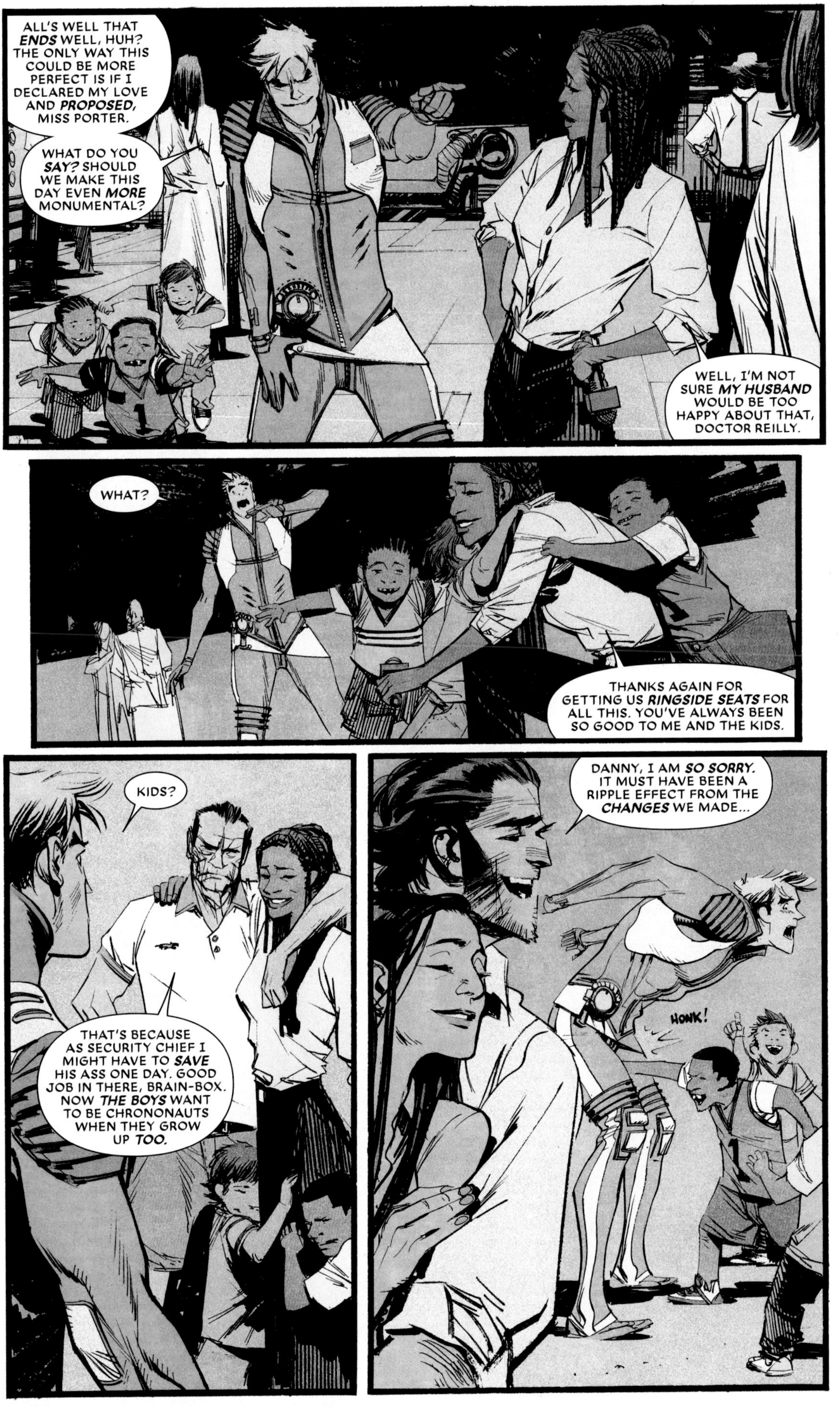
ALL'S WELL THAT ENDS WELL, HUH? THE ONLY WAY THIS COULD BE MORE PERFECT IS IF I DECLARED MY LOVE AND PROPOSED, MISS PORTER.
WHAT DO YOU SAY? SHOULD WE MAKE THIS DAY EVEN MORE MONUMENTAL?
WELL, I'M NOT SURE MY HUSBAND WOULD BE TOO HAPPY ABOUT THAT, DOCTOR REILLY.
WHAT?
THANKS AGAIN FOR GETTING US RINGSIDE SEATS FOR ALL THIS. YOU'VE ALWAYS BEEN SO GOOD TO ME AND THE KIDS.
KIDS?
THAT'S BECAUSE AS SECURITY CHIEF I MIGHT HAVE TO SAVE HIS ASS ONE DAY. GOOD JOB IN THERE, BRAIN-BOX. NOW THE BOYS WANT TO BE CHRONONAUTS WHEN THEY GROW UP TOO.
DANNY, I AM SO SORRY. IT MUST HAVE BEEN A RIPPLE EFFECT FROM THE CHANGES WE MADE...
HONK!

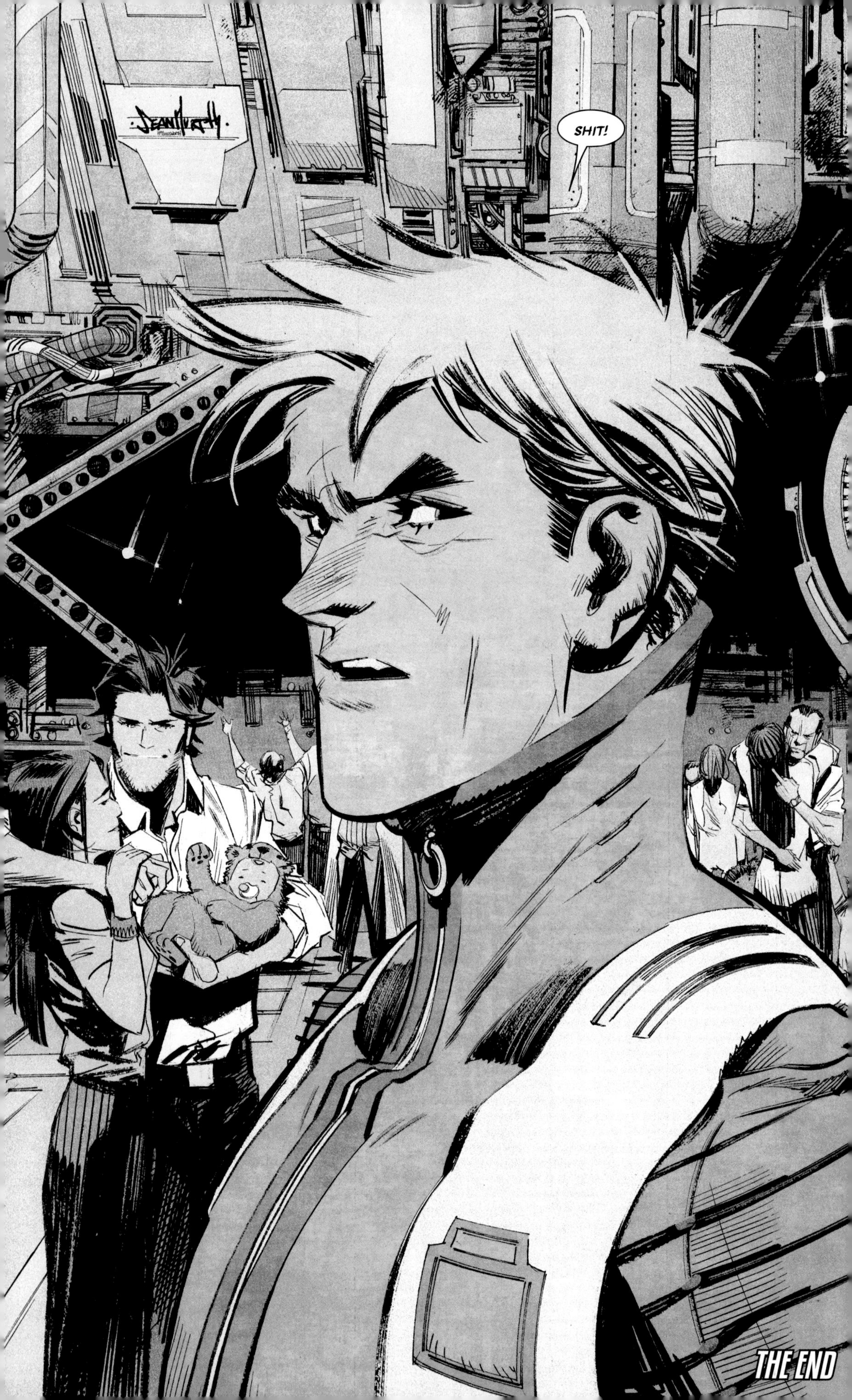
SHIT!
THE END

MILLARWORLD®

THE COLLECTION CHECKLIST

KICK-ASS
MARK MILLAR
JOHN ROMITA JR.

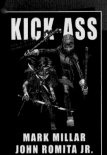

KICK-ASS
Art by John Romita Jr.

- ☐ Kick-Ass #1-8

HIT-GIRL
MARK MILLAR
JOHN ROMITA JR.
TOM PALMER and DEAN WHITE

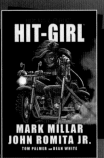

HIT-GIRL
Art by John Romita Jr.

- ☐ Hit-Girl #1-5

KICK-ASS 2
MARK MILLAR
JOHN ROMITA JR.

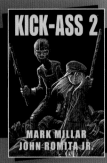

KICK-ASS 2
Art by John Romita Jr.

- ☐ Kick-Ass 2 #1-7

KICK-ASS 3
MARK MILLAR
JOHN ROMITA JR.

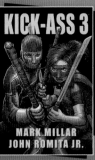

KICK-ASS 3
Art by John Romita Jr.

- ☐ Kick-Ass 3 #1-8

MILLAR MURPHY
CHRONONAUTS
#1
$3.50

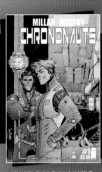

CHRONONAUTS
Art by Sean Gordon Murphy

- ☐ Chrononauts #1-4

MARK MILLAR DUNCAN FEGREDO
MPH

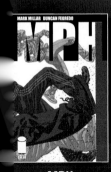

MPH
Art by Duncan Fegredo

- ☐ MPH #1-5

MARK MILLAR GORAN PARLOV
STARLIGHT

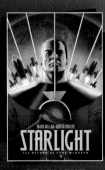

STARLIGHT
Art by Goran Parlov

- ☐ Starlight #1-6

MARK MILLAR DAVE GIBBONS MATTHEW VAUGHN
KINGSMAN
THE SECRET SERVICE

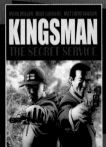

KINGSMAN: THE SECRET SERVICE
Art by Dave Gibbons

- ☐ The Secret Service #1-6

MARK MILLAR · WILFREDO TORRES
JUPITER'S
CIRCLE

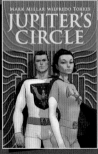

JUPITER'S CIRCLE
Art by Wilfredo Torres

- ☐ Jupiter's Circle #1-5

MARK MILLAR · FRANK QUITELY
JUPITER'S
LEGACY

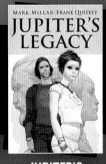

JUPITER'S LEGACY
Art by Frank Quitely

- ☐ Jupiter's Legacy #1-5

MARK MILLAR LEINIL YU
SUPER
CROOKS
THE HEIST

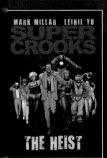

SUPER CROOKS
Art by Leinil Yu

MARK MILLAR & LEINIL YU
SUPERIOR
FROM THE
WRITER OF
KICK-ASS

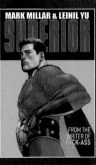

SUPERIOR
Art by Leinil Yu

MILLAR & McNIVEN'S
NEMESIS

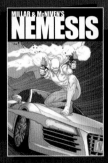

NEMESIS
Art by Steve McNiven

WANTED
MARK MILLAR • JG JONES • PAUL MOUNTS
UNIVERSAL PICTURES

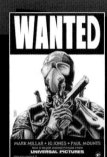

WANTED
Art by JG Jones

AMERICAN
JESUS
BOOK ONE : CHOSEN
MARK MILLAR · PETER GROSS

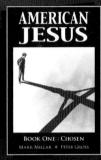

AMERICAN JESUS
Art by Peter Gross

MARK MILLAR

is the **NEW YORK TIMES** best-selling writer of **WANTED**, the **KICK-ASS** series, **THE SECRET SERVICE**, **JUPITER'S LEGACY**, **NEMESIS**, **SUPERIOR**, **SUPER CROOKS**, **AMERICAN JESUS**, **MPH**, **STARLIGHT**, and **CHRONONAUTS**. **WANTED**, **KICK-ASS**, **KICK-ASS 2**, and **THE SECRET SERVICE** (as **KINGSMAN: THE SECRET SERVICE**) have been adapted into feature films, and **NEMESIS**, **SUPERIOR**, **STARLIGHT**, **WAR HEROES**, and **CHRONONAUTS** are in development at major studios.

His DC Comics work includes the seminal **SUPERMAN: RED SON**, and at Marvel Comics he created **THE ULTIMATES** — selected by **TIME** magazine as the comic book of the decade, **WOLVERINE: OLD MAN LOGAN**, and the record-breaking **CIVIL WAR** event, which redefined the Marvel landscape and is now being filmed as the next Captain America movie. Currently, he is working on **JUPITER'S CIRCLE**, the second volume of **JUPITER'S LEGACY**, and the upcoming series **HUCK** for Image Comics.

Mark has been an Executive Producer on all his movie adaptations and is currently creative consultant to Fox Studios on their Marvel slate of movies. His autobiography, **GO WEST, YOUNG VAMPIRE**, will be published next year.

SEAN MURPHY

was born in Nashua, NH in the fall of 1980. He got interested in comics in grade school and spent many afternoons of his childhood drawing instead of making friends. His formal education started in Salem, NH as an apprentice to Leslie Swank, local painter, cartoonist and WWII vet. After graduating Pinkerton Academy high school in 1999 he attended Massachusetts College of Art (Boston) and then the Savannah College of Art and Design.

Before graduation, Sean was already working with such publishers as Dark Horse on their Star Wars titles. After getting his BFA, he moved out to Hollywood to pursue concept art for video games and film making while paying the bills with additional titles like **STAR TREK**, **TEEN TITANS**, and **BATMAN/SCARECROW: YEAR ONE**.

His first creator-owned book, **OFF ROAD**, was released by Oni in 2005 and won an American Library Association award. Soon after, Sean signed an exclusive contract with DC Comics and moved to New York. His DC published work is what he's most known for currently — **HELLBLAZER: CITY OF ANGELS**, **JOE THE BARBARIAN** and **AMERICAN VAMPIRE: SURVIVAL OF THE FITTEST** helped boost his career greatly. His latest book for DC/Vertigo, and creator owned mini series called **PUNK ROCK JESUS**, is in stores now.

Sean lives in Brooklyn with his wife Colleen, and their two dogs, Red and Bebop.

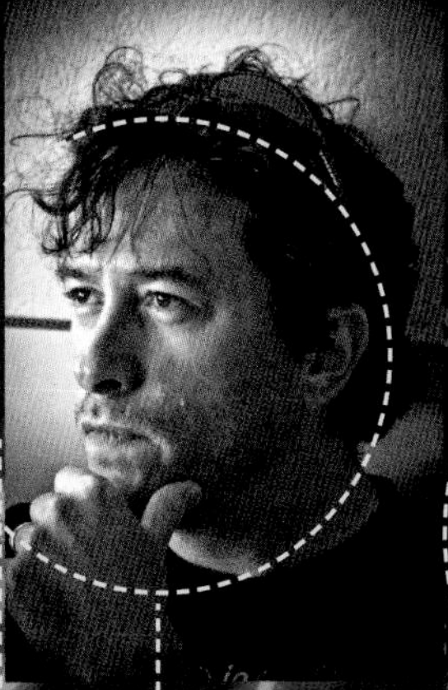

MATT HOLLINGSWORTH

is an Eisner Award-winning colorist for Image, Marvel and Vertigo Comics. He graduated from the Joe Kubert School for Cartooning in 1991, landed work at Marvel and DC two days later, and has been working on comics ever since. His work includes doing the colors on **PREACHER, HELLBLAZER, DEATH, DAREDEVIL, HAWKEYE, THE WAKE, HELLBOY, WYTCHES, GRENDEL TALES, CHRONONAUTS**, and a ton of other books. Current works include **WE STAND ON GUARD** and **TOKYO GHOST** for Image Comics and **SUICIDERS** for Vertigo.

He had a two-year hiatus from comics from 2004 to 2006 when he went to work in visual effects for the movie industry, working at Stan Winston Digital, Rhythm & Hues and Sony Pictures Imageworks primarily as a texture painter on 7 feature films, including **SKY CAPTAIN AND THE WORLD OF TOMORROW, SERENITY** and **SURF'S UP**.

Born in California, he currently lives in Croatia with his wife Branka and young son Liam. He is a multiple award winning homebrewer of beer and is heavily involved in the beer scene in Croatia.

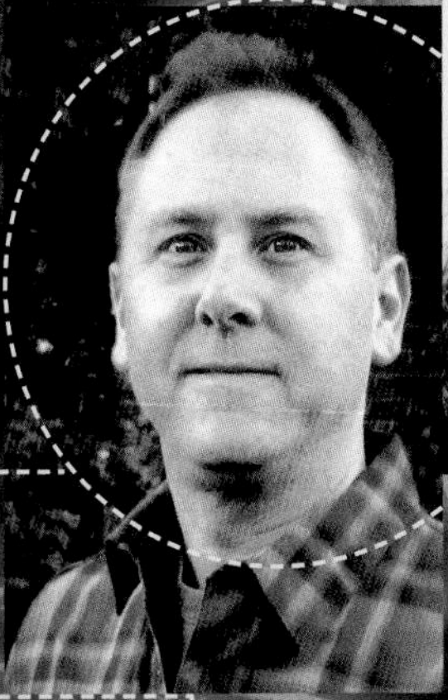

CHRIS ELIOPOULOS

(www.chriseliopoulos.com) began his illustration career as a letterer for Marvel, and has worked on literally thousands of comics. But along with that, he is also the author/artist of many comics, including the popular series **LOCKJAW AND THE PET AVENGERS** and **FRANKLIN RICHARDS: SON OF A GENIUS**, for which he was nominated for multiple Eisner Awards and received a Harvey Award. He also co-created **COW BOY** which was optioned by Dreamworks. He currently illustrates the **ORDINARY PEOPLE CHANGE THE WORLD** series with Brad Meltzer. He lives in New Jersey with his wife and their identical twin sons.

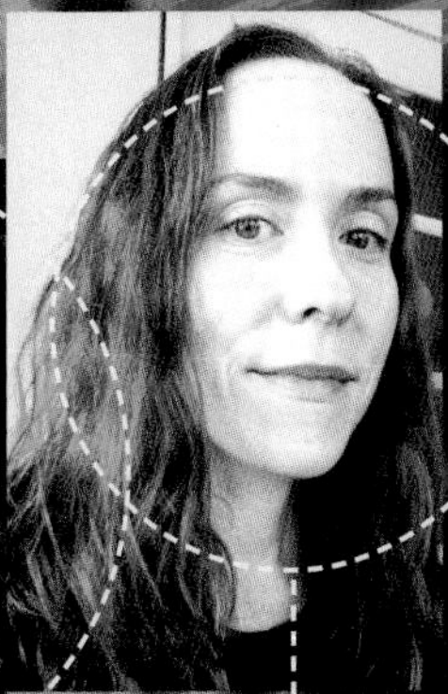

NICOLE BOOSE

began her comics career as an assistant editor for Harris Comics' **VAMPIRELLA**, before joining the editorial staff at Marvel Comics. There, she edited titles including **CABLE & DEADPOOL, INVINCIBLE IRON MAN**, and Stephen King's **DARK TOWER** adaptations, and oversaw Marvel's line of custom comic publications.

Since 2008, Nicole has worked as a freelance editor and consultant in the comics industry, with editorial credits that include the Millarworld titles **SUPERIOR, SUPER CROOKS, JUPITER'S LEGACY, MPH, STARLIGHT, THE SECRET SERVICE**, and **CHRONONAUTS**. Nicole is also Communications Manager for Comics Experience, an online school and community for comic creators.

Born in Philadelphia and a long-time New Yorker, she now lives near Cleveland, Ohio with her family.

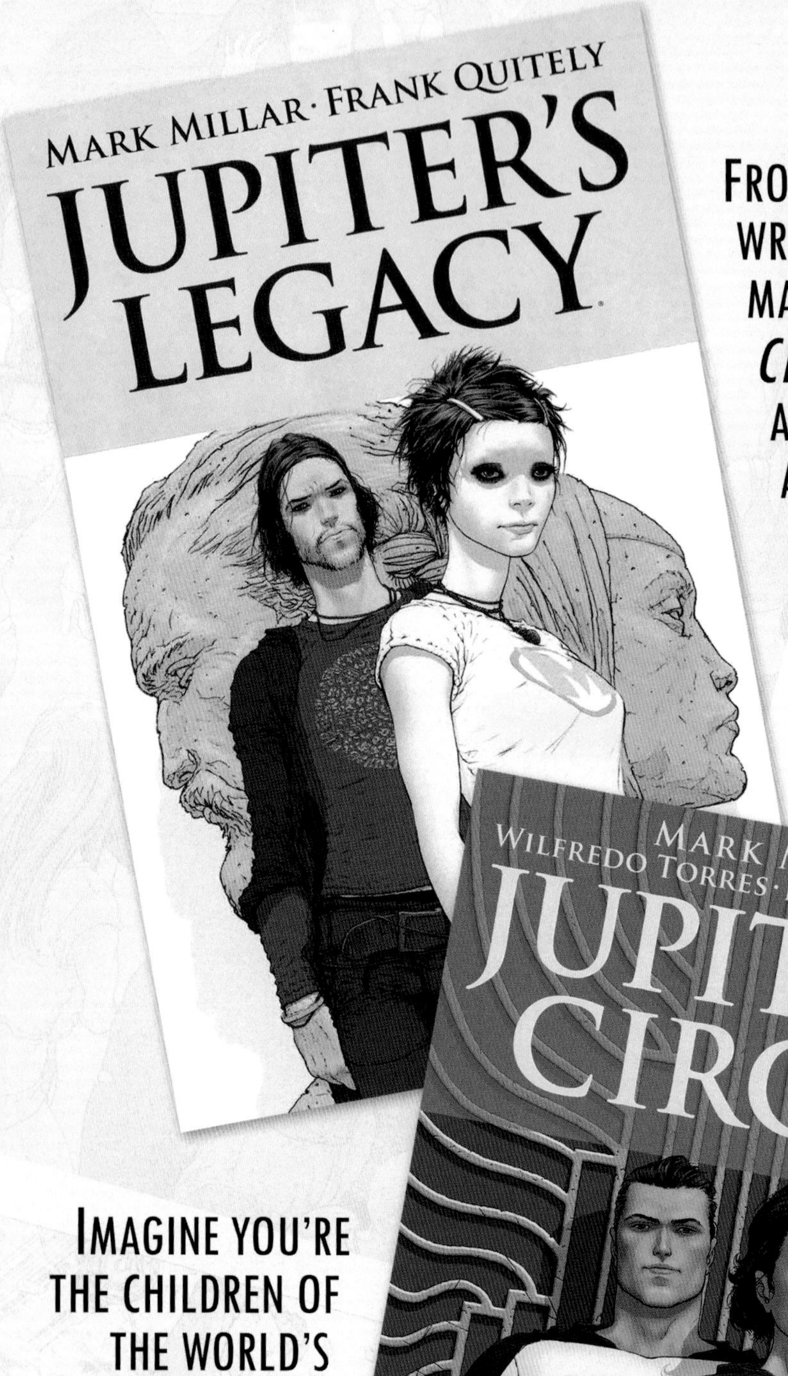
MARK MILLAR · FRANK QUITELY
JUPITER'S LEGACY

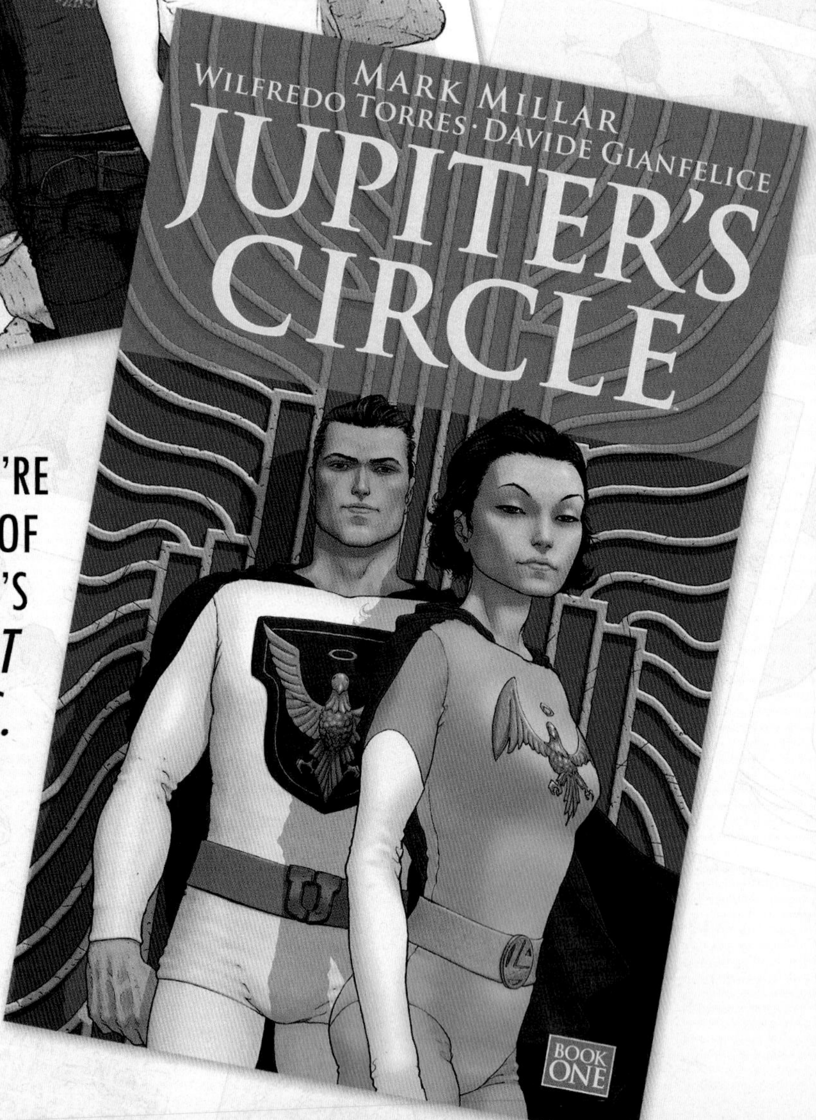
MARK MILLAR
WILFREDO TORRES · DAVIDE GIANFELICE
JUPITER'S CIRCLE
BOOK ONE

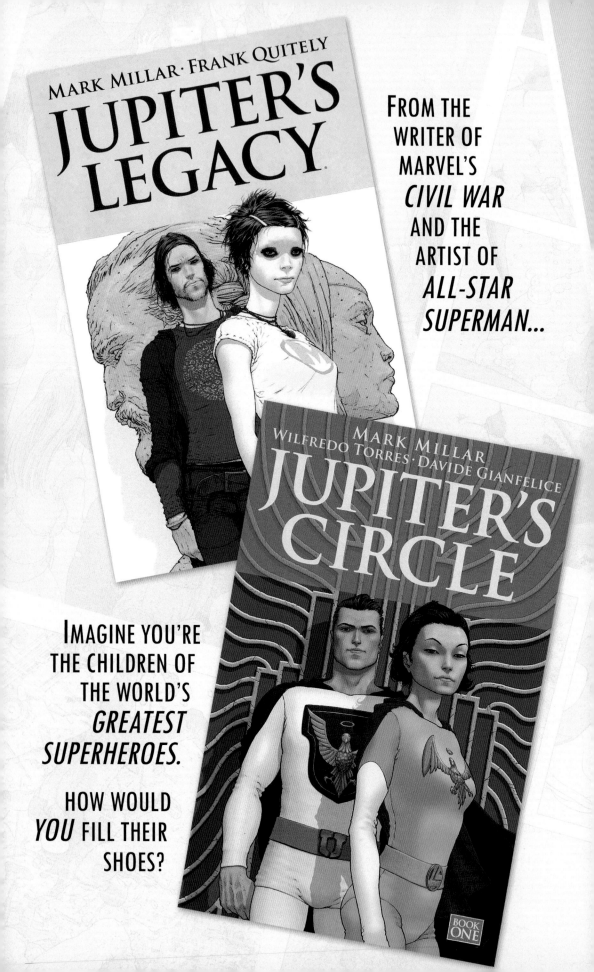

"★★★★★"
NEWSARAMA

"★★★★★"
COMIC VINE

"★★★★★"
GEEKED OUT NATION

"★★★★★"
FOLLOWING THE NERD

"★★★★★"
FORCES OF GEEK

"★★★★★"
FLIP GEEKS

"★★★★★"
COMIC BOOK THERAPY

"★★★★★"
UNLEASH THE FANBOY

"★★★★★"
IMAGINATION CENTRE

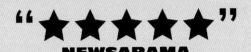

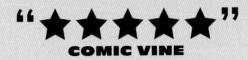

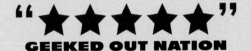

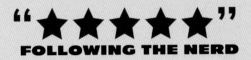

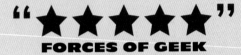

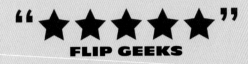

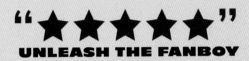

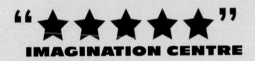

"Just when you think you've seen every corner of the superhero genre explored a hundred times over, here come Millar and Quitely to remind you why you fell in love with capes in the first place. A game changer!"

Robert Kirkman, *The Walking Dead*

"Chain-smoking, philandering superheroes drunk on their own power and unrepentant in their use of it? Yes, please. Oh YES!"

Damon Lindelof, *Lost, Prometheus*

"Jupiter's Legacy is an instant modern classic. A wild, gorgeous, intimate epic, it shows superheroes battling with politics and family, and ultimately facing the most deadly enemy of all– the passing of time."

Russell T Davies, *Dr Who, Queer as Folk, Cucumber*

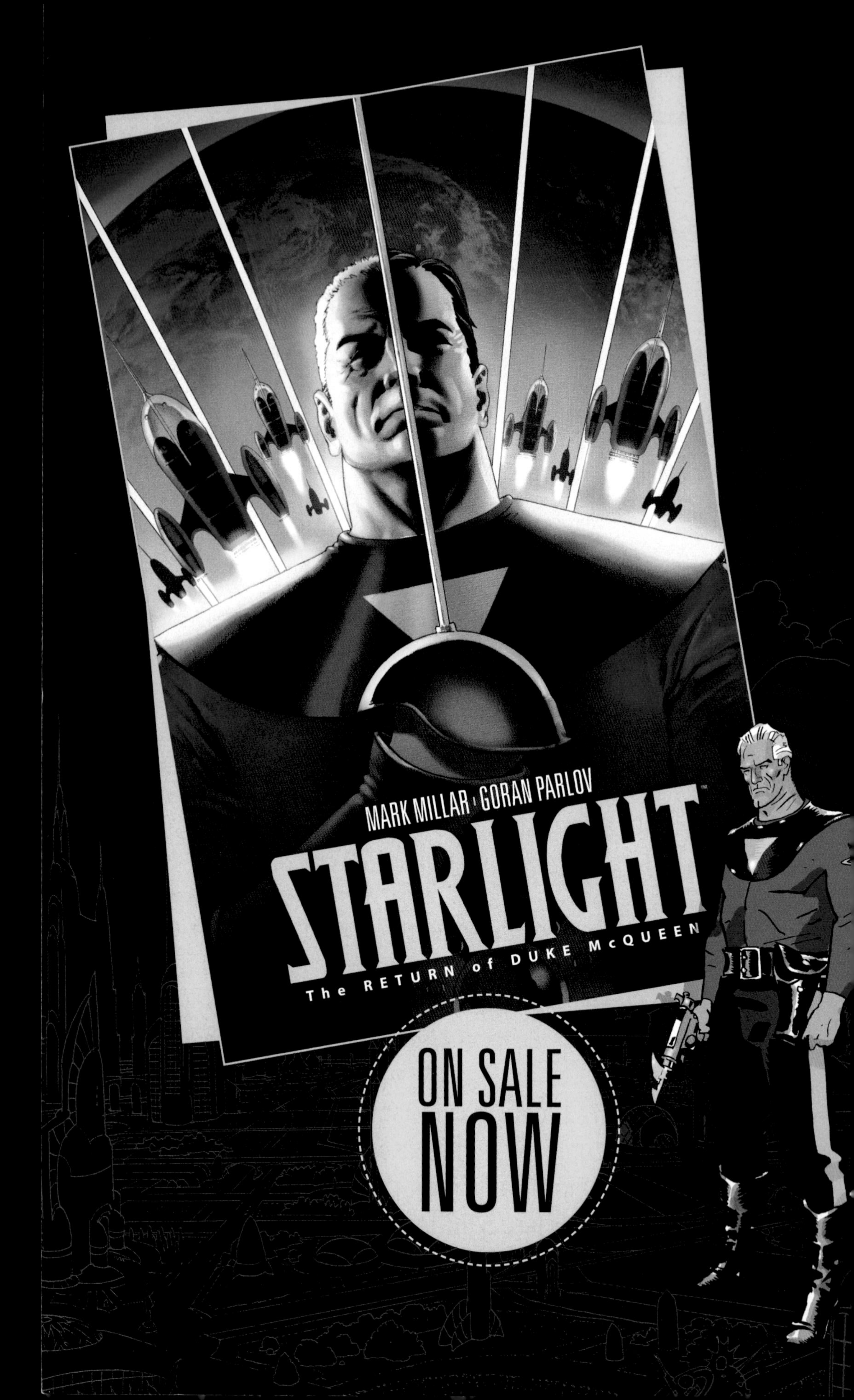
MARK MILLAR · GORAN PARLOV
STARLIGHT™
The RETURN of DUKE McQUEEN
ON SALE NOW

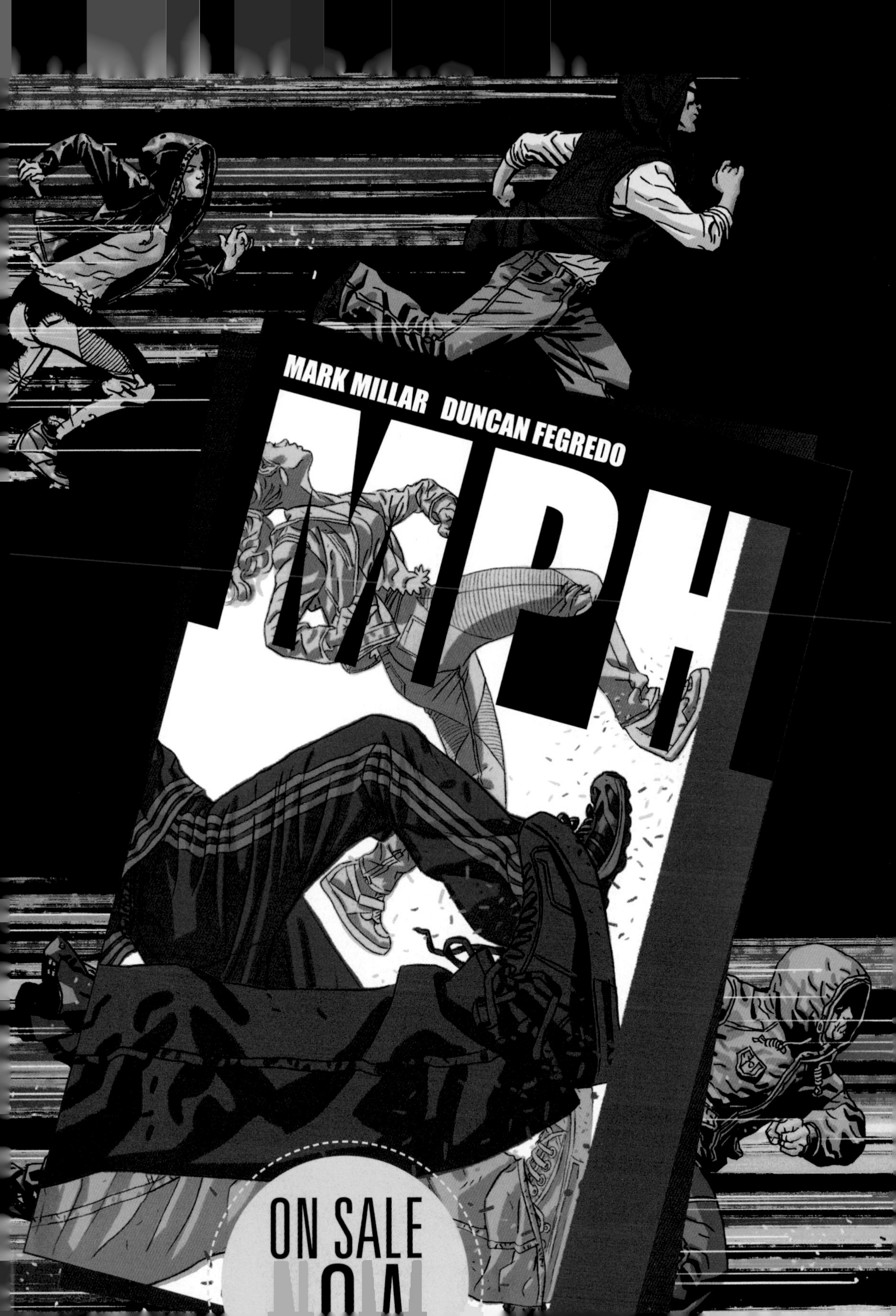

MARK MILLAR
DUNCAN FEGREDO
MPH
ON SALE
NOW

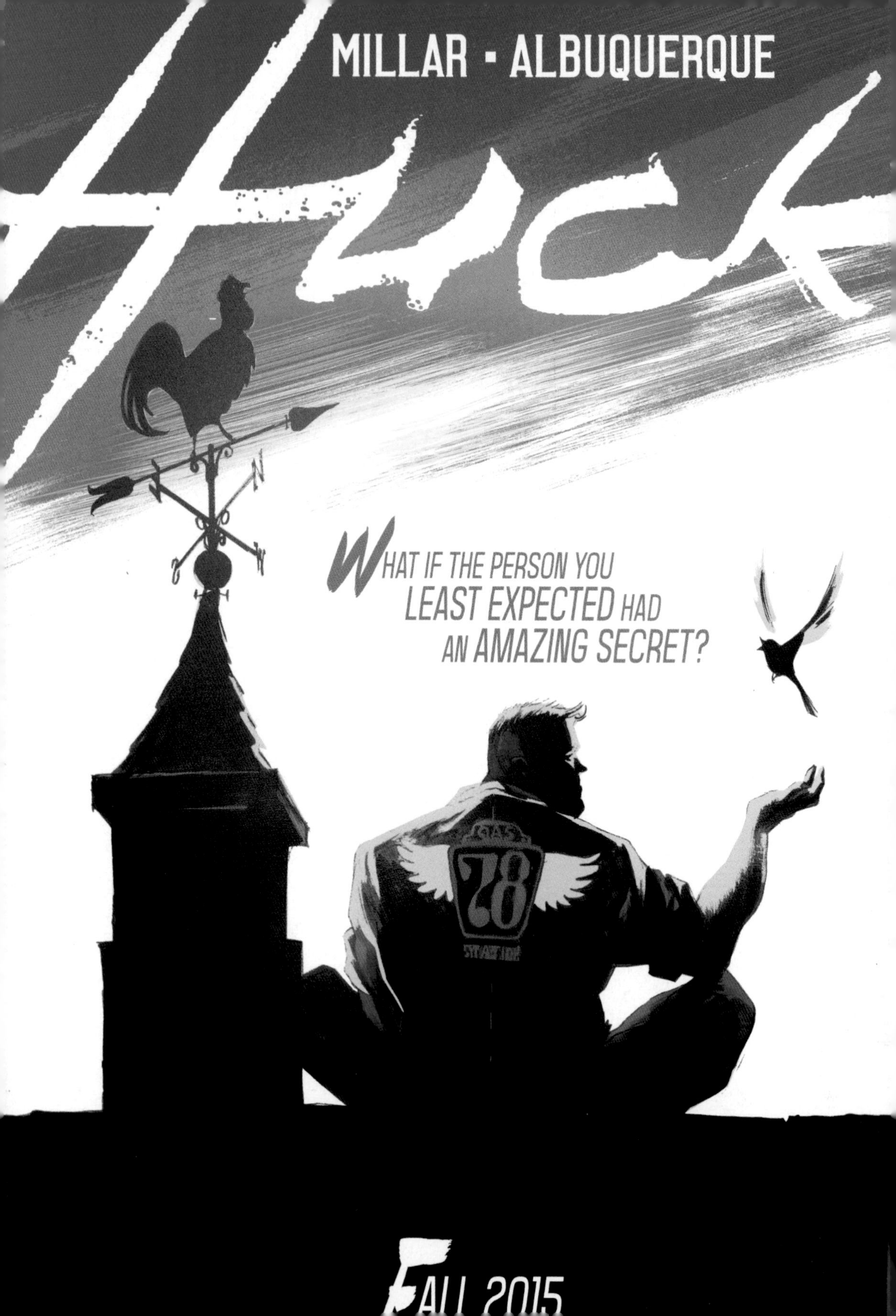
MILLAR • ALBUQUERQUE
Huck
WHAT IF THE PERSON YOU
LEAST EXPECTED HAD
AN AMAZING SECRET?
FALL 2015